Theodoros Kolokotrones, Elizabeth Mayhew Waller Edmonds,
Ioannes Gennadius

Kolokotrones the Klepht and the Warrior

Sixty years of peril and daring. An autobiography

Theodoros Kolokotrones, Elizabeth Mayhew Waller Edmonds, Ioannes Gennadius

Kolokotrones the Klepht and the Warrior
Sixty years of peril and daring. An autobiography

ISBN/EAN: 9783337030001

Printed in Europe, USA, Canada, Australia, Japan

Cover: Foto ©Raphael Reischuk / pixelio.de

More available books at **www.hansebooks.com**

KOLOKOTRONÊS. THE KLEPHT AND THE WARRIOR. SIXTY YEARS OF PERIL AND DARING. AN AUTOBIOGRAPHY

TRANSLATED FROM THE GREEK WITH INTRODUCTION AND NOTES. BY MRS. EDMONDS, AUTHOR OF "GREEK LAYS," "RHIGAS PHERAIOS," ETC., ETC.

WITH A PREFACE BY MONSIEUR J. GENNADIUS, GREEK ENVOY TO THE COURT OF ST. JAMES'S

LONDON: T. FISHER UNWIN, PATERNOSTER SQUARE. MDCCCXCII

PREFACE.

THE Greek text of the autobiography of which a talented and muse-inspired lady has given, in the following pages, an abridged English version, may be considered as one of the most noteworthy contributions to modern Greek literature. It is remarkable as a specimen of the terse and graphic idiom which prevails with the illiterate portion of the Greek people; it is valuable as an historical document; and it is characteristic both of the hero and of his amanuensis, who wrote it under his dictation.

Kolokotronês gives, in his own narrative, a pretty faithful picture of himself; and to that picture some additional touches will be attempted later on. But a few words may here be prefixed with regard to George Tertzetis, who actually wrote and published these memoirs.

Tertzetis was a native of Zante, a man of much talent, of considerable culture, and gifted with a peculiar grace and sweetness of diction. He was a poet and an orator; and, though himself possessed of a classical education, he was one of the most uncompromising and, as far as his own writings are concerned, one of the most successful apostles of the so-called "demotic school" in modern Greek literature; the school namely of those who aimed at preserving, in the written tongue, the spoken vernacular, unchanged and unimproved, and who were opposed to all progress or epuration. *

* The chief service rendered by the advocates of the "demotic" tongue consisted in the proof they afforded of the futility of endeavouring to tie down to the thraldom of a restrained and unserviceable idiom. the awakening conscience and the daily increasing requirement of a people able to fall back upon an immortal language in order to supply such requirements. Few words need here be wasted on the essayists and philosophers of the kind of the late Lord Strangford, who are either sufficiently naïve to imagine, or ill-disposed enough to assert, that an entire nation have somehow conspired, at much personal inconvenience and loss of precious time, to make use of an unnatural and stilted idiom in order to vindicate a patrimony, of which, apparently, only such should be deemed the rightful heirs as choose to pronounce Greek in a manner which is as arbitrary as it is ludicrous. To quote Lord Strangford is to prosecute a *post mortem* research of an uninviting description. But many accept and to this day repeat his delusions as dogmas of an infallible faith; and as his remains in literature have been mummified into a two-volume "Selection," it will be no fault of ours if his diatribes be shown to constitute but a sorry epitaph on his erudition:

"It must be owned that this word [*Hellene, Hellenic*] does not read quite comfortably and easily." "The nation is simply mad." "The Greeks, one and all, write in an artificial language;" "an extraordinary lingo . . . to which they are sacrificing their own satisfactory vernacular bow-wow." "This factitious language is the symbol of Hellenism," which, "with much rattening and house-burning," is forced down the throats of "the Romaic-speaking Byzantine agriculturists of Thessaly. . . . It [their education] teaches nothing of any kind except a barbarous and factitious literary jargon, made up out of the grammar and the words of a dead language, from which it is a point of honour to divorce the idiom of the true spoken language; and this jargon is taken up and inculcated everywhere as the symbol of Hellenism and the uniting bond of the race. . . . If I were a rich man I would set a premium on the head of any Greek in the kingdom who could be shown to have lived to the age of fifty without ever speaking a word of book-Greek, . . . just as you give a blue coat

For many years Tertzetis was the librarian of the Greek Parliament (which, under King Otho, was still composed of two Chambers), and in that capacity he came into close contact and intimate

and brass buttons to the virtuous labourer at home as a reward of merit."

It is to be feared that but few Greeks would have availed themselves of this tempting offer. Kolokotronês himself, at an age even more mature than fifty, appears so lost to a sense of the fitness of things as to use "book-Greek" the moment he finds himself confronted with the necessity of giving expression to any idea rising above the limited vocabulary of his "vernacular bow-wow." As for Tertzetis, he, in common with the rest of the now all but extinct vernacularists, failing to give adequate expression, in the demotic idiom, to the subjects he had to treat, used at every step whole phrases from "book-Greek," and persuaded himself he was writing in the vernacular by simply dropping terminal ν's and by maiming harmless words. Lord Strangford might have endangered his pecuniary resources had he offered his prize of a blue coat and brass buttons to such Dorsetshire rustics as would not use the English of the *Times* even to the day of their death; but in Greece his proffered munificence would have remained untouched. Those who for their own egotistical enjoyment advocate the continuance of a picturesque barbarity in language, remind one forcibly of that sickly school in art, who, little caring whether the people of Venice needed St. Mark's as a useful place of worship, lamented and protested against the restoration of its contorted pavement, the upheavals of which, they boldly affirmed, had thus been originally fashioned, in order to represent the waves of the Adriatic! The Greek people were guided in the progressive development of their language by practical and urgent needs. The movement which has made, within the last century, such rapid and giant strides, was not the result of scholastic pedantry or of political fanaticism; it was not imposed or forced; it was not mechanical. It was the result of the spread of education and of the gradual re-civilization of the country. It is a remarkable fact that it preceded political emancipation. The culture of the Greek language and the study of Greek literature have undoubtedly had, at all times and places, and still have, as an immediate result, the awakening of a sense of individual dignity and of national freedom. But that is one of the primary reasons why the study of Greek is advocated the world over as an indispensable adjunct to a liberal education. Such an influence may be esteemed, by some, a regrettable drawback; but Lord Strangford's reprinted diatribes will not help to cure it.

relations with all the great survivors of the War of Independence. On the 25th of March (6th April) of each year, the anniversary of Greek Independence, coinciding as it does with the festival of the Annunciation, was celebrated in the Chamber by an oration which Tertzetis delivered, never failing to move his audience to enthusiasm and tears. It was on one of these occasions that he announced the forthcoming publication of the reminiscences of Kolokotronês, and related how he had succeeded in persuading the old warrior that he owed it to his country to leave a written record of his sufferings and of his deeds of valour in her cause. He had repeatedly begged him to do so, but Kolokotronês refused, pretexting his inability to write. He could read, in a fashion; but in the way of writing he could not do more than scratch his signature. At last one day Tertzetis said to him :

"General, you will remain like a musical instrument, which brings forth sounds men listen to and enjoy, but which does not itself comprehend the value of .its own voice. If you do not yourself record your deeds, they will hereafter appear as the play of chance, not as the works of your own wisdom and conscience. Deeds of heroism and acts of devotion are befitting a Greek; but they must be recorded in writing, as of old. You hesitate lest you should do injustice to others. Speak the truth, as you know it to be ; be not concerned lest you fall into errors ; you will not lead the world astray; truth will herself appear foremost. And if your memory fail you as to details, who will put it down to you as a sin? You object you are illiterate; you know enough and to spare. Speech is literature. Speak, and I will write; for there lived many a brave man before Agamemnon and Achilles, who, having chanced no chronicler, now lie forgotten, unpraised and unmourned. Do not trust the record of your own deeds to others than yourself; but fear the adventurer in literature as you have shunned him in other walks."

"He scrutinized me," Tertzetis goes on to say, "with his glance, now wild, now soft and caressing, and then he said to me, 'Come to-morrow.' 'Come early,' he again cried out to me from the window as I was leaving."

So the dictation began in the summer of 1836, and a part of these reminiscences was privately printed in 1846, three years after the death of Kolokotronês. The printing was continued in 1850, but the whole was not published till 1852.

Tertzetis noted down these memoirs, not in shorthand, with which he was unacquainted, but by writing as fast as he could follow Kolokotronês, who did not precisely dictate, but narrated his tale as he usually talked.. He was already bowed down, more by the terrible hardships which he had endured, than with years. Besides, his idiom and mode of expression was peculiar, and, as Tertzetis relates, often a gesture, the intonation of his voice,

or the expression of his countenance, indicated
and explained more than his rugged sentences.
The original manuscript must therefore have
been of a very fragmentary description; and
Tertzetis adds that he marked with dots many
gaps which he had intended to request Kolokotronês to supplement, had he been spared to do so.

The fidelity with which Tertzetis accomplished
his self-imposed task cannot be disputed. On the
contrary, the style used is only too faithful a re-
presentation of the idiom of Greek mountaineers
of the times to which the narrative relates. It is
an idiom as peculiar as the English of the Scottish
highlanders, with a large admixture of barbarisms,
and with many abbreviations and the suppression
of such explanatory words or sentences as may be
suggested by the context, or may be easily understood by one conversant with the habits of thought
and life of the speaker, but which compel the
ordinary reader to halt and consider at every
sentence. Moreover, Kolokotronês was address-
ing his remarks to one already familiar with the
general course of the events of which he was
offering rather his own version, than a connected
and systematic recital. For all these reasons, even
to a Greek the perusal and thorough comprehen-
sion of this remarkable book is no smooth reading.
It requires, in any case, some acquaintance with the
general outlines of the history of the Greek War
of Independence. The courage, therefore, with
which Mrs. Edmonds has undertaken to grapple

with difficulties, in many cases hopeless, is as admirable as the apparent shortcomings and hiatuses of the English version are conceivable and almost inevitable.

The narrative begins with the birth of Kolokotronês in 1770, and ends in 1836, when he was living peaceably at Athens. The first question which will present itself to one who has read it through is to what extent does it possess an historical value. Of its sincerity there can be no doubt. Kolokotronês dictated it when many of those concerned were still living. It was not addressed to the outer world; while in Greece itself everything relating to the War of Independence is eagerly scanned and jealously criticised. Nevertheless, while supplementary statements or rectifications of unimportant incidents may have been offered, no material contradiction has appeared with respect to Kolokotronês' narrative of his individual action in the war. It cannot, of course, be maintained that his narrative is absolutely impartial. He was an active participant in the events of that time; he was mixed up, however involuntarily, in the intestine troubles and strifes which considerably reduced and almost crushed the great object of the Greek uprising. But on the whole his account of these events is dispassionate, fairly impartial, and singularly sober and unpretentious. In fact Kolokotronês' countrymen esteem his deeds and the glorious part he took in the liberation of the country far higher than he himself appears to appraise them; and the verdict of history will confirm their appreciation.

As regards their literary merit, these reminiscences can lay claim to no sort of artistic finish. There is no trace of scholarly ability or of careful composition. On the contrary, the style, as already stated, is rugged in the extreme, indicative not of the affected ruggedness of the professional philosopher, wearying and repellant in its too manifest effort, but of the unconcerned directness and unconscious force of a natural rhetoric. In one sense we have here the modern counterpart to the narratives of Homer and Herodotus. All three relate the same tale, each in the particular manner of his age—the secular struggle between Greece and Asia. Kolokotronês, however, had this advantage over his predecessors in the narration of this ever-recurring strife: that before consigning to writing the deeds he relates, he engraved them on the page of history with the point of his sword. His story may well be said to have been written not with ink, but with the blood which flowed in torrents for the freedom of Greece.

He was born and destined to this holy work. His family, which dates three centuries back, first appears in history as a living protest against foreign domination. They waged war against the Turk from their native crags and fastnesses, bequeathing from father to son the choice between blessing and curse, to continue or abandon the sacred tradition. Each succeeding generation is decimated in holocausts of martyrs; but it persists in the firm belief and inextinguishable hope of ultimate triumph.*

The abortive revolt of the Morea, in which his father, Constantine Kolokotronês, had taken a leading part, had just been suppressed, when on April 3rd, the Easter Monday of 1770, Theodore was born† under a tree on the hills of Rama, in Messenia,

---

* How deeply rooted this belief was in the traditions of the entire nation, how imbued Kolokotronês was with the conviction that the Turkish dominion, however powerful, was insecure, incomplete, and transitory, and that the nation, as a whole, had never been reconciled to it, and never recognized it, is conclusively shown by the following anecdote, which is given in his reminiscences, but which Kolokotronês himself related on another occasion in the following more detailed manner. In 1823, after the fall of Nauplia, three English warships anchored in the bay, and the commander of the squadron, whose name is given as Hamilton, after congratulating Kolokotronês on his victory of Dervenakia and the capture of Nauplia, urged upon him the opportuneness of appealing to the English Government, so that, through its mediation, Greece might be constituted into a principality, vassal to the Sultan. Kolokotronês replied that the Greeks had never recognized the Suzerainty of the Sultan; and on the English commander expressing his surprise at this assertion, he added: "The Turk has come upon us as a rapacious marauder; he has put to death some of us and has made slaves of others; but when our king fell in battle he had made no treaty with the Turks, but left a will bidding his garrison carry on the war and free the nation. His garrison has never given up the struggle, and our two fortresses have never capitulated." Hamilton again asked who were the garrison and which the fortresses; and Kolokotronês replied: "The garrison of our king are the so-called Klephts, and the two fortresses are Maïna and Suli."

† Tertzetis points to certain parallel incidents in the lives of Washington, Napoleon, and Kolokotrones, all three having been contemporaries, great strategists, and leaders of nations. Kolokotronês was in his fifteenth year when Washington signed the treaty of peace with England; and in his thirtieth when Napoleon was proclaimed Emperor, whose junior he was by one year. The mothers of both were driven by war to mountain refuges in their pregnancy; but Napoleon died an exile in his fifty-second year, while Kolokotronês attained the age of seventy after seeing his country free.

where his clan had sought a refuge. The child of a struggle for freedom, he was reared up amidst the mountain songs of the Klephts and within echo of the wailings of the bondsmen of the plains.* His father having been, some years later, seized and put to death by the Turks, he was sent by

* It would have required a good-sized volume—one that might well have figured in this series—to set forth with adequate detail who the Klephts were, what their origin, their organization, the patriotic and religious motives of their desperate mode of life, and how the Porte entered into compacts and alliances with them at times, the more effectually to hunt them down at others. The interesting introduction in the following pages, offers some elucidation of the subject. But those who are desirous for more ample information, can find no better guide than the unrivalled historial retrospect with which C. Fauriel has prefaced his classic work, "Les Chants Populaires de la Gréce Moderne: Paris, 1824." Although inaccurate on some points of minor importance, it remains the best monograph on the subject; and in perusing it, the reader may fancy himself carried back to the heroic times of ancient Greece. No doubt the Klephts degenerated in later years into bands of marauders and brigands. When the great chiefs, who served only Faith and Freedom, had disappeared, it was but natural that their following, having been persecuted into the conviction that the governing caste were their natural foes, should continue to regard a life of armed opposition to all government as the only one worth leading. The poisonous seed of secular slavery and misrule cannot be eradicated in a generation. Yet, whatever brigandage may have existed in Greece—and it was never a more rampant evil there than in other and more favoured countries, both of the old world and of the new—it existed mostly as the outcome of incursions from over the frontier, for which the government of the country could not well have been held answerable. The Klephts of old may have been guilty of acts of cruelty; theirs was a life and death struggle, bequeathed from father to son. But their sense of chivalry can compare favourably with that of the much-vaunted knights of the West. They certainly never proved themselves capable—not even towards their Mussulman foes—of such acts as those of the later Crusaders, who, starting with the avowed object of freeing the tomb of Christ, ended by enthroning the harlots of their camps on the holy altar of Saint Sophia, by way of mockery of the Virgin of the "Schismatics," and who, for many centuries afterwards, infested and victimised the Levant as depredators and adventurers.

his mother, now an orphan of twelve, to sell a load of wood in Tripolitza, and bring back flour and salt. On his way thither he was waylaid and beaten by a Turk—the usual reminder to a Christian that he was but a giaour and a slave. Kolokotronês managed to sell his firewood, but he brought back neither flour nor salt, but a sword, vowing vengeance to the tyrant. Who but his own stout heart would then have hoped that forty years later, on the memorable 22nd September, 1821, he was destined to enter Tripolitza as a conqueror!

Yet he seemed marked out by Providence to work out such a revenge. His whole life was typical of the sufferings, the struggles, and the resurrection of Greece. The influence, the prestige of the name of the Kolokotronês was so dreaded by the Turks, that the extirpation of the entire clan was ordered by the Porte in 1804. Thirty-six of Theodore's brothers, cousins, and relatives, and one hundred and fifty of their followers, were butchered in the struggle that ensued. But he remained undaunted; and after compelling the Turks to recognize him, at the age of sixteen, as chief of the Armatoles of Megalopolis, he found himself again the object of a perfidious conspiracy, intending to entrap him. He was thus forced to take refuge in Zante in 1805.

Once in safety, his first care was to organize amongst the Greek refugees in the Ionian Islands a memorial addressed to the Emperor of Russia, entreating him to intervene in favour of Greece.

No answer was received, but the Russian Governor of. the Islands urged Kolokotronês to recruit a Greek corps for service against Bonaparte. "What wrong has Bonaparte done to us?" was the reply. "If you want men to fight for the freedom of Greece, I bind myself to muster a body of ten thousand." For his inextinguishable hopes made him cling even from afar to his beloved mountains; and oft and again he would ascend with his young son the castle hill of Zante, and, pointing to the Morea, he would tell the boy that those were the fastnesses of their forefathers, which must again be free.

The English occupation of the Ionian Islands opened up for Kolokotronês a new and brilliant prospect. With that far-sighted sagacity which guided all his resolves, he seized the opportunity to lend brilliant services to the British Government during the siege of Santa Maura, and his bravery was rewarded with the grade of major. It was then he acquired tactical knowledge and experienced the advantages of regular warfare. It was then he became acquainted with, and conceived a devoted friendship for, General Sir Richard Church. It was there, in the Ionian Islands, that Lord Guilford and General Church laid the first germ of English philhellenism, the one by the revival of learning in Greece, the other by his resolute endeavours for the liberty of Greece.

It was a long and dreary waiting. But at last

the day, which fourteen generations of Greeks had longed and prayed for, dawned with the spring of 1821, when the proclamation of Alexander Ypsilantis resounded throughout all Greece. "When it reached my ears," said Kolokotronês, "when I heard 'the war-trumpet of the Fatherland calls you,' I fancied that heaven and earth re-echoed the trumpet blast. I donned on my fez gallantly, I grasped the hilt of my sword with fervour, and I inscribed in my heart with letters of fire the immortal name of Alexander Ypsilantis!"

The long-expected hour had now arrived, and of the result he never doubted for an instant. "Fear not," he was wont to say; "God has pledged His word for the liberty of Greece, and He will not retract." He declared, "We have been baptized once with holy ointment; we shall again be baptized in blood for the freedom of the Father-land!" The faith and piety of this rough and hardened warrior was that of an ascetic. In 1803, passing by a Convent of the Virgin, ruined and devastated during the last revolt, he halted there and prayed fervently, making a vow to rebuild the shrine in its pristine grandeur, if but the Blessed Virgin inspired him how to free the country. The second year of the war, after his heroic successes, he returned to the sacred spot and fulfilled his vow. And again, after his great victory at Valtetzi, it being a Friday, he ordered his troops to fast that day and offer up a thanksgiving prayer to God.

But not these qualities alone endeared him to his men, over whom he exercised a magic influence. The prestige of his name, his ardent patriotism, his consummate knowledge of the country, were powerful agencies in his favour. Above all, he was a born soldier and a great strategist. The troops which he led to battle were composed for the most part of raw recruits, badly armed, and inferior, always in numbers and often in physique, to the splendid armies which the Turks poured into the Morea from Asia and Egypt. Yet he gained one victory after another— never a more glorious one than over the dreaded force of Dram-Ali, whom he outwitted and out-manœuvred. He was full of resource, especially in times of crisis and reverses. Memorable and most characteristic is the feat by which pretending, in the midst of a precipitate retreat, to have suddenly routed the Turks, he set up a cry of exultation, and he deceived his own men, whom he thus rallied and actually converted from fugitives into pursuers. On another occasion, during the siege of Tripolitza, one of his officers drew his attention to a body of Turkish troops lurking in the distance. Kolokotronês looked around unconcerned, and replied that they were only birds of prey who must have just feasted on the body of Hadji-Koulélé (a dreaded Turkish commander who had been killed), and they were now resting to digest him!

In fact, he was the Odysseus of the Greek War

of Independence,* and he was befittingly nick-named "the old man of the Morea" (O' Γέρων τοῦ Μωρέα), not on account of his age, which was not great at that date, but owing to his unrivalled experience, his unerring judgment, and his in-exhaustible resource. In common with many great men, he was extremely superstitious, and, like all good Klephts, an adept in divining by the bones of sheep. He believed in the portents of dreams, so much so, that he often took military measures in accordance with the inferences he drew from his dreams. Yet he was full of dry humour, and many of his sayings remain fresh in the minds of men in Greece. It is related of him that, when suffering from an abscess on the back, he asked his men how it looked. One told him it was no bigger than a pea; another, that it was the size of a cherry; while a third assured him it was as large as an egg. "Strange," remarked Kolokotronês; "the distance is but from my head to my back, yet I cannot learn the truth!" And again, when the Bavarian Regency committed the fatal blunder of condemning Kolokotronês to death on a trumped-up charge of treason, on the sentence being commuted to twenty years' imprisonment, the decree was read to him. "I shall cheat the Regency," he said; "for I shall not live the

---

* Une fois que je rencontrai à Argos, si je ne me trompe, Koloko-troni sortant de chez lui, il (Comte Capo d'Istria) me fit, avec des passages l'Homère qu'il savait par cœur, le portrait du fourbe Ulysse, et me dit: "Ne le trouvez vous pas bien resemblant?" (Bory de Saint Vincent, "Expedition Scientifique de Morée." Paris, 1836).

twenty years." Being himself a humorist, he knew well how to frustrate attempts at scorn. At Tripolitza, on a Sunday, a lampoon directed against him was found nailed to the door of the church, where a large crowd soon gathered. Kolokotronês going into mass, took down the placard and put it in his pocket; but at the conclusion of the service he compelled the priest to read it aloud to the congregation, whom he then asked whether he had merited the insult. He was greeted with cheers, and returned to his house amid an ovation.

He was inexhaustible also in fables, by means of which he would convey much of his caustic and pregnant criticism. For he loved to examine the philosophical aspect of things, and he used to say that philosophy is observation. His rhetoric, rude and unadorned as it was, had great persuasive powers. His strategy would not have availed alone against Dram-Ali's campaign. It was by haranguing his soldiers that he encouraged them to hold fast to their entrenchments and despise the onslaughts of the enemy. And when, after the establishment of peace and order, the rising generation were to be exhorted and urged to imitation of the deeds of their fathers, George Gennadius called upon Kolokotronês to address the young students of Athens. The scene was one never to be forgotten, when, on the feast of the Asomati in 1838, the grizzly old General stood up on the Pnyx and related to those, who were now fortunate enough to be educated as free citizens, by what sacrifices the Fatherland had been redeemed and liberated. The voice of Greek liberty then re-echoed on those sacred rocks for the first time since the days of Demosthenes. The whole assembly was filled with enthusiasm, and was moved to tears when he told them, in conclusion, that he had but one regret, that he had always prayed to fall sword in hand in battle, but he was now condemned to end his days on his couch.

His own want of education made him even more eager that the rising generation should receive enlightenment. He often attended the lectures in the University and the Gymnasia, sitting himself on the benches by the side of the scholars, so as to excite pride in their studies. It was his wont to pace up and down the room while his son prepared his lessons; and on one occasion, stopping short, he asked him suddenly: " Kolinos, which do you take to be the great house of the nation? " " The king's palace," answered the boy. " No," said he; " it is the University." He had in him the innate love and admiration of the Greek for learning. He, however, knew well how to discern times and seasons. On the eve of the Revolution, while at Zante, he attended as usual the lectures of the Master, Nicolas Kalyva; and, being filled with enthusiasm at the mention of a free Fatherland, he snatched the book from Kalyva's hands, and, tearing it up, " This you should now teach them," he said, " how to make cartridges with the paper."

His whole mind and soul was indeed that of a
soldier. His very appearance announced him as
such. He was rather short in stature, of a thin,
wiry frame, sunburnt and weather-beaten to a
degree that he might well have been mistaken for
a man of colour.* He had a stentorian voice,
and an irresistibly piercing glance, to which his
hooked nose lent the aspect of an eagle; and
with the long hair, traditional to the Palikar,
floating about him, he looked, as Pechio says,
like one of those splendid rocks which project
from the Ægean.

Dressed in the Greek fustanella, he wore during
the whole of the war, not a fez, but a helmet,
declaring that his mind was with the Greeks of
old. And while, prior to the war, he served under
British rule in the Ionian Islands, he would never
consent to hang a tassel to the hilt of his sword,
testifying thereby his strict obedience to the
literal interpretation of Rhigas' immortal war-
song.†

Though hardened by a life of cruel wrongs,
by the terrors of slavery, in the midst of which

---

* Kolokotronês was of so dark a complexion that when, in 1804,
the Turkish authorities sent word to the primates of Messenia that they
must deliver up his head or they would forfeit theirs, they sent in the
head of a gipsy, declaring it was Kolokotronês'.

† Κάλλια γιὰ τήν πατρίδα κανένας νὰ χαθῇ,
᾽Η νὰ κρεμάσῃ φούντα γιὰ ξένον στὸ σπαθί.

"Better to lose one's life for the Fatherland, than hang a foreign
tassel to one's sword." This referred to the many Greeks who at that
time, fleeing from Turkish oppression, served as mercenaries in Euro-
pean armies.

he saw the light of day, by the untold horrors
of a barbarous war of rapine and extermination,
yet he had a child-like meekness and tenderness
of heart. So that when the death of Karaïskakis
was announced to him he wept and wailed long
and bitterly, repeating himself the dirges said to
the brave slain in battle.

He was of a truly Spartan simplicity, and in
fact he took pride in the extreme poverty in
which, in spite of his hundred victories, he had
lived, and in which he was destined to end his
days. He glorified in his achievements, and the
liberation of Greece was his recompense. Speaking
in the Assembly at Nauplia in 1832, he said:
"As commander-in-chief of the Peloponnesus I
have led many thousands of men, I have conducted
many campaigns and have fought many battles;
but I confess in all conscience that during the
whole duration of the struggle I did not spend
a single obole of my own; for I had none. The
people fed me, and supplied my troops with all
they required; my sword supplied the rest, for
all the horses and arms we needed we took from
the Turks."

With his small savings he at last built himself
a house in Athens, and there he retired to pass
the last days of his life in a room, about the
only furniture of which consisted in the couch on
which he lay. To those who called to pay their
respects, "You see this room," he said; "it has
no ornaments, the walls are bare, the windows

ungarnished. Such is Greece as we have entrusted her to you, of the younger generation. In 1821 we cleared the ground, we brought together the stones and the mortar, we built the walls and covered them in with a roof. It is for you now to deck the naked walls, to bring in the furniture, to hang the mirrors and light the lamps. This your advancement and enlightenment will do; and the blessings of your fellow-men will earn for you a place of rest in the abodes of the just."

He appeared to have felt his own end approaching; and daily he took leave of his friends and compeers, bidding them pardon him that he might depart in peace. He was reconciled with his old comrade, Peter Mavromichalis, and he actually sailed to Hydra and Spetzæ to make his peace with the aged Lazarus Countouriotis, his old opponent, with Mexis and others. On the very eve of his death, which occurred on the morning of February 4, 1843, he was present at the court ball, and there bid King Otto farewell.

Many of those who will read these pages may well say of him:

> "D'autres ont eu plus d'influence
> Sur mon esprit et mes idées,
> Lui, m' a montré une ame héroïque ;
> C'est encore à lui que je dois le plus." *

---

* These lines are from Victor Cousin's sublime dedication of his translation of Plato's "Lysis" to Count Sanctorre de Santa Rosa, the Italian patriot and great philhellene, who fell at Sphacteria on May 9, 1825, for the independence of Greece.

For such, indeed, was the heroic generation of the men who fought for the freedom of Greece. Nowhere on earth, and at no time in history, was the issue between wrong and justice, darkness and light, tyranny and freedom, placed before the world more clearly, than when, in 1821, the Greeks rose up against their oppressors, in a struggle all but hopeless. Not alone the power of the great Turkish Empire was still unbroken and dreaded; but the Cabinets of Europe were, one and all, opposed to the liberation of Greece at that time. Yet they braved all, and with their trust in God, with unshaken faith in the justice of their cause, a whole people marched to what then appeared certain destruction. At Messolonghi, when they issued forth amid the drizzle of the night, feeling their desolation and their doom, they said to one another: " The Almighty Himself weeps for us to-night!" But they went on, sword in hand, to fall for their country, greeting her with the gladsome cry: " Arise, thou dearest mother!"

And as they fell they saw around them the old heroes of Greece, arrayed in their panoplies, bathed in the light of their immortal glory, rise up from their tombs to receive into their ranks those who had died to make the name of Greece live once more.

J. G.

London, *October*, 1891.

CONTENTS.

LIST OF ILLUSTRATIONS.

INTRODUCTORY AND HISTORICAL SKETCH OF THE KLEPHTS.

 GENERAL survey of the Klephts, both in regard to their origin, and also in relation to their historical and political influence, is almost demanded before the following "Autobiography" of Theodore Kolokotronês, one of their most famous captains, can be duly appreciated. Although the far larger portion of this "Autobiography" refers to a period when Kolokotronês was no longer a leader of Klephts, but a leader of armies, this latter portion cannot be rightly understood except in connection with the former. At the very outset it must be borne in mind that in any historical consideration of the Greek Klephts, however brief and cursory its nature, the bodies of men so called ought not to be confounded with ordinary bands of brigands and robbers, but should be critically dissociated from them. Historians have not always clearly defined this difference, and the political import of the events in which the Klephts played so

prominent a part has thus in a great measure been overlooked. Some continental writers, however, and especially the modern Greek historians, have been careful to discriminate in this matter by employing the word λησται to describe the brigands pure and simple whose object is plunder alone, and who live solely for the purpose of robbery, whilst they reserve the name of κλέφται as a distinguishing mark whereby to designate the free mountaineers who carried on an open warfare against the oppressors of their nation, and who, by their unsubdued state upon the hills, justified the assertion occasionally made that Greece was at no time wholly conquered. Thus viewed, the Klepht truly typifies a free and unconquered Greece, and when his life is closely studied through the medium of a few examples which will be given presently: in his independent haughtiness, the austerity of his morals, his undying enthusiasm for liberty, his fidelity to his religion, and in his inveterate and uncompromising hatred for the Ottoman rule, the real value of such an assertion and its full significance will be readily seen.

It is not the intention here to assume that those hills which the free Klepht made his home were altogether unpeopled until after the taking of Constantinople by the Turks in 1453. Discontented or turbulent men fled thither at different epochs, for a time at least, to escape from the trammels of a despotic government, whilst some possibly, who were persecuted on religious grounds, sought and found there a welcome refuge. Such has been the opinion of competent writers on the subject. The Klephts, however, who are now to be considered did not make their appearance until after the fall of the Western Empire, and through the fanaticism of the Turks, these mountaineers—her declared and open enemies—increased from year to year, until Olympus, Pindus, Pelion, and Agrapha were peopled by them.

In the first years of this occupation the defiant attitude which the Klephts assumed towards the Ottoman Government was greatly encouraged by the Venetians, who held some of the maritime ports in their vicinity. Through the open as well as the covert aid thus derived, they quickly became a terror and a scourge both to the Sultan and his Turkish subjects alike. In point of fact the war-like education which these denizens of the heights in the countries extending from Olympus to Cape Maleas received during the Frankish occupation, became the heritage of a race of men who never bowed their necks to the Ottoman yoke. As often as Venice took up arms against Turkey she asked for their assistance, and when she made peace with that power, many of them remained in her service with the hope that another opportunity would soon arise for striking at their common foe ; whilst others—probably the greater number —returned to their rugged hills to renew the old struggle with more vigour than before. Their strength at length became so recognized a fact in the Peloponnesus, and throughout Macedonia, Epirus, Thessaly, and Akarnania, that the whole of the hill country was practically resigned to them, and was commonly spoken of as κλεφτο-χώρια—the abodes of the Klephts. The attractions of such a life, whatever its dangers and hardships, when viewed in comparison with the humiliations and degradations to which those who followed peaceful occupations of whatever kind were exposed, can easily be imagined. The restlessness of youth, its natural dislike to restraints of any sort, and its love of adventure, without any more powerful motives (which, however, were at no time wanting), furnished a never-failing supply of the most vigorous and the bravest of the sons of Greece to fill the ranks of the mountain armies. It may without any exaggeration be affirmed, that the flower of Greek manhood, which had been formerly seized upon by the child tax to furnish material for the Janissary Corps, was, after the abandonment of that levy, to be found arrayed in arms upon the heights.

The feeling of repulsion which every healthy-minded young Greek must have experienced towards all his political surroundings, is forcibly and pathetically described in the opening lines of one of the popular songs—" Mother, to the Turk I cannot be a slave ; that can I not endure. I will take my gun and will henceforth be a Klepht ; I will dwell with the wild beasts on the hills and the high rocks. The snows shall be my coverlet and the stones shall be my bed in the stronghold of the Klephts. I go, but weep not, my mother, bless me rather, and pray that I may kill many Turks."

In this way was the Klephtic force on the highlands of Turkey maintained, a force which professed open warfare, and which gloried in the name of Klepht, for that name carried no dishonour with it, and thus became every year more formidable to the Ottoman Government. A declared enemy in her midst which entered into no treaties with her, and which, from the fortified position which it held seemed to be almost invincible, it was still more dangerous to the safety of the Turkish Empire from the one fact that it was an internal enemy ever ready to assist a foreign foe.

In view of this danger which was ever present, and always threatening, the Porte, in imitation of the Venetian Republic which at different times had enrolled as many Greeks, and especially Klephts, as were willing to enter her service, and having found by long experience that the abodes of the Klephts were not to be reduced either by arms or by subtlety, offered them terms, which in their details contained no token of subjection, but assumed rather the forms of a tributary sovereignty.

This measure was introduced between the years 1534 and 1537, during the reign of Souleiman the

Magnificent, through the instrumentality of his Grand Vizier Ibrahim. This man, afterwards to become so noted, was the son of an obscure Christian sailor of Parga, and had been taken from his parents among other children of the inhabitants of that island, in order to be brought up and enrolled in the army of the Janissaries. On account of his great ability he rose by quick steps until he reached the post of Chief Vizier. He had always been well disposed to the Christians, and was a far-seeing man. Upon his promotion to the high office of Vizier he issued a firman which divided Greece into fifteen districts, at the head of which there was appointed a Christian man of arms—an Armatolos in fact—with the title of Captain, whose duty it was to keep order and to repress outrages in the roads and passes under his jurisdiction. This regulation remained intact until the reign of Amurath, who, in 1627, in order to weaken the increasing power of these Armatoli, abrogated the employment of them, and destroying all their forts on the defiles and passes, filled up the Armatolik posts with Ottomans.

The Armatoli, in revenge for thus being driven out, gathered themselves together and attacked those who had entered upon what they considered to be their lawful inheritance, despoiling the districts, and slaying the Turks who had been put into their places. "On this account," says the Greek historian Sathas, "they first received the name of *Klephts*, from κλέπτειν—to steal or rob—by which name they were ever afterwards known to the outside world." In vain did the governors of these districts use every means to quell those excesses, but at length finding that the attempts they used increased rather than abated them, and that the employment of force was of no avail in checking the exploits of their opponents, another firman was issued, which reinstated the Christians as the guardians of the roads. Besides keeping the passes free from robbers they were now required to collect the taxes on flocks, and received as before the name of Armatoli, which name, merely signifying armed men, was originally employed by the Venetians. By this arrangement the possession of the hills was virtually ceded to the Klephts for the payment of a small tribute, on condition of their being formed into a kind of militia for defence against Albanian brigands.

This was a wise and politic measure on the part of the Porte, and the proffered posts were accepted by large bodies of Klephts who were enrolled as Armatoli. One of the most important rules to be observed in this enrolment was, that the Armatoli were to be composed exclusively of Greeks, and that neither Turk nor Mussulman should be admitted to serve. The fertile plains of Thessaly, which the ruling pashas had been hitherto unable to protect from devastating hordes, were the first to feel the benefit of the institution, as their husbandmen were now able to till their lands in safety, and those districts at once became more prosperous. In a short time, therefore, the whole of Continental Greece experienced the advantages arising from the different cantonments of Armatoli. A great number, however, of those Klephts who had taken up their abodes, and whose haunts were, in the more inaccessible heights, utterly and haughtily refused to make any compact with Turkey, and, rejecting every kind of compromise, remained as before in a state of defiant hostility.

In the organization of the Armatoli the chief military command was held by the captain, whose title was hereditary, dependent, however, upon a diploma obtained from the pasha of the district, whilst the men of his band received the name of *pallikars*, which word is derived from the Greek verb πἀλλομαι, I bound or leap; and *pallikar*, at first representing a vigorous youth, came at last to denote a brave warrior in the flower of his age. All these bands were composed of men schooled in temperance and inured to every hardship and privation, whose strong healthy bodies enshrined spirits as lofty and unbending as those of their leaders. Such, briefly described, were the Armatoli. Their wild brothers on the heights disdaining all acknowledgment of the authority either of bey or pasha, also governed their several districts, either singly or as a confederacy, with a form of republican administration and with due regard to the maintenance of order and justice among themselves.

These two bodies of Armatoli and Klephts were, however, never fixed or stationary. Their numbers were continually changing, and causes were constantly arising which impelled either the Armatoli to become Klephts, or the Klephts to take up the Armatolik (=circumscription of Armatoli). Those who were the most celebrated among the Klephts, and whose prowess was an unmitigated source of terror to the authorities, were frequently on that very account invited to become Armatoli, great inducements being held out in order to win them over; whilst the Armatoli, on the other side, frequently threw up their posts, and fleeing to the heights became in their turn Klephts, so often as the petty vexations and annoyances customarily received from the pasha of the district, made their position in the Armatolik wearisome and distasteful. Thus it will be seen in the lives of many of the most renowned leaders, that the change from Armatolos to Klepht, or from Klepht to Armatolos, occurred several times during their careers.

The principal stations of the Klephts were upon those ranges of hills in Ætolia, which separate Thessaly from Macedonia, and on the mountains called Agrapha, but the most renowned of all their strongholds was on the far-famed Olympus, the abode of the old gods. In one of the popular ballads this mountain is represented as boasting of its ancient claims for reverence, asserting its pre-eminence thus: "Am not I the ever-enduring, the world-celebrated Olympus ? I have forty tree-crowned heights, and sixty-two fountains, and every fountain bears a flag, and every waving bough a Klepht."

There was no difference in the costume of Armatoli or Klephts except that the latter had a rather significant addition in a cord which was wound several times around their waists, and tied in front, the use of which appendage was to bind their Turkish captives. The dress of both was handsome and picturesque, and in prosperous times carried with it an appearance of wealth, in glittering weapons and ornaments taken from the Turks. The *pallikars* were almost as richly dressed as their captains, the *fustanella*, or white kilt, and the amount of embroidery on their leggings and jackets, being the distinguishing features. Rows of silver buttons on their vests were much esteemed, and form the subject of remark in several folk songs. "Two rows of silver buttons " are mentioned as worn by Niko-Tsaras. Thus accoutered, with the fame of their exploits preceding them in song—it can well be understood how they were admired and followed by the simple peasant class when they came down from their heights to mingle in the church festivals. In the homely language used commonly to distinguish the Armatoli from the Klephts, the former were denominated tame Klephts, ἤμεροι κλέφται ; and the latter wild Klephts, ἀγρίοι κλέφται.

The wild Klepht or Klepht proper was necessitated to plunder as a means of subsistence, and occasionally, in default of his natural enemies, the Turks, he was inclined to pillage those of his own countrymen who were obnoxious to him. The principal of those who fell victims to his discrimination in this respect were the *proesti*, or primates of the different districts = the Cogia Bachis of the Turks, who were responsible for the taxes which they often farmed out. This office could be purchased from the pasha of the district, and unhappily the desire for self-advancement often caused weak or unprincipled men to league with the pashas in every act of oppression. The second class, whom the Klephts had no scruple about despoiling, were the wealthy prelates, and especially the monks—and their monasteries, for the monks, from a fear of incurring the anger of the governing pashas, were indisposed to render them any assistance in times of need, and very often from the same motive gave information which led to their being captured and slain.

Regarding death in the battle-field when in arms against the Turks as the greatest of all blessings, whilst they recoiled in horror from being captured, and falling alive into the hands of their enemies, it was their custom at all festivals and rejoicings in their strongholds, to drink to the "good bullet." When this welcome shot had prevented the dreaded possibility of being made a captive, there was still another wish only second to the first, which their comrades were enjoined to perform as a sacred and friendly duty after death, namely, to cut off the head of the fallen warrior, and carry it with them from the field so that it might not fall into the possession of the Turks.

In religion the Klephts were strictly orthodox, and Kolokotrones himself is a good example of the form of piety that was characteristic of them, although few were inspired with so fervent a veneration as that which was natural to his strong spirit. They went down to the festivals glittering in arms and ornaments, crossing themselves, and kissing the priest's hand—they were liberal in their offerings to the saints, and, fully assured that Heaven was on their side, invoked God to consecrate their arms. "Bless, O Lord Christ, bless, O Master, our good swords."

If the Klepht robbed the monks, he abstained in his utmost needs from touching the vessels of the sanctuary. He was so temperate in wine that a drunken Klepht or Pallikar was almost unknown, and would have been regarded with the greatest contempt. Far more chaste than the legendary knights of chivalry, the honour of a woman—Turkish as well as Greek—was safe in the keeping of these fierce sons of the hills. The daughter of a wealthy functionary of the church or of a primate might be carried off for the sake of ransom, but she was invariably treated with respect. Captain Taskas alone rescued two thousand girls whom the Albanians had carried off in the Morea. It is related of Androutsos that learning from a maiden who had been captured that she was betrothed, he took her immediately without waiting for any ransom to the house of her future father-in-law. The exceptional notoriety in this respect of the courageous and otherwise much honoured Captain Zacharias of the Morea is supposed eventually to have cost him his life. Both Klephts and Armatoli married young, and from all derivable accounts appear to have ever been both faithful and affectionate husbands.

A retrospective and historical glance at the first indications of revolt emanating from these mountaineers, with mention of the several chiefs who inaugurated them, leading up to the time when the inveterate persecutions of the Porte, and the Pasha of Juannina hastened on the Revolution, is here necessary, as it will make manifest that attempted risings were initiated by them, although generally with the most lamentable results long before 1821, and it will also serve as a corollary to the "Autobiography," showing what kind of men were those who were perpetually held before the eyes of all Klephts as examples for them to follow, in the heroic songs with which they solaced themselves in their leisure hours. These songs to which Kolokotronês himself alludes in this "Autobiography" were inspired by the long series of wars carried on in the heart of the mountains, and narrate in the most vivid and often most poetical language the glorious deaths of their chiefs on the field, or their heroic martyrdoms if they were made captives, and in this long succession of short ballads may be found the whole history of their struggles.   The popular poet was in many cases one of their own class, and this added a double stimulus towards fortifying the courage and accentuating the stern resistance of both Klephts and Armatoli, as often as the latter were in revolt.

Many of the chiefs whose careers will be briefly narrated were the contemporaries of Kolokotronês, and a few were personally known to him. If any portion of the details as recounted appears somewhat repellent, it must be remembered that only by a knowledge of those facts can the attitude and conduct of the revolted Klephts he fully justified, and it will also serve to show that the crushing out of every rising by barbarous means only inspired fresh motives for successive attempts.

Mani, the southernmost part of the Morea, was by its configuration, and the sterility of its soil, alike qualified to be the natural home of brigandage, and its people, hardy and warlike, and but little disposed to industrial pursuits, was the most suitable material possible out of which to make Klephts and pirates. With these proclivities, only a slight stimulus was required at any time to set them in motion, and such incentives to activity were never wanting after the Ottoman conquest. It seems, therefore, highly probable that the statement is correct which alleges that the Klephts first appeared in the

Peloponnesus. Of what class of men other than Klephts could those large bodies of troops which were perpetually aiding the Venetians in their wars with Turkey be composed? For besides being a service which was ever acceptable to their feelings as Greeks, Venice was a country which afforded them a ready refuge from Turkish persecutions so long as those countries were in open warfare.

As early as 1479 there is mention made of one Klados who, having been in the service of the Venetians during her conflict with the Ottoman power, after peace was made between the two countries, transferred himself and his band to Mani, and carried on the struggle in the Peloponnesus as a leader of Klephts.

It is almost a century later before there occurs any notable example of this irregular kind of warfare against Turkey, when Theodore Vonas Grivas of Vonitsa and Loris, who had been enrolled as an Armatolos by the Venetians, rose up in revolt against the arbitrary rule of the Venetian democracy. Although he raised his banner in Akarnania and Epirus in the first instance—not against Turkey, but against Venice, the Turks in a very short time became the chief objects of his attack, and falling suddenly upon Vonitsa and Loris, he and his followers in one night killed all the Turks who were found in those two places. This outbreak was quite sufficient to fire the discontent of all the other

Armatoli who were living in Epirus, and was
followed by a descent into Arta and Juannina
under Poulios Drakos and "Captain Malamas,"
the latter of whom is the subject of one of the
earliest songs of the Klephts or Armatoli which
are extant. Being thus threatened by so sudden
and unexpected a danger, the Turks of Thessaly
and Macedonia flew to arms to help Juannina, in
which they had the assistance of the Pasha of
Naupraktos, and at the head of several thousand
men they went to Akarnania. Grivas encountered
the Turkish force at Achelous, but he was completely defeated, and was obliged to take to flight.
He took refuge among the hills, grievously wounded
as he was, and sent for one of his brothers,
bidding him to come to his aid with all possible
speed. Suffering in body and anxious in mind he
awaited the arrival of this brother from hour to
hour, until at last the news came to him that the
insurgents had again been routed, and were dispersed, and that his brother had fallen in the
battle whilst fighting valiantly. Upon the receipt
of this sad information Theodore Grivas hastened
to secure his own safety by fleeing from the dangers
immediately surrounding him, and effected his
escape before the arrival of the enemy who was
diligently searching for him. He, with a few
faithful followers, reached Ithaca, where he died
very shortly afterwards in consequence of his
wounds.

In 1684 a large proportion of the Corfiotes and

other inhabitants of the Seven Islands, enlisted under the banners of the brave Morosini when he sailed from Venice upon an expedition to Dalmatia, and about this time a daring exploit is recorded by which three Armatoli who were being conveyed to Venice for punishment, not only escaped the fate which awaited them there, but were also instrumental in saving the lives of their captors.

These men were Angelos Vlachos from Juannina, Panos Meitanos from Akarnania, and Metros Chortopoulos from Agrapha. These Armatoli had been inculpated by anticipation, and were treated as open rebels apparently before they had even meditated becoming such. In consequence of this suspicion they had been surrounded by a body of Turks that had been sent against them into Akarnania, which itself had very narrowly escaped being captured. There was peace at this time between Venice and Turkey, and as the result of this, these three Armatoli after the above event, being on the shores of Vonitsa, were betrayed into the hands of the former power, and were seized, thrown into chains, and put on board a galley which was to convey them to Venice. On their voyage thither, an Algerine piratical vessel appeared in sight and called upon the Venetians to surrender. Upon their refusal they were summarily attacked, and an engagement ensued, which was carried on with much vigour on both sides for some time. The Armatoli who were lying manacled and fettered below heard the tumult without understanding the cause. Inquiring of one of the sailors what it meant, and receiving his explanation of the occurrence, the three entreated him to go to the captain, and pray him to remove the chains of his prisoners who offered themselves willingly to fight on the part of the Venetians. The commander of the galley, who had just seen that victory was on the side of the Algerines, thought he could do no wrong by granting their request now that his own destruction was imminent, and knowing the prowess of the men he ordered their chains to be struck off. The moment they were freed, they sprang to their feet with wild shouts of joy, and seizing their arms they began to fire at the very moment when the corsairs were about to take possession of the galley. Their impetuous attack was so contagious that the Venetians followed it up with the same ardour, and in a very short space of time the Algerines themselves were entirely overcome; those who were not slain being taken prisoners, and their vessel thus becoming the prize of the Venetians, the commander fastened it astern his own boat, and sailed on to Venice highly elated. He did not forget upon his arrival there to extol highly the bravery of the Armatoli who had rendered him such signal service, nor did his government neglect to reward them, for lands and position were at once assured to them in perpetuity. This occurrence gives the occasion of one of the earliest of the historical folk-songs, in which the white banner with the red stars upon it, which the revolted Armatoli were about to raise in Akarnania, is thus alluded to in the opening lines, after the usually figurative language of the popular poetry of Epirus :—

" Is yonder snow upon the hills—or are those sails outspread ?
  It is Angelos, it is Meitanes, with white flags and stars of red."

Between the years 1689 and 1694 the Armatoli rose up in arms again, drove the Turks out of the districts which they considered as their own, and asked the aid of the Venetians in their projected revolt. The Venetians promised to lend them their assistance (but no help came from them), and in consequence of their failing to do so, large numbers of Armatoli deserted from the service of the Venetians, when many Slavs, who were attracted by the hope of Turkish spoils, joined the insurgent body. The perpetual danger to Turkey which accrued from the Venetians, in conjunction with the Greek Armatoli and Klephts, determined the Ottoman Government to create a Prince of Mani for the purpose of keeping both these inimical forces in check. For seven years a once notorious pirate had been languishing in the prisons of Constantinople. This man, Gerakares the Liberian, usually called Liberakes, from the junction of both names, the Porte resolved to raise from his dungeon to the government of Mani, with full powers of action.

The revolted Armatoli had placed themselves

under the leadership of Meitanes, who had united with two other chiefs—Spathogianni and Loudo-rekas. The new Prince of Mani led a powerful force against them but was repulsed with great loss, and being driven back was pursued as far as Karpenesi. Thence he issued the most menacing circulars to the inhabitants of those parts, and especially to those of Salona, threatening with condign punishment all who should in any way aid the insurgents, but at the same time offering an amnesty and remission of taxes, with other favours to them, if they would submit. The answer to these offers was sufficiently daring or insolent, for, despising equally both his threats and his promises, they stated that it was not their intention to pay any taxes. In consequence of this, Liberakes a second time led out a large force in order to punish them, which force was met by Kourmas and Bishop Philotheos at the head of all the Armatoli, who were also joined by the inhabitants of the surrounding districts. Libe-rakes was again repulsed, and forced to retreat a second time to Karpenesi. Bishop Philotheos however, was badly wounded in the battle, and died in consequence; but not before he was enabled to give this dying request to his brother Demetrius who succeeded him in the command: "Hide my bones, and when the Greek revolt is a thing accomplished, dig them up and inter them with all due solemnity in the church of our native place."

No permanent advantage came from these successes beyond the barbarous satisfaction of cutting off a number of the heads of the slain Turks—an evil practice which the Klephts had learnt from the Turks, and unhappily followed down to much later times. This action was amply retaliated by the Prince of Mani who ravaged and burnt a great number of villages in reprisal, and thus obliged the wretched inhabitants to flee to the hills.

Demetrius Charitopoulos, the brother of Bishop Philotheos, who took the command, as above narrated, died eventually at Zante, whither he was obliged to flee, and in his will, made shortly before his death, he narrates many interesting circumstances in connection with the bishop. After some preliminary observations upon his *most Christian parents*, he tells us that his elder brother had been named Philip in his baptism, but took the name of Philotheos when he became a monk. Being deeply imbued with a longing desire to emancipate his countrymen, it was not long after he was raised to the episcopate, before he exchanged the spiritual staff for the sword militant, and having joined himself with the Armatoli captains, "killed many Turks." The chief, Kourmas, was slain during his hot pursuit of the Prince of Mani, whom he was hoping to take prisoner on the occasion of his second retreat to Karpenesi, and the bishop himself badly wounded in the shoulder, died, it is seen, in consequence, a few days afterwards. Demetrius took care that the bishop's bones should *not* be desecrated. He concealed them, he says, "in a sack deposited in a cave which is known only to myself and my brother Georgios." He enjoins this brother, to bury his own bones " temporarily, without any expense, clothed only in my breeches and black shirt, to be disinterred when God thinks fit to free our country, and then to be reburied along with this bishop in the church of his birthplace—*but not whilst the nation is enslaved.*" He promises that his own blessing and that of good Bishop Philotheos " will follow upon this being fulfilled, whilst the curses of both will fall upon any one who infringes it, because," he adds, " I swore to it myself on the gospel when the blessed Philotheos lay a-dying."

To Georgios was also entrusted the silver cross of the bishop, which he was enjoined to take at once to the same village, and to present it to the church to be used in the sacred offices, " lest, if it be kept (as men are liable to fall into error), under some great necessity it might come to be sold." After leaving some money to free slaves, and to build a hospital, Captain Demetrius concludes his will by having " nothing more to say."

At the beginning of the eighteenth century there was a rapid increase in the numbers of the Klephts, and a corresponding diminution of the Armatoli, and for this result the Porte was largely responsible. With the suspicion which is common

to all despotisms, the Ottoman Government after
a time began to regard the effectiveness of the
Armatoli with apprehension, and jealous of their
increasing power, devised a fresh plan, and instituted a new office, with the view of checking
their growth and ultimately crushing them. For
this purpose it created inspectors of roads, who
were called Derven-agas, and Mussulman Albanians
were appointed to fill these posts. Mussulman
Albanians were of course the natural enemies of
the Christian Greeks, and the secret object for
employing them was that dissensions would be
sure to arise between them, whereby the strength
of the Armatoli would be gradually weakened.
That which was hoped for, and reckoned upon,
took place. This measure was effectual in
destroying the independence of a brave and useful
body, and by a series of cruel hostilities on the
part of the Derven-agas, the Armatoli were
frequently driven into rebellion, whilst the gorges
of the high hills became densely populated with
Klephts.

Although for two centuries there had been
initiatory attempts at a rising, the first most
decidedly planned revolt was inaugurated about
the year 1750, by the Armatoli Chrestos Meliones,
the two Tsekouras, and Vlachamatas, who raised
their standard in the districts of Parnassus and
Doris. How many were concerned in this insurrection has not been ascertained, but it is
conjectured that the number was considerable.

The usual religious enthusiasm accompanied the movement, and the Virgin was invoked to descend and fight with them.

On account of that disunion which was a prominent feature among the leaders in every rising, the chiefs above named soon separated, each taking his force in a different direction, by which course each was necessarily weakened. Chrestos Meliones led his men off to Ætolia. After this departure, · Lambros Tsekouras and Vlachamatas had a brief flash of success together, for meeting with a detachment of Turks on a road between two places of some importance, they attacked and completely routed it. Elated with this victory, they directed their march towards Salona and encamped for the night below the rocks of Agia Euthemia, which lay on their way, when a considerable body of Turks unexpectedly fell upon them. Their position was most disadvantageous; nevertheless they fought courageously and killed some numbers of the enemy, although they were eventually compelled to retreat. In this conflict one of their principal captains fell, whilst Vlachamatas and another chief were severely wounded. Lambros Tsekouras was enabled to carry off these two disabled men in safety to Krissaros, an islet in the bay of St. Konstantine, after which, being joined by his brother Metros with twenty-five Armatoli from Parnassus, they both ravaged the whole country round. The Bey of Salona naturally desired to rid himself of foes so troublesome, and sent repeated invitations to the two brothers to submit, promising them both riches and honours if they would do so. After very many solicitations they went down to Salona together, to confer with the bey on the subject. The place of meeting that was agreed upon was an olive-crushing factory on the plain of Salona. Lambros stationed his Armatoli outside, and entered the building with only four of his men, and was received by the bey; but in a moment he found himself surrounded by a large body of armed Turks. His brother Metros, sword in hand, rushed out by the door; but Lambros and his followers, transported with rage, threw themselves savagely on to their intending assassins. After a short, but fierce struggle, Lambros, seeing that two of his companions had fallen, and that terribly wounded as he was, all further resistance was vain, leapt from a window, but was met on his descent by a shower of bullets from a body of Turks who were concealed beneath, and fell. His comrades were able to obtain possession of the still breathing body of their chief, and bore it away to his stronghold on Parnassus, where he expired in great agony, rejoicing, notwithstanding, that he had been brought to die on his beloved mountain. After his death, Vlachamatas having recovered from his wounds, took the leadership in conjunction with another chief, and from their stronghold on Parnassus made frequent descents on the neighbouring Turkish districts. In one of these inroads they were completely crushed, after a violent conflict, by a large body of Turks, falling, however, on heaps of their slain enemies. Vlachamatas, fleeing to a chapel in the monastery called Jerusalem in that district, was eventually betrayed and put to death in a barbarous manner, when his body and that of his fellow chief, who was also slain in the battle, were impaled on a cross-road leading to Salona. After their deaths, Metros Tsekouras again joined himself to Chrestos; their reunion and the meeting between them being thus described among the songs which record the deeds of Meliones: "The sun rose high upon the hills, on the mountains' topmost peaks, when down beneath a fir-tree, by a fountain cool and fresh, Metros made him a halting-place with Chrestos Meliones, and the two captains formed again a bond of faithful union."

Thus reunited, these two Klephts went shortly afterwards to Arta, and carried off a Kadi and two Agas. This daring deed made a great sensation, and the Sultan issued a firman ordering them to be pursued, and directed that the Aga of Akarnania should produce the head of Meliones without further delay. The Aga, however, being well aware of the desperate character of the man as a fighter, did not care to have anything to do with him, but preferred to kill him by subtlety. Through the offer of a good bribe, he procured one Souleiman, who had formerly been a friend of

Meliones, to go and assassinate him. Souleiman
reached the quarters of Meliones at night and was
received in a friendly manner, which touched him
with such a feeling of remorse, that in the morning he told Meliones the purpose for which he
had come; whereupon the two men arranged
themselves for combat, and firing simultaneously,
their shots took effect at the same time and they
both fell dead. Metros Tsekouras, the last of
the chiefs concerned in that useless rising, still
continued fighting in Akarnania; but his exploits,
it is said, excited the envy of the inhabitants, for
he was assassinated after a time by some of them
for a bribe of two thousand grosia from the Turks,
which is thus recorded: "O Captain Metros!
Captain Tsekouras! could I not have told thee
so? Why didst thou come hither to a place
which was strange to thee? The Beys and the
Mavromati have killed thee by treachery for
two thousand grosia. All the Klephts bewail
thee; all Galazeidi mourns thee. Thy mother
is weeping for thee, and thy friends all droop
with grief."

The year 1770 follows as the most conspicuous
era of revolts on a larger but equally disastrous
scale. At this time large bands of Albanians
began to overrun Continental Greece, directing
their course towards the Peloponnesus. Many
Armatoli of renown at this juncture, instead of
opposing themselves to these savage robber hordes,
were content to enter into treaties with them in

order to remain in their several Armatoliks; but their example was rejected as quite unworthy of being followed by Chrestos Grivas, one of their number, and as soon as he heard· that the Albanians had entered Akarnania he raised the siege of Vrachoria, which he was prosecuting, and flew to bar if possible their further progress. The Albanians, under the leadership of Souleiman, had united with bodies coming from Vrachoria with their chief, Achmet, and all moved towards Angelo Kastro. Grivas finding himself unable to intercept their march thither, immediately drew back to St. Elias, outside Angelo Kastro. He posted his brother Tsegios with fifty men to hold a place called Rangaverka, and Captain Georgios Lachores was directed to keep the bridge of Angelo Kastro and the adjoining wood, whilst Chrestos Grivas himself at St. Elias made ready to receive the expected onslaught.

The Turco-Albanians marched forward in two bodies—the one which was commanded by Souleiman Bey throwing itself upon Tsegios and Lachores, whilst Achmet opposed the other force under him to Grivas at Angelo Kastro. For three hours Tsegios and Lachores fought bravely, but at last Tsegios fell, and then Lachores, seeing that it was of no avail for him to attempt carrying on the conflict alone, cut away the bridge, and made all possible haste to unite with his commander Grivas, who as yet had not engaged with the forces led by Achmet. A desperate contest ensued, and whilst the issue was still doubtful, Souleiman came up with the troops which Lachores had declined to meet at the bridge. Despairing of the possibility of achieving any success they determined to cut their way through the enemy sword in hand, to which in any great crisis the Armatoli and Klephts often resorted, and sometimes with signal advantage. This rush —*giourousi*—as it was called, at first spread a sudden panic amongst the troops of the Turkish commanders, but the arrival of another band of Albanians at this juncture completely changed the aspect of affairs.

The heroic band was completely surrounded in a very short space of time, but they undauntedly fought on with a determination to sell their lives dearly. Grivas and Lachores fell among heaps of slain, and three hundred of the flower of the Armatoli lay dead after the battle of Angelo Kastro. Only six escaped from the field, led by one Mavodemos, and they also were afterwards taken and killed. By the commands of Achmet, the bodies of the Armatoli were not to be buried, and the heads of their leaders placed on three spears were erected as trophies on the cross-roads near the place where they had fought. The spot where these devoted chiefs were slain is still called " The Ashes of the Grivas."

Russia now shows herself as the undoubted encourager, if not the promoter or instigator, of the rising that followed in the year of 1770 upon a larger scale, and upon more general grounds. Among the prominent leaders in this revolt was old Vlachothanases, who had been an Armatolos for nearly half a century, and who is especially worthy of mention as the adopted father of Androutsos, for famous beyond all the Klephts or Armatoli stands the name of the renowned Androutsos of whom we will now speak. Every Greek remembers him with mingled feelings of admiration and respect as one who through the whole of his life combated for the independence of his country at a time when that country was not awakened to a knowledge of her real strength. He was a native of Livadia, and is said to have been descended from a long ancestry of Klephts or Armatoli. He attracted the notice of old Vlachothanases whilst he was yet a youth, when the courage and other virtues which he showed so early, won the heart of the aged chieftain, who took him under his command and cherished him as his own son. Vlachothanases, however, being now seventy years of age, after having served forty years as an Armatolos, wished to retire from the service, therefore Androutsos, who had proved himself to be a good soldier, asked a blessing from his adopted father and left him. But Vlachothanases was not allowed to be inactive or to rest in his old age. Several Armatoli who had long served under him, and with him, begged him to resume his former life, and he yielded to their solicitations. Before long these very same

Armatoli, having dissensions among themselves, separated, and then the venerable chief hastened to enroll himself with his much-loved Androutsos, who had now under him many Armatoli of good report in arms. Androutsos at once launched out into a fierce struggle with the Ottoman power. In the first engagement with the Turks the Armatoli were unsuccessful, for to their body, which numbered only sixty men, the Turkish Pasha opposed a force of many thousands. Being surrounded in a monastery, whither they had retired, they managed to defend themselves against their besiegers for twelve days, but at last cannon being brought against them, they threw open the gates, and issuing out sword in hand cut their way through the Turks and escaped. The folk-song, which narrates this exploit, states that *two thousand* Turks were killed during the time of their defence and in the *sortie*, but only *five* pallikars.

Androutsos some time after this event was promised the Armatoliks of Livadia and Salona, and whilst he was under this expectation he ceased carrying on any hostilities. Selim Bey, the Derven-aga of Salona, deceived him in this matter, for after great delay Androutsos discovered that John Levkadites, a wealthy and influential Turk, had been nominated in his stead. Incensed at this deception, he again declared war, and called upon all the Armatoli to gather round him, which the greater part responded to with eagerness; the Armatoli, it was said, becoming day

by day more and more encouraged by the numbers
which flocked to the standard of Androutsos, as
the Turks were dispirited by the same spectacle.
Selim Bey at length summoned a large force to
march against Androutsos, but the Armatoli, as
usual in their methods of warfare, avoided meeting
the Bey in a pitched battle, contenting themselves
with skirmishes and a course of irregular conflicts.
One day, however, thirty of them came up with
Selim Bey, who had at that time only about two
hundred men with him, and they resolved to venture a hand-to-hand engagement. As Androutsos
was absent, Vlachothanases, being the oldest and
the most experienced chief among the little force,
took the command. For a long while victory
inclined neither to one side nor to the other, but
the Armatoli at last making a sudden rush with
drawn swords, the Turks began to retreat, and at
the same moment Androutsos, arriving on the
field at the head of twenty Armatoli, the Turks
found themselves between two opposite bands of
combatants, in consequence of which only one
half of them were able to seek safety by flight.
The Armatoli hotly pursued, when the Turks,
seeing no other way open to them, shut themselves up in a deserted little church which they
came up to on the road. For three days and
three nights the Derven-aga, Selim Bey, remained
there with the remnant of his men, whilst the Armatoli were closely besieging this little church. At
length, wearied out and exhausted, the Turks

surrendered. The haughty Selim Bey, a man who had always been proud of his good descent, now bowed himself down to the very earth, and kissing the hands and feet of Androutsos and the other Armatoli called upon them for pity, beseeching them to spare his life, and offering an enormous ransom. The Armatoli, suddenly seized with a generous impulse, at once released all their prisoners, and altogether declined receiving the proffered price for their redemption. " He bows down his head," says the folk-song, "bending to his feet and kisses his hand. ' I am Selim Bey, the renowned Bey, yet grant me now my life, and I will send to thee my mother, who will pay thee much money for me.' ' I care not for florins; I care not for grosia ; I am the renowned Androutsos, and I will release thee—go to thine house— go back to thine own people,' " was the answer. Old Vlachothanases was still longing to cease from this life of warfare, and he again strove to detach himself from it that he might go to his native place and die in peace ; but it was Androutsos this time who, appreciating the value of the veteran both in counsel and in war, besought him not to leave his comrades. As he listened to the warm persuasions of one whom he so much loved, the heart of the old man was suddenly stirred to its very depths, and overcome with strong emotion, he seized his gun, calling out that he would die fighting, " for to war he was born, and in war he had grown old."

Their first attacks after this occurrence were made in the district of Malandrinon, and their course was one marked out by fire and slaughter. Androutsos went to Naupaktos solely to meet Mouchtar Pasha, to whom he bore an intense hatred on account of his adopted son having been killed in a brutal manner by the Pasha some time previously. Mouchtar Pasha had put himself at the head of a large force, and when the encounter took place, it was maintained on both sides for a considerable time with obstinacy and vigour. Old Vlachothanases went raging about, sword in hand, to find Mouchtar, in order that he might himself engage with him in single combat, whilst his long white beard floated in the breeze, and made him a conspicuous figure. As he was thus ardently seeking his foe, two bullets struck him—one wounding him in the right hand, and the other striking him in the neck. The Armatoli rushed forward to defend him, followed by the noble John Xikiliotes, also an Armatolos, who fell almost immediately under a shower of bullets, whilst Vlachothanases himself, as he was turning round towards him, received a bullet in his head. Summoning all the strength into his voice which he could command, he was just able to articulate—" Comrades, secure my head, and take my blessing," when he expired, falling upon the body of Xikiliotes. Seeing the old chieftain prostrate on the ground, Androutsos, with a body of Armatoli, rushed to protect the body, whilst at the same

LAMBROS KATZONES.

time the Turks made every effort to get possession of it. Many on both sides fell over the corpses for which they were contending—the one party to preserve them from the desecration they so much dreaded, the other longing for the triumph of obtaining the blanched head of the aged Armatolos. None left the field ; the Armatoli against unequal numbers being determined to possess themselves of the heads of their two comrades, or die in the attempt.

The centre of the army of Mouchtar was at this juncture on the point of taking to flight, when the Aga of Naupaktos brought a large reinforcement to its aid. No longer were the Armatoli able to stand, when this additional force was brought into the field, and they were forced to abandon the bodies of their two dead comrades, and retreat. The head of the old Armatolos was borne away in triumph amid acclamations of joy, and treated with every mark of indignity.

At this point in the life of Androutsos it is necessary to speak of Lambros Katzones, the Klepht of the Seas, as he may be called, with whom Androutsos now connected himself. A native of Livadeia, in Bœotia, and born in 1752, Katzones was also concerned in the disastrous rising of the Peloponnesus in 1770, upon the failure of which he entered a Greek regiment in the Russian service, and acquitted himself well in their expedition against Persia.

In 1788 (the expenses being furnished by

Greeks) he fitted out and armed a small fleet, with which he carried on a piratical war on the coasts of Syria, doing fearful damage to the Turkish possessions. The Porte, alarmed at the ravages which he committed, sent out a large squadron in pursuit of him, which Lambros met outside Karpathos with his own six ships and two transport vessels which he had captured. The French consul at Rhodes seems to have derived much pleasure in witnessing the destruction of the Turkish vessels which ensued, as he congratulated Lambros upon his victory, telling him that he was *a worthy descendant of Themistocles.* This event was communicated to the Russian Government, when his ships were enrolled as the fleet of the Russian Empress, and were entitled to carry the Russian flag, whilst he himself was to be considered a Russian officer. After this encouragement, Lambros, triumphantly hoisting the Russian flag, sailed forth and scoured the Archipelago even to the Hellespont. He now received one of those letters so characteristic of the Porte in those times—which came to him from the Sultan through his dragoman, Stephen Mavrogenés, and which addressed him as " *Most brave hero.*" This letter *complimented* him upon his *valiant deeds,* and offered him an amnesty, and the government of any island which he might choose, free of taxes, and with a present besides of two hundred gold pieces, if he would leave the service of Russia.

This letter was not answered in writing, but

was replied to by an expedition in search of the enemy's fleet, which Lambros encountered between Mykonos and Syra, and completely defeated. Shortly afterwards, hearing that six Algerine vessels had gone to Hydra, he set sail, and drove them thence to Nauplia.

It was at this epoch, in the beginning of 1790, that he was joined by Androutsos at the head of some five to seven hundred Armatoli. This transformation of mountaineers into seamen may seem strange, but it was not unusual. The occurrence is considered by some writers to be alluded to in one of the folk songs which record the deeds of Androutsos, where "the mother of Androutsos rejoices, the mother of Androutsos is glad, for her sons are all Armatoli, and great captains."

The Algerine vessels sent out by the Porte were afterwards engaged, and in an obstinate battle, where the enemy lost heavily, Katzones was wounded in the head, and two of his vessels were captured, whilst a great number of the Klephts under Androutsos were killed. In the following year Lambros and Androutsos endeavoured to systematize a regular rising in Mani, but the Maniotes rightly observed that enthusiasm alone was useless, and that money was wanted. Russia promised some aid both in money and soldiers, but gave none; and in the year succeeding this the usual termination to all coalitions of Greeks with Russia arrived; peace was made between Russia and Turkey, and Katzones was told that he must desist from any further operations against the Turks. Lambros and Androutsos however thought that they could carry on the war on their own account, and after several minor engagements, met the combined French and Turkish ships off Tainaros, where they came to close quarters, when the French sailors opened fire from their ship, to which Androutsos and his Armatoli responded with so thick and dense a volley that many French officers were killed, and upon this they retired. On the third day afterwards the Capitan bey effected a landing, which was not opposed by Katzones, who left him to be settled with by Androutsos and his Pallikars, and after the Turks were all disembarked, Androutsos and his Pallikars discharging their guns suddenly, fell upon them impetuously sword in hand, and routed them with great slaughter, four thousand of them being slain; twelve of their boats were captured, and out of the whole force about a hundred only were able to save themselves on the three boats which remained. Upon this crushing defeat the Capitan sent to the Bey of Mani, and commanded him to secure and deliver up Katzones immediately either dead or alive. The Bey ordered a large force to be made ready for the purpose of effecting his capture, but at the same time sent a monk to Katzones with private information concerning the intended expedition. Katzones was able to save both himself and his sailors in consequence of this warning, and eventually re-entered the service of Russia, where he died in 1804 at the age of fifty-two.

The valiant Androutsos was less fortunate. For forty days and nights he was pursued by a force of six thousand men. As they fled through that difficult country they often turned and skirmished, and so great was the skill of their leader that in these encounters there were fifteen hundred of the enemy slain, and although his own numbers were reduced to ninety-six, yet that remnant of the five hundred Armatoli which he had brought to Katzones was at last carried over in safety. A foreign consul is reported to have likened this passage to the celebrated march of the ten thousand in Xenophon. Androutsos himself contemplated going to Russia, but disregarding some friendly warnings, he trusted himself on Venetian territory, when he was immediately seized by the Government, and transported in the first ship at hand to Constantinople.

Upon his arrival there he expected to be immediately beheaded after the manner of so many other Klephts, who deserved no severer treatment by the Porte for their acts against her than himself. Instead of which he was thrown into the filthy bagnio—the convict prison. Repeated offers of advancement were continually held out to him if he would abjure Christianity, and take office under the Sultan, but they were always indignantly refused.

In the year 1798 the Ambassador of the French Republic at Constantinople made a special request to the Porte to restore Androutsos to liberty. "You could as well ask for three millions," was the answer, "as to require me to set Androutsos free." So the redoubtable chief, whose noble figure and fine face, as well as his skill in all manly exercises, had been the theme of many a song, languished for the mountain air of his native hills during several years, until he at last succumbed to the plague. There is no authentic picture of Androutsos, who is always described as being exceptionally handsome; his moustaches are represented to have been of so great a length that it was his custom whilst fighting to tie them at the back of his head. It was these moustaches which gave him the fierce aspect ascribed to him, but it is nevertheless said that he was naturally of a calm temperament and gentle-hearted. Possibly for a long time the mountaineers who adored him might have been ignorant of his fate when they sung, "The mother of Androutsos is sorrowing, the mother of Androutsos weeps; she often turns to the hills and upbraids them. 'O, ye wild mountains of Agrapha, what have you done with my dear son, the Captain Androutsos?'"

The personal bravery and influence of Androutsos was contagious, and three men who had been his proto-pallikars carried on a strife for a short time after Androutsos was lost to them, which could have no other than a tragic termination.

These men were the two brothers Georgios and Joannes Karaples, and Alexis Romanes, more commonly called Alexis the Monk. The latter had lived several years as a monk in the monastery of the Prophet Elias, but upon receiving some annoyances from a Turk, he had fled and joined himself to the Armatoli.

The above chiefs having gathered others around them directed their course to Chrysos, where they were met by the Governor of Salona with a large force. Those of the Armatoli who at that juncture found themselves near the monastery above mentioned, shut themselves up in it and were there laid siege to. Firing was kept up on both sides vigorously for some time, when the Turks, having invited the besieged to surrender, and receiving from them an insulting reply, they set fire to one side of the building, and the flames spread rapidly, when the Armatoli seeing how great was the danger which threatened them from within, threw open the gates and rushed out sword in hand. Striking at their foes on either side in their headlong passage they cut their way through the midst of the Turks. Fifty of the Governor's men, among whom was his own son, were killed during the siege and sally, and seven only of the Armatoli, Joannes Karaples being wounded.

The Governor of Salona, smarting under his defeat and enraged at the loss of his son, sent express orders to Lambros Kasmas, the *Derven-aga,* as guardian of the roads, to drive out all these

Armatoli from the district. Lambros, however, did not care to encounter them alone, and got the Bey of Loidovikos to unite with him for that purpose. Their two forces made between them no inconsiderable amount, and the Armatoli against whom they were directed were comparatively few in number, their chief strength lying in the zeal by which they were inspired. The engagement that immediately took place was carried on for three hours unremittingly, without the balance of victory inclining either to one side or the other, when Georgios Karaples with a sudden rush cut off the head of the Bey of Loidovikos, which at once decided the conflict, as the Turks took to flight instantly. In a subsequent encounter with the Turks Georgios was slain. After his death many of their followers left the service, and Manikas, the Derven-aga, who superseded Lambros after the defeat recorded above, undertook to be a mediator between the hostile combatants.

The then Bey of Salona, hearkening to this mediation, offered to them different posts as Derven-agas. For some time they had many doubts as to his sincerity, notwithstanding the oaths with which he accompanied his offers, but at last they were prevailed upon to go to Salona, where they were most graciously received by the Bey, who invited them to partake of his hospitality. Alexis the Monk was made Derven-aga by him, and the others were engaged as his soldiers. During the repast which followed, the Bey disarmed every suspicion by his courteous manners, and they all ate together as though in perfect ease, after which he dismissed them to their several posts. They had scarcely, however, reached the monastery of St. Elias when a foot messenger brought them an order to return immediately to Salona. The mediator Manikas meanwhile in his office of Derven-aga had been sent away to quell some alleged inroads of Klephts. In obedience to this summons Alexis and the others returned to Salona, but had no sooner entered the Bey's palace when the doors were closed behind them and they were fired upon and the whole of them were slain.

It is not perhaps too much to say that the most celebrated and best known names among the Klephts are those of men whose deaths have invested every one of their actions with that deep interest which follows the hero of a tragedy through all the minor scenes up to the dread consummation in the last act. There were hundreds, perhaps thousands of Klephts who lived the lives of heroes, but whose deaths on the battle-field had nothing more exciting than the ordinary death of soldiers dying in the fulfilment of their duty. Of all such, nothing more can be said than that they lived and died in their career of opposition to a tyrannical government; no particular act of individualism, either in their deeds or in the manner in which their lives were terminated, distinguishing them. The names of two men only, names which have called forth not only from the poet historian of the people, but from the educated poets of modern Greece, some of her best ballads, are examples of this. Diakos and Katzantonês are remembered in verse which will not be easily forgotten, with as much love as admiration. The first of these two, as Mr. Papparigopoulos justly remarks, differed in no wise from many others who threw themselves ardently into the cause of the rising, but "he was young and he was handsome," and those two simple facts exhibited his sufferings or stronger contrast.

Athanasius *the deacon*—as his surname, Diakos, the name by which he is generally alone called signifies—was designed for a religious life, and was educated in a monastery. It is seen that he had already taken the first orders in the priesthood, but like many other young men who were originally destined for the church at that time, he was so stirred by the tyranny around him, or possibly still more disgusted with the abject life that the majority of the peasant class to which he belonged was forced to lead, that he was impelled to throw aside all the bonds of a religious life and to join himself to the Klephts. After some few years he became the protopallikar of Odysseus Androutsos, who was then the Captain of the Armatolik of Livadeia, which post he held under Ali Pasha. A few words in passing is due to Odysseus, although it is only with pain that the gifted son of so celebrated a father can be alluded to.

ATHANASIUS DIAKOS.

Possessed of most of the external qualities of the first Androutsos, equally handsome, and possibly equally clever—a brave and brilliant figure in the first years of the revolution—Odysseus did not inherit either the incorruptible patriotism or the integrity of his father, and not being proof to the seductive offers made to him by the enemy, became a traitor to his country and fell accordingly. At this time, however, no stain had darkened his career. He entertained also a great friendship for Diakos. It was during the absence of Odysseus that Diakos raised the standard of independence in Central Greece. If it be a merit to be recorded as the first who had ventured to do so the merit is his, but it was as undoubtedly rash as other previous declarations of the same kind had been.

His success was at first brilliant, but it was brief. Omer Vriones and Kiose Mehmet, with a Turkish-Albanian army of nine thousand cavalry and infantry sent out from the camp of Kourchid Pasha, advanced against him. Diakos and two other captains with fifteen hundred men endeavoured to hold two roads which led the one to Bœotia by Thermopylæ, the other to Phokis, but the troops which they commanded shrunk from the unequal contest with so large a force, led by two leaders of so deserved a renown as the two warriors above mentioned, and they fled precipitously, all but a faithful band of fifty followers. Diakos scorned flight, and he fought on until the whole of this small but brave guard was slain. Then he was taken prisoner. It is now that the martyr completes the picture of the hero which to this day fascinates the Greek peasantry. Life was offered to him, but the offer was flung back with scorn, for the price was apostasy. He was therefore sentenced to be immediately impaled. It was a beautiful May morning in the year 1822 when Diakos was led to the stake. For a few moments the loveliness of external nature and his own age, as he was still under thirty-five, called forth an expression of passing emotion, "What!" he is reported to have said, "has death come for me in the time of flowers and green leaves?" On the stake, however, he gave forth no expression of pain, but hurled out defiance to his foes. "It is but one Greek more," he cried; "as a Greek I have lived, as a Greek I will die. Odysseus and Niketas are left." It is consoling to reflect that Odysseus was not faithless to the memory of his friend. He achieved a brilliant victory in revenge for the death of Diakos. "Would that he had died then!" is the remark of a Greek historian.

Katzantonês, the second of the two Klephts who are classed together on account of the brilliancy of their short careers and their alike most painful deaths, preceded the appearance of Diakos upon the scene for nearly twenty years, and belongs rather to the close of the eighteenth century. He was the eldest of five brothers, who were the sons of a shepherd in Agrapha. The nomadic life of the shepherds in Greece is still to a very great extent the same as in primitive times. In the summer months they lead their flocks over the mountains from pasture to pasture, and only when the winter approaches do they come down to the plains. This was the manner in which the early years of Katzantonês were passed. In following this life he had made acquaintance with the Klephts, with whom those wandering shepherds were generally in good accord, and who, in this pastoral state, would have been equally as free as the Klephts if they had not been oppressed by cruel exactions. Ali Pasha levied frequent and heavy confiscations on the flocks; he had shepherds and flocks of his own which were bound to consume the produce of others, and thus the pastoral life became by degrees odious to Katzantonês, who was not of a temperament to bear vexations patiently. He had frequently said that he would become a Klepht if it were only to avenge himself upon the tax collectors of the Pasha, who in that case would be obliged to be ransomed from *his* exactions in the future. This asseveration was always received by his intimates and companions with derision, on account of his very small stature and slight frame. Although his appearance has often been descanted upon in disadvantageous terms, and the epithets " mean " and " insignificant " have been freely indulged in as regards his personal appearance, Pouqueville, the French consul at Juannina at that time, speaks in terms of admiration of his fine black eyes and his soft silken brown moustaches. Strength and agility, and a frame capable of supporting great privations and hardships, he undoubtedly possessed; these were natural qualifications for a Klepht, but those who knew him personally, ignored those qualifications on account of his comparatively diminutive form. It needed only time, however, to show how mistaken was the common estimate regarding him; he was brave almost to temerity; was possessed of a marvellous suppleness and lightness in all his movements; had an inexhaustible fund of resources within him, and owing to the early part of his life having been spent with the flocks he knew every pass in the mountains. At last he resolutely made up his mind; he sold his flocks, and burnt all his huts and folds; then he armed himself, and followed by his four brothers, he went forth as a Klepht to those same hills of Agrapha whither he had so often led his sheep. For some time Katzantonês was inspired by no other feelings than those of revenge joined to a desire for pillage, and he treated the Greek villages lying at the base of Agrapha with as little consideration as those which were inhabited solely by Turks, so that in this respect he is not to be placed in comparison during the early part of his career with those captains who acted solely from motives of patriotism, and a desire to accomplish the liberty of their race.

His endurance, his courage, and the indomitable hatred with which he pursued the Turks were for some years the admiration as they were the terror of the Ottoman Government. Ali Pasha, who was now invested with the headship of the Derven-agas, sent out his ablest generals successively in search of him; but either by his valour or by his adroitness he always managed to defeat or to baffle them. As one instance of his prompt ingenuity in finding a way out of very present danger, it is related that, being pursued to a stronghold, which was accessible only by two narrow defiles, whilst in every other part there were only steep and rugged precipices, and having discovered that both these passes were occupied by Albanians whom treachery had led to his retreat, he cut off a strong branch of a fir-tree with his sabre, and mounting upon it astride, launched it over the face of the rock—the foliage and his own weight keeping the branch steady, and thus he reached the ground in safety. The Klephts who were with him were not slow in following his example, whilst the Albanians only learnt his flight by the consternation which his sudden appearance caused in the district below.

Veli Guekas, the Derven-aga of Akarnania, was one of the most formidable of all those who arrayed their strength against him. With a courage equal to that of Katzantonês, and with immeasurably more means at his disposal, Veli had been ravaging all Akarnania in search of the notorious Klepht, and irritated that he was so long able to elude him, he suspected that the villagers around were in complicity, and renewed his devastations upon the surrounding district with increased vigour. Being informed of these proceedings on the part of Veli Guekas, Katzantonês had the insolence or temerity to write him a letter couched in the following terms: "You seek me—come to Krya-vrysis; I will await you there."

When Guekas received this defiance he was not in motion nor in preparation for any march, but he was so piqued by it that he immediately ordered his Albanians to reassemble, and so great was his impatience that, without even waiting for them, he started off with only a few of his men, and flew with the rapidity of lightning to the place where Katzantonês had appointed to meet him. Katzantonês with his Pallikars was there lying in ambuscade awaiting his coming. After a few insulting words on both sides the combat began, when Veli Guekas fell dead almost instantaneously, having received several balls at once. After this event the name of Katzantonês was held in still greater dread than ever, and the fury of Ali Pasha was redoubled. Fresh bodies of men under other Derven-agas were sent forth to vanquish him, fresh dangers encompassed him everywhere, but he was still invincible.

The island of Santa Maura had always been an asylum for Katzantonês in his every need. Thither he would go to get cured of his wounds, or occasionally, if there was nothing much to be done in the career which he had chosen, to rest. Whenever he came there he was followed by crowds who thronged to gaze upon the terrible Klepht.

In 1805 he went thither with nobler thoughts throbbing in his breast than any which had hitherto made their abode there. He was now bent upon promulgating a general rising of the Greeks for the independence of their country. The Russians who then held the Ionian Isles secretly encouraged the project. All the chiefs of Ætolia, of Epirus, and of Western Thessaly were assembled there, and here at last was a real triumph for the shepherd of former days; for Katzantonês, who had a great love of display, glittering with ornaments of gold, and costly silver weapons, the spoils of many a well-fought fight, and conspicuous by his haughty carriage despite the smallness of his stature, inspired involuntary respect from all the other captains, who acknowledged him as one whose bravery was unsurpassed.

At this time, however, in the very height of his elation Katzantonês was seized with an attack of smallpox. It seems that when struck down by this virulent disease, he was impatient of the necessary confinement, for having always breathed the fresh mountain air, he chafed at being held within the four walls of a chamber. Anyhow, he left Santa Maura before he was well, and hastened to attain his native hills once more.

Very shortly afterwards he paid a visit to a monastery on Agrapha in order to raise some contributions, and whilst there he was again taken ill. After remaining a few days in the monastery, being still sick, and not feeling quite assured as to his safety, he left and concealed himself in a cave, George, the youngest of his brothers, staying also with him to nurse and tend him. Food was brought to them daily from the monastery, and it is conjectured that one of the monks gave information concerning the place of his retreat to Ali Pasha, who, upon receiving it, without a moment's delay, sent sixty picked Albanians with orders to bring him both the brothers *alive.*

George was just about to issue from the cave when he saw an Albanian posted at the entrance. Family love is strong among the Greeks, and fraternal love is possibly stronger with them than with any other people. Be this as it may, there is no more beautiful example of fraternal love in the world's history than that shown by the Klepht George to his sick and helpless brother, the once dreaded Katzantonês. Rushing back to the recesses of the cavern he hastily told his brother what had occurred; and catching him up in his arms, threw him over his shoulder, holding at the same time his sword in his mouth and his gun in his hand, and made for the entrance to the cave, where he discharged his piece at the Albanian who attempted to bar his passage, and took his way to a forest at no great distance. He was pursued by the Albanians, but he was swift of foot, and kept for some time in advance, whilst he occasionally laid down·his precious burden to reload, when he would turn to face his pursuers and fire, and then again, charging himself with his brother's enfeebled body, fled onwards. In this way he killed several of his pursuers, but at last ten of the foremost of the Albanians, infuriated by the deaths of their comrades, rushed forward with a sudden bound, and the two brothers were captured, and taken to Juannina together.

A brother of Veli Guekas was in the service of Ali, and the Pasha in the refinement of cruelty handed over to him the slaughter of the Katzantonês, trusting that a desire to revenge the death of his brother would nerve him to execute them in some barbarous fashion. Guekas went to them in their dungeon, and began to pour a volley of savage reproaches upon Katzantonês, accompanied by many taunts upon the fate which was now awaiting him. "Veli was a Pallikar," answered Katzantonês, "and I am a Pallikar; he did his duty, and I did mine." This reply so touched the soldier's sense of justice, that he hastened back to Ali and asked that Katzantonês might be set at liberty, adding that he would meet him as a free man, and fight him as a soldier should, but that he could not murder him whilst he was a captive and in chains. Ali, however, was not the man to be stirred by any such generous impulses, and he had too long thirsted for the blood of the defiant Klepht to release him now that he at last had him in his power. He therefore ordered that both the brothers should be beaten to death by sledge hammers. It has been said that the hitherto heroic firmness of Katzantonês, whose nerves had been somewhat shattered during his wasting illness, gave way under this dreadful torture, and that he uttered cries of anguish, whilst George, upbraiding him for thus complaining like a woman, endured all in silence until every bone in his body was broken, and expired without a sigh.

Lepenotis, the second brother, who had received his name from the place of his birth, followed the career of Klepht for some little time after the deaths of George and Katzantonês; but harassed by continual pursuits, he at length submitted to Ali; and, as it usually happened with the Klephts after they had been induced to make their submission at Juannina, he was waylaid and murdered on his journey back.

Among the large gathering of Armatoli and Klephts that took place at the island of Santa Maura in the year 1805, for the purpose of concerting an universal rising of the Greeks, when "all the captains of Olympus," as Kolokotronês remarks, "were there," there was none who was more conspicuous, or who attracted greater curiosity and admiration from the inhabitants of the island than Niko-Tsaras. Kolokotronês with characteristic brevity only mentions his name with those of others as being "there," and nothing further; but no historical sketch of the Klephts, however brief, can omit the name of one whose encounters with the Turks whether on sea or land, as well as his feats in athleticism, excite our marvel, and almost our incredulity. Skill in running and jumping is not worth recording in a biographical notice of any gravity, were it not that such skill may be explanatory of other feats accomplished in hardly contested fields, where pith and endurance count for something against many odds. Whether he did or did not, as related, leap over seven horses in a line, or spring over a barrier of three waggons drawn abreast, and piled high with thorns to bar his passage, is not of much moment in itself except that such feats if accomplished explain the victory at the bridge of Pravi.

Nicholas Tsaras, or Niko-Tsaras, as he was more generally called, was a Thessalian by birth, his natal place being in the neighbourhood of Elassona. Both his father and his grandfather had been Klephts, and it is probable that he had descended from a long generation of those wild warriors; and if such were the case, his exceptional agility and athletic prowess could readily be accounted for as being inherited gifts. His father, Tsaras, had held the post of Captain of Armatoli for a considerable period. There happened to be a monastery at no great distance from his station, which was fortunately under the direction and superintendence of an Archimandrite, Father Anthemos, who was possessed of excellent literary attainments, and who was moreover a very good man and an enthusiast for Hellas. Tsaras grasped at this opportunity, and sent his son, Nikos, to be educated by him. Some knowledge of science and general literature, with a more perfected acquaintance with his mother tongue, Nikos soon acquired, and he had already made some progress in the study of the ancient language, and was advanced to reading the Iliad, when an event occurred which scattered all his learning to the winds, and at once changed the whole course of his future life.

Tsaras, the father, being an able man, was in the usual course of things, soon marked out as a suspect in the opinion of the Turkish authorities. To make sure of him therefore, and to prevent him from becoming dangerous, two detachments of Albanians were sent out secretly, with orders to bring back Tsaras, dead or alive. It was a dark night which was chosen for performing this duty, and Tsaras had only his children and two or three of his Pallikars with him when the Albanians reached his abode; but he was aware of their approach, and being ingenious and quick-witted, he cast about to see how he might be able to save himself. Hastily binding some of his own clothes together, so as to make the semblance of a figure, he dangled it by a cord from a window. A shower of bullets greeted this appearance, and whilst the Albanians were rushing to seize it as it fell, contending who should be the first to secure the head, Tsaras, followed by his people, made his escape by the door, and under cover of the darkness of the night eluded them, and succeeded in gaining the heights, as the stations of the Armatoli were always on the lower hill-slopes. In this way young Nikos passed suddenly from the peaceful monastery school and his Homer to a rough apprenticeship for the calling of a Klepht. His new career seems to have fascinated him more than his books, to the study of which he never returned. His father was slain in an encounter with the Turks when Nikos was only fifteen years old. He was present at his father's death, and was able to save the head from being taken, and, young as he was, immediately took up the leadership of the band, and sallied forth upon a series of expeditions which made his name both famous and dreaded in the gorges of Kissarvos, and in the whole vicinity of Mount Olympus.

The strength of his arms, and the renown which followed upon his daring, were sure soon to attract the notice of Ali Pasha. Henceforth all kinds of means were employed to subdue him, or to win him over, from threats of vengeance to promise of reward and station. After a time, Nikos was induced to hearken to solicitations for his preferment, and went to Juannina to make his submission in person, with the hope of obtaining his father's Armatolik. It was always the custom of Ali, as before noticed, to receive every Klepht who went to him for that purpose with the utmost graciousness, but after he was dismissed to have him waylaid and murdered on the return journey. Niko-Tsaras, however, was aware of this, and was as wary and shrewd in such matters as Theodore Kolokotronês ever showed himself, so he trod his way back very cautiously. All kinds of snares had been set for him ; but he went out from Juannina at night, and choosing paths and byways that were known to very few, he got safely into Thessaly. When there, he used less precaution; and it is said that crowds of Greeks followed him as he passed along, regarding him with as much awe as admiration. Nikos did not return to the hills at this juncture. A wave of gentler emotions and thoughts of the pleasures of peaceful occupations must at this time have passed over him ; for, like every other Klepht, he now married, and would probably have settled down on the beautiful coasts of Thessaly, and have led a quiet, uneventful life in the future, if he had not speedily discovered that he was in perpetual danger of assassination from the emissaries of Ali Pasha. Thus menaced, he began to long again for the comparative safety, and also for the freedom of the rocks, and he determined to take up gun and sabre and renew his former life, not, as before, merely to rob and harass the Turk, but to achieve the liberation of his country.

It is conjectured that about this era he had some communication with Ypsilanti, the Governor of Wallachia, which led him to form certain definite plans towards carrying out the aims which he was now entertaining for the purpose of promoting a general rising; all of which, however, resulted in nothing more than a display of heroism and powers of stoical endurance. A descent upon Macedonia was what he first had in contemplation, and he crossed from Karpenesi to Skiathos, and took ship to the base of Olympus, intending to move thence into Macedonia. The Pasha of Thessalonica sent to ask him who he was, and whither he was going? to which he replied, that he was going to join Mouchtar Pasha, who was fighting with the Russians, and hoisting the Turkish flag, he was allowed in consequence to proceed. The deception was discovered after a time, when he at once lowered the Turkish banner and raised that of the cross. He was pursued by three thousand Turks, but managed to reach the hill Rilos, which he found occupied by a still larger body of the enemy, and then, as he had no guides, he resolved to return to those parts with which he was better acquainted. So he regained the valley of Nestos, which he had before traversed to reach Rilos, and after fighting day and night for two days, he was successful on the third day in being able to force a passage by which he reached the Bay of Kontessa.

Russia had promised to aid him in this expedition, and the Russian Admiral Piniavin had agreed to await him with help in the Bay of Kontessa, in order to take him and his men away in his ships, if the expedition failed. There was no Russian fleet there. The Klephts had the ocean before them, and behind them was the enemy in considerable force, to the right was the unfordable river Strymon, and there was no other passage but the bridge of Pravi. Pravi itself is situated on a tableland between two high hills, on the left by the sea is the plain of Sychna. The bridge is stated to have been a thousand paces in length, and either end was closed by strong gates closed by chains.

It was in 1804 that his brilliant exploit at the bridge of Pravi, now to be narrated, called forth eloquent bursts of song from the historians of the people. In pursuance of the designs which he had projected of making an expedition into Macedonia, he had taken with him a body of three hundred Klephts, all picked men. The Turks had been forewarned, and had occupied all the most important passes. Upon his arrival at the narrow bridge of Pravi, he found the passage barred by iron chains drawn across, and a force of three thousand Turks opposed to him at that advantageous post, with the full expectation of effectually crushing him. He took up his position on an eminence, but in a short space of time was so completely surrounded that he was neither able to advance nor to retreat. For three days and for three nights, Nikos and his Klephts kept the Turks at bay, but in the evening of the third day they began to drop down with faintness and exhaustion, and, more than all, their cartouche-boxes were emptied. Nikos rightly conjectured at this point that there was nothing left for them to do but to attempt to force a passage through the enemy, sword in hand. Desperate men can achieve desperate things. With a sudden rush they burst right through the body of the Turks, broke the chains across the bridge with blows from their Damascus blades, and flew forward to the town of Pravi, whilst the Turks dispersed and fled.

Nikos and his men stopped at Pravi just long enough to appease their hunger and obtain a little rest, when, hearing that all the defiles before them were occupied by the enemy, they retraced their steps, and again sought the mountains of Thessaly, which they reached in safety after so great and useless an expenditure of energy and courage.

This expedition having signally failed, and Nikos seeing that his position in the mountains as a captain of Klephts was one full of uncertainty and danger, all hope of obtaining the Armatolik held by his father being completely abandoned, he considered what way he could best damage the Turks, and at last resolved to carry on the warfare against them by sea. For this purpose he fitted out two ships and reinforced his men. His first act was to seize upon a building on the coast of Thessaly, which he made his head-quarters; and in a short time the Gulf of Thessalonica resounded with his exploits.

It was not long before other leaders of Klephts imitated his example and joined themselves to him, among whom was Gianni Stathas. Two at least of their ships, if not more, were painted black and had black sails, whilst Stathas himself was also clothed in black; but they floated the Greek white and blue banner above their funereal-looking vessels. Pappas Euthymios, during the same time, was concerting measures with him for the overthrow of Ali Pasha, but before their plan could be carried into effect, Nikos was killed almost accidentally. Some of his sailors and Pallikars, having landed in order to take in supplies of water, fell in with a party of Albanians, by whom they were attacked, and some sharp fighting took place between them. Nikos, who was in the building before alluded to, looking down upon the encounter, issued forth to take part in it. When the Albanians saw him approaching they all fled, with the exception of one man, who in former times had been one of his own Pallikars, and who having been punished for some misdemeanour whilst under his command, bore him a grudge in consequence. This man hid himself behind a tree, and as Nikos was returning after the Albanians had taken flight, he fired upon him. Nikos fell, the bullet having struck him in the hip. He was carried back to the building, where he died in the course of a few days, when he was borne in one of his own ships to the island of Skyros, and was there buried by his Pallikars with much ceremony, and his sword was taken to his widow, who put it reverently aside to keep for his son. At the time of his death, Nikos was about thirty-seven. His personal appearance is described as very handsome and imposing. The culture of his youth was not without its effects, for besides imparting a dignity to his manners, the letters written by him were remarkable for correctness and elegance. It was his physical attainments, however, which attracted his Klephts to him, and they loved to talk of his swiftness, which could surpass that of any horse. They were superstitious in their estimation of his powers, believing that he had a charmed life, and that a ball would glance off if it should touch his skin and would leave him unhurt.

The priest Klepht, Pappa-Thymo, as he is generally called, has just been alluded to as concerting a rising with the pirate Klepht, Niko-Tsaras. A Christian priest figuring as a Klepht may at first sight seem a strange anomaly until it is remembered that throughout this introduction the word *Klepht* is synonymous with *patriot*. Under the domination of Ali there was, in fact, no more determined leader of Klephts throughout all Thessaly, than this Pappas Euthymios, nor was there one against whom the Pasha of Juannina felt a more rooted hostility. When it is taken into account that this priest came from a generation of Klephts, that he was the eldest son of the renowned Blachavas, who was for many years a captain of Armatoli, at Khasia, the transition from priest to Klepht is not to be wondered at. The blood of the warrior rather than the ascetic flowed in his veins. Blachavas, his father, possibly from pious motives, devoted his eldest son to the service of the Church, whilst he brought up the two younger ones to be Klephts or Armatoli. It is quite evident that Euthymios was never attached to his sacred profession, as immediately upon the death of his father he assumed the leadership of the Armatolik, and was acknowledged as their captain by his two brothers and his father's Pallikars.

Ali Pasha, who was possessed of great shrewdness and perception in his judgment of the characters of men, immediately regarded this step with mistrust, and Pappa-Thymo was at once an object of suspicion. All his usual methods of alternating threats with cajolery, and attempts to destroy him with promises of advancement were resorted to. The Pappas listened to none of them. It was not as an Armatolos or a Klepht that he was intending to work; he had probably been laying his schemes during his quiet life in the priesthood, and he at once aimed far higher than in maintaining the post he derived from his father, or in making raids for the sake of spoiling the Turks.

His whole heart and mind was set upon a rising,
and for this end he consulted with Niko-Tsaras,
and for this end he also went down to the confederation of chiefs, which met at Santa Maura.
That confederation, as it has been shown before,
resulted in nothing; but Pappa-Thymo, after that
had collapsed, determined to act by himself. In
addition to his own Pallikars he had he thought
gained over a number of Albanians who were discontented with their service under Ali, and he
prepared for a descent into Akarnania, when he
hoped to be supported by the Souliotes and other
bodies; for the captains of Klephts in different
parts of Greece, as well as many Turkish Agas,
had promised him their adherence. All the
arrangements which he had prepared were
frustrated by the treachery which gave Ali full
information of every one of his projects. He
had fixed upon the 29th of May, the anniversary
of the capture of Constantinople, for the day of
the projected rising, but the Turks of Thessaly,
who had promised to join him, wavered when the
time for acting drew near.

His fellow plotters in Epirus hastened to give
him information concerning the peril in which he
was placed, but he, nothing daunted, rashly anti-
cipated the projected movement, and raised the
standard of revolt at Khasia on the 5th of May,
when with six hundred of his followers he went down
to Kalabaka to cut off all communication with
Epirus. By a special messenger he announced the

course events had taken, and summoned all the Armatoli to assemble themselves. He also wrote to those Turks of Trikkala who had promised him their assistance, but they were no longer disposed to give him their aid. At this juncture Blachavas left his brother Theodore in command at Kalabaka, and flew to Olympus to rouse the Armatoli there, and to gather more supplies of men. Meanwhile, the other brother, Demetrius, who had been sent with three hundred of the insurgents to the bridge of Baba, where the Derven-aga Jousouf was stationed, was at first able to drive him back into Hani; but Jousouf, uniting with some Albanians under Veli Bey, and other forces also combining, turned again, when a terrific contest was renewed.

At the same time, Mouchtar, Ali's other son, was moving on at the head of five thousand Turco-Albanians with a commission from Ali to lay the whole country waste. The same traitor who had been disclosing the intentions of Pappa-Thymo from the beginning, now guided Mouchtar to the pass, which Theodore was to hold as a post of the utmost importance. On the 7th of May in the early morning these two unequally matched forces began the combat. The advance guard of Mouchtar was at first repulsed, when Mouchtar himself, sword in hand, barred its retreat. The battle was waged for two hours, at the end of which the whole of the six hundred Greeks, as well as their brave captains, were all cut to pieces. Blachavas arrived on the spot with a reinforcement of five hundred Olympians, only in time to see that the sacrifice had been consummated. A ghastly convoy of the remains of these heroes went to Juannina on mules, where their heads were cemented into a pyramid.

Pappa-Thymo would not risk the lives of the reinforcement of five hundred men which he had brought from Olympus by engaging with Mouchtar Pasha and his many thousands, and he, therefore, led them back in safety to Olympus.

It was at this time in the midst of his anguish and rage, at the waste of so many brave lives, that Blachavas determined to unite with Niko-Tsaras and other fugitive Armatoli from Olympus, and by fitting out a fleet, to carry on the war by sea. Hundreds of disaffected men swelled the numbers who daily flocked to join these piratical ships, which carried on their devastations even in sight of the Sultan's fleet. Alarmed at the prospect of affairs, the Sultan issued a firman, commanding them to cease their ravages, and offering them an amnesty. To Ali Pasha this firman also counselled abstinence from such a display of enmity as he had lately been showing, whilst the Patriarch put a seal to this advice by a letter, composed in synod, which he sent to Pappa-Thymo exhorting him as a Christian priest to abstain from so sinful a life, and offering him absolution for all that was past.

Blachavas was prevailed upon; he immediately stopped all his piratical courses, dispersed all his fleet, and disbanded all his Armatoli.

Without entering into every detail it is sufficient to state that through fraud, having held out some promise of restoring him to his father's Armatolik, Ali got possession at last of the person of Blachavas. In great pomp the unfortunate man was conducted to the Court of Juannina, and delivered up to the Pashalik. It was in the court-yard of the Palace where for two days he was exposed to the insults of a fanatical mob that Mons. Pouqueville, the French consul, saw him, and thus graphically describes the bearing of the captive :—

"I had once met Blachavas at Milias on Mount Pindus, in all the pride of freedom, and surrounded by his warlike companions; I saw him again for the last time bound to a stake in the court of the seraglio at Juannina. The rays of a burning sun fell full on his deeply bronzed forehead, down which the sweat of agony and exhaustion was flowing in copious streams. Even in death his eye still flashed defiance; and turning on me a look more serene than that of the monster who directed his torments, he seemed to call on me to witness with what calmness a hero can die. Without a moan or a shudder he received the last blows of his executioners, and his manly limbs severed from his body and dragged through the streets of Juan-nina, showed to the terrified Greeks the remains of the last of the chieftains of Thessaly."

This outline of the lives of a few of the most re-markable of the Armatoli and Klephts is a picture of them as a whole, and is presented to us again almost word for word in the scenes which Kolokotronês has jotted down from his own personal experience. It is the same thing throughout several centuries of endurance—heroism and daring, perils and escapes, betrayals and death. In his generous appreciation of the captains who had been sacrificed before the rising of 1821, Kolokotronês remarks, that had THEY lived, the liberation of his country would have been effected during the first year of the struggle. This is rather more than doubtful, although if the ranks of the insurgents had not been so reduced by the loss of those capable leaders, Theodore would have found coadjutors more worthy of himself, if, it must, be added, he could have controlled himself into acting in conjunction with them, but his inability to submit his will to that of others is tolerably well shown in his " Autobiography." The terseness and abrupt brevity of these utterances, bear the stamp of truth in every line. They are the frank outspoken statements of an uncultured man of exceptional natural ability, who was not careful to conceal anything, least of all his contempt for indecision and weakness. Descended from a generation of Klephts, the son of a most renowned captain, looked up to by every scion of the Kolokotroni as head of the family, it is not surprising that he was so little amenable to a provisional government of professors and priests. He was not, nor could he ever have been, popular with the heads of parties. He was irritable and passionate to a degree, and he occasionally gave vent to feelings of displeasure in a rather strong manner, as can well be inferred from an anecdote given by his editor in some notes appended to his "Autobiography," who relates that whilst he was in Zante, he took up an English edition of the Greek New Testament and began to read from it, when a young man who was present, and who was a reader in the Greek Church, began to expostulate with him for so doing, bidding him to remember that it was forbidden by the Patriarch, " and, therefore, you will be accursed of God." Koloko-tronês, upon hearing this remark, was so trans-ported by a sudden access of anger, that he sprang up, and seizing the young man by his thick black hair, hurled him to the ground, when some by-standers rescued him from the chief's fury. It was conjectured by those who witnessed this occurrence, that the reference to the authority of the Patriarch had brought to the remembrance of Kolokotronês the excommunication fulminated by that prelate, which had been the occasion of so much suffering to himself and his kinsmen.

That he was placable and forgiving, and that his wrath, if quickly aroused, was as easily appeased, is evident from the fact that he could tolerate as colleagues men who had not been un-willing when he was a Klepht to deliver him up to death for a certain number of grosia. That the tender emotions were occasionally as readily called

forth as his fiery ebullitions of temper, the torrents
of tears which he shed when the death of Karais-
kakes was announced to him are proofs sufficient.
At the funeral of Zaimês with whom he was always
in contention, his sorrowful demeanour occasioned
some surprise to one who was present who reminded
him of his continual disputes with that politician
whilst he was living. "True," was his answer,
" I always differed from him, but I never bore him
any ill feeling." It is related of him that his
despatches showed his temporary moods, for it was
only when he was angry that he employed the
capital letter Θ in his signature $\Theta\epsilon\grave{o}\delta o\rho o\varsigma$, whilst if
he were pleased, that condition of mind was
evidenced by a small initial being used, and his
name Theodore then appeared written $\theta\epsilon\grave{o}\delta o\rho o\varsigma$.

Although it must certainly be assumed that
there were many who personally disliked him, yet
on the other hand it is distinctly evident that he
was also capable of inspiring a very strong and
remarkable devotion. Apart from the duties of
sonship, how beautiful is the conduct of Gennaios
in every campaign in his obedience to an exacting
leader! Apart from this unquestioning obedience
which Kolokotronês required and obtained from
his son, there are everywhere marks of an exceptionally strong attachment to him, which probably
was accentuated by the behaviour of Gennaios
before Tripolitsa, when he was a youth of only
seventeen years of age. He made a conspicuous
figure upon that occasion, during the siege of the

city, when the Turks came forth from the gates in full force, thinking that the mere sight of so large a host of cavalry and infantry, fully equipped in all points, would of itself be sufficient to terrorise the undisciplined and badly-armed rebels, and cause them to take instantaneous flight. This result did not occur, and the Greeks met them boldly, when there was a desperate conflict, and a consequent repulse of the Turks. Young *Gianni* Kolokotronês, who till then had been known by his baptismal name Gianni (John) only, here exchanged that name for *Gennaios* (brave), which was bestowed upon him by his fellow combatants and others for his heroic conduct in the field, and by which name alone he was ever afterwards called.

Amid much base desertion in numbers of the colleagues of Kolokotronês, the noble constancy of Koliopoulos remained unmoved throughout, and through all temptations and trials he never once swerved from his fealty; and that of his nephew Niketas—the *Niketaras*, "with the swift-winged feet" of the folk-songs, and of his own familiar moments, is unrivalled. Of Niketas, the *Turkophage*, or Turk-eater, as he was surnamed from his exploits, he, whom no horse could overtake so agile a runner was he, Dr. Howe, the American, who detested Kolokotronês, has nothing but praise. "Of all those who fought in the war of liberation," he says, "there was no more high-minded or perfect a character than he," adding that his devotion to his uncle was so remarkable that he identified him absolutely with the cause of his country, as an embodiment of patriotism itself, and never questioned but that the old chief was always in the right, and that swayed by this feeling, and thus judging, he chose the welfare of Kolokotronês, good patriot though he was, to mean the welfare of his country. From the entire absence of self-seeking in his character, and from his probity, Niketas has been called the " Aristides of the Revolution." When fortune favoured the Greeks, and a fortress was stormed or a citadel taken, there have not been wanting those who have censured the needy victors with greed in their partition of the spoils. So timeless an accusation cannot be brought against Niketas, who in all his campaigns never asked for, and never received more, than *one Damascus blade.*

Diakos in his dying moments found solace in the remembrance that "Niketas was left," and there must have been some consolation to the oppressed heart of the hunted-down Captain of Klephts when, after his flight to Zante, he recounts in anguish "out of thirty-two Kolokotroni only seven remained," that Niketas was one of that seven.

The amount of influence which the Kolokotroni exercised over the people of the Morea when their power was at its height, which may be assumed to have been somewhat before 1770, is evidenced by the number of popular ballads which are dedicated to recounting their family annals. These folk-songs, which were first inspired by the prowess of Kostantês the father, followed the son Theodoros through his whole career down to the very hour of his death, whilst the relations, whether uncles or cousins, like lesser luminaries or satellites, also invoked severally a recognition from the heroic muse of the Peloponnesus. The tragic events of 1780, when Kostantês and several of his brothers were slain, were fruitful in calling forth folk-poetry of the above kind, whilst every circumstance of any note in the lives of the twenty-five Kolokotroni whom their chief and the head of the family laments as having fallen in consequence of the firman of 1803, has been made the subject of a separate poem.

The imagery in this poetry is extravagant in its expression, but underlying all its metaphors there is truth in the narratives as they stand, and they testify to the devotion borne by the peasants. A reverse of fortune which had happened to this family, and their temporary absence in consequence from their accustomed haunts, calls forth the following rhapsody—"The sun is shining brightly on the hills—On the plains and on the strongholds of the Klephts; But where are the Kolokotroni who have silver, yea, silver in plenty? They had five rows of buttons below, and six rows above. When they went to church they disdained to walk the earth; They went on horseback to worship. The horsemen kissed the cross and the priest's hand; They dismounted from their horses, and went in one by one," &c.

Although in consequence of the firman, and the excommunication which the Patriarch felt compelled to fulminate by command of the Sultan, it might almost appear that every one's hand was against him, and ready to deliver him up to torture and to death; yet the passionate laments that these songs exhibit at this time for the dangers which surrounded "Theodoraki" show very clearly that the men who were willing to betray him, and who were pursuing him, belonged to a different class to the poets. "O God! where are the Kolokotroni gone, that they come no longer to weddings or to feasts?" would not be sung by any other than the peasants who were generally on the side of the Klephts. The following, which is chosen for its brevity, but which is only one out of a number of others, may serve to exemplify how great was the fascination by which the Kolokotroni held the people of the Morea—"How heavy is that cloud which ready now to break doth lower; the waters cover all the plains, snows on the hill-tops shower. It is not rain, it is not snow; they are tears and bitter weeping, in which the firman which hath come the Morea is steeping—Roumaics, Turks, are all in arms, our Klephts beloved betraying—the Klephts, the Kolokotroni brave, now eager to be slaying."

The imputations which have been so often

brought against Kolokotronês, that he only aimed at freeing the Morea, in order to become its ruler, derive all their plausibility from his almost extravagant attachment to the place of his birth. Apparently he was never happy when he could not tread its rugged mountains, and whilst he was in Zante he was daily in the habit of ascending a height whence he could see the Peloponnesus, and there he would stand and gaze upon the outline of her hills with mingled feelings of pleasure and pain. "There," he would say, "is my home; there was I born; there are the graves of my kindred; and there have my brethren been slain."

But the remote idea of kingship, if not indulged by himself was one not unfamiliar to the people of the Morea in respect to him. The Klephts assumed a kind of sovereignty among themselves, and in one of the "heroic songs" dedicated to sing the praises of the Kolokotroni brotherhood, there is a bold renunciation of the authority of the Sultan and his firman, and an assertion that Theodoraki is King of the Morea—a king equal to the Sultan, and that his brothers are Kadis and Viziers. Theodoraki is also always described as "wielding the sword of Leonidas." It will be seen in his "Autobiography" that one man out of a body of Klephts who had submitted, and who were serving under the Turks, refused absolutely to march against him—he would march against any one else, "but not against our king." This popular idea, aided by his own assumptions of independence, would naturally strengthen any suspicions which the provisional government might harbour at times as to his ultimate designs.

As strong and unbending in will as he was undaunted in prowess, there is, nevertheless, seldom to be seen in the autobiographies of public men so much restraint as is exhibited in this man. He hardly speaks of himself at all apart from his actions. A few words record the plain fact that he marries, and not once afterwards is his wife mentioned. That this was not the result of indifference may be gathered from the reverence which he displayed at her obsequies; for she dying whilst they were in Zante, Theodore, when the usual requiem service was held, himself bore the funeral cakes (κόλυϐα) into the church, carrying the salver which contained them upon his head. Of his children nothing is mentioned until they are of an age to bear arms. He is reticent of his feelings throughout, except when he speaks of his country, and sixty years and more of travail and exposure to every danger, from the time when he was born under a tree on the mountain till the day when he was brought to judgment by a faction and heard sentence of death pronounced against him, had left him unchanged. On that day he was not voluble in his own defence, and he made no appeal to his past services. " Lord, into Thy hands I commend my spirit " were the only words which fell clear and unfalteringly from the lips of the old warrior in the near presence, as he then thought, of death from the hands of the executioner—saying which he crossed himself, and then *took a pinch of snuff*.

The people, however, never swerved from their love to him. When some years before this last trial he had been dismissed from the generalship, all the reverses that afterwards befell the Greek arms in the Peloponnesus were ascribed to his withdrawal, and the senate was obliged to restore him to the command in answer to the reiterated cries of an angry mob—"Give us back Kolokotronês! give us back Kolokotronês!"

It is gratifying to reflect that the old chief lived ten years after his condemnation to death, and that he enjoyed the full confidence of the young monarch, Otho, whose first gracious act after attaining his majority was to release him from confinement. Only a few days before his decease, which occurred in February, 1843, he was present at a ball given at the palace, and death seems at last to have come to him very gently upon the evening of the same day, in the morning of which he had attended the marriage of a friend.

In translating the following "Autobiography," which was not written down by the hand of Kolokotronês himself, but dictated by him to Tertzetis, who transcribed with exact fidelity the words as they fell from his lips, the same course has been followed, and no attempt has been made to modify the original.

The authorities which have been consulted are the Greek works : "The History of the War of Independence," by S. Trikoupês; "The History of Greece," by Paparregopoulos ; "Greek Miscellanies," by Sathas ; "The Risings of Greeks against Turkey," by Sathas; "The History of Epirus," by Aravandinos; "The Songs of Epirus," by Aravandinos; "Chants Populaires," by Fauriel; "Sketches of Actors in the Revolution," by Dr. Howe; "History of Modern Greece," by Tennent, &c.

THERE was a certain person from Roupaki, near the village Tourkoleka, whose own place having been destroyed, departed thence and went over to Libovisti. This happened some three hundred years ago. He appeared to be intelligent, so the chief elder there made him his son-in-law, and the heir of all his possessions. His name was Tzergines, and sixty families of that name can be found in Messenia at the present day. A son was born to him who was very handsome indeed, but he was seized and carried off by the Albanian chief Bouloubasês, who put him in fetters. This young man's name was Demetraki. The Albanians who were guarding him amused themselves by jumping in threes *—when Bouloubasês told him that if he liked to jump also, he would remove his chains. Demetraki replied to this offer by saying that he would jump with his irons on, if the chief would give him his freedom if he surpassed the others. As the Albanian thought that it would be utterly impossible for him to do much in his fetters, he readily promised to set him at liberty if this should happen. He accordingly, having his chains on,

* Three consecutive jumps—a common game in Greece.

jumped with the others, and by his superior skill won his freedom again. He afterwards married and had three sons, who were named Chronos, Lambros, and Demos. They became the possessors of five hundred sheep and sixty horses and cattle. These were taken from them by their rivals and killed ; upon which they went to Roumêli, and, becoming Klephts, were there for twelve years, after which they went back to the Peloponnesus, taking twelve Roumeliotes with them. The Turks when they heard of their return attacked them, and one of them was killed, but the others managed to save themselves. Demos, the younger of the two who were now left, married the daughter of Captain Chrones from Chrysovitsi, a great house. This was when Morosini governed the Morea. He was not one of the Venetian captains. The son of Demos was called Botsikas, instead of his family name of Tzergines, because he was small and dark-skinned.

In Botsikas' time the Turks came into the Morea. The Chrysovitsioti, the Libovisioti, and the Arkourodematiti went to Pyrgos of Dara, and made war against six thousand Turks ; they were defeated, however, but Botsikas himself escaped. He had one son, Gianni, and an Albanian said to him concerning this son, " What monkey have you here ? " For truly *his back was like a crow's*, and so the name *Kolokotronês—κῶλος*, back ; *κοτρών*, crow—remained with him and his descendants. Botsikas was killed, Gianni was hung at Androusa, and thus from 1553, when the Turks came into our parts, they never admitted their supremacy ; but there was always war.

KOLOKOTRONÊS,

THE KLEPHT AND THE WARRIOR.

CHAPTER I.

WAS born in the year 1770. It was the 3rd of April, and it was Easter Tuesday. The revolt of the Albanians in the Peloponnesus had taken place in the previous year of 1769.* I was born under a tree on the hill called Ramavouni, in the district of old Messenia. My father, Kostantês Kolokotronês, had been a captain of the Armatoli in Corinth, a post which he held for the space of four years. He left Corinth, however, to go to Mani, and whilst at Mani he harried the Turks greatly.

In the year 1779 the Kapitan Bey and Mavrogenês † came down and overrun Mylos and Nauplia. They sent papers of submission through all the Peloponnesus, and the people went up and made their submission in person to the Kapitan at Mylos. He forwarded to my father a special and separate paper of submission, and asked him to join them in their endeavour to expel the Albanians,

* See Note A.   † See Note B.

assuring him that the rayah should have his rights. My father straightway moved forward with a thousand of his soldiers and took possession of Trikorpha, near Tripolitsa, but did not go to the Bey because he feared to do so. The Kapitan then rose up from Mylos, and with a force of six thousand regulars and three thousand Klephts marched through Doliana towards Tripolitsa and encamped. As my father was still at Trikorpha the Kapitan Bey sent to him again, commanding him to go to him by himself in order to make his submission, but my father gave this reply, " This is not a fitting time for me to go and make my submission. The Albanians are at Tripolitsa, and they can seize upon all the wild part of the country and disperse themselves over the whole of the Peloponnesus, and get possession of it." My father, nevertheless, sent the Bey a present of a capote for himself and twenty jackets for his captains.

Whilst the Turkish army was advancing upon Tripolitsa in order to besiege the Albanians, a body of four thousand Turko-Albanians came down for the purpose of driving my father from his encampment; but he repulsed them, and pursued them for some distance, and then returned to his former position. The Turkish army commanded by the Bey had moved away to Agio Sosti, a place some little way off, when an additional force of Albanians, six thousand in all, again attacked my father, and were again driven back.

The Albanians saw that it would not be possible for them to hold Tripolitsa because it was not walled; so they gathered all their forces together against my father ; but he made a furious onslaught upon them and drove them into the open plain, where he was joined by other captains. They rushed into the fields, and the cavalry cut them down on the plain as reapers mow the wheat; the horsemen fell upon them and reaped them—the cavalry on one side and my father and his troops on the other. Whilst they were fighting the Albanians cried out, " Kolokotronês, do you not give any quarter ? "

" What quarter should I give to you," he replied, " you who have come here and despoiled my country and made slaves of us, and done us every evil which it was possible for you to do ? "

" It is your turn now," they replied ; " ours is to come."

Out of a force of twelve thousand men, there were only seven hundred who made their escape to Dadi.

They built up a tower at Tripolitsa with the heads of these Albanians, and the Peloponnesus was at peace for a time. The next year, however, namely in 1780, the same Kapitan Bey came down again and endeavoured to destroy my father. A squadron arrived at Marathonisi, and armies were brought over both by sea and land. The colony of Kastanitsa, where Kostantês Kolokotronês and Panagiotaras were established, was six hours distant from Marathonisi. Upon the coming of the squadron Panagioras, who was a Maniote by birth, solicited his countrymen to lend him some assistance, and the Maniotes promised that they would go and aid him, but no help ever came to him from them. The dragoman Mavrogenês was a Greek born, and he was a man of ability. He had made the Maniote, Michael Tropaki, a Bey, and by making him a Bey he secured his aid for himself, and a force of fourteen thousand men was brought down to besiege them.

The Seraskier, Ali Bey, sent a writing to the besieged summoning them to surrender, and demanding that both my father and Panagioras should each give one of their sons as hostages, and in that case he would remove his hand from themselves, but they both answered—

" We will not surrender—we wish for war—and he who is conquered, let it be for him to submit."

Panagioras still hoped that help would come from Mani.*

The Turkish army then prepared to besiege them vigorously; they brought up cannon and bombs and poured upon them an unceasing fire both by night and by day. Their bombs and their cannons, however, did not inspire the besieged with any dread, and for twelve nights and for twelve days they stood out nobly and bravely. When, however, they saw that no assistance was forthcoming, they determined to flee from the towers in which they were besieged. There were two towers, the one being held by the father of Panagioras, and the other by my father and Panagioras himself. Now the father of Panagioras was an old man of eighty years, and his mother, who was there also, was about the same age, and she by reason of her many years was not able to flee with the other women during the sortie. Panagioras' old father therefore called out from his tower to my father and his son, " Set fire to the other towers, but I shall remain where I am." He did remain there with one servant only and his wife, who also had her one maid, with the full intention of fighting, but hoping nevertheless that his sons would eventually be able to go and help him. The battle was thus carried on by him and his servant, but he had great skill.

They who held the other tower made a rush through the camp of the Seraskier sword in hand. There were only three men killed in the sortie, and a part of the women, but many children were captured and taken for slaves, and among them were my two little brothers, one being three years old, and the other only a year old. Both of these were carried off into slavery (but they were afterwards redeemed). When they sallied forth they found that the Turks were occupying the hills for the night; and about

* See Note C.

the middle hour of the night the moon shone forth, and her rays lightened up every place. It was therefore a very short night, and there was consequently no time for them to reach Mani, for when they got to the hills it was daytime. Panagioras was captured alive, and was afterwards killed by the Bardouniotes. My father and his two brothers, Apostolês and George, were also slain, the one on the hill, and the other when he was alone, because he had been wounded : my uncle Anagnostês, who was one of the four Kolokotroni who had been shut up together in the tower, was saved. Myself, with my mother and sister, were saved by my father's pallikars. Kostantês Kolokotronês, my father, was wounded by a sword-thrust at the time of the sally, and was afterwards killed through the treachery of a Turkish friend. His head was never recovered. The murderers who slew him concealed his body for the sake of the property which they found upon him. Three years afterwards his body was dug up, and every one knew that it was the body of Kostantês Kolokotronês because one of his little fingers had a crook in it, in consequence of a cut from a Turkish sabre years before. They had hidden him in a hollow between Arna and Kotzatina, and he was afterwards interred again at Melia. My father was exceedingly dark and very thin, so swift of foot that the most speedy stallion could never overtake him; he was thirty-three years of age at the time of his death, and was of middle height, black-eyed, and slim. The Albanians held him in so great a terror that they swore by his name. "May I be saved from the sword of Kolokotronês!" was their favourite oath. It was said that before he was slain he had killed with his own hand seven hundred Turkish irregulars.

Panagioras was a man of a gigantic stature, also young, with black hair; a man of noble breeding, of about thirty-

seven or thirty-eight years of age. Old Gianni Kolokotronês was killed at Androusa—his hands and his feet were
cut off, and he was then hung; but his son some time
afterwards avenged his death. As for the old father of
Panagioras, who was left alone fighting in the tower, his
servant, who surrendered himself up, bore witness to seeing
him persistently lighting his fusee, but the old man was
captured alive. When brought before the Kapitan Bey he
was asked, " Why did you not make your submission ? "

" I make my submission now," answered the old man,
" because the heads of those who submit are not cut off."

The hands and feet, however, of the aged warrior were
amputated, and he himself was afterwards hung.

We remained some time at Melia in Mani with my uncle
Anagnostês, and I bought back the two enslaved children,
my brothers Gianni and Chrestos. One of them had been
taken to Hydra ; and we stayed in Mani three years. We
had sustained many losses, and our other uncles on our
mother's side, who were called the Kotsakaioi, came to us
and took us away with them to Alonistaina. We managed
to get away without being recognized, for we were in great
fear of the Turks. My uncle Anagnostês afterwards went to
Sampazika, in the district of Leontari, which is at the
extremity of Mani. He there allied himself with George
Metaxa, a native of the place, and a prefect, and a good shot,
to whom he gave his daughter in marriage, and he then built
himself a house. Hearing that my uncle had established
himself at Akovo, we left where we were and went and settled
ourselves there. We stayed there some time, and the submitted Klephts appointed me Armatolos of Leontari to act
against the other Klephts, and I managed the province
with leniency. I was then fifteen years old.

When I was twenty years of age I married the daughter
of the chief primate of Leontari, a man who had been ruined

by a Pasha in Nauplia. As I received in dowry both olive-trees and a vineyard, I built houses and settled down as a householder, but I still took care of my Armatolik, and always went about with a gun, for the Turks envied us and wished to slay us all; they were not able to do so because our place was situated on the heights. They therefore kept up a continual warfare against us by craft and subtlety. At one time they sent out one hundred, and upon another occasion two hundred soldiers to attack us, but as these were not able to get us wholly in their power, they did not carry out this attempt. I saw, however, that if they continually found that artifices failed they would at last come against us openly. We received information of this, and fled away from the place. After we had left, the Turks went and destroyed all our possessions, and issued orders that wherever we were found we were to be destroyed likewise.

I now found myself with twelve of the Kolokotroni, all younger than myself, so we took our families to Mani and left them there ; and then we rose up openly as Klephts, and got together our soldiers, sometimes sixty in number, and sometimes less. We remained Klephts for two years straight off, and afterwards, when they found they could do nothing against us, they offered us the Armatolik again. I had Leontari and Karytaina given into my charge, and I remained there as an Armatolos four or five years.

My uncle Anagnostês Kolokotronês gave himself up to drink as a means of forgetting all the past events of his life, and he, my father's eldest brother, was killed in Leontari some time afterwards. They carried off his head. (One of his hands had been cut off in his youth.) He had led an active life for forty years, and was fifty-two years old at the time of his death. He left behind him three sons, Giannaki, Georgaki, and Demetraki, and seven daughters.

At his death he was the last of my father's six brothers.

When we were Armatoli, our children were left in Mani, at Greater Kastania, but during the time that we were in the service we always went down to Mani on special days. We always went to Mani to help the Bey Koumountouraki in his needs, and we also gave our assistance to the party to which he belonged. Captain Konstantine Douraki, who had been a friend of my father, had begun a feud about this time with the Kitriniari, and we had sent him reinforcements.   We had at one time shut up Nicholas Kitriniarês and besieged him, and whilst his brother and cousins were having a meal he discharged his gun in the air.   The Maniotes had caused him to be in great straits, and he therefore desired to deliver the place up, and asked for me.   His design, however, was not to surrender, but to kill me if possible by an act of treachery.   He came himself outside the gate of the tower in order to surrender it, but he had placed some men inside, and these men discharged six guns full at me.   I was struck, but not hurt; I fell down under the roof of the tower gate, and my own men thinking that they had killed me, wanted to slay the relations of Kitriniarês; others, however, called out, " No, let us look after Theodoros. "   The brother of Kitriniarês came up, and I took him by the shoulder and protected him, and at night I threw fire into the tower, and it was then delivered up.   His brother was with us.   The brother then asked me what I meant to do to them for their treachery, and I answered him, " God has preserved me, so I grant them their lives."

Zacharias * was helping the other side.   We fought with each other for a space, and then we had a conference outside.   I supported the Bey.   Mourtzinos was in opposition

* A celebrated chief of the Morea. See Introduction.

to the Bey and my friend the captain.   One must help one's own people for one or two months during the summer.

During the six years described above I removed my children to the village Gianitsa, near Kalamata, because it was better for me on account of provisions.   Mani was envious of the Bey, so Seremet Bey went to drive out Anton Glegoraki Bey.   The Bey Koumountouraki came into Kalamata with sixty men, and I had eighteen with me; but I was prevented from giving any assistance to Koumountouraki, although for friendship's sake I was bound to help him, because the Turks and the Maniotes had assembled three thousand strong against Koumountouraki.   I foresaw that there would be large bodies of men in the captaincies, and it was my advice that we should not go into Mani. We wished to occupy the fort of Koumountouraki, which was four hours distant from Kalamata.   The chieftains and other Maniotes fought with us, and I was wounded, but we took possession of a tower, and afterwards, during the night, we reached the fort.   The sloughing of my wound was internal.   I wrote a letter, therefore, to Panagiotês and Christeas Mourtzinos to obtain from them some agreement by which I could go to Mani to be healed.   The Mourtzinoi told Seremet Bey that they would drive out all the Klephts, which would weaken the power of Koumountouraki, and they made merry with Seremet Bey about my going down in their very midst, and told me that I had better take all my men with me.   I deferred going with my men.   As my men remained behind, one Petrounês became a mediator, with the object of persuading Koumountouraki to make his submission, assuring him that he would suffer nothing; but I said, "When Petrounês comes, do not listen to him, otherwise he will destroy you."

Koumountouraki did not think so: he entered into a

treaty with them, and our people went away. Koumoun-touraki was delivered up, and the squadron took him away captive.

I got healed of my wound, and went back to my Arma-tolik. The primates and Deligianni caused me to do this, for they said, "It is not well that thou dost endanger thyself in Mani; take thy family into Karytaina." So I took my children to Karytaina, and settled in the village of Stem-nitsa.

In the year 1802 a firman came, which commanded that we two, Petimeza and myself, should be killed. This was set in motion by a voivode in Patras. The firman said, " Either your two heads or the heads of the chiefs." Whereupon the vizier of Tripolitsa summoned the father of Zaimês and Deligianni. Zaimês obeyed the summons, but Deligianni was very much afraid. He took an oath to them both that it had nothing at all to do with them. I had accompanied Deligianni as far as Tripolitsa, and as we were returning together I said to Deligianni, " I do not believe that the firman is for us;" and he replied, " Do not fear." The Pasha, however, only sent for those two, and he read the firman to them. "You must give us time," they said, "for these are wild men." Old Zaimês Asemakês, however, had Petimeza quite in his power, be-cause he went down to Kalavryta daily, but for myself I never went to Karytaina. The two primates said that they must make themselves masters of the wild one (Koloko-tronês), and that afterwards they could easily get the tame one (Petimeza). Deligianni made two of the primates take an oath that they would kill me. That was rather difficult to manage, because I was always very cautious. They had a conference with Velemvitsa, and swore him in first; but he replied, "I do not agree with the killing of those men; we shall destroy the province." They did not change their minds, however. They then brought one Bouloubasês with his Albanians into Karytaina. I had my suspicions about this proceeding, and went to pay a visit to a primate in Stemnitsa. "What do you want with the Albanian Bouloubasês here?" I asked; "ho won't become of your opinion." The Albanian then came into Stemnitsa, and I went there also, taking with me fifty of my men. I had an interview with Bouloubasês, when I said to him, "They are trying to set us at loggerheads: tame fowl cannot chase away wild ones. Though all fly away, the sparrow still remains."

That circumstance fortunately brought old Kolias to me, who came with his son Koliopoulos. We now numbered two hundred, and our own men joined us at Magoulia. Anagnostês Bakalês, a primate at Garzeniko, derided the Turks and sent me continual information. I wrote to the two primates (before-mentioned) to send me news also, and to advise me what to do, but they only wrote me lies; and I procured some guns and ammunition from Demetri. Bouloubasês, with his force of two hundred picked men, surprised us, however, at Kerpeni, when we were only forty altogether. I marched outside the village and shut myself up in a monastery at Kermitsa; but if I had remained there I should have been utterly lost, so I left and got away to the wild parts of the country.

Meanwhile they slew Petimeza in Kalavryta, and sent his head to Tripolitsa. We killed some Turks, however, at Magouliana, and we also burnt some of their villages. The primates whereupon appealed to Kolias, asking him to persuade us to make some agreement, whereby everything might be pacified. I was therefore taken back into the Armatolik service again. Deligianni had been trying for three or four months to effect our ruin, but he had not succeeded.

So, in the month of September, I again entered the Armatolik. Deligianni at this time found an opportunity of wreaking his spite. He had a friend in Lala, one Hassan Aga Phida, and he besought him to slay us— treacherously, of course, because we were Armatoli. We had placed our families now in Palouba, and old Kolias, who had discovered the treachery, sent us information that the Lalians were coming down upon us. I was in a village called Tourkokerpeni when I received this news, and I cast about in my mind how I could unravel this secret movement which was astir for the purpose of óverthrowing us, and I thought it over during the whole of the night. The Turks came up and seized upon two roads, sending out two separate bodies, each with two hundred men, in order to entrap me in an ambuscade. I had a traitor about me, and he came to us to see if we were on the move, or if we were sleeping. I had hoped to have been able to send a defiance to them in the morning, but in the morning we found ourselves surrounded in a village. I had given my clothes to an adopted son. We were rejoicing at the return of day, when lo! I saw the Turks drawing nigh. We seized our guns, but as we were endeavouring to get to the back of the hill, my adopted son had eight balls fired into him. My brother Gianni was also wounded. We then shut ourselves up in three houses, and I stationed myself in the cellar. In all we numbered thirty-eight. The second body of two hundred coming up they surrounded us. We fought through the whole of that day, but at nightfall we sallied forth and fled. This occurred on the 7th of March, in the year 1804.

In the year 1805 I left for Zante. The Emperor Alexander of Russia had sent an invitation to the Greeks to take service in his armies.

All of us, both Souliotes and Roumeliotes and we Peloponnesians, had framed an address to the Emperor to ask him to give us help so that we might set our country free. Anagnostaras was very active in getting up this address. The Souliotes and Roumeliotes were in Parga, but Anagnostaras got together a force of five thousand Peloponnesians for the army at once. I went to Zante. When the answer to the address came—that was in August—I had an interview with the general of the Russian army, and he told me that he had arranged to receive into the Russian service as many Greeks as chose to enter, for the express purpose of fighting Napoleon.

"Then, for my part," I answered, "I shall not enter the service. What concern is it of mine in regard to Napoleon? If you, however, want men for the purpose of aiding us to free our own country, I can promise you from five to ten thousand soldiers. We were once baptized with oil, and we have since been baptized with blood, and yet again will we be baptized in blood for the deliverance of our fatherland!"

I stayed in Zante a fortnight, but I would not consent to that measure. I left twenty-eight of my comrades behind, and my nephew Niketas, a son of my brother Gianni Kolokotronês. The other Greek soldiers enlisted, and were sent to Naples.

When the Turks saw this movement they sent information to the Sultan, and expressed to him all their suspicions about it. The Sultan thereupon conceived the idea of taking some summary acts of vengeance on the people. The patriarch (of Constantinople) intervened, saying, "What have the people done? Better that we kill the prime movers and the evildoers;" and so he was turned away from his purpose.

The opinion of the Turks coalesced with the convictions of the French Cabinet, which had advised Turkey to make an end of all those captains called Klephts, and to get rid of the captains of the sea-vessels also, or else at some time or other they would cause a rising.

The Sultan, following this advice, issued a firman to slay all the Klephts. At the same time the patriarch was compelled to issue an excommunication against them, in order to stir up the whole people; and by these means the Peloponnesians, whether Turks or Romaics, were all excited against the Kolokotroni.

I had gone to Zante in August, and I had left it in September, and returned, and in the following January, in the year 1806, came the orders to hunt us all down. Petimeza, Gianni, and Zacharias were already gone from us, and we were now only a hundred and fifty men in all.

We went to the monastery of Velanidia, near Kalamata, and I wrote a letter to the abbot asking him to send us provisions. The Turks seized the letter, and Deli Achmet with a thousand men came down and laid siege to us. We issued out, sword in hand, and put them to flight, pursuing them right into Kalamata, and took their flags, many of their men being slain.

This Deli Achmet had been a noted man in Roumêli. He had been ill-treated by Ali Pasha, and had fled to the Peloponnesus. The Pasha of the place gave him five hundred paid men in order to hunt out the Klephts. As soon as I heard this, having eighty men with me at the time, I went out on purpose to try my strength with him at Akovo (Sampazika), but he was afraid to fight with us. So we then marched on to Vlachokerasia and despoiled it, because *there* were the possessions of that Chaseki who had destroyed and burnt our houses. At another time we went down to Tzepheremini, and when the Turks of Androusa learnt where we were they came up with a hundred men for the purpose of having some blows with us, but we drove them back and frightened them into saving themselves. The same men made a stand at Paleo-Kastro in Melia, when we fought against them all day and at nightfall we escaped. They advanced again into Marmaria, and all the Turks from the different districts joined with them; they surrounded the hill where we were, but we engaged with them the whole of that day also, and in the evening we again drove them back. The nephew of Deli Achmet was present at the conflict at Akovo, when they declined to fight, and on his return to his uncle the latter spat in his face for rage because he refused the encounter. The young man's answer to this affront was :

" May God grant that you yourself may fight with them, and then you will see what they are like."

After that last repulse Deli Achmet departed to Kalamata, where he stayed three months. Being fearful whilst he was there that we might advance against him and give him some trouble (for we had written to him to that effect), he went and had an interview with the Pasha, and said that as *he* could do nothing with us, the best thing would be to make us Armatoli again and thus obtain a little peace. So for this time the matter was passed over.

When I heard that the firman, together with the ex-communication, had actually arrived, I gathered all my hundred and fifty men together and said that we had better go back to Zante; but they having heard that the Russians had taken the whole of the Greeks who had entered their service to Naples, answered with one voice: " We will not go to France; we wish to die in our own country!" and my brother Gianni cried out,

"I would rather be devoured by the birds of our country!"

I then proffered other advice, which was that we should separate into parties of four and five, and keep ourselves concealed during the months of January, February, and March, after which time the snows would be dissolved, and we could then resume our old career. I gave this counsel, because by that time our pursuers would also have dispersed, and the present danger would therefore be averted for awhile; but they would not hearken to me, saying, "We do not wish to spend what few pence we possess!" adding, "Why do you send your captains away from their districts?" "Only do this now," I said again, "and when March comes back we will meet together, and then I will repay you all that you have spent;" but they would not heed me, and went about through every part of the Morea displaying an open flag. This flag bore upon it a X with stars and a half-moon, X signifying Christ.

They had some chiefs of the Morea, namely, the Kou-mountouraki, as hostages in Tripolitsa, and the friends that we had in Mani, as the Mourtzinoi and the rest had been banished by Anton Bey to Zante, therefore we had no longer any refuge in Mani. The hills were covered with snow, so that we could not take to them. On this account thirty of our comrades separated from us and went to Pygadia, and we others spread abroad our flag and marched to Agio-Petro. We sent into Vervena an order that it should forward to us both supplies and bread. "We have powder and shot for you here," was their answer; so we fell down upon the place and despoiled it. Thence we retired to Sampazika, but the Pasha had issued orders throughout every district that all, whether Turks or Romaics, should drive us forth.

From Sampazika we went again to the monastery of
Velanidia, and sent into Kalamata asking both for bread
and guns, but the Kalamatans were afraid to supply us,
so we moved on to Kalamata straightway with the intention
of striking a blow at the Turks, and then the primates
brought to us at Agio-Elias, which is close to Velanidia,
both food, ammunition, and guns. We marched thence
the same day to Pêdema, at the extremity of Kalamata,
and in the evening went on to Tzepheremini. We
were then about an hour from Skala, whither came down
Kehayas Bey with two thousand Turks and cohorts. We
got away that evening to Alitouri, and whilst there the
Androusani and the Leontarians and others, to the number
of about seven hundred, assembled against us. When the
dawn came we began the conflict, drove them out of the
village, and pursued them for a whole hour. We captured
four stallions; many of their men were drowned in the
river, and we also killed many and took a large amount of
provisions and ammunition.

When the soldiers who were in Skala heard that there
was fighting going on, they came to give help to their own
people. We retreated and shut ourselves up in the village
Alitouri, and defended ourselves during the whole of the
day, and in the evening, sallying out with drawn swords,
were able to reach Arcadia. We entered one village and
found it occupied by three hundred Turks, so that we were
not able to get any bread there. The Turks who came to
Alitouri, finding that we were absent, turned round and
came and sought us nearer.

Kehayas Bey now began to oppress the Christian popu-
lations, in order to inspire terror everywhere. The Turks
came upon us from above, but as they were inhabitants of
the district they sent word beforehand for us to flee,
because we were still feared by them. We had built an

encampment in order to fight them. We fled thence and went to Kontovounia to seek for bread, and then returned to a hill to rest. We sent to our friends to find us a boat, so that we might embark in it and get right away, but they answered that all the boats from Pyrgos to Neo-Kastro were retained. As we had no means whereby we could flee to Zante, we returned to the interior of the Peloponnesus. We were able by pillage to procure bread, but the Turks arrived in Psari also, and we were fighting all day.

My comrades now began to flee away from me and became insubordinate, for during this time they had been fighting through the whole of every day, and walking through the whole of every night. So forty left me all at once, and from a hundred men we were now reduced to sixty. The next day we who remained went down to Leontari, but back they came upon us there. We fled on to Sampazika, and there we met again with four hundred Turks, whom I had not expected to find in that place.

We fought with the Turks and we saved our guns, but we had but little bread. At night I told my comrades that we could no longer keep together, and that we must disperse; so we parted, each saying the one to the other, " A happy meeting in some other world."

I only kept with me nineteen of my own relations, and Georgio, one of my captains who had no place to go to. In five-and-twenty days not one of those who left me was alive. Of the nineteen who remained with me, my two first cousins, who were unable any longer to endure hunger and privations, stayed behind and hid themselves, but in a few days they were discovered and were killed; so then there only remained seventeen.

Not knowing whither we were going, we went and took up our quarters by chance close to three companies of soldiers.

Fortune so far favoured us that they did not see us until it was nearly dark, so that we had a little breathing time. They discovered us, however, at last, and we were obliged to make a stand, and to pass through them fighting, in order to save ourselves in so great a peril. We marched all through the night as far as the plain of Leontari; we heard much firing off of guns, and the sounds came from all parts; but we did not know what it meant. Firing off a volley was a signal that Klephts were taken. The next night we went over to Anemodouri to obtain food, but we only found the women there, as all the men were at Drasila, and it was guarded by the Turks. The dogs, who began to lick us, caused some suspicion, and the Turks came and laid siege to us. When the Turks were drawing nigh, the dogs began to bark, and then I knew that the Turks had come up. We took away our families at that time, and by whatever road we found open we managed to get them to Tripolitsa, which we entered quite publicly, and afterwards we went to the heights of Valtetsi in order to take up our quarters there. The women of the village recognized us, and immediately went about saying, "Kolokotronês has just passed through here;" and so we were again pursued. We fled at nightfall, and retraced our way towards Karytaina, and, lest they should know us at that place, we sprang from rock to rock till we came to a sheepfold, when we were told that it was full of Turks. Then I determined that we should divide ourselves into four parties, and go and hide with our friends.

Antony Kolokotronês with one other was concealed by our relations. Demetrius Kolokotronês and three others went down to Visino to hide, for we had relations in that place also, and my brother Gianni with four comrades descended into Demitsana, in a village of which district we had a trusty friend with whom they were to be concealed.

Antony was preserved, and is alive at this hour. Demetraki*
only stayed two days at Visino, and then went away.   He
was captured. They cut off Demetraki's head and his hands
and his feet, for they thought it was I myself, because they
found letters upon him.

My brother Gianni could not find his friend at Demitsana,
so he and his comrades went to a monastery at Aimyalous
and asked a monk who was pruning the vines for food and
shelter. The monk gave them food, and they concealed
themselves in a vat in the vineyard. The monk then went
and gave information to the Turks, who came and besieged
them in the vat, and my brother was killed.

I, who was left with the other four, went to a friend
of mine who was a primate at Pyrgaki, K. Paraskevas by
name, in order to hide. I found his son, whom I had kept
with me in Karytaina.

"I guarded you for a long time," I said to him; "now
you must take care of me."

He took me to a cave, and then I sent him into Vytini to
learn what had occurred there. It was the month of
January. We had been hunted down for twenty days, and
yet we were still alive.

The son gave the news to his father. The father himself went into Vytini, and reported it to the Turks, telling
them that he would lead them straight to the cave where
we were concealed, so that they might seize us. In order,
however, to make sure that we were still there, he came on
beforehand; he was armed; I said to him therefore, "Zacha-
riah, why art thou armed?" And immediately suspecting
him I added, "Fellow, hast thou betrayed us?" "That will
not happen," he answered. Whilst he went back to speak
with them, I, with the other four who were with me, sped

---

* Demetraki, a familiar name for Demetrius; aki being a kind of
affectionate termination, as Georgaki for George, &c.

away to the hill. They pursued us the whole of that day, but Fate was kind to us, for there was not much snow upon the hill, and we were able to walk with ease; but they followed us as far as Zygovisti.

That was the day on which they killed my brother, when the Turks made great rejoicings. I knew directly that they had killed him when I heard volleys fired off, which was a sign of their joy.

I then marched through Liodora to old Kolias and Demetrius, my son-in-law. They had got them at Karytaina as hostages, so I only found my brother Georgaki at the sheepfold. I had some conversation with Georgaki, and he brought us food, and I besought him to go to Zatouna and obtain some information for me. He learnt there that they had killed all our people.

The Turks gave him an order, which had been issued to the Psarai, the Paloubaioi, and to the people of other villages, that if Kolokotronês was killed by them they should have an indemnity for their villages of so many years; but if they did not kill him the sword should not be taken away from them for the space of seven years. The Turks, who had been pursuing me in every direction, considered that there was clearly no other to whom I could flee for refuge except the Kolias family, and therefore they issued this decree. Georgaki came to me and told me everything, so I left him and directed my way to Langada. We went to Kalyvia, in Chrysovitsi, we killed a lamb, and there they betrayed us. We went thence to Arachamitês, and there we again found Turks; we fled onward, and at last reached the monastery of Kaltesia. We knocked at the door: there were two hundred Turks inside. They knew us at once, and immediately set forward in pursuit, but we got safely to Gianitsa, in Kalamata, where we met with one of our comrades, who had been there four days, being quite unable to walk any further on account of great prostration from hunger. We found Turks everywhere, but we could not find either any place of rest or any food.

Roubês was in Gianitsa with four hundred Bardouniotes. I went into a house by chance, and again I found Turks within. I raised my gun quietly and turned away without being discovered, as they were all asleep. I entered another house, but there were Turks everywhere. I managed to get away to the house of my godmother at the far extremity of the village, and she offered me three okas * of bread, for which I gave her a Venetian florin. We marched on to Selitsa. The bread, however, so oppressed our stomachs that we were hardly able to walk.

From Selitsa we journeyed on to Kustanitsa, to my old friend, Captain Konstantês Douraki, whom I trusted greatly, because I had taken care of his family in former times, and because he was, as it were, my co-father-in-law, for I had betrothed my daughter to his son.

Out of the five we numbered, two Maniotes left us and fled to their homes, so now there were only myself and two Roumeliotes.

I remained a month concealed in the house of Douraki. Whilst there, one Niketas came to me from Tourkoleka with twenty-five comrades, and I said to him, "Let us only find a boat, and we will all get over to Zante." But he thought that there need be no longer any fear about going into the interior of the Morea, and therefore turned back again. The Turks killed all of them excepting one, who was captured alive and was taken to Tripolitsa. The Pasha there inquired of him if they were all slain, and he answered, "All except Theodoraki Kolokotronês;" whereat the Pasha flew into so great a rage that he killed very many Turks and Romaics who had

* An oka is 2½ lbs.

declared to him that Theodoros Kolokotronês was destroyed.

The report of my death had given the Turks great satisfaction, but when the Pasha discovered that I was still alive, and actually in Mani, he sent Papazoglou with fifty thousand grosia (about £565) to the Bey of Mani, at Agio-Petro. As soon as he arrived there the Bey summoned Captain Konstantês Douraki to go to him at Kytria, when he said, " I will give you so many thousands (*grosia*) if you will give up this Kolokotronês. I have received most strict orders, and I am told that if I do not succeed in seizing upon Kolokotronês, that he—the Pasha—will write to the Kapitan Pasha, and that you will be dismissed from your position of Bey." Douraki, when he looked upon the *grosia*, determined to betray me, for the Maniotes will do anything for *grosia*.

At a previous interview, after the Bey had discovered that I was concealed in Douraki's house, Douraki had said, " He must be concealed; it will never do not to preserve one who belongs to our family; " but when he saw the *grosia* he forgot everything.

No one except Douraki and the abbot of the monastery there knew that I was living up in Douraki's tower. Douraki at this juncture sent for the abbot, whom he took, together with his eldest son, to see the Bey at Kytria. It was then March, and I had gone there in February. The Bey promised the abbot that he would make him bishop and give him other privileges if Kolokotronês was delivered up alive, and the Bey also wrote a letter to myself, which they brought back with them, which said, " Thou must come hither, and we will talk it over, and I will write to the Kapitan Pasha to send thee a ticket of submission; thou canst come with thy kinsman Douraki." The sole meaning of all this was that they wished that I should be taken alive,

When the abbot and Douraki's son came together to pay me a visit, I suspected that there was some artifice in hand concerning me, but I did not know what form it would take. I therefore sent a boy to little Kastanitsa, about six miles distant from the place in which I was. (It was the place where my father was surrounded.) I sent him to my nephew, Basil Panagiotoras, who came to me that same night with three others. I then told him all that was going on, as well as my suspicions, and I proposed to go away with him. He made answer, "I will go back and sell some oil, and will return in the evening;" but he did not return in the evening.

The next morning my co-father-in-law with the abbot came to me. I rose to greet the abbot. "Welcome," I said. His reply was, "I wish you had come across me." I asked him to speak of something else, but he made no answer. In the evening my co-father-in-law came again, with his brother and two other relations, and gave me the Bey's letter. His brother had some suspicions, and was no party in the plot. I took the writing and read it, when I understood immediately that the desire was to get possession of me alive. "How can we go in the daytime," I said, "when every one will see and know who we are?" "Oh," replied Douraki, "you can dress yourself like a Maniote, then no one will recognize you." His brother then made a sign to me to be careful.

"I will consider the matter until the evening," was my answer. About noon on the same day, however, I gave my answer: "I am one of your own people, and I can go to make my submission at some other time; I am one of your own people, and you have some knowledge of me."

I gave this in writing and handed it to Douraki, who took the writing from me, and opened it, and read it, when he saw that I did not wish to go; and afterwards therefore tried

THEODORE KOLOKOTRONES.

to put some opium into my wine. His wife and sister saw him do this before he took it to the tower where I was, and one of my men also heard the wife say to her husband—

"What is this that thou art doing? Dost thou not remember all the good that Theodoraki has done?"

Douraki, however, only insulted her, and came and offered me the wine, but I had been forewarned by my man, and as he gave it to me I managed to knock over the can which held it, so the wine was spilled. "What do I want now with wine!" I cried. I then told him that it was my intention to leave the place. He tried to persuade me to go into his house and take wine with him before I left, and went in to prepare it, and at the same time he ordered some men to fall upon me and secure me whilst we were drinking together; but his brother prevented me from going in, and he also kept the dogs from barking whilst we got away.

As soon as Douraki discovered this, he himself called out all the villagers, and told out a hundred to keep the roads. I knew the place, however, quite well, and we fled by another way, and got safely to little Kastanitsa, where I found Basil, with whom I had proposed to flee.

We departed thence to the village Pasava, and got to the house of an adopted brother of mine, where we stayed two days. We then sent him to find out Maria, the mother of Tzanetakês; she was the daughter of Panagiotaros. When she came we asked her to procure a boat for us at Marathonisi, so that we could embark in it and get away to Cerigo. Three days afterwards we went in company with Maria and took ship somewhere between Mavrovouni and Marathonisi. We hardly made any sail, as it blew strongly from the north, so that we made very little way. (Palm Sunday was on the morrow.) We touched Souli and sailed back, but the wind was contrary and drove us Elaphonisi. We at last made Cerigo in the face of a violent

storm, and were carried to a village called Potamo.   There
we met with one of the Giatrakaioi, and he said that he
thought it would be better not to declare myself as Kolokotronês whilst I remained in that village.

We went to the governor of Cerigo, whose name was Al-
banitaki, and he scolded us for going about armed.   Whilst
we were there we were recognized by a boy from Pyrgos.
(The day on which we came there was the Great Thursday.)
I then proceeded to the Russian commandant and told him
straightway the whole truth—who we were, and to what we
were reduced, when he immediately gave orders that we
should be well cared for, and supplied with everything that
we needed.

I had been once to a festival at Agia Monê.   This monastery had been a large one, and had been destroyed by the
Turks in a former war.   When I again saw it—the ruined
and desolated church turned into a stable, and roofed with
branches of trees—I made this vow: " Blessed virgin, help
us to deliver our country from the tyrant, and I will build
thee up as thou wast before."

She did help me, and in the second year of the rising.
I fulfilled my vow and rebuilt it.

The kind of life which we had already led aided us much
throughout the war of Liberation, because we knew all the
passes on the hills, and we knew the habits and ways of
men.   We had been accustomed to hold the Turks in contempt, and we were inured to hunger and thirst, suffering,
filth, and every other privation.

CHAPTER II

I ARRIVED in Zante in May. After a month's sojourn there I learnt that Pappadopoulos, the general of the Russian forces, had come into the island of Corfu, and he sent for me and asked me to enter the service. I replied, "I do not intend to enter the Russian service, because my purpose is to return to the Morea and avenge the slaughter of my kindred, and the injuries which I have sustained myself. I could not take an oath, and afterwards become a perjurer by fleeing away secretly." So I returned to Kastro, and remained there ten months without any employment.

I entrusted a letter to one Rontikês, a native of Magoulia, which he was to take to my family, in order that he should obtain and bring me all the property which I had placed with different men. He took it and went, but he showed it to Deligianni, and Deligianni showed it to the voivode, in consequence of which all my goods were lost. That was in 1807.

All the soldiers, and captains, and the Roumeliot Klephts in a body had fled to the seven islands about the same time as my own flight took place. Russia had declared war against Turkey, and commanded all the soldiers to go into Roumêli to attack the Turks. I immediately tried to go to Santa Maura, where they were all assembled, and get as many of them as I could for myself and then return to the Peloponnesus. There were two regiments in the service of Russia, one composed of Maniotes, at the head of whom was the son of Pierrakês Samet Bey, and the other was a body of Peloponnesians commanded by Anagnostaras. These were still in Zante. Pappadopoulos had ordered them to fit out a vessel of war. When they had made it ready and I could go in it to Santa Maura, Anagnostaras, the Petimezaioi, Giannaki Kolokotronês, Melios, and others came down to me and said, "Do not go, we shall get permission to have a ship for ourselves, and if thou desirest, thou canst go in her." They found a Turkish boat with two cannons, and they bought her and appointed me to be captain.

I took out passports, and went to the government office of the Republic of Corfu, and there they gave me permission to attack the Turks either by sea or land. I took eighty soldiers for land service, and went down to a place called Achaia, near Patras, and burnt the houses, possessions, and magazines of Saïtaga, and returned to Zante. The inhabitants of Zante, however, were obliged to import food from the Peloponnesus, and therefore they petitioned the government and begged it not to attack the Morea, as in consequence of that the Turks would not admit any of them who went thither for the purpose of trading. The government prevented me in consequence from making any assaults by land, and ordered me only to carry on the war at Santa Maura.

I met Pappadopoulos with Synevi at Corfu. He was making preparations to attack Constantinople in conjunction with the English. I gave him a little of my opinion—namely, that there were twelve hundred Russians and five thousand Greeks in the service of the seven islands, that they had twelve vessels in the Baltic and the Black Seas, and forty other vessels, both brigs and frigates, which had been got together for the purpose of attacking Buonaparte, so that with ten thousand of the islanders we should number altogether twenty-five thousand men with six ships in the Gulf of Corinth, and others at Egina, and that with these forces we could sail away, and then I would undertake that in two months I would free the Peloponnesus.

General Pappadopoulos received my proposition, and laid it before Synevi Motzenigo, the national primate, Benakês, the vice-admiral, Deli, and General Atrem. Pappadopoulos took it to the council, and Benakês opposed it, saying, "I will not have my country lost a second time even for my father's sake." Motzenigos said, "We must go with the English and strike at the head, which is Constantinople, and afterwards, when we have struck the head, all the rest is ours." This opinion was therefore accepted and mine thrown over.

Synevi went to Tenedo, and the English to Constantinople, but rather as if they were going upon an excursion than for any warlike purposes. The Turks were met by the Russians at Tenedo, and after one battle the Turkish fleet was destroyed.

After the battle of Austerlitz the Russians gave up the islands belonging to Napoleon, and Synevi was ordered to retire from the sea, and the Russian army to evacuate the land. The war was then virtually over, and as many warships as had been taken into the service of the Republic received their discharge, and I returned to Zante in August. On the 27th of July, 1807, an order came for the Russians to deliver up the forts to the French. I put myself under Captain Alexander in the Levant, who was against the Turks, for ten months, and afterwards went to Mount Athos. Three Turkish warships, two corvettes, and one frigate laid siege to us at Skiathi. We gave information to an English frigate, and she came to our assistance. The two corvettes were shelled, but the frigate was captured uninjured. There were about fourteen hundred of us Greeks, among whom were all the captains of Olympus, as Pappa-Blachabas, Liolios, Lazopoula, and the captains of Tsaras. These were all in Skiathi, having been driven there by Mouchtar Pasha and other Turks. As the winter was now coming on, we went over to Mani and returned thence to Zante.

CHAPTER III.

IN the spring of 1808 Veli* Pasha alarmed Ali Pharmakês by demanding that either he should deliver up his tower, or give himself or his son as a hostage into his hands. He was stirred up to this by Deligianni. Deligianni, not really desiring that Ali should even exist, told Veli that he must demolish his tower, and thus he would demolish all his strength. To Ali he said: "Do not go away, for Veli intends to kill thee." So Ali Pharmakês made preparations to oppose himself to Veli Pasha.

My grandfather, Gianni Kolokotronês, and the grandfather of Ali, had been friends and adopted brethren. My grandfather was killed, but the friendship was continued between my own father and the father of Ali; and we also were sworn friends. Remembering this friendship, and counting upon it, Ali wrote a letter to me to this effect :—

"DEAR FELLOW-COUNTRYMAN,—Veli Pasha is making ready to destroy me—come, and give me your help."

I answered it immediately, thus: "I do not come to you at this moment, because by so doing I should injure you, for if Veli Pasha has no intention to do you any harm, as soon as he learns that I have gone to you, he will come then; but if you can see no

* A son of Ali Pasha, Vizier of Epirus.

other way but to declare war against him, and if he
advances against you, let me know, and then I will come."
Veli Pasha did muster his forces against him ; and Ali
wrote to me again that the soldiers were advancing, and
bade me thus : "If thou art really my friend, come."
When I received this second letter I made ready to go
with a hundred men, but their officers prevented me, saying
that I could not take the men away to another part, because
I had previously given my word that I would not do so.
The French also hindered the soldiers from joining, so that,
instead of a hundred men, I only had sixteen, myself
making the seventeenth. I embarked near Glarentza and
directed my course to Monasteraki.

The same day on which I arrived at Monasteraki, eight
thousand Turks arrived before it, and we were obliged to
wait until the middle of the night before we could cross.
Ali Pharmakês had four hundred men, but so many had
left him, out of fear, that at this time there only remained
ninety with him. The conflict was opened at dawn, and
was carried on vigorously both by night and day for the
space of thirty days. They had four cannons. On the
thirtieth day of the siege proposals were made to Ali that
if he would deliver up Kolokotronês to them, all his possessions and his tower also should be guaranteed him.
Ali answered : "If it be according to the laws of honour
and those of the Pallikars to give up a friend who has
come from the islands to help me, of course I can do it."
They answered him : "That is true, but it is a great
matter for a Romaic to be ruined by Turkey for the sake
of one man." Ali Pharmakês replied again : "Were I a
Pasha, I might become unfaithful ; but I cannot do it ; so
make your mine, and if you can overturn us, the issue
rests with God." And fighting recommenced.

We had a council in the evening, and, having gathered

all the Agas together, he told the heads of the corps what the Turks had proposed—namely, to give up Kolokotronês. They all cried out together, " We will all be lost, but this we cannot do." "You had better deliver me up and have done with it," I said. "I have eaten my bread." * Ali Pharmakês replied, "It is not thy service—it is ours." And they all determined to die together.

At the end of sixty-four days they began to cast fire into the mine, and the mine had thousands of okas of powder in it. We dug down twelve feet outside the tower three and a half cubits in width, with the view of seizing the miners. The mine began to tremble, and the ground to quiver in one quarter, on account of our having dug away the earth, and then the earth fell in ; but the tower had suffered no damage. The Turks, who were hoping that the tower would be overturned, and that we should be buried under the stones in its fall, shouted ; but we, as the mine was destroyed, fired off a volley as a sign of rejoicing, to show that we had received no harm.

Then they began to treat with us.

In the course of sixty-five days more than three thousand cannon shots had been fired at us, and when they saw that neither their cannon nor their mine had done us much injury, they proposed a treaty, and asked what terms would be sought for. Ali Pharmakês demanded that the tower should not be destroyed, and that Kolokotronês should go out unharmed, requiring hostages until he should arrive safely in Zante, and that he, Ali, would remain in the tower until he had received a letter from Kolokotronês, announcing his safe arrival ; after which Ali would leave the tower, and would go and make his submission to Veli Pasha.

This arrangement was entered into by the army and its

* I have run the course of my allotted life.

commander without any consultation with Veli Pasha upon the matter. The writing was drawn up and signed by Paso Bey, and the Agas and all the chiefs took the required oaths. I departed on the morrow, taking with me my own men from Lala and three hostages from the best among them, with the agreement that if we were attacked they should be slain. So we embarked and got to Lala, when I sent the son of Ali home, and I myself went to Pyrgos in Gastouni. The treaty was forwarded to Veli Pasha, and he was greatly enraged at it, and gave orders to take possession of all the landing-places, and to seize me. The ticket of submission was sent to Ibrahim Aga, who was Ali Pharmakês' cousin, and a voivode. When, upon his reading over the submission paper, he came to where it said they must seize Kolokotronês, he made a jest about it to Tatarês, saying, "We do not understand the Turkish language here; so thou hadst better take it to Gastouni, where there is a kadi and a voivode who can read it, and then what the vizier has ordered in this paper we are ready to carry out." Tatarês laughed out, and I immediately took my hostages with me, and, being accompanied by Ibrahim Aga, went to Pyrgi and embarked, when I released my hostages, and sent a letter to Ali Pharmakês, acquainting him of my safety.

Pyrgi is about two hours' distance from Pyrgos and six from Gastouni, and we had scarcely got two miles outside it when some Turkish soldiers, who had been dispatched after us from Gastouni, arrived there to seize Pyrgi; but we were gone. When the news reached Ali Pharmakês that we were embarked, he himself went down to Tripolitsa to make his submission in person to Veli Pasha. I went to Zante, and shortly after Ali Pharmakês found a way to leave and come to Zante also. Veli Pasha had also written to me, asking me to go to him, but I would not;

and he did not kill Ali Pharmakês, because he endeavoured to make him deceive me into going to Tripolitsa; but he made no such attempt. The reason why Ali Pharmakês entered into this treaty was due to some compulsion from the Turkish inhabitants, who feared for their lives and property. He had scarcely got away from Pyrgos when his ruin was compassed.

All the Agas, with Paso-Bey and Veli Pasha, wrote to me to go to the Morea, and Pharmakês wrote also; but he put a ball above his signature as a sign to me not to go. The brother of Ali Pharmakês, therefore, when he came into Zante with the men of Veli Pasha, tweaked me by the ear, and I understood his meaning, so I said to them: "Go; I will come."

Ali Pharmakês then came to Zante. He had asked permission to go and see his villages until Kolokotronês could come, he said, and he took with him five hundred thousand *grosia;* and we sent a boat for him, and that is how he got to Zante. We planned to go to Paris together in order to have an interview with Buonaparte, and we went to Corfu in the first instance; but Donzelot, the governor there, prevented us from so doing. "Stay here," he said, "and I will write myself, and state that you require an answer. We must, however, arrange our plans before the answer of the Emperor arrives." The plan which we made in conjunction with Donzelot was as follows: that Buonaparte should give us the command of five hundred gunners clothed in fustanellas (for there were five thousand Greeks in the French service), and that he should also give us *grosia* in order to make enlistments in Tsamouria, where there were enemies of Ali Pasha. We crossed over to Tsamouria and got three thousand Tsamides for pay, and then went to Parga and embarked them for Santa Maura. The gathering was intended to take place at Santa Maura and Zante. I crossed over to Santa Maura myself with six hundred men.

At this time (on the 9th) the English came to Zante, and, disembarking, they established themselves there, and sent away the French to Corfu. About four hundred Greeks were put into the boats as prisoners of war. They also took Cephalonia, Thiaki, and Cerigo, and made them their own. General Oswald had orders from the generalissimo of the English forces, who was then in Palermo, to take into the service all the Greeks who were willing to join, and to put Church (who was then major) at their head.

When we saw that the English had come into the islands we sent word to Parga to enlist no more soldiers, as our plans were frustrated by their arrival. Our scheme was to get all the forts in Messenia, Parga, and Monemvasia placed in our hands. All the Turkish inhabitants of those places had agreed at a conference we had with them, that we should form a government, consisting of twelve Turks and twelve Greeks—the Turks to be governed with the same impartiality as the Greeks. Donzelot had framed the laws in conjunction with ourselves. Our flag was to have been a cross on one side, and on the other a half-moon and stars. This plan also formulated that when we had secured the Morea we should write to the Sultan to assure him that our action was not against him, but against the tyrannies of Ali Pasha, and Donzelot had already advised with the minister at Constantinople to prevent him from making any movement.

It was my own private intention, however, that when we had got possession of all the forts, we should then make it a more national movement, and throw over the Turks ; but what I resolved upon doing would have to depend upon circumstances. Our measures would have necessitated raising fifteen thousand of the islanders. Donzelot, myself, Ali Pharmakês, and a secretary were three days and three nights laying out our plans.

Ali Pharmakês was at this time forty years old. His skin was very dark and yellow, and on this account he had received his cognomen from *Pharmaki* (poison). He was shorter than myself and thin, but a most sensible and trustworthy man—very silent, but irritable. He died at Lala. He was ill in Zante with dysentery, and his relations advised him to go there. The English sent him a physician, but when they saw that he must die they gave him permission to go anywhere outside of the Morea, for the English, being on good terms with Ali Pasha, would not grant him the liberty of going to the Morea, lest Ali might be displeased. When I heard that he was dead I went over to the Morea and also to Lala to condole with his family. [Kolokotronês, in his narrative, is here anticipating events.] We then stopped at Cerigo until Sunday, the Feast of St. Thomas. A Cephalonian boat, belonging to Alexander Raftopoulos, coming in, we embarked on her for Zante. The captain found out who I was, and paid me great attention. In Zante they had given me up for lost, and all who were there—the Petimezaoi, Anagnostaras, Melios, Gianni Kolokotronês, Niketas, and the rest welcomed me back. This was in 1806. In order to be in safety I had changed my clothes, and had only taken the most wretched-looking weapons with me, so as not to excite the covetous to kill me on their account.

I was born in the year 1770.

When I was saved at Kastanitza I was ten years old; I lived at Mani two years, three years at Alonisthaina, and twelve years in Sampazika. I was married when I was twenty, and I was twenty-seven when they first began to hunt me down. The royal firman against Petimeza and myself came over in 1802, and the second firman with the patriarchal excommunication in January, 1806. I was thirty-six years old when I went to Zante, and fifty years of age when I embarked in the war of liberation.

When we were Klephts and Armatoli our chief officers were always chosen for their courage and ability. Whilst we were Armatoli we had our pay, and when we were Klephts the half of the spoils. Prizes were given to those who distinguished themselves. If any of them committed a fault his hair was cut short, and his arms were taken from him. Reverence for women was our law : whoever insulted a woman was driven out from us. We had games and drums to amuse ourselves with, jumping, dances, heroic songs, and quoits. The country people made our songs, and we sung them .to the lyre. The songs were our hymns and our military newspapers.

Our arms were pistols, daggers, and swords carried in our belts. We had jambes on the legs, and in the winter we wore breast-plates, and we also had large buttons on our waistcoats. The captainships descended to the sons— not to the first-born, but to the most worthy.

Our flag had the same cross as that upon the Russian banners. The monasteries gave us help, and the husband-men and shepherds always sent information to the Klephts, as well as giving them ammunition and provisions. When any of us was seriously wounded in a battle and could not be carried away, we all kissed him and then cut off his head. It was thought a great dishonour to have the Turks bear away one's head. Among the thirty-six first cousins whom I had, only eight were preserved ; the others were all destroyed. There is not a spot where there is not a Kolokotronês buried. Besides those, there were my second cousins, my uncles, and many friends who were lost. The name of *Klepht* was a boast. "*I am a Klepht,*" some would say vauntingly. The prayer of a father for his sons was that he might become a Klepht. The Klephtship afterwards lost its authority. In my father's time it was a sacred thing for a Greek to undertake. When the Klephts had a collision with the Turks all the husbandmen left their oxen in the fields, and went to help the Klephts—every time the Greeks were disposed to ally themselves with the Turks. When Androutsos, the father of Odysseus, came, I was well known in Mani, and I accompanied him to Corinth. During the time that we were being pursued, for fifteen days we neither slept nor tasted food, and we had fighting every day, but we saved our guns.*

From September to January, 1809, I was staying at Santa Maura. The English had cast the son of Ali Pharmakês and others into prison. Upon learning this, we disbanded our army and only kept twenty men. The minister Forrest, and Oswald, the general of the English army, invited all the captains, and also asked them if they could not bring Kolokotronês to Zante with them. The English, seeing so many assembled at Santa Maura, had some fears about them. They answered, " When you like to do so, you can send a letter to him by a trustworthy man, and we hope that he will follow us." On account of this reply Oswald and Forrest wrote a letter and sent it to me by a native of Zante named Pomonês, who passed over in the *Clarence*, and embarking under a Turkish flag, came to Santa Maura. This letter invited me to go to them, and with it was a circular invitation to all the chiefs, both on land or sea, offering to give us what we asked, and that they would send boats to fetch us to Zante.

It was difficult at that time for any one to go about, because the middle islands of Greece were in the hands of

* This sentence has no reference to Androutsos,

the French, and the others were held by the English. We went, therefore, to General Camus, a Frenchman, and asked his permission to go to Mothokorona, and we manned a boat, and hoisted a French flag. We had scarcely got out to sea when a contrary wind met us and drove us to Thiaki, which was guarded by English sentinels, and they summoned us—"Who are you?" "Kolokotronês!" we answered, when they made preparations for attacking us. I asked them if they had any commander with whom I could confer. They answered that they had an English officer who was resident there; he had come to those shores in 1810. So I got into a boat and went to him and produced General Oswald's letter. The moment he saw that, he became very friendly and treated me with great respect. He gave us some Cognac, and we then stayed at Thiaki. The commandant of Thiaki gave us an invitation, and we remained there four days. Ali Pharmakês and myself had some misgivings about the English as they were the friends of Ali Pasha, and so we both agreed that the two of us would not go to Zante together, but that one of us should remain in the boat at Skrophai, and that I would go to Zante, and if I saw that matters were on a firm basis I would then write to him, and he could come. This was carried out. I went to Zante and left Ali Pharmakês in the boat, together with my nephew Niketas.

As soon as I arrived in Zante I went both to General Oswald, to Forrest, and to Church,* and they questioned me as to how affairs were going on at Santa Maura during my five months' stay there. I then received permission to go to Kastro and release all the native Turks belonging to Ali Pharmakês who were imprisoned there. I saw that

* Sir Richard Church, commander of the National Corps in the Ionian Isles,

everything was quite fair and straightforward, and I sent a special boat to Skrophai to fetch Ali Pharmakês, who then came to Zante also. I entered the service with the rank of captain, and after a few days had passed, General Oswald again sent for me, and asked me in what way we could gain over all the Greeks who were at Santa Maura belonging to the French service, informing me that we were to fight only against the French. Lepeniotês, who was the brother of Katzantonês, came into Kalamo and Meganesi at that time with two hundred men, he having been driven out by Ali Pasha. Meganesi belonged to the French, and they drove him out. Lepeniotês said, " I wish to take service with the English, but I will not put faith in any one except Kolokotronês." The general then showed me the letter, and sent me to Kalamo, and gave me a brig to be under my command. "One brig has come," I said to him, " but I want a gunboat in order to go to Kalamo," and I told him to send me three days afterwards a gunboat in any case, and three days after the brig the squadron with the soldiers were to make a move. That was our plan.

I went to Kalámo and met Lepeniotês, and took him and all his two hundred men and the boats; and we made a descent on Meganesi, and routed the French, and made a halting-place. Whilst there I made a signal for the brig to come. Moore and Lowe, the Governor of St. Helena, were in the brig. They made a signal for me to go to them, and so I went, taking only four men with me, and the others remaining at Meganesi. Whilst I was at Meganesi I sent over to Santa Maura, and many Greeks came to join us, and I told them what they ought to do. We went to see where the fleet was stationed. We arrived at Vagina—I, Lobis, and Konstantine Petmezas. As soon as the French saw us they sent a regiment with four cannon and cannonaded us, and in one detachment I met with some Greeks who were in the French service. I cried out to them, "What are you doing here? The English fleet is coming." But their answer was, "We have taken our oaths, and we must fight." "Ah! is it so?" I cried; "then go back to your ranks, for we must fight also."

The fleet came, and we went to the harbour to see the general. Whilst I was making my report they made a signal for a landing, just two hours before nightfall. As soon as I understood it I said, "General, we must not make a descent now, because we are gathered together from different parts, and our soldiers do not comprehend it, and, between ourselves, we may be killed; but we will go at daybreak, and I promise you that by noon we shall have taken the place." The general accepted my recommendation, and ordered the soldiers to go to their ships. There were four thousand soldiers in all—English, Corsicans, Sicilians, and Greeks. The French prepared for war, and as the soldiers began to disembark I also landed, and the Corsicans seized me as a prisoner of war, and carried me off to Church! Then we marched forward and took the place.

We took the first battery of nine cannon; the five hundred Greeks, with Church at their head, did all this. The general came with the English soldiers and Lowe with the Corsicans, and went into the country; and the general ordered Church to go and take another battery still more powerful because it had twelve cannons, with the marsh on one side, and on the other shoals and the sea, and so there was only one part left on which we could advance. We sent a scout forward. The Albanians took him and scourged him. I went with ten men to a height. They called to me, "Who is going to attack?" "I am."

Two captains then came to me. I told them to march forward, and they were not disheartened. "We will fight," they said. The conflict began, and we repulsed the enemy. We planted the cannon in the windmills. The French retired to Gyra, where they had erected a strong battery.

We led the Greeks first, the Sicilians second, and the English last. As we neared the battery it began to discharge ball and guns upon us. The brother of General Church was wounded, and a captain of the frigate, and altogether thirty-five Greeks were wounded and killed. We took the battery by assault, and in this conflict the Corsicans signalized themselves greatly. We besieged the fort where the French were collected. On account of some suspicion they did not wish the Greeks to enter the fort, and so they came out to surrender to us. We had not attacked them thirty days before we had thrown forward ten cannon and ten bombs; and in eight days four hundred bombs had been discharged day and night. Major Clark died; the French surrendered, and the soldiers were sent prisoners to Malta.

We returned to Zante, and then I was promoted to be major. That was in May, 1810, when we had been absent from Zante a year. We then embarked on a frigate with fifty Greeks and fifty English, under the command of Church, and made a descent upon Paxos. We disembarked and formed the Greeks into two companies, and went into the country, being aided by the two frigates, when both the Greeks and the French surrendered. We took the French as prisoners of war, and the Greeks entered the service. Ali Pasha at this time sent to besiege the French in Parga. The Pargiotes called for our aid, so we went over, and the people forsook the French and hoisted the English flag. After this we returned to Zante, when the general, being jealous of Church, displaced him in favour of his brother.

Church then prepared to go to London, and being at perfect liberty to do as he chose, he dressed himself in Greek clothes. As many Greek captains as we could find in Zante now joined us in making an address to the English Government asking for its assistance in freeing our country. This address was found among the State papers when we framed a second one in 1825. Church took this first address to London, and got permission there to form a regiment of a hundred and fifty Greeks, and in five or six months he organized a body of six hundred Greeks. In the meantime Napoleon fell, and an order came to disband the Greeks and other foreign soldiers. They gave about eight hundred dollars to each officer, and twelve hundred to be divided among the captains, when they were discharged. I remained, however, for two years afterwards in the position of major, when I also was dismissed.

I then saw that what we had to do we must do by ourselves, without any hopes of help from foreign Powers. Church went to Naples and became a general there. He sent me two invitations to join him, but I now knew that the Hetairia (secret society) was formed, and I determined henceforward to devote myself only to freeing my own country.

Pangalos spoke to me about the Hetairia, and Aristeides came, and afterwards Anagnostoras brought me a letter from the Hetairia, and I began to act in concert with many in Zante and Cephalonia, and also with the captains of the Speziote and Hydriote vessels; and twenty letters at least came to me from Ypsilanti, bidding me hold myself in readiness with all my people, as the day of the rising was fixed for the 25th of March. The English heard that I had received some letters, and the police came at night to search me, but I had taken good care of my letters.

On the 6th of January I went to Mani to the house of Captain Panagiotês, the son of Mourtzinos. But at this juncture, before I went to the Peloponnesus, I passed over to Corfu, with the view of seeking from Maitland my four thousand dollars, the pay due to me, and also to meet Kapodistria. I met him, and stayed with him eighty days, after which I returned to Zante. We talked much about the position of affairs.

Here ends my past life—at the commencement of the rising. Whatever foreign service I had before entered into, I only entered it upon these conditions: that I was never to be sent far from the seven islands, never to fight except upon Turkish ground, and never to lay aside my national dress. In the islands I met with the Botzarês, and took Markos for my adopted brother.

In my youth, when I had time to learn, there were not many schools. There were only a few schools where I could learn reading and writing. The primates of the different districts hardly knew how to write their own names, and even archbishops knew scarcely anything beyond their ecclesiastical duties—they had studied nothing more than the psalter, the Octoêchos, the book of the months * and the prophecies; they read no other books. It was not until I went to Zante that I met with the history of Greece. The books which I often read afterwards were the history of Greece, the tale of Aristomenes and Gorgo, and the story of Skenter Bey.

According to my judgment, the French Revolution and the doings of Napoleon opened the eyes of the world. The nations knew nothing before, and the people thought that kings were gods upon the earth, and that they were bound to say that whatever they did was well done.

---

* Books of the Orthodox church service.

Through this present change it is more difficult now to rule the people.

In my time commerce was very limited, money was scarce. I gained three grosia on a dollar. It was thought a great thing if a person possessed a thousand grosia.* Any one with such a sum could command as much service for it as he could not procure now for a thousand Venetian florins. The community of men was small, and it was not until our rising that all the Greeks were brought into communication. There were men who knew of no place beyond a mile of their own locality. They thought of Zante as we now speak of the most distant parts of the world. America appears to us as Zante appeared to them. They said it was in France.

* 1,000 *grosia* = piastres were then worth about £22; and 1,000 tallera = dollars represented as nearly as possible £225.

CHAPTER IV

AT last the secret of the Hetairia began to be divulged among every class of men, both good and bad, and thus we were unhappily forced to commence the rising prematurely. Diogos had communicated it to Ali Pasha. On this account I left Zante on the 3rd of January, and arrived in Skardamoula upon the 6th, going at once to the house of my friend and countryman, Captain Panagiotês Mourtzinos. Our general move took place on the 22nd of March, but from the 6th of January I was working and employing all my energies at Mani, in endeavours to unite different Maniote houses after the usual custom, and we did succeed in uniting them, and took them into the brotherhood. The rising took place at Kalamata. I also sent to the districts of Messenia, Mistros, Karytaina, Phanari, Leontari, Arcadia, and Tripolitsa, bidding all the inhabitants to come whither we were, and then I instructed them to be all ready on the festival of the Annunciation, and that each district was to attack the Turkish inhabitants simultaneously, storming them in their different fortresses—namely, that the Arcadians should besiege Neo-Kastro, the Mothonai Mothon, and so on.

Whilst we were making ready and gathering them all together, it was necessary that Zaimês and others should go to Tripolitsa and remain there, where they attacked the

Voivode of Kalavryta. The Turks found out that I had
come, and thought that I had arrived at the head of five or
six thousand men. I had four men with me. The Arcadians
and Mistriotes, clothed in the rayah cloaks, came down to
inspect us in order to see how many there really were. I
was playing at quoits when they came, so they went back
and reported—"We only found an old man playing at
quoits."

I went to Mourtzinos as to a friend and of the same
district. Mavromichaelês had the title of Bey, but Mourtzinos had the power in Mani. Mavromichaelês asked
wherefore I had gone there, and Mourtzinos answered that
I had been unfortunate in Zante, and had come to get
some assistance amongst my friends, after which I should
return thither again. He behaved himself tolerably well
towards me, and it is not true that he betrayed me to the
Turks, for he had not the power to do so even if he had the
will, for besides my friendship with Mourtzinos, it is a
custom in Mani to help every one who goes there for a
place of refuge.

On the 23rd of March we fell upon the Turks at
Kalamata. They were led by Arnaoutoglês, a man of
some importance in Tripolitsa. We had two thousand
Maniotes, with Mourtzinos and Petro Bey. Western Sparta
also was moving. The Turks remained at about a hundred
men, report stating them to be ten thousand. Eastern
Sparta began to move at the same time. When I first
arrived the Turks had sent for the primates and chief
householders, and they went, but they were not killed. The
Spartans, when they had done some pillaging, went off and
laid siege to Monemvasia. We had a meeting at Kalamata
to consult whither we should move the armies in the first
instance. The Kalamatans inveighed against the Bey,
wishing us to go to Koron lest the Turks should put the

Christians to the sword. I said in answer, "If you give us help for this army I will move off to old Arcadia and give aid to the centre of the country." I had received a letter from Kanelos, who invited me thither, saying that he had ten thousand men, and in arms, and that I was to be placed at the head of them. Dionysios, the son of Mourtzinos, was ill, and therefore all the Maniotes did not rise at once. I received two hundred from him and seventy from the Bey, and Captain Voidês came with his thirty men, so we made three hundred in all, and I prepared two flags directly, putting a cross on them, and moved forward. The Androusian Turks, hearing that we had a force, fled in a body to the fort of Messenia.

As we went along all the Greeks showed the greatest enthusiasm; they came out and met us everywhere, carrying the sacred pictures (ikons), with the priests chanting supplications and thanksgivings to God. Once I could not forbear weeping, on account of the ardour which I beheld. So we went on, followed by crowds. When we came to the bridge of Kalamata we exchanged greetings, and I marched forward.

On the 24th of March we arrived at the village of Skala, in Messenia—a village of about five hundred families. As many men as I could get were sent forward as scouts. "Go to the forts, besiege them, and I will follow with three thousand men;" but that was only a *ruse.* At daybreak on the feast of the Annunciation, March 25, 1821, they heard in Leontari that I had arrived at the head of many thousand Maniotes, so they seized on the animals belonging to the rayahs, and went away into Tripolitsa. Upon leaving Skala I fired off some thousands of small shot in three volleys so that the people might join us upon hearing this announcement.

The Garantzaioi, hearing the guns, killed their Beys,

who were preparing for flight; so the first slaughter began with them. I then marched to Dervenia, in Leontari, to go to old Arcadia, and met a messenger from the Greeks, who told me that the Leontarians fled and went towards Phraukovrysi, but had since returned and killed two or three Greeks. They had seventy horsemen. I said, "Go and shut them up there," and turning back, I came to Leontari.

The Phanarites, on this same day of the Annunciation, met and told the Turks that they should go to Tripolitsa, because they did not know what all this might mean. The Phanarites, Mountrizani, and other tribes where the Turks had intermarried with the Christians, got together seventeen hundred guns. They assembled two hours off Andritsaina, near a brook called Soultina, having carried off amongst them three thousand animals belonging to the rayahs.

The islands now made a proclamation that no one was to go out of any of the islands to help the Greeks. Some, however, fled secretly from Zante, both peasants and proprietors, and became co-partners in every danger : their property was therefore confiscated. Western Turkish Roumêli was then in amazement about Ali Pasha, because the Souliotes had seized upon Souli. (The downfall of Ali Pasha helped us much ; it was needful that he should be removed, he was a great brute.)

Spetsai was the first island which joined in the rising, and she sent immediately to Hydra to follow her example. The landholders were indisposed to rise, but Captain Anton Koulodemas and Ghikas, the brother-in-law of Miaoulês, had a meeting with the people, and addressed the chief men amongst them thus : "You will either join the rising or we shall set fire to you and burn you out; so all you have to do is to get your ships in order." So they were forced to submit, and laid out their grosia and embarked.

Psara and Samos rose of their own accord.

When I left Skala on the 25th, going on to Dervenia, I met a scout who was sent to me by Basil Boutouna, and who brought me a letter. "The Turks of Karytaina and Mustapha, the Voivode of Iblakios, are shut up in the old fort of Karytaina, and the two prefects, not having been among the number of the Hetairia, and knowing nothing of what has occurred, have persuaded the Turks not to flee, but to remain in the fort. The people of Karytaina's plains have not taken arms." Such was the writing which I received. I lost no time, but straightway issued the following proclamation : "Fire and sword to every place that does not listen to the voice of the nation."

Hearing that I was going down to Dervenia, seventy horsemen rode off immediately to Tripolitsa, and I moved forward to the village Tetempes, between Léontari and Karytaina. My Maniotes said, "Let us go to Leontari." "What—to polish copper pots!" I said [in irony of a Maniote calling].

On the morning of the 26th, as soon as it was light I got a thousand men together and made a move towards Karytaina, in order to await the coming of the Phanarites and Karytainans. Hearing the volleys, every one was aroused. On the road I met another messenger from Basil with a letter. "Look at this letter from the Phanarites," it said, "who are stopping at Soultina." " To-morrow we leave Tripolitsa with a force of so many ; make ready to join us. Kolokotronês has gone forth with several thousand Maniotes." Basil had killed the Turk bearing the above at the bridge of Karytaina, and had taken the letter from him. Upon reading it, I determined to take up a position and lay in wait for the Phanarites.

The Turks, when they arrived before Karytaina and saw the flags (which not being unfurled did not show the cross), thought that they were Turkish banners, and that we were a reinforcement for them. I marched through a defile, for I said to myself, if they try to pass to-day I will attack them. I questioned a rustic whom I met in the pass about the Turks and Phanarites, and he said, "They have had no information of anything, and are going to sleep to-night near the spring, and can easily be surprised." I wrote a despatch directly to Panagiotês Giatropoulos of Andritza to go forward and take them in the rear, whilst I should await them in front. When I saw that the Turks were not intending to make a move that day, I went on to Karytaina and surrounded the Turks who were in the fortress. On the morning of the 27th I rose up at sunrise, and leaving a body of fifteen at Karytaina, went back to the defile. The same night that I was at Karytaina a message came from Panagiotês: "Send us troops because we have not assembled any yet."

On the same day that I began my march—that is to say, on the 27th—a despatch came to me from the late Beyzadè Elias to say that he had arrived at Leontari with two hundred Spartans, and I wrote to him to come quickly, "because to-day we shall have a fight." From the place where I wrote to Leontari is a four hours' walk, and by chance it happened that we could only send an old man on foot, and he did not get there in time, so that they did not arrive to take part in an engagement, therefore I went up the defile as far as St. Athanasius. In the morning the army of the Phanarite Turks was before us, a mile in extent, in a narrow pass, and with a great deal of baggage, so that the entire line occupied two miles. Upon seeing us they immediately opened fire in front, and as we had entrenched ourselves we fought for six hours. The Spartans that day had a battle in which they imitated Leonidas, for they were three hundred, and the Turks seventeen hundred. After six hours they ceased firing, Voidês was wounded, and five or six were slain. It was noon when they ceased firing, and the army said to me that we ought to open upon them. Koliopoulos was then six miles off, at the river Achelsous. Hearing the firing, he moved forward. He did not, however, arrive in time, but half an hour afterwards. He had four hundred men with him. The Turks killed fifteen of us; they fought with determination because they had their property and their women and children with them. If Koliopoulos, Georgaki, and Demetrius had come up, the Turks would have been routed there. The Turks took our position. Hearing the volley fired by the Kolians they went opposite to look out. The Spartans, perceiving that a reinforcement was coming to us, went away carrying off their wounded. Upon hearing the volley, we made a rush upon the place with twenty men, so that the Turks should not pass over the bridge. I hoisted a banner so that Koliopoulos might know me. I had got quite a stiff neck from shouting all day. We drove back the Turks, who, with their women and children, not being able to get to the bridge which we had seized, were lost; five hundred were drowned in the river alone, not being able to cross it. The Greeks took possession of the mules and all the wounded stallions; the remnant fled to Kastraki as to a hive. (This was our first victory, and the first which the Kalavrytians gained over the Turks.)

We besieged them. In the evening Elias arrived from Leontari, and on the 28th Kanelos came with two hundred Karytainans. Anagnostaras and Pappa Phlessas moved forward to Arcadia with five hundred men, and as the Arcadians were fleeing, they turned back and went into Karytaina together, one thousand strong. In two days we had amassed six thousand men. The Turks who were shut up had left their animals outside, and the Greeks took them; they had neither water nor food. I had stationed Niketaras with a hundred soldiers at Phranko-vrysi, in Tripolitsa, two hours off. In the first two days that we were there, Mustapha Aga clothed two Turks as rayahs, and gave them five hundred grosia to go to Tripolitsa, and ask that a reinforcement be sent, announcing that all who came should receive pay for their help. The two messengers, when they had got two hours on their road, were met, but were not seized. The letter was delivered, and two thousand men were despatched to the help of the Karytainans and the Phanarites. As soon as I learnt about those two messengers, I suspected that a reinforcement would arrive. I had a conference with the army immediately, and gave it as my opinion that Anagnostaras should go to Salesi, which is four hours equidistant from Tripolitsa and Karytaina, taking two thousand men to Salesi, to prevent the reinforcement from Tripolitsa from moving forward; and if it could not prevent that it was to keep them from going back; for the Turks were inspired with fear that they would pass over to Karytaina. But he answered, "It will not do to break the force we have gathered together." I then made another suggestion, "Let me have five hundred;" but he had different views, so that plan was abandoned. We could have hemmed in the Turks so completely that not a shadow could have passed us.

On the next day, the 1st of April, the reinforcement started from Tripolitsa at daybreak, passing by the place where I had told Anagnostaras to station himself, and setting fire to the districts before them. When we saw the fires we said, "It is the reinforcement." I then ordered that scouts should go forward and reconnoitre. They went and returned, saying that they were not coming against us; but I persisted in my opinion, and said, "Take possession of three heights that we may await these Turks and do battle with them." So I mounted a horse, and, taking a flag in one hand, and also my glass, I told them that if they who were advancing were Turks, I would furl my flag, and that if they were not, I would display it. Two men followed me on foot. As soon as I had reached the hill, I dismounted from my horse and tied it to the bough of a tree, and ascended to a cliff and looked through the telescope. When I saw that they who were approaching were Turks I furled my flag. As soon as the Greeks saw this signal they all began to flee. As it was cold with a fresh breeze, and as I was in a perspiration, I took from a young shepherd a small white capote, and returned to find my army. My men were gone, and Kavadias had taken my horse. I went back to where the regiment was stationed, and found there the late Elias, who had been fighting. The other regiment had taken to the hills. The Koliopoulans had been fighting on the rear of the fort. I removed Elias thence because he was alone, and we all went to a height. "We will hold this height," I said, " because if the Turks dislodge these men we can fall upon them in the rear and drive them into Tripolitsa." Anagnostaras took possession of the bridge with a thousand men, Pappa Phlessas and Kanelos kept the upper road, and I remained alone. The Greeks were broken. I concealed myself beneath some branches of trees with my two heavy pistols. Twelve Turks pursued one part of the Greeks, ten some of those from the bridge held by Anagnostaras, and others went in pursuit of Pappa Phlessas and Kanelos. The Greeks thought that they were followed by the whole Turkish force. The Turks passed over; I saw them, for they passed quite close to me. I was saved by the capote which I was wearing; for I had on a red scarf, and the capote concealed it.

When the sun rose high I came in front of my own men at the bridge. As soon as they saw me they cried out, "Where have you been?" "Where you left me," I said, "but concealed." I proposed that we should now march on to Tripolitsa, but the Greeks would not consent to do so. The Koliopoulans went to Heliodora, Pappa Phlessas and Elias to Demitsana, and Kanelos to Langadia, to take their families to Megaspelion.

I had some conversation with those who were upon the bridge. Night at last overtook us, it was one o'clock, and quite dark. I made the sign of the cross, and said, "All ye who love your country, come with me." I then moved on, followed by Anagnostaras with two hundred of his men, and Bouras and I led them by a pass I had known for twenty years. When we were near the monastery Agio-Gianni we met the people of Stemnitsa, who were going to take refuge there with their wives and families. I called out, "Whither are you going, Stemnitsians?" "We are forced to flee," they answered. "Come here," I said; "I am quite able to meet those Turks."

I then went forward to Stemnitsa, which is a mile distant from the monastery. I sent a messenger so that no one should be troubled about me.

When Phlessas and Elias heard that I was at Stemnitsa they came to me at once. At sunrise the next day I said, "We will go and take possession of Langada; the Turks will pass that way, and we will fall upon them." Near Langada is the village Chrysovitsi, and I went there with three hundred men. On the road the Greeks concealed themselves, for as we went into Chrysovitsi the moon's rays revealed a hundred of them. In the villages of the Vlacho district the people were still absent in their winter quarters, and there were no men there. We met one man, however, and we asked him if any Turks had gone into

Langadia, and his answer was, "Yesterday seventeen went there and carried off five or six thousand sheep, and there was not a man to fire a shot at them."

Niketaras, who was at Phrankovrysi, had attacked many bodies of Turks, had taken some prisoners, and had killed about five or six; but all the Turks had marched back again into Tripolitsa.

At daybreak the captains said to me, "What are we doing here? Let us leave and get on to Leontari, and gather some soldiers together there, and just see what the world is doing." "I shall not go," I answered; "I shall stay here on these hills where the very birds know me; better that they, my neighbours, should eat me than any others." I had not one man of my district with me. I had a horse.

Anagnostaras, Elias, and Bouras went to Leontari. I was left alone, I and my horse at Chrysovitsi. But Phlessas turned back and said to a boy, "Stop with him lest the wolves devour him."

I sat down until they had disappeared with their flags. After some time I descended the hill until I came to a church on the road, dedicated to the Blessed Virgin (the Panagia at Chrysovitsi), and there, where I threw myself down, I wept for Hellas.

"Holy Virgin!" I cried, "help us now, that the Greeks may take heart once more."

I then took the road leading to Piana, and on the way I met my cousin Anton, the son of Anastasius Kolokotronês, and seven of my nephews: these with myself made nine, and my horse made the tenth. I had not even a gun. Anton told me that there was nobody in Piana, that they all had fled. I threw myself into Alonistaina—they knew me there—and about twenty came down to me. I made them all messengers (runners), and sent into all the villages in order to form a regiment. In three days I assembled a force of three hundred men, and went with them to Piana, three miles from Tripolitsa. A despatch was immediately sent to Tripolitsa: "Kolokotronês with three hundred men is in Piana."

Early on the morrow a body of Turks four thousand strong was despatched from Tripolitsa. When I saw them through my glass I said, "The Turks are very few in number." I said this to encourage them, for I never allowed any one but myself to use my telescope. They opened fire; but our men were routed. I was left with my horse behind, and alone. I took the road leading to Alonistaina, and on the way found Nikolo Boukouras standing by himself, so I took him up on the crupper.

We on the one side, and the Turks on the other, were both going to Alonistaina. The Alonistainans were firing from the heights so that the Turks should not get into the place, and wasted their time. As I was going along with Boukouras, I called out, "Come here, you dirty dogs!" "Do not anger them," said Boukouras. Kanelos Deligianni came up with a hundred national guards and baggage; but the Turks fell upon him and carried off his baggage. I joined Kanelos, but the men which he had brought all took fright, and, dispersing, went to their own villages, and I was again left with Kanelos and eleven of his men. The Turks burnt the village and went back to Tripolitsa. I took Kanelos away with me at night, going from place to place, until one day at dawn we reached a village at the extreme end of Karytaina. The men of the plains and the mountaineers passed over the other part of Phanari to the hill Dragomano. Out of sheer hunger we killed, roasted, and ate a lamb, and it was the Holy Wednesday.* I sent scouts to Leontari,

---

* Wednesday in Passion Week. To eat flesh, except in extremity, was a great sin.

where some captains were assembled, with this message, "Pappa Phlessas, Mourtzinos, and Anagnostaras are drawing near Tripolitsa; they are at Marmaria." Kyriakoulês with the Mistriot army, and Vrysthenes with the Agiopetrikan force, were going to Marmaria; there were two thousand men at Vervena, and Kyriakoulês brought some thousand men down to Vlachochoria, opposite us. I wrote to him to come to me, and so unite into one force; but he would not. "I have got a very good position," he said, "and if the Turks come down upon us you must send us a reinforcement."

Kyriakoulês on the very day of Easter had set as sentinel some man of the place who betrayed them, and at daybreak two thousand Turks came down and attacked them. They fought for a short time, when fifteen Greeks were killed, amongst whom was the celebrated Anton Nikolopoulos and Panagês Venetsianos. Kyriakoulês went away with the other part of his army to Mistra. When we heard of the conflict we went with a reinforcement, but it was two hours off, and when we got there we found no one, neither Greeks nor Turks, only burnt houses, and fifteen headless bodies. We therefore retired to Marmaria.

At this time my son Panos of blessed memory came to seek for me, also my son Gennaios, bringing thirty followers. The other regiment was at Vervena under Vrysthenes, Giatrakos, and Zapheiropoulos. Upon the arrival of Panos and Kanelos Deligianni, I sent him to Karytaina, with orders to burn the houses of those who did not rise.

They gathered a force in Alonistaina and Chrysovitsi. They did not delay enlisting in all the villages round, and got together six hundred men, and sent the whole of them to strengthen the place. The Koliopoulans and Kalavrytians were laying siege to Lala with cannon, and we assembled at Marmaria quite twelve hundred in number, and went thence to take possession of Valtetsi, which was opposite the encampments at Vervena, Chrysovitsi, and Alonistaina. Mourtzinos, Niketaras, and others went to Valtetsi, and I put myself at the head of them. When we were all collected, I stationed myself there with two hundred, with another three hundred in the village to give assistance. The encampment was near to aid either the one part or the other. This was the commencement of our warfare, and they did not know how to fight.

The Turks about this time took over ten thousand men to the port of Nauplia. We thought that they would go to Vervena, which was opposite Nauplia. I had gone to Kalogerovouni to give a signal where a reinforcement should be sent, for if they had gone to Vervena I should have taken a reinforcement there myself, whilst those who were in the encampments at Chrysovitsi and Piana were to seize upon the post of Valtetsi; but the Turks did not go to Vervena, but to Valtetsi, so that I had to turn the battle round, as it were, and go thither. The Turkish body was attacked by Giatrako, Kyriakoulês, and Niketaras. They wavered, retired, and fled. I came up from the rear, and went to take their place. The Turks began to burn the village. I shouted out, "Hold fast! be firm! or we shall be destroyed." Thirty of us stood firm, and smote a standard-bearer, when reinforcements coming from Vervena, Piana, and Chrysovitsi, we turned round and drove them into the plain, pursuing them down as far as Violetta, half a mile from Tripolitsa. There were two thousand Kalavrytians in Levidi, and they received no information about it. If they could have come to our aid we should have gone into Tripolitsa with the Turks; but we went back each to his own regiment. The next day, upon some pretext about getting soldiers, Mourtzinos went away, and I was left with twenty men of my own. They all marched to Leontari, and I with those twenty men went and divided the Karytainans into two bodies, one of which I put under Koliopoulos, and the other under Andreas Papadiamando-poulos. The whole were about twelve hundred men.

When ten days had passed I wrote to those in Leontari : "Come, and we will take possession of Valtetsi." About twelve hundred Petrovaioi and Messenians moved thither with Elias. I also went to Valtetsi, and said, "Build up close breastworks. At the end of the village is a church, which we made use of as a breastwork, as well as two of the heights which defend the village, so that if the Turks come," I said, "shut yourselves up." "We are lost men," they answered. "Shut yourselves up there," I repeated, "until I come with a reinforcement ; I'll be answerable for you."

At the very time that we were building up these entrenchments, Kehayas came from Juannina to Vostitsa with four thousand men, burnt Vostitsa, and then crossing over to Maura Litharîa without a gun being fired at him, he burnt Corinth. Phlessas then burnt the houses of Kiamil Bey, whereupon Kehayas went and burnt Argos, and afterwards marched for Tripolitsa. When he had entered Tripolitsa he was told of the first battle of Valtetsi, where we routed Romaics and his picked Turks. The old Turks related it thus : "They were Russians, and we drove them into the plain of Sinanos, where they surren-dered." That was the plan they had laid out for themselves.

Kehayas, who was a warlike and able man, made a scheme to the effect that Roubês, whom he had sent to Bardounia with five thousand men, should go to Valtetsi and drive out the Greeks, whilst he would send a separate force of fifteen hundred by night, who should take posses-sion of Valtetsi from the rear, and if the Greeks were broken as the Turks had been previously, they were to fall upon them, whilst he himself with two thousand cavalry should also come up from the rear of Valtetsi, the same course as was followed when the Greeks routed them, and to throw a thousand men into Kalogerovouni to oppose the army of the Verveni men if they moved forward with a reinforcement. The one army at Chryso-vitsi, where I then was, numbered eight hundred, and the other, commanded by Koliopoulos, consisted of seven hundred men.

We had made Kanelos Deligianni with four others military inspectors in order to keep a regular *surveillance* over the armies. When the Turks at daybreak moved on to Valtetsi, our sentinels had been all through the night passing over the several positions. I slept at Valtetsi, dined at Piana, and supped in Chrysovitsi, making the round of the three camps, and fixed to remain this day in Chrysovitsi. We had sentinels posted at Pano-Chrepa, above Tripolitsa, who were to give us information when the Turks were to advance. They made a signal that day, by lighting fires to indicate that the Turks had marched in the direction of Valtetsi, when I immediately moved on with eight hundred men, and consequently, as the Turks were arriving in Valtetsi, we were arriving there also.

The battle of Valtetsi began. The five thousand of the enemy attacked us. Opening fire as we came up on the flanks of the Turks, we gave a volley to encourage our men in the middle, and they being much emboldened, repeated it; the Turks replied with another, and a great conflict ensued. The Turkish advance guard, who were expecting the flight of the Greeks, awaited it for two hours, and hearing the terrible engagement that was going on in the rear, concluding that the Greeks were surrounded and were still fighting, came up also to give their aid in laying siege to them, and with ten flags took possession of a height, and thus prevented our communicating with those in the middle. We, with our eight hundred, strengthened the place so that the Turks could not take us in the rear. Kehayas himself persevered, but seeing nothing coming from it, brought two cannon to Valtetsi. The Greeks enclosed there fought on. Koliopoulos came up and so surrounded Roubês and his five thousand men that he was not able to hold any communication with the other part of the forces. Roubês had brought cannon against them, but did them no injury with it. The battle was sustained vigorously throughout the whole of the day, as the Turks hoped that by their persistence the Greeks would ultimately be compelled to evacuate Valtetsi, and we kept up our resistance with the expectation that the Turks must soon retreat.

When twilight was coming on I took a few men with me, and ascended to a height where the Turkish flags were planted. I went close to them and fired, and they gave me four shots in return. The Greeks behind could not comprehend it.

" I shall take you alive ; I am Kolokotronês," I said.

" Who art thou ? "

" Kolokotronês."

They evacuated the position, and then we went into Valtetsi and distributed ammunition and food to all who were in need of such. At two o'clock at night two hundred of our own men came and fired a volley ; we thought that they were Turks, instead of which they were Greeks. We passed the night, therefore, divided into two parts, each endeavouring to put the other to flight. When the morning came we were still at war. I levelled my glass to take a survey of what was going on, and saw that the Turks were in one place, and that Roubês was surrounded. Kehayas brought his cannon against the breastworks of Elias the Beyzadè, but the cannon passed over Elias' breastworks and traversed those of Roubês. Had they been pointed lower they would have reached them.

Roubês being in sore straits determined to make a sally through the breastworks of the Greeks. I was persuaded that he would try to flee, and so moved nearer. Roubês made a rush; they left their guns behind them in their fear.*

They fled between the two bodies; three hundred were killed; we were in the rear. We fell upon them in close quarters. The Greeks who had been surrounded we massed together, and followed them for a whole day.

The Greeks fell to spoiling and slaying, and did not pursue them with ardour. Niketaras, who was in Vervena with eight hundred men, came up, but just an hour too late. We pursued them, however, as far as the plains. This battle established the good fortunes of our country; if we had lost it we should have had some difficulty in making another stand.

Elias was on the heights, and his men were in the church; Metropetrovas was on another height, and the Leontari men had the other breastwork. It was Koliopoulos who surrounded Roubês. We were all engaged in the pursuit of the enemy.

This was upon the 13th of May, and the battle had lasted twenty-three hours.

That day was a Friday, and I gave an address to the following effect: "We must all fast, and render up thanksgivings for this day, which should be kept holy for ever, as the day upon which the people made a stand, whereby our country achieved her freedom."

* They were richly ornamented, and they thought very truly that the Greeks would stop to pick them up instead of pursuing their foes.

Kephalas and Papatsonês were in the battle of Valtetsi. After this victory the Karytainans returned to their places at Chrysovitsi and Piana, and the rest remained in Valtetsi.

Bouboulina crossed over ten days afterwards, and Tsokrês and Staïkos wrote to me to send them assistance, and a leader also; so I sent Niketas with fifty men from Chrysovitsi, and fifty from each of the camps of Valtetsi and Vervena. He went over to Doliana to take his fifty from Vervena and slept there. The Turks held a council at Tripolitsa. The Mistriotes and Bardouniotes proposed that, as they did nothing at Valtetsi, they should go and destroy the camp at Vervena, and thence march to Mistra. The Turks took to this idea, and getting into motion directed their march towards Doliana, in order to spoil our camp at Vervena. Niketas had hardly gone a quarter of an hour's distance from Doliana when it was told him—"The Turks are coming!" He turned back and gained the village, which the Turks surrounded. Whilst some bodies of men enclosed Niketas there, others marched on to Vervena. The regiment at Vervena was prepared for them, and at their first volley they killed a standard-bearer, when the Turks, being seized with a panic, fled at once. When they got near Doliana on their retreat, the Turks, who were besieging Niketas, were broken, and Niketas coming forth with his men set upon them and drove them into the plain. Two cannon were taken and seventy men slain, and the Turks were so discontented with the result that they made no other expedition of the kind.

Niketas then marched into Argos and despoiled the mosques, and minarets, and sent us the lead which he took from them, for we were in want of lead and paper, and we had therefore made use of the library of the monastery of

Demitsana, and also those of other monasteries, in order to make cartridges. The brothers Speliotopouloi had made an agreement with themselves to supply us with powder, and on account of their serving us thus with powder we did not make any requisition on the Demitsanians for the army, but left to them this service instead.

When the Spetsiotes and Hydriotes heard of the progress the war was making, besides giving us ammunition they also sent us leather for shoes. They sent these things to me, so I gave them out wherever I saw that there was a need.

I rose up one night after the battle of Doliana, and in conjunction with the Karytainans seized on the heights of Trikorpha, where we had shepherds, and we kept all war material and provisions and other things in Zarachova, at which place there was a strong tower.

I built a breastwork on the summit of Trikorpha. This was the first time that we had been so near to Tripolitsa, as it was only half an hour distant. I stimulated their ambition to go forward, and I reminded them of the proverb of the serpent.

The next morning, when the Turks saw that we had made breastworks opposite Tripolitsa, they came out and attacked us with two thousand men, but we both repulsed and pursued them. For the succeeding five or six days we had battles continually. We were eighteen hundred strong. Our position helped us much, and since the defeat of the Turks at Valtetsi and Doliana, the Greeks had become much more courageous, and went out frequently for a little skirmishing. When this warfare had gone on for some time, a reinforcement came to us from Valtetsi.

I had given out orders in the district that whosoever should leave the camp should be seized and scourged, and that he should be sent back and his house burned.

Kanelos Deligianni was to arrange for our supplies, whilst
I was to order and supervise all military matters. The
Greeks began to feel so great an enthusiasm for the cause
that they threshed the corn, and afterwards leavened the
flour, and baked the bread which they brought on their
asses and mules to the camp. We had, however, national
ovens at Piana, Alonistaina, Vytina, Magouliana, Demitsana, and Stemnitsa. They brought us sheep from twenty
to thirty, forty, and fifty at a time, and gave them to us
with their heartiest good wishes. Kyriakos Tsolès made
us a present of a hundred and twenty goats from
Zarachova. We also had cuttlefish sent, which they had
collected for us. This example was also followed in respect
to the other camps, which were treated alike.

Ten days later I ordered the armies to move from
Valtetsi and come on to Trikorpha, which was done.

Anagnostaras, Elias, the Messenians, the men of Leontari, and others, to the number of fifteen hundred, came
and built breastworks above the mill of Tripolitsa. We
then sent for the Tsakonai and the Agiopetritai who were at
Vervena, and they took up their position at Steno. There
they made both breastworks and entrenchments, Zapheiropoulos commanding. The Turks came out and skirmished
with them occasionally.

Meanwhile the siege of Patras had been raised because
the Turks had defeated the besiegers on several occasions.
During the time that we had been occupied, as detailed
above, the Lalians had written to us to send them a reinforcement. One was sent, and there were many engagements at Lala, and in one of them the brother of Koliopoulos was killed, and Andreas Metaxas was wounded.
Upon this the Lalians removed their families to Patras.
The interior of the Peloponnesus was evacuated, Patras
was then strengthened, and the Kalavrytian army re-

treated and came over to our assistance at Pano-Chrepa. I went to them and instructed them how to build breast-works at Perthori, in order that we might press Tripolitsa. These sent me a lying letter, saying that a great many Turks had suddenly come to the Black Rocks, wherefore they had removed themselves away six miles further from Tripolitsa.

A council of a part of the chiefs took place at Kaltezia, in the district of Mistra, and it was thought desirable that we should have Mavromichaelês with us; therefore Kanelos Deligianni and Poneros brought him from Kalamata into Stemnitsa, and he was made President of the Senate. They then wrote concerning it to Spetsai, Hydra, and the Seven Islands. Meanwhile we were having skirmishes every day. The forces within Tripolitsa amounted to fourteen thousand foot and eight thousand cavalry. Ypsilanti came to Aspros in June, and all the governors of the Peloponnesus gathered together for a conference — to wit, Andreas Zaimês, Petro Bey, myself, and the rest. I left my son Panos, Giannaki Kolokotronês, and others at the camp. We received him with a guard of honour, and the Spetsiote chief being there, we all accompanied him to Vervena. There Ypsilanti happened to do certain things which displeased the chiefs, and so they quarrelled. Ypsilanti had Vamra and Anagnostopoulos with him, and fifty Greek students in Europe. He wished to become the head of the national commissariat, and the chiefs not desiring it, Ypsilanti was offended and withdrew to Kalamata.

There were five thousand soldiers gathered together at Vervena, and these all seized their arms in order to kill the whole of the chiefs. They came and laid siege to us in Petro Bey's tent, where we were all assembled. I heard the uproar, and was going out when Kanelos Deligianni prevented me, saying, "Do not go out, lest it might give rise to something; for a gun might go off, and then we should all be killed." I had not got soldiers of that sort, so I went out and called to them: " Greeks, what do you want? Come hither!" They ran to me directly and bore me into the open air. They said, "We want to kill the chiefs because they have driven away Ypsilanti." " Come," I answered, " let me first talk to you about that, because I must be your fellow-helper in the matter if you kill them." I then marched them all away with their guns at full cock to a fountain, and then I stationed myself upon a piece of rock so that all might hear me. " Why do you wish ruin to come only through ourselves? We have taken up arms against the Turks, and therefore it is regarded by the whole of Europe that we Greeks have risen up against tyrants, and all Europe is looking on to see what will be the upshot. At present the Turks are skilful in fortresses and the open field, and we in warfare on the hills. If we kill our primates, what will the kings say? Why, that these people have not risen for freedom's sake, but to slay their own colleagues, and that they are bad men, and *carbonari;* and then the kings will give help to the Turks, and we shall have a heavier yoke than that which we have borne hitherto. We will write a letter, and Ypsilanti shall come back again."

Thus I pacified them.

The chiefs and Mavromichaelès sent Anagnostaras to Ypsilanti, and he was brought back, and everything went into its proper channel. At this time Monovasia surrendered. The Maniotes and Tsakonoi had been besieging it by land, and the Spetsiotes with their boats by sea. A few days afterwards Neokastro was also given up. This place had been laid siege to by the Arcadians, Messenians, and also by the Maniotes and the Spetsiotes.

As we were now returning to Trikorpha we asked Petro

Bey to send to Mani and to procure us more help; but he replied that the Maniotes would not leave unless they were paid. Then came five hundred Maniotes, for all the districts agreed to pay them whilst they were besieging Tripolitsa, and Karytaina especially undertook to pay for three hundred under Mourtzinos. We brought a cannon from Mistra, and began to cannonade Tripolitsa from a distance.

At that time our rulers were sitting at Sarakova. I do not remember what Ypsilanti had asked from them, but the rulers did not agree to it. As soon as the army heard of it it wanted to go to Sarakova again to kill them. A petition was presented to me to this effect: "The chiefs do not want to sign what Ypsilanti has presented to them for their signature;" and they came to ask my opinion as to "*whether they should not go and kill them!*" I only replied, "Keep yourselves quiet; I will finish this business." So I went off at noon to Sarakova by myself; and finding the chiefs all together, I said, "What are you after now? Whatever you do you must sign what Ypsilanti requires, and make an end of this breach." And so it was at last settled.

On the festival of St. Elias, on the 20th of July, the Turks came upon us and upon the Agiopetritai and Tsakonoi. That was a most unfortunate day for us, for fifteen Agiopetritai and ten Mistriotes were killed. We had fighting from noon till evening, and in the evening we got right into their midst. We approached so near that we brought the Kosmitai to make a mine in the great fir grove of Tripolitsa. Provisions were beginning to fail there, so they drove out all the Greek families in order that they should not consume their rations, and thus we had news every day of what the Turks inside were doing or not doing. They brought all these people into my camp, and I interrogated them. Water was failing, for we had cast foxglove into the running streams.

The Greeks went up to the walls of Tripolitsa. One day I learnt from a Greek that Kiamil Bey was making ready to go into Corinth with from three to five hundred men, and that he intended to pass through Mytika. As soon as I heard of it (only it happened to be false) I took ten of the cavalry with me and went to Mytika in order to reconnoitre this body; but instead of two hundred Tripolitsans I did not find thirty. I spoke to them at sunrise, and they went away. I upbraided them because they were so few, when they told me that the others had not come, and that they had kept guard there for twenty days. Dagrês, with two hundred men, was at Tsipiana and on the rocks. Some shots were fired at them, when they came down, and I took them with me to the village of Louka. As I had acquired these two hundred men of Dagrês, I threw them into Mytika, opposite Kapnistra, and they made breastworks there. I examined the ground, and found that it would be easy to dig from Mytika right up to those parts of Kapnistra where I had left the soldiers belonging to Dagrês. It was about a mile long, and for half a mile of the distance there were trenches for vines. I then sent an order, "Make a trench here." I also despatched other orders to the villages round about Tripolitsa to summon from seventy to two hundred men to dig a trench, and to throw the earth which they dug out towards Tripolitsa, as I did not expect that they would cross at any other part of the trench; and in three days they had completed it right up to the breastworks, where it terminated. It was seven hundred paces from the base of the hill where the breastworks were situated.

Kehayas, three or four days after this, went to Doliana with six thousand soldiers, and as he was returning he pressed Dagrês very hard, and almost destroyed his regiment, twenty-seven of his men being killed and twenty wounded. The Turks, however, did not notice the newly-made trench because it was night, but, seeing only the end of it, they said, "The Giaours are making frontiers; they are parcelling out the land." Dagrês was shut up in a cave with four of his people; but when I heard the firing I knew at once that he had been attacked, and moved on to help him. I ordered all the regiments of Karytaina to march near me, and sent them to Chomatovouni, opposite Mytika, with my adjutant Photakos, and also despatched a band of about three hundred of the swiftest to hold the trench and give assistance to Dagrês. These were followed by two hundred others, who came up shortly, and a thousand Karytainans also arrived.

The Turks who had been left in Tripolitsa sallied out to skirmish for the purpose of preventing the Greeks from going to aid Dagrês. The soldiers, however, whom I had despatched on that service attacked the enemy from above, scattered them, and eventually saved him. The greater part of the Turkish army went to the village Louka, and procured six hundred mule loads of provisions. Kehayas sent three hundred cavalry to cross the trench; our men pressed down upon them, and then opened out so that the three hundred Turks crossed over, five being killed and ten wounded; fifteen horse were likewise wounded. I went forward to strengthen the Greeks, when Kehayas again brought out another thousand. The Greeks then formed themselves into two divisions, opposing front to front, and attacking in both parts. About five hundred of the enemy were killed, and many wounded, both horse and men. At last followed the main body of the Turks with their laden mules and horses to the number of six hundred, with foot-soldiers and cavalry accompanying.

The Greeks who had been sent to the assistance of Dagrês approached them fighting from behind. Both the cavalry which had crossed the trench, and that which had not, made a rush. Eighty of the cavalry were slain, and all the animals laden with supplies remained in the hands of the Greeks. The Greeks gave themselves up to pillage, and so the Turks were saved because they were not followed up. I threatened the men with my sword, I tried flattery and cajolery to move them, but they did not heed me; and so the Turks were saved. In this battle the Turks numbered six thousand and the Greeks one thousand—all Karytaina men. The brother of Kehayas Bey was wounded, and a hundred and twenty of the enemy were killed, besides the many that were wounded. Of the Greeks there were two or three who were wounded, but only two were slain!

The Turks did not again venture forth from Tripolitsa. This was the last time. They now fought only from the walls, and they despaired of being able to procure any more provisions. This battle took place on the 15th of August—a month before Tripolitsa was taken.

I went forth one night and seized Mantzagra. We made trenches, and Demetraki Deligianni came with his forces and occupied the village, which is ten minutes off Tripolitsa. The Turkish horses now began to succumb because they had nothing to eat. I therefore sent out Gennaios, and he, gathering together Tsakonitai and Agio-petritai, joined with Panagiotês and Tsakona, and took possession of Voulimi (there was no cannon there), and at the same time Kephala with the Messenians were ordered to go and encamp at Agio Sosti, so that we left them no possibility of obtaining any more.

The Albanians now began to open communications with us. There were three thousand of them, and theirs was

the whole strength of the Turkish fort. They proposed to
me that I should allow them to pass out, and I promised
that all the Turkish inhabitants might also leave, only
without their arms, but to the Albanians I granted their
arms. I first spoke about this to the primates and the
chiefs and to Mavromichaelês, and then I gave my word of
honour to the Albanians that they might go forth unhurt.

In the month of June, whilst we were besieging Tripolitsa, I summoned Panos of blessed memory from Dervenia.
Panos, Ypsilanti, Gennaios, and others were at Vasilika, a
district of Corinth, because I had told them that the Turks
had gone there.

The army, consisting of seven hundred men with Ypsilanti from Agia Irene, met the fleet which burnt Galaxeidi.
The Albanians during this time were making their
arrangements. There was a secretary with the Albanians who
was on the staff of Veli Bey, and also on that of Almas Bey,
and he came to act as a mediator between the Albanians
and ourselves. When the other Turks heard about the
treaty that was thus being negotiated, they wished to
take part in it themselves. Petro Bey and Deligianni and
others acted for our side, and told them that they might
go out, but that they must leave their arms behind, when
we would embark them for whatsoever place they desired
to go to. Their answer was, " *No ; with our arms !* " We
sent Koliopoulos to the Albanians as a hostage, so that
they might trust in us. The Greeks, who knew that
Tripolitsa must fall, had assembled there from all parts
to the number of twenty thousand.

Whilst the Albanians were going out, some Greeks
jumped right into the place amid the redoubts of the
palace. The Albanians were to go out, taking Koliopoulos
with them. As the body of them was issuing forth, I sent a

public crier to announce that we were not to slay the Albanians.

Inside the town they had begun to massacre. My horse from the walls to the palace never touched the earth. The Albanians who were then shut up in the fort did not trust my words.

I rushed to the place. The affair of the Albanians had been settled in my tent three days previously. Upon reaching the fort I found that the Greeks were endeavouring to attack those Albanians. "If you wish to hurt these Albanians," I cried, "kill me rather; for whilst I am a living man, whoever first makes the attempt, him will I kill the first." I then went in front of them with my body-guard, and had a conversation with the two leaders, Veli Bey and Limas Bey, and demanded two hostages on their side, when I gave up their property to them, which amounted to as much as thirteen animals could be laden with.

The chief men among all the Greeks had joined in this treaty. I was faithful to my word of honour. I took Koliopoulos from the Albanians, and gave them Giannaki Kolokotronês, Chrystakês, and Basil Alonisthiotês as hostages in his stead.

I ordered Koliopoulos, with three hundred men, to escort them, and he accompanied them to Kalavryta and Vostitsa, and then returned.

Tripolitsa was three miles in circumference. The host which entered it, cut down and were slaying men, women, and children from Friday until Sunday. Thirty-two thousand were reported to have been slain. One Hydriote boasted that he had killed ninety. About a hundred Greeks were killed; but the end came : a proclamation was issued that the slaughter must cease.

The family of Sechnetzi Bey remained under my care;

they were twenty-four people in all. Giatrakos took Kiamil Bey, and Kehayas was also a prisoner, and with his harem was taken charge of by Petro Bey.

After the victory of Valtetsi I had written to Kehayas, and I told him therein: "I knew you to be a man of skill, and that you came to fight as with a Klephtic horde. I hear that you have papers of submission for the Romaics; it is not now the time for Turks to offer papers of submission, and I hope to be able to give you, if you are saved, a permit to go to your own country. Hold out if you can, and *au revoir* in your own palace." And God brought this about, and we met again in his palace.

"I have been a slave among the Russians," said Kehayas; "it is better for me to fall into. the hands of the Greeks; if not, the Sultan will send orders, and I shall be lost."

"Do not fear; we never kill those who surrender." We then delivered him to the keeping of the Mavromichaeli.

When I entered Tripolitsa they showed me a plane tree in the market-place where the Greeks had always been hung. I sighed. "Alas!" I said, "how many of my own stock—of my own race—have been hung there!" And I ordered it to be cut down. I felt some consolation then from the slaughter of the Turks.

When we started to go to Valtetsi I remember that three hares crossed our path, and the Greeks caught them all. "Now, lads," I cried, "victory is certain." The Greeks have a presage either of conquest or defeat when they meet hares as they set out from a camp. They did not kill them, and if they had not been able to catch them the hearts of the Greeks would have been so depressed that they would have lost the battle.

Once, whilst we were at Trikorpha, Anagnostês Zapheiropoulos, who was then my secretary, saw that I was working hard for twenty-four hours straight off. At the end of the twentieth hour I went to my tent and ate a small piece of bread, when he said: "Beseech thee, Kolokotronês, to study thyself—study thyself; thy country will reward thee."

"My country will banish me rather," I replied; and fate brought this about, and verified it.

We had formed a plan of proposing to the Turks that they should deliver Tripolitsa into our hands, and that we should in that case send persons into it to gather the spoils together which were then to be apportioned and divided among the different districts for the benefit of the nation, but who would listen?

Karytaina, from the commencement of the siege until the fall of Tripolitsa, had given from the flocks of those who were well-to-do in the district forty-eight thousand animals.

CHAPTER V.

AFTER ten days had elapsed all the Greeks carried off their spoils, and went to their different districts with their captives, both male and female. In those ten days which had been granted to the Greeks to secure their spoil we had a council which Ypsilanti, Petro Bey, and others attended. I spoke to this effect: " It is time that we made another campaign, and as for myself I will go to Patras," and they thought well of the proposal. I then set forward with only my body-guard of forty men. I issued a command to the district of Karytaina to gather the forces together for Patras, and when I arrived at Magouliana, six miles from Tripolitsa, I had collected seventeen hundred soldiers, and by the time I got down to Gastouni ten thousand were assembled. Hearing that I was mustering the armies for Patras, the chiefs who were besieging Patras, namely Zaimès, Soter Charalampès, and Patron wrote a letter to Ypsilanti, in which they said, " We hear that Kolokotronês is coming to Patras; Kolokotronês can stay away, and assistance can be sent to us, as, for instance, three hundred national guard, either with Deligianni or Mavromichaelès, and in six days hence we shall have taken Patras "—which was, in short: " It does not suit us that Kolokotronês shall come and carry off the spoil here as he did at Tripolitsa." Their intention was that I should not go and strengthen them at Patras, although, if they had allowed me to go at once, the Turks would have given up the keys to me immediately out of very fear.   Let them be Anathema.

They wrote to me from Tripolitsa that I had better turn back, because the Patras business was over. "Return, and we will go to Nauplia." I turned back with the forces which I had massed. As I was approaching Tripolitsa I wrote to know what we could do at Nauplia, and their reply was: "We are quite efficient of ourselves to take Nauplia, because they are hungry there." Tsokrês, Staïkos, and others were the leaders of the besieging forces. At the very same hour in which they wrote that letter an Austrian boat laden with ten thousand measures of corn arrived at Nauplia; and therefore, as that had happened, the army wrote : "Come, for a boat has arrived with provisions, and we cannot do anything by ourselves." We started for Argos at once, Ypsilanti, Petro Bey, and the then Senate. The Tripolitsans petitioned me that Panos should be left behind to keep the fort for the preservation of order in the city. I therefore allowed him to remain with them. We then embarked for Argos in order to take the field, carrying with us Kiamil Bey and his son. When we disembarked at Argos we found the siege in a fair state of progression.

Bouboulina * with her brother guarded the blockade. When we had called together all the chief people from Hydra, Spetsai, and the Peloponnesus, we formed a government. At the same time we also determined upon making an assault on Nauplia. I rode over to Mylos to look at the ships there, and whilst on the road my horse threw me, and I became unwell in consequence. I gave my advice in regard to the projected assault. The army

* The warlike widow of a Spetsiote shipbuilder and captain.

on land was to attack Palamedi and the port, and the ships were to cannonade the castle, and the Five Brothers and five hundred were to fall upon Kranidiotika from the shore. My advice was not followed. "If thou art not equal to it," they told me, "stand aside awhile." "Stand aside, while my brothers are being killed!" was my rejoinder.

The forces assembled at Areia. Josaphat sent word to the soldiers, "Whoever is killed or wounded, the country will recognize his value."

We were four thousand in all. I took a thousand of them, and with Niketas, Giatrakos, and others, went down to attack the port from the shore. The Philhellene Tarelle had a hundred men with him.

I told them that if they had an opportunity the boats should make the first attack, but if there was not an opportunity we would not attempt it. They answered: "The boats are there, and we will attack the first." I resolved to attack Palamedi myself at night until daybreak, when they could bring down a force from the country, and then strike at the port on the land side. I decided to take the thousand men; four hundred followed me, but the others thought it better to go down country. I began the attack at daybreak with those I had, and opened fire. We seized the landing-stages at Pronoia, and attacked Leuko in the same way. The boats to the shore had no wind, as it blew from the shore, and was therefore contrary, so we made no way. The Turks were strengthened between their platoons, and the Greeks kept sinking in the earth of the Turkish cemetery. The battle lasted two hours. Seeing that the boats could do no service, I sent my adjutant, Photakos, to bid them retire at once, and therefore the whole of them retired in a body. A few were killed, and we had a little fighting with the Turks, but we returned to Argos with nothing achieved. The Greeks were not equal to the taking castles such as those by assault; it was folly to attempt it. We sent word to the different districts that we ought to have an assembly. Mavrokordatos and Zaimês came to arrange the meeting in order that we might form a government.

Mavrokordatos, with his son Karatza, was at Patras, where he had been some little while, and we met him at Argos for the first time. Upon our return to Argos all the chiefs and rulers from the various districts and from the islands of Greece met there together.

Ypsilanti was a man of fixed opinions, honourable and brave, of small intellect and vain; also he was easily deceived. He was small in stature and slim. His name was very useful to us in the beginning, but he had an idea that he should be made head of us all, and his brain did not furnish the necessary qualifications for the position in which he was placed. Had his brother Alexander come to us he would have been of real service, because he would have been able to strengthen us. For myself I did not bow down my shoulders to one of them. I was not going to make myself a crupper for the leaders to ride upon. They were there, and there was myself, but there was no third person. There were no dissensions at the meeting. Anagnostaras was a man of great sense, but envious, heavy to move, and fat. Krebata was also a clever man, and very useful to his country.

We were quite agreed about making a government, but we quarrelled about the place where it should be held. The soldiers who were gathered there made a petition to me asking for my consent to their killing all the chiefs and primates. Some of them thought that there was no necessity to have an assembly at all—for every one to jeer at. At noon I went and argued with them. "What are you doing now?" I asked. "Take your oaths, because this which they have in hand must be done for you, and then you can go to a place where you can begin the assembly." I led them straightway to the church of St. John; they took the oaths, and thus this boiling over was stopped. The people always have a fancy for killing their governors whenever the smallest cause for discontent arises.

The politicians went to Epidauros and began to frame their laws, and we with our soldiers departed for Corinth. Giatrakos had his Leontarians and men of Tripolitsa with him, and he also took there Kiamil Bey and twenty braves from Leontari. Ypsilanti and Anagnostaras were also there. Giatrakos with his Turkish prisoners went to Examilia, and the rest of the forces set themselves to besiege the castle. One day I took a journey down to Examilia, in order to ask Kiamil Bey to write a letter to his lieutenant and to his wife also to bid them deliver up the castle. Either he did not write to that effect, or they would not listen to this request, because the castle was not surrendered. The army which was in Corinth killed twenty Turks. There were several Lalians and Albanians among them, and I sent down Karachalios, and asked them once or twice to surrender, and they always said, *to-day or to-morrow*, and in that manner twenty days were passed. The fact was that they were expecting a reinforcement from Omer Vrioni, who was in Eastern Greece. They went to the Corinthians and persuaded them thus: "Do not surrender to Kolokotronês, because a reinforcement will come to you." Their intentions also being, that when we were gone away and they were left there alone, they would partake of the spoils: there was envy in it all.

After twenty days I sent Karachalios again to the Lalians, and two of them came to my tent. I told them to go out of the castle and to let the other Turks remain in it. This was in order to make a beginning; so sixteen of them took their arms and came out, and I put them into my own camp. We went on treating with them; and after five or six days had passed over, a Lalian came to me and cried aloud against the deputy of Kiamil Bey, against the Kadi, and against two other Turkish officers whose names I do not remember. We again spoke with them about the terms, offering to allow them to take two changes of raiment with them, when we would see that they were put aboard different ships, some going to Roumêli, and others to be sent either to Galaxeidi or to Salonia. Their answer was, "We must first have a conference with the others, after which we will send you our reply."

The next day they spoke with me again in reference to my making a covenant with them. We were preparing to do so, when the whole army, from its utter want of discipline, began to move nearer to us. Seeing its undisciplined state I misdoubted this, and galloped off with only Captain Anagnostês Petimeza, and went to a castle in some Turkish cemetery, when I announced, " The chiefs must sent a body of thirty national guards to attend me; " and so they did.

We two being there, I sent word to the fort that they must come down to me, and then I would speak to them again upon the matter, because the previous bond which I had made in the past days had been made of no effect through the conduct of the Turks. Four came out upon this suggestion, and we sat and conferred together. As I had got these well in hand, I sent to the Kadi by my thirty men to announce to him that all the Turks must deliver up their arms, and place them all together in one house. The Kadi gave his word that he had had them sworn upon their faith not to conceal any of their arms, but to give them all up; so they were all disarmed. As regards the assembly, as soon as it was known that the Turks were going to surrender, we demanded that five or six members of the Government should be sent to receive the spoils, and to divide it among the nation. Soter Notaras and others were therefore sent. The Archimandrite of Arcadia also arrived from the Senate in order to get our signatures for the laws which it had been framing. I would not sign them because there was a clause which said, " The executive will conclude a proposition, and at the end of six days it will render an account of it to the assembly." All except myself appended their signatures. A supplement was put to that clause when it was brought back to me, and then I signed it.

I sent the thirty men into the fort to disarm the Turks, which, being done, I gave information of it to the deputies from the assembly, and taking three hundred men from different regiments, I went to the gate and crossed it with a Greek flag, and then planted the flag on the top of the fort. The army and myself then went into the interior; we numbered six thousand men. Ypsilanti, Giannaki Kolokotronês, Apostolês Kolokotronês, my son Gennaios, Anton Kolokotronês, Anagnostaras, and others were at the fall of Corinth.

News was then brought that the squadron of Kapitan Bey with nine thousand men had arrived at Patras. Upon hearing this I gave the necessary orders and marched directly for Patras. I passed from Argos to Tripolitsa, and when at Tripolitsa I ordered that regiments from Karytaina, Phanari, and Arcadia should get into marching order for Patras.

When I arrived in Tripolitsa the news had come that Ali Pasha was destroyed, and many members of the Senate said, " Now that Ali Pasha is dead, the eighty thousand men who were besieging him will fall upon us."

" That rests with God," said I.

Then one Nicholas Tzanetos from Phanari remarked—

" We have done well, and have made a senate and a parliament, and now, as the old writings say, let ruin come upon us."

" Well said, Sir ! " was my reply.

I ordered Gennaios to bring his Tripolitsans and Phanarites near. At Vytina I received the orders of the first systematized government of Greece ; and I also received from it a diploma as general. On the 1st of March I arrived in Patras. I had gone through Karytaina, Pyrgos, Gastouni, and had collected six thousand men.

I· have now related the events up to March 2, 1822. Niketaras and Acholos had gone against Omer Vrioni. When I first arrived in Patras,* on the 28th of February, I was ignorant of the country ; the Turks had been making raids into and pillaging Achaia, having a force of about five thousand men, and the advance guard of Gennaios came up with ·them. Koliopoulos went to his assistance, and routed them, driving them outside Patras, when I came up upon their rear, when we all massed together at Saravali, and I immediately sent a hundred to take possession of the monastery of Gerokomeios, and also to carry there a cannon from Patras. When the Turks saw that we had seized upon the monastery they prepared directly for a battle, thinking that it was the same with us now as formerly. We moved up our armies quickly, and a terrible battle ensued. We took about eighty heads.

The Greeks had arrived and gone into the interior.

* Kolokotronés had with him a force of about 4,000 men ; Zaimês, and other chiefs, about 1,500

They signified their intention of remaining there ; but I told them to go to their several posts. The Kalavrytian body of a hundred men stayed at Gerokomeios, and four hundred of the Tripolitsans remained by the vats of Saitaga ; whilst Kanelos Deligianni was to occupy Pournaro-Kastro with six hundred. I placed Gennaios with three hundred Phanarites at Paleopyrgo. I had the Gastounaioi at Obria, and the most effective part of the army I held back in Saravali as a reinforcement. Saravali was half an hour distant from our breastworks, and three-quarters from Patras. I saw the regiments of the Turks, who, when they heard that Kolokotronês had come, they sent immediately to Jousouf Pasha, who was then at the castle, saying that Kolokotronês had brought over a force of many thousands. Before we came to a battle, Miaoulês had made frightful havoc among the shipping, which had fled in consequence and gone to Constantinople. We, with our own men, stayed where we were and prepared for battle.. As the Turkish vessels were gone, Jousouf Pasha sent to Epakto and to the castle of Patras and levied all the Turks, and with as many as he could muster marched into Patras. The assembled Turks numbered twelve thousand ; nine thousand of these were Eastern Turks, and three thousand of the others. On the 9th of March the whole of them were set in motion, and when I took a survey of them from Saravali, and saw how great a host it was, I summoned all our troops, with the Kalavrytians, who were at Gerokomeios, and the Tripolitsans, who were stationed in Saitaga.

The battle was commenced beyond the hills. When the engagement opened, I sent Gennaios forward with his Phanarites, and the Gastounians from my own regiment. As soon, however, as the reinforcement arrived it was broken, and Gennaios with his six hundred was surrounded in the vat grounds of Saitaga ; the Turks were very numerous, and they enclosed him there, and endeavoured to force him thence. Koliopoulos in the meanwhile, with the rest of the army, took possession of the vineyards where the vats were situated, and with the help of the Gastounians held them. The army of Patras, under Kanelos, was engaged also at Pournaro-Kastro, and Zaimês made a stand there, but was routed and pursued for half an hour, when he reached the river by the mills with the remnant of his army.

I was alone, for I had sent out my whole force, so there I was with the master of Arta from Western Greece, Andreas, Kalamodartês, and the secretary, Michaelagês.

Seeing clearly that the Turkish forces were preparing to force the vats and the monastery, I said, " I will leave the mules with the shepherd here ; if we break the Turks, come on, and if not, flee with the mules, and I go trusting in the help of God and in yours."

I went forward alone, not even having my adopted son with me. A quarter of a mile off I met old Anagnostês Lechoritês, whom Zaimês had sent to me. " Run, brother, run ! " he cried ; " we have lost the battle." I accompanied old Anagnostês along the road leading to Paleopyrgos. When we arrived at the high ground just above Paleopyrgos, I saw a little flag, and there was Evangelês, Koumanitês, with fifteen others, stationed all together and forming a line. I called to them—

" What men are you ? "

" Greeks," they replied.

" Do you not know me, then ? " I asked. " I am Kolokotronês ; come hither."

At that time I was wearing a red jacket and a red fustanella. They descended, and I sent them forward, and then went myself straightway towards the Turkish centre, and some straggling Greeks, who heard whither I was going, joined me, and I thus got together about fifty men, and these I placed at a post in front of the Turkish centre. I said to them, "Fix your flag here." "We are lost men," they replied. "I will send you a reinforcement." I then galloped off to the vineyard of Kol, and told those who were there to take their flag and go and place it by the side of the other.

Gennaios and the Kalavrytians were all this time surrounded. I looked forward to the line of flags, and saw a lime furnace, so I ordered Paraskeva, the brother of Koliopoulos, with twenty men to go and seize it, as there were only about fifty Turkish cavalry who could oppose them : they also said, " We shall be lost."

" Go ; I will see to you."

As soon as the centre was well strengthened, Karachalios and my adjutant, Photakos, took up their station where I could observe the battle. I saw that we should not be able to break the Turks from the centre, and that if we defeated them we must defeat them in the wings. Taking Karachalios and Photakos with me, I went to another part which the Turks were holding, near the water source (but there were only two there). I raised my voice : " Where are you, you silly Greeks? Come down ! come down ! " Hearing my voice, those that had fled came down, and when they had all descended, I put up my glass and called out (it was merely a trick, for I saw nothing), " The Turks are broken." The Greeks rallied at once, and the first ranks were broken where were the Turks, who had surrounded Gennaios in the vat grounds.

I was on horseback, and fortune was good but not my horse, in order to take them alive. The wing of the Turks that was near to the water springs was scattered ; we followed them up. Sikerês was commander over the Tripolitsans. My own centre now attacked the Turkish centre, and an officer was killed; the Koumaniotai also attacked, and we got two hundred and fifty heads. What became of the wounded I know not, and we then returned to where they had been drawn up. From that day they did not advance forward to engage us, for they said that our flight was only a stratagem.

We then approached nearer. All through the day there was skirmishing with bodies of Turks; Karachalios was wounded in the head, and therefore he gave up his flag. "You go ahead!" he cried; "I am stunned."

The food for the whole army came from Gastouni, and the supply of provisions was most regular. We had altogether four thousand beasts, eighty head of cows, besides bread, all coming from Gastouni. Gastouni was an inexhaustible hive. Sissinês sent them all to us. As many as we ate during the week the number was made up again, so that we always had four thousand.

I now wrote for the Arcadians to come. The Arcadians had chosen Metros Anastasopoulos to be their leader; their force numbered twelve hundred. Poneros also arrived. He had wished to have led the army of the Arcadians himself, and to have exchanged into that service, and had asked me to put him at their head when the Arcadians came first to Saravali, where my camp was. I told him at once, "I cannot do such a thing without asking the rulers." I did ask, and he was not accepted by them. "Now what can I do for you more?" I said. The Arcadians came alone and carried on a good war, fighting bravely, and they killed somewhere about ten Turks. In fifteen days, however, all the cohorts, whole cohorts of twelve hundred men, went away secretly; the captains alone remained. I seized some of them and put them to shame.

As the Arcadians had gone off, and the captains only were left behind, I dismissed them also. An order now came to me from the minister of war, telling me to move my armies into Western Greece. I immediately replied that I could not go away and leave twelve thousand Turks in Patras. "I must first," I said, "put out the fire in my own house before I go to quench that of my neighbour." He wrote to me again, saying, " The letter which thou hast forwarded I have not shown to the Government, as thou wouldst have been seriously damaged by it; take, however, this second order and fulfil it and begin the campaign." I then left Koliopoulos at the head of the armies and went straightway to Corinth, to stay there for three days. Having gone five hours on my journey, I sent information to the Government that I should not go to Western Greece; but I received no reply. I then went on my road. I had continued my journey for about a quarter of an hour longer, when I received an order to leave behind the eighty men whom I had taken with me and to enter Corinth with five only. I did so. I had a tent given to me for my use with no floor, and at night they left me so uncared for that I went to the village to sleep.

When it was known that I had gone away thus, the executive began to quarrel among themselves, saying, "It's your fault." And the others, "No; it is you who are to blame, and you ought not to have acted thus." However, they sent a commission of inquiry from Koletês, Korinthos, Soter Notaras, and from some of the Hydriotes. Replying to them, I said, "If you do not receive a general when he is coming to confer with you in a proper manner—well, I go away; and I shall betake myself to Tripolitsa, and what I have to say I shall say it there to the Senate." "No, no; go back," was their answer; "do what thou proposest, because it

MARKOS BOTZARES, A SOULIOTE CHIEF.
Surnamed "The Leonidas of the Revolution," killed during the Siege of Missolonghi.

was wrong that there should be any want of proper tents."
I said openly to Koletês in answer, " You ought to be
minister of war at Juannina, and not here."

The ruler of Corinth and the others who were there,
sent for me and I went to them and laid some
propositions before them, which the Government accepted.
I represented to them that if I left and went to Roumêli,
the Turks of Patras would swarm all over the Peloponnesus
directly, and their numbers being twelve thousand it would
be utterly wasted by them. The Government saw by these
representations of mine that there was a necessity for my
presence there, and it therefore gave me a fresh order to
go to Patras.

I passed through Argos and Tripolitsa, and reached
Patras in the beginning of May. I met Markos Botsarês
in Corinth; he was staying there in order to make a
change for his family. He told me to go to Western
Greece, as if I did so they would make me the general
of all the forces. But I gave him my own ideas upon
the subject, observing that I had proposed to the Government that Mavrokordatos, who was then president of the
executive, should be sent with a thousand trained Philhellenes. In consequence of this, Mavrokordatos and
Markos Botsarês took the Philhellenes and went to the
camp at Patras, where I found them; after which they
passed over to Western Greece, and wrote to me
thence that they wanted me to send them more help;
so I despatched my son Gennaios to them forthwith with
two hundred picked men. Giatrakos coming over afterwards, I sent him also with the hundred which he brought
with him—the rest of his troops having gone away—and
Kanelos Deligianni was sent also with another two
hundred. I remained behind to fill up the vacancies
caused by those whom I had sent away to Roumêli,

having about six thousand altogether. I put down thresh-ing-floors to lay the currants on, and ordered the Greeks to harvest the currants in order that they might be rewarded for their exertions, as we took the currants under a sense of national justice; so the Greeks came and applied themselves to the work. The Turks in the fort were much distressed for water, and on account of the extent of their sufferings they would be obliged to surrender before a month was out.

About a thousand Turks were killed in the different skirmishes which we had with them, and as many more were ill in consequence of wounds received. (Kanelos was made a general secretly by the Executive; the great battle of Saravali took place on the 7th and 8th of March.) I sent Koliopoulos to Karytaina to raise fresh levies. Now, however, when the Parliament and Executive suddenly heard that Dramalês had come over to Trikala in Thessaly, they met and despatched Krebata to Mistra with one thousand soldiers, in order to carry on the campaign in Eastern Greece. Soter Notaras was also to take the Corinthian force to Eastern Greece, and with him were associated Zaimês, Soter Charalampês with the Kalavrytians, and Anagnostês Deligianni with two hundred Karytainans, all of whom were ordered into Eastern Greece. The order ran thus: " Whoever disobeys, and does not follow these commands, the same is to forfeit to the nation one-third of his estate."

When I received the commands of the rulers, I sent to different captains, who were with me at the siege of Patras, that we might all assemble and pass over together. The captains showed me these orders, when I told them plainly, " It is not befitting that we raise the siege of Patras at this time, as the Turks will then go forth and lay the districts waste. The fall of Patras is now imminent." They replied, "We dare not stay behind because the order expressly says that if we do not obey we shall lose one-third of our possessions." "If that be so," I answered, "give me a writing to the effect that I do not discharge you, but that you go away of your own free will—and God be with you!" So they gave me such a writing. This was in the middle of June. The soldiers went away, and I was left with only six hundred men, and the consequence of this was that the Turks came down and burnt our quarters. I fought with them a little, but at noon the same day I moved off to Gastouni. The intention of the Government was that I should not take Patras, and therefore it sought to weaken my military resources as much as possible.

Whilst I was at Gastouni, Sissinês became so alarmed that he shut himself up with three hundred men in different houses belonging to him. I therefore sent a man to him with the following message: "Sissinês, if it be true that Dramalês is come, my opinion is that we should all assemble the Corinthian armies into one body and await him at Dervenia, and thus be really looking after the affairs of the nation." Whereupon Sissinês at once agreeing with me, said, "I am ready, and will act when I receive your next orders." I sent general commands to all the districts of Arcadia, Phanari, Leontari, and Messenia to collect their soldiers and go to Tripolitsa. I then moved on towards Karytaina, and walked day and night till I arrived at Demitsana, gathering soldiers as I went along.

Having reached Demitsana, a special messenger came to me with an order from the minister of war, which was worded thus:—

"Most brave general, Theodoros Kolokotronês, receive here the orders of the Government, namely, that you are to strike at once with your usually powerful arm, and gathering your forces, go directly to Patras. The Government is much disconcerted because you have raised the siege of Patras, and it has taken the necessary measures for the safety of Dervenia."

At the same time the courier who brought me the above also took a writing to K. Anagnostês, which said : "Most well-born Kyr * Anagnostês, take your forces and go to Greater Dervenia, because Dramalês has come into Thebes." And at this time Kyr Anagnostês was in Lankadia with his servant. The Government sent Rhêgas Palamedês to Greater Dervenia with eighteen hundred Corinthians and Tripolitsans.

Loukopoulos gave a thousand gold pieces, which were to be divided among the Maniotes, who would not move a step forward without money. I arrived in Tripolitsa with two thousand men, and the Senate happened to be there at the time ; but some of the senators were so frightened on account of my going there that they fled away. I, however, as soon as I got into Tripolitsa, put in others from their own districts, and in this way strengthened the Senate.

It so happened that the Senate had not heard anything about the coming of Dramalês. I therefore sent foot-messengers to all the districts with orders to make themselves ready. I remained four days in Tripolitsa, when men came from Argos informing us that Dramalês had really arrived; but to myself, who was then in Tripolitsa, the Government wrote not one word, neither did it send the six thousand men it had promised to Dervenia. Since I heard nothing from the Government direct, I did not forward any soldiers, for I thought that the report was probably nothing but lies. In my anxiety, however, I sent two horsemen to Agio-Georgio, who were to let

* Abbreviation of Kyrié.

me have all the information that they could acquire, bidding them to go to Corinth, Dervenia, and even to Thebes, and to seek out Ypsilanti and Niketas, and thus procure for me true and reliable information concerning all that was going on. (Niketas had gone away in January with Zapheiropoulos.) As soon as these horsemen approached Corinth they came up with some Turks, and it was with great difficulty that they escaped being captured; so they returned.

Rhegas was at Dervenia, and when the Turks were moving from Megara thither he abandoned the two or three flags which were planted there, and fled without firing off one gun. When the Turks saw the flags displayed they made sure that there was an army somewhere, and began to slacken in their advance, but when they found that there really was no army, the Turkish cavalry made a movement to get nearer the Greeks, some of whom fled directly to Ægina, and others to Sophikos. The Turks slew a few Greeks. Rhegas paused to take breath when he got to Argos, where he gave out that Dramalês had brought up sixty thousand men to Dervenia—just as if he had stopped to count them. "What has become of your army?" they asked. "All are destroyed; only I myself have escaped." The Government had kept a monk named Achilles, who was a teacher of literature, in the citadel of Corinth, and he, when he saw the Turks approaching, fled along with the soldiers. The soldiers before they took to flight killed Kiamil Bey. Dramalês then took possession of the deserted fortress and sent forty-nine cavalry men to carry the good news to Nauplia.

Nauplia only a month before had made an agreement with the Government whereby the Turks were to give up the castle, and ten Turkish officers as hostages, to thirty of our own people, with a promise that we would send provisions to the fortress until they could be taken away in

Greek boats, after which the spoils were to be divided according to rule. The Government, however, when it saw the Turks arriving, and bringing to the fort the joyful news that Dramalês was coming to their aid, fled and embarked on the boats belonging to the members, whilst the army stationed there dispersed. The two horsemen whom I had sent out brought me word that Dramalês had embarked for the Peloponnesus, and had reached Corinth, but it was not yet known that the fort was in the hands of the Turks, and we hoped to bring it help.

A messenger came on foot an hour before sunrise. Upon the receipt of the letter he brought me I went to the Senate and said, " As many among you as have any acquaintance with letters, let them come hither." Then we sat down and wrote all through the night and sent to every district to gather men together as quickly as possible, because Dramalês had come into the Peloponnesus. I gave an injunction to the Senate to remain: " Stay here and help us with food and ammunition, and I will go forward with the armies, and if I see that I can do nothing towards crushing the enemy, I will send you word, and you can then depart."

In the morning I addressed the soldiers. " Greeks," I cried, " do not fear the Turks; we have killed so many of the native Turks in battle, that why should we not do the same by these? There are not so many Turks either as you have been told. Let us go and fight and slay them far away from our children and our families; do not take with you either mules or capotes, they will bring you all those things."

I directed Koliopoulos and Anton Kolokotronês with seventeen hundred men to march to Agio-Georgio, and to go opposite and fire off two or three volleys, so that the Greeks who were in the fort of Corinth might be emboldened when they heard them, because I hoped that the fort was still standing out. I myself marched on with only three hundred men, because I knew that there were five or six thousand soldiers at Argos, whom I took with me when I reached that place, and then went forward to meet the Turks at Dervenia. Upon reaching Partheni I met Rhegas with Kolios the Dareiote. I asked them to tell me what they knew, and they told me that sixty thousand Turks had met them, and that only he (Rhegas) was saved. I scolded him right well, and bade him not to carry such tales to Tripolitsa. He, however, had scarcely got into Tripolitsa before he spread this report all over the city, and every one immediately fled, only the Senate remaining behind.

The soldiers also whom I had assembled around me lost heart when they heard this, so in order to put a little confidence in them I began to sing. Lower down I met Lycurgus Krestinîtês with fifteen men, and asked them whither they were going. Their answer was that they were going to Pyrgos, but that they should come back. The Maniotes got out of Argos and fled. I met them on the road and asked them whither they were going. They all said, "We are ill, so we are obliged to return." "One or two among you may be ill, but not all of you," I said. At Tavouli I met Ypsilanti, Krebata, my son Panos, who was in the Senate, and Mavromichaelês. "Where are you going?" I asked. "Can you see the Turks with your open eyes?" "No, but they tell us that fifty troops of cavalry have gone to Nauplia." "And whither go ye? Have we no fort to go to? Have we no force to march forward? Are the Turks to enslave the world?" And in this way I restrained them from going.

I then called out for Petro Barbitsiotês, Theodoros Zacharopoulos, and Anton Koumoustiotês. "Go and take possession of the fort of Argos," I said, "and hold it with a hundred men, and, having got possession of the fort, make a light to show that the fort is being held." They all answered, " We will go, but we shall be lost men."

" Go," I cried ; " I will be answerable for you."

They accordingly went and exhibited a light. Immediately afterwards I sent Panos with another hundred and fifty to seize Mylos, and to give orders that the vessels of his mother-in-law (Bouboulina, the heroine of Spetsai) should come near so that they might help him with their cannon if there should be a battle. We stopped at Achladokabo for three days, and wrote for the armies to move forward, when the Agiopetriti and the Mistriotes arrived under Zapheiropoulos, and we made together some thousands. I then ordered Petro Bey and Ypsilanti to go also and occupy Mylos, and send help to Argos thence, whilst I would march over to Corinth and see what the Turks were doing there, or whither they had gone. I formed them into two columns, one to go to Vasilika, and the other to Argos. These went to, Mylos ; Panos and Georgakês Beyzadè passed over to Argos, and were shut up there ; I marched towards Corinth and met with Koliopoulos at Skenochori ; Anton was at Agio-Georgio, and the Turks were preparing to make a descent upon Argos. Koliopoulos encountered some Turks at Charvati, and killed twenty of them. Koliopoulos had a single combat with one of their cavalry and slew him, after which he returned to Skenochori. Many of them came out of the fort of Argos and skirmished and fought with the Turks who were arriving from Corinth, and about ten were killed. The Koumountouraioi and Sissinos remained with Anton Bey who was also lying in wait at Agio-Georgio for the Turks who were expected to arrive from Corinth, and they slew about séventeen. The day after that occurrence two thousand came up in a body and fought with him, when he was repulsed and some houses were burnt. For myself, when I had sent forward others to Mylos, I made haste to get to Corinth, and going by Skenochori, I sought out Koliopoulos, when he informed me that Anton had departed from Agio-Georgio by the way of Malandrino ; we met ten of the Turkish cavalry, who, seeing us coming, shut themselves up in a house, and as they would not surrender we burnt the house and them inside it. One of our soldiers seeing a gun standing against the door took possession of it. I then marched on to Agio-Georgio. The village was full of oil and other things. I seized upon the village, and as I advanced further I saw that the Turkish forces were moving from Corinth in the direction of Argos and Nauplia.

When the Turkish armies had arrived they at once laid siege to the old fort of Argos. There were two Pashas among these troops, and they said to the soldiers : '' Here lie the riches of the world ; if Nauplia is ours, we will soon have all the rest,'' and they began the siege.

There were quite five thousand men assembled at Mylos. Koliopoulos, with his Phanarites and Karytainans, and Deligianni also, were shut up in the old fortress there. They sent word to me that I must go to their aid because the fortress was surrounded, and they had no provisions. The following day Antonaki Mavromichaelês was made general of the army that was in Mylos. As he was made a general he wished to have a battle with the Turks, and did not warn Koliopoulos, who was just on their side, so the engagement was forced and took place at the end of the vineyards, when the Turkish cavalry, ten thousand strong, broke the Greeks, and a hundred and fifty of them were slain. As they were losing the battle they sent a note to me bidding me—even if I were eating my bread—to leave it and go to their assistance ; but I was at Agio-Georgio, therefore the country suffered,

I lost no time, however, in moving up a hundred soldiers, and I left Anton Kolokotronês at Dervenaki with some thousands. When I reached Mylos I found all the Argive soldiers sorrowing and despondent on account of the battle of the day before, in which many of the army had been killed. I did not fail to speak to them, and tried to encourage them by saying, that if the Turks had killed a hundred and fifty, we had slain our thousands, and that we would yet avenge those others, with many other things of the kind to put them in heart again. I very strongly upbraided them, however, for the undisciplined conduct of the engagement, and for their not communicating with Koliopoulos. Mavromichaelês and Krebata were at the Aphentikos Mills. The next day twelve hundred Arcadians came up.

The Turks threw bombs into Argos, and placed two cannon on a rock, in order to lay close siege to the old fortress. They who were shut up there had nothing with them, and were much distressed for want of provisions. On the 20th of July, the festival of St. Elias, I summoned all the regiments to the Argive Mills, and harangued them for the space of two hours. " We must fight," I said ; " we must relieve those who are shut up there : the Turks are all mere ballast."

I decided to attack the Turks in the evening on all sides ; for no one could get through to communicate with the besieged, but we depended entirely on signals. I therefore ordered the different districts to attack the enemy each from the position it held, and I placed Koliopoulos and the Arcadians in the centre to make for the Turks holding the guns. The Arcadians, as I was going round in the evening, attacked on different sides, rose and destroyed their breastworks, knocking them down with their feet, and left them because the other Greeks did not move; they remained shut up in the old fort. The next day, becoming very anxious about the besieged, I had recourse to a stratagem; I decided that we should all go right round to the other side, and while discharging a couple of musket shots make lights so that they who were in the fort might find means to sally out. In this way we approached the fort, and the whole of them were able to come on without loss to the Mill of Argos; * the only provisions left in the fort being a skinful of cheese.

The Turks went to the fortress at daybreak and found nothing. It was told to them that we had all moved away and whither, so a force of about ten thousand cavalry rode off to the Argive Mills to see the truth of the matter. When the cavalry were seen approaching I formed my own men into two columns at the base of the hill, and also sent out twenty horsemen to skirmish on the plains, as the Turks had come to reconnoitre, not to fight. They then turned into the vineyards where the grapes were showing and gathered them. I instructed the soldiers at the Argive Mills to occupy that place, and to light about twenty fires, and I threw the Tripolitsan force on the heights opposite, and gave them orders to do the same. Koliopoulos, with his army, was to be at Skenochori, near the roads leading to Tripolitsa.

The Turks seeing so many fires all round decided that they could not pass through Tripolitsa. They were lacking supplies, because Tsokrês had burnt the plains of Argos beforehand. They therefore resolved to turn back to Kortho, and, crossing through Vostitsa to go to Gastouni, in order to obtain provisions, as they had none. I summoned all the captains to a meeting at the Argive Mills, and said, " The Turks will turn back towards Kortho; they see that from this place they are not able to cross; you remain here, and I will go and occupy Dervenaki, which the Turks

* See Note D.

will endeavour to pass over." I left Giatrakos with the main body which was at the mills. They did not desire this arrangement; they asked that I should stay there. I told them they must go. I marched on with all haste to Dervenaki, being quite certain myself that the enemy would pass thence and not by Tripolitsa.

"Kolokotronês has gone to the hills to become a Klepht again," said Petro Bey. I moved on and reached Agio-Georgio.

On the 26th of July, the festival of St Paraskevy, a sentinel of Anton spoke with three hundred men, who told him that the Turks were advancing in two columns. I immediately made my arrangements at Agio-Georgio and commanded the Tsaousadoi to collect all the supplies and to place them in four different houses, with this direction, that if I saw the two columns approaching I would give a signal, upon which they were to set fire to them all, so that they should not fall into the hands of the Turks, and with the other part of my force I then occupied Dervenaki. I had sent Niketas, Pappa Phlessas, and Ypsilanti with five hundred men to occupy Kinari, a strong village on the road to Corinth. The advance guard of the Turks came up to Anton, and when they saw the Greeks in front of them, the Turks ordered them to leave the road free. They wanted to pass behind into Roumêli, our own place. I sent a foot-runner to Skenochori, where Koliopoulos was, to tell him to come and bring us all the aid he could. The distance between Dervenaki and Kinari was six hours' journey, and it was two hours from Agio-Georgio where Niketas was stationed, whilst Pappa Nika with the Corinthian soldiers was in another village. I sent to them all to come with reinforcements.

When I got to Dervenaki I picked out eight hundred men, made them into four columns, and sent them to the post which was being held on the rock, whilst Anton, who held the chief command, was in front. The Turks meanwhile had left the fort, and the foremost ranks waited until the whole had assembled. As soon as the Turks began to move I threw down all our flags and capotes upon a height, and brought hither all our animals, piling them up so that they might think that there was a large body of soldiers ready to come down, and for that reason would not attempt to mount to the positions to rout us. I stayed on the top with ten men, my adopted sons with the mules in line. A foot messenger belonging to Niketas told me that the Turks were on the move, but that they were not going to pass by Dervenaki. The Corinthians dispersed. Koliopoulos was six hours' journey off in a straight line : it would be night before a man on foot could reach him. About three o'clock the whole of the Turks were gathered together, the Pashas being in the hindmost flanks.

The six thousand men who were at the mills had no sentinels to look out and see if Argos was evacuated, so that they might advance nearer. I had ordered that the four columns should not begin the battle until they heard ten shots, and that then they were to stand.

When the entire forces of the Turks were met together, a Pasha ordered the advance guard 'to move forward, and therefore the Turks galloped to take the position and moved on with the baggage. Anton was entrenched. As soon as the Turks advanced within a hundred paces, Anton attacked them, and held about ten Turks engaged. The force turned their flanks and made for Agio-Sosti. Streams of water at that place, however, prevented their passage, so that the whole Turkish host ascended the rocks. Antonaki did not throw himself upon them in close quarters, but taking a banner with thirty men he reached Agio-Sosti before them. The Turks now formed into three columns—

one behind, then the Pashas, another in the middle, and
the third was opposed to Antonaki—there were ten thousand men opposed to Antonaki—but he and his thirty killed
very many, only two of them being slain, and those two
were my nephews.

The whole of the Turks who remained passed at Kourtesa
and there made a stand. Niketas, Ypsilanti, and Phlessas,
hearing of the conflict, arrived at Agio-Sosti and took
possession of the most powerful post there. The middle
body where the Greeks had been slaying also made for
that place, and fell upon Niketas, when a thousand men
were killed. This column succeeded in crossing into
Kourtesa and united with the others; but the Pashas who
were left behind were not able to pass over, and night was
coming on. They then opened a colloquy with the Greeks.

"What captain have you forward?"

A pappas from Chrysovitsi answered, "Kolokotronês."

"Ask him," answered the Pashas, "to allow us the
means whereby we may pass, and we will give him whatever he may choose to ask."

Pappas Demetrius sent a person to speak with me, and
as soon as I received this information I prepared to
go on at once, for I was planning in my mind how I should
be able to delay them, so that in the morning we might
destroy them. We had some horsemen with us; there
were Photakos and Speliopoulos, Kotsos Boulgaros, and
one other nephew of mine. These galloped forward, and
the Pashas, seeing these horsemen of ours, thought we had
a large body of cavalry, so they turned back towards Tiryns
and left all they had, for night was at hand, and we could
just see the dust that rose as they went.

When day dawned Koliopoulos with two thousand and
Deligianni with his Phanarites came up. Our own
men had fallen upon the spoils and gone to the hills.

The Turks, who were at Kourtesa, tried to learn what had happened to the Pashas, and sent out a thousand men, who were to go to Agio-Sosti and find out what had become of them. Our own men were lying in wait for them, and after firing some volleys drove them back again. The Pashas who had gone on stopped when they reached Tiryns, and Niketas marched on to Agionori with Pappa Phlessas, and was the first to arrive at Agio-Sosti. Dervenaki is at the side of the tomb of Agamemnon.

When day dawned Koliopoulos and ourselves mustered four thousand at Dervenaki. Giatrakos and Tsokrês soon arrived also at Dervenaki, and I asked them, " Where are the other armies ? "

" They are at Koutsopodi and Charbati," they answered.

" Well, then," I said, " the Pashas who are in Tiryns will soon prepare for a campaign in Corinth ; you therefore must take your soldiers, and go to a village on the road leading from Agionori to Corinth, and there you must station yourselves and make your observations so that the Turks shall not get to Agionori. If they come on to us you must then advance on the rear, and we will await them in front ; you are to come up on the rear if they try to pass near us, so that we may seize upon the Pashas alive ; if they act as I am now describing, give some signal and we will come to your assistance."

These men did as I said, and went to their army, and the army fled away, going off to the Aphentikos Mills (it appears that Giatrakos urged them to go). Giatrakos, when his army departed, certainly did not inform me of it, but I hoped that he would go whither I had directed him, and consequently I remained waiting, and had placed sentinels everywhere to look out for the signal which I expected them to make.

The Turks went forward, and the Pashas and the army marched straight to Agionori. The advance guard of Niketas, however, came upon them, and his advance guard began the battle, when Niketas himself went forward to reinforce them, and they were not able to sustain the combat, but the whole army turned back and took possession of the village. The Turks fought all the way to the extremity of the village. The Turks had no intention of engaging with Niketas; their sole intention in the first instance was to pass through Klenia; but when the Turks began to descend upon that place, Niketas went forth with the inhabitants and even the women to oppose them. At that point Niketas gave me information at Dervenaki of the occurrence, and when I heard of the battle I sent Demetrius Koliopoulos with two thousand men to occupy Klenia. Niketas threw himself upon them in close conflict at Klenia, and about five hundred of them were killed, among whom was a Pasha. They got possession of all their camels and baggage. Koliopoulos did not arrive in time to occupy Klenia. When the forces which were at the mills saw the Turks in flight, they advanced somewhat nearer, but they did not engage in the battle. So much for Giatrakos. The Turks who were left endeavoured to reach Corinth. When I heard that the Turks and the Pashas had resolved to get to Corinth, I was persuaded that they would pass by the Black Rocks, and through Vostitsa and Patras, in order to procure supplies; so I immediately ordered all the soldiers to follow me, and went forward and occupied Vasilika. Our army numbered seven thousand.

In the evening, as darkness was coming on, I warned the soldiers to light ten or fifteen fires, for where we were was directly opposite Corinth, so that all the hills were lighted up, and the Turks in consequence thought that we had many thousands of soldiers. In the morning the Turks made a movement with fifteen thousand to try to cross over, but we attacked them vigorously, and they were unable to pass us ; a few were killed ; and in the evening they returned to Corinth. As they were going thither they were attacked on the roads by the Greeks, and several skirmishes took place. One day two thousand sallied forth again with the object of fighting their way across. The Greeks obstinately opposed their passage, but their cavalry made a rush and broke through the Greek breastworks, destroying them to their very foundations, and thirty of the men were killed, among whom were Anagnostês Petimeza and his son, who was commandant, and also a pappas, a man of some importance, from Mistra. The other breastworks being broken down helped the fugitives. The Turks returned the same day without having done much.

Dramalês chose out four hundred Turks and left them with rations for six months with a commandant at Palamedi, with orders that none of the other Turks were to go either in or out. He made a resolution not to send them any reinforcement. The main body remained for a time inactive with the exception of a few skirmishes. The Corinthians had previously asked me to send them a commandant, which I did, and he put the Corinthians under discipline, and harassed the Turks. An order now came to me from the Senate to go to Tripolitsa, and therefore I left Gennaios and Anton Kolokotronês in the Vasilikan district. (I had also a regiment at Klenia.)

CHAPTER VI.

FROM Corinth I went to Tripolitsa to support the
Senate. The chiefs were envious of my successes
with Dramalês, and the Senate also was envious even
whilst it upheld me. When I routed Dramalês at
Dervenaki the army voted me to be the commander-in-
chief, and the Senate sent me a diploma as generalissimo.
The members and the executive had no power and used no
exertions at that crisis. (Kanákarês even said, "Let us
save the Archives and let the nation perish." What
madness !)

The chiefs tried all they could to have an assembly, with
the view of overturning the Senate (which had done the
greatest service), and its generalissimo, and for this purpose they made every effort to call a meeting. Whilst
I was in Tripolitsa, I learnt that two hundred loads of
supplies had gone from Dervenaki into Nauplia. I was
ill at the time, but I was much annoyed. Within five or
six days afterwards ten thousand men with four hundred
baggage loads came over and occupied Agio-Sosti, and,
sending the supplies on to Nauplia, remained there until
they who took them should return. I had left Niketas,
Panos, Gennaios, and others at Dervenaki. When I
heard that provisions had been sent down twice, I marched

forward to the Aphentikos Mills, and wrote thence the following letter to the Beys and Pashas who were in Nauplia. "If you are willing to evacuate Nauplia, I will embark you all, and you can go whither you will, wherever you can have supplies, but if you are not, and, out of mere despite, stay on with your families and your children, I shall not hereafter treat with you, and you need not expect any more supplies from Corinth, because I am going in person to Dervenaki, and shall not allow any provisions to pass; so if you do not now listen to me, the punishment will fall upon your own heads."

From Mylos I went to Dervenaki. I had a regiment at Klenia, and another at Stephani, which was an hour's journey in a straight line from Agio-Sosti. Hadji Chrestos was at Stephani, Zapheiropoulos at Klenia, the brother of Giatrakos at Agio-Georgio with three hundred Mistriotes, and Niketas with the Kranidiotes was at Agio-Sosti. Alexis Kolios was commander of the Tripolitsans. I had brought with me to Agio-Sosti masons, who built me up a tower and breastworks, so that no supplies should be transported that way. Gennaios and Panos with the Karytainan army were above Dervenaki, and I was in their rear.

When the Turks went over to Nauplia, taking supplies thither, and afterwards returning, the Naupliotes accompanied them back, and went with them to Corinth, with the expectation of their being despatched back again with further supplies. The resident Turks knew the locality, and ten thousand made a move to pass through Agio-Sosti. They sent five hundred in advance to fall upon Niketas, and the baggage and supplies remained behind on the height above Agio-Sosti. The engagement began: they who were on the flanks fell upon them in the rear, our soldiers were broken, and

Pappas Arsenios killed. Niketas was surrounded in the tower. Chrestos now came up with assistance and pressed upon the flanks. The Turks were broken, and Niketas came out of the tower (the tower saved him), and in conjunction with our own men the enemy was vigorously assailed, and followed up for the space of two hours; about forty of them were slain, and they were effectually hindered from taking on the supplies. After this the Turks made no further attempts to carry provisions into Nauplia, because we held every post. Moreover, Giamsakês and Apostolês Kolokotronês in the space of one month had made raids and collected more than three thousand horses. The Turks at Nauplia were now getting much distressed. Autumn had arrived. On the 26th of November Dramalês died. All the other Pashas who were left were weak and exhausted. Death and slaughter encircled them on every side, and they were now very few. Twenty-seven died in the month of December from hunger alone.

I had left my nephew Nikolas to be commander at the siege of the fort of Nauplia. One day the Turks made a sally; there was some fighting, and Nikolas was killed, when Staïkos became leader. Before long the Turkish squadron came as far as Astro, but our vessels frightened it with their fireships and it was driven out by the Spetsiotes. On the 26th of December the Turks had a communication with Staïkos, when they asked him to send for Kolokotronês to enter into a treaty with them, and Staïkos sent it on to me by his brother. I wrote to them thus: "You ask for a treaty: it is my will that you deliver up all the forts; that you leave your property behind you; I will then embark you on Greek vessels, and will send you whither you desire to go: for this you must give hostages. When I wrote to you from Mylos I told you that you could go and take your things with you ; but now, a-hungered and wearied out though you be, you must go as you are. Such is my will, and if you do not listen now, in ten days the whole of the Turks at Corinth will have gone, and the armies will return and will come hither and will take you by assault, when you will all be put to the sword."

As the Turks were so weakened at Nauplia, I left very few men there with Staïkos, and guarded and strengthened Dervenaki so that no help could get to them from Corinth. I gave the above letter to Staïkos, and he summoned the Turks, and delivered the writing to them on the evening of the 27th. As soon as they had received the letter they summoned a meeting in the village, and called for Teztaraga and other of their principal men who were to take the answer to Palamedi. They left nine men at the redoubts in Beziera, and about ten others with two or three Albanians at the Giour redoubts. I had left so few men at Palamedi, that those at Nauplia had no fear of the Greeks, because they were so small a number. Two Albanians dropping down from the redoubts went to Staïkos, and told him that the Turks had gone down to the village, and that they could go and take the fort, adding, " If we do not tell you the truth, keep one of us here, and if it be false, kill us." Staïkos upon this took some soldiers, and sprang over. The Turks who were in the other redoubts went down into the village also.

This happened at midnight. Daybreak was the festival of St. Andrew. Cannon was fired off, and I knew directly that Palamedi was taken. I galloped there immediately, and as I was on the road I met a foot-runner who was sent by Staïkos to give me the information. I had left Panos, Gennaios, and others with the regiment. I sent the messenger on to the army to carry the news to the others. As soon as I got to Palamedi I found that Staïkos had purged it from the Turks. I went into Palamedi, and found that our men had planted fifty cannon there. As soon as I saw that I ordered them to be turned round and directed to the village and Its Kalé. I then sent to the village and invited the Turkish chiefs to a parley. The Beys came to Palamedi, and with them was Albanitês, a leader of Albanians. I said to them, " What will you do now ? Deliver up to me all your forts and arms, and I will save your lives and those of your children. You must take with you only two changes of raiment, and I will embark you in Greek vessels to go whither you will. When you give up the keys to me I shall put my own men in possession, and give you a body of soldiers who will conduct you in safety, and put you on board at the Five Brothers (Penta Adelphia).*

The Albanian answered to this, "We will not give up our arms. We will fight, we will burn up the country, and we will not leave one stone upon another." I said to him, "You wretched Albanitês, to whom do you speak thus ? Let us once fight on horseback, and you will see. As to burning up the country which our forefathers made, we shall rear it again, but as for you, we will put you all to the sword."

The Beys called out, "Do not listen to him, because he is a single man; treat only with us who have families; we will come down to you, we will make a contract with you, we will put our signatures to it, and we will send it to you with the keys; you on your part must do the same, and give us your oath upon it."

They then went down and made an agreement, and sent me the bond that they had signed, and also the keys at the same time. Ali and another Pasha did not sign it because they dreaded the wrath of the Sultan, and I

* A name given frequently to plantations of firs.

therefore accepted them with forty-five other lives as prisoners of war.

Three or four days after the feast of St. Andrew I despatched some soldiers to occupy Its Kalé, the Five Brothers, and the redoubts both on the seashore and on the land, and to gather together the Turkish properties and put them in the mosques. I also wrote to Hydra and Spetsai to send boats, which they did. I had shut up the fort in order to prevent any excesses. I sent also to all our own forts and to the forces wherever they were stationed, and embarked the Turks for Smyrna.

The Senate had likewise been summoned there to be present at the fall of Nauplia, and the division of the spoils. I realized, at a bazaar which was held in the ships, a hundred and ten thousand grosia. Whatever articles that remained were put back into the mosques, and the Greek soldiers seized upon the rest. There was only a moderate amount of money found at Nauplia, because the besieged had spent so much in procuring provisions. There were a good many silver vessels and also clothing, and these I gave as freight money for the ships. After three days had passed I went down to the houses of Aga Pasha in Palamedi. The spoils were all disposed of for the public benefit, and every district and each island had its allotted portion. By this means I preserved Nauplia from the consequences of any inadvertence.

During this time the Turks who were left at Corinth, and who numbered something like three thousand men, had heard of the fall of Nauplia, and leaving four hundred men in the fortress they prepared to go to Patras. The Kalavrytians were quarrelling among themselves. Zaimês, Charalampês, and the Petimezaioi made ready to attack, but when they heard of the Turks they forgot all their dissensions, and falling upon them, routed them, and laid siege to them at Akrata. When Panos and Gennaios whom I had left with the army at Dervenaki learnt that the Turks had fled from Corinth they also came to Nauplia, but as soon as I found that the others were being besieged at Akrata, I equipped Niketas, Panos, and Gennaios in order to despatch them to their aid. The chiefs, however, sent me word to send them war material only, and not to forward an army (they were thinking about the probable division of the spoils). They had been laying siege to Akrata for two months. The Turks were much distressed, and made several agreements without fulfilling any. The Turkish vessels brought them reinforcements and took them all off in safety to Patras. Out of the thirty-two thousand men and the seven Pashas which Dramalês brought over, there were only saved the four thousand who were in Athens and Euboia, and these two thousand at Akrata who were taken away to Patras. I asked Ali and some other of the chief Turks (prisoners of war) about it, and they said that the number of those who entered the Peloponnesus was twenty-eight thousand, with twenty thousand saddle horses, thirty thousand baggage mules, and five hundred camels. All these were left in the Poloponnesus, and thus the Greeks became possessed of many very costly weapons and other treasures. That army was very rich, because it had seized upon the valuables of Ali Pasha when they were besieging him.

I had often represented to the Russians and the French (as well as to the English) that I had contemplated the revolt of the Peloponnesus, not because I limited the movement to that place alone, but because at that time, as there was no general information, the enterprise could not at once become national, because the people were not prepared. I saw a little about what means were available, and my plan was, first, to make the Peloponnesus free, and when that was done we should have a basis for operations, which we could carry on outside the Peloponnesus: for the Peloponnesus was like an island, and it was easy to defend it.

Between the epochs of 1805 and 1821 there was a very great difference. When I first took refuge in Zante in 1806, the Turkish Power offered fifty thousand grosia to Russia if it would seize upon me and deliver me up. The Russian consul sent me word about this, and told me to hide myself; and in consequence I kept myself concealed for a month, whilst he told the Turks that Kolokotronês had fled, for he could not be found in Zante, and therefore he must have gone away. At one time Ali Pasha* sought me, and made me a thousand grand promises to induce me to go to Juannina; but I never paid any attention to them.

* See Note E.

CHAPTER VII

A S the districts were preparing to send representatives to the second assembly which was about to be held, I wrote to them to say that I considered it would be better to hold it in Nauplia. The chiefs, as a body, did not wish to go there: first, because it was a fortress; and secondly, because I held it. I left Koliopoulos commandant there, and went to Tripolitsa to join the Senate and Mavromichaelês, and we made an agreement that the Senate and the office of generalissimo should be retained in the forthcoming assembly. We took oaths that we would retain the existing order of things. It was at last settled that it should take place at Astros, and part of the repre-sentatives met there. They wrote thence to Mavromichaelês, telling him that they would appoint him president as soon as he arrived. Then Mavromichaelês forgot the oaths that we had taken, and so did Pappa Phlessas and others. I went also to Astros, and then I saw clearly that we were divided into two parties, one of which might be called the Primates' party, and the other the party of Kolokotronês. The most of them were for the Primates. There were a hundred and fifty representatives and six thousand soldiers, Odysseus, Mourtzinos with eight hundred men, and forty other representatives were with me.

They brought soldiers to support their opinions by force,

and I also made use of force to overturn their opinions. We established ourselves in a tent at Melegitika, and the other party was at Agiannetika—a gun-shot off. They had a sitting, but we did not attend it. They desired and they voted that fifty generals should be made, and also a hundred and fifty more deputies. This excess of a governing power did not please me at all, because this excess was with a view of destroying our power, which it would have done, for they thought that by voting for fifty generals my influence must certainly be demolished. They also voted for alienating the land, with the purpose of reimbursing themselves for whatever they laid out just as they willed, and by such a course the land would suffer loss, and the people, whose only hope was in the earth, would be left destitute. Tho people then became of my opinion in this matter, for they saw how evil a blow this alienation would cause, and they obliged them to expunge that article. They then began to cajole my friends and supporters, and won them over to their side one by one.

They called upon me to go to them, and I went to a garden wherein their assembly was held and thus addressed them:—"Reverend assembly, the votes which you have made are not good, for it is not well to have so many generals and members, because they will bring upon us many expenses and many cares, for the nation is poor and is not able to pay for so many unnecessary politicians and soldiers." Zaimês at once rose up and called out, "Kolokotronês, Kolokotronês, it is in thy hands whether Greece shall be ruined, or be made free if thou wilt unite with us." I then asked him three times, "Does it rest with me?" "Yes," he replied, "with thee." I then went and gave my signature, saying, "Look to it, and see if evil does not ensue to our country from this plurality of chiefs."

Upon returning to Tripolitsa all kinds of intrigues recommenced. It was evident that they intended to give every post, whether political or military, to their own party and relations. We had called an assembly for the benefit of all Greece, and they had employed it in the interest of family connections and partisanship. I gave my opinion upon it, saying, " What is this which the ministers propose that you should do ? Your assembly swore that you would regard the whole nation—that was the proposed condition, and that you would put those people into office who would serve the country and be useful in times of misfortune, but I see that you have elected representatives out of a party, and thus the politicians and the military will be disunited."

They answered, " If that occur we can rectify it."

Both in word and deed it was their full intention to appoint their own people in order to weaken me. Seeing that things were getting worse, I proposed to have a meeting of my own adherents.

A vote had passed in the assembly that no strangers should be elected, except Mavrokordatos, as minister for foreign affairs. Everything had been conducted at first in a friendly spirit, but those things to which we had put our signatures were forgotten. So when I got our meeting I said, " What is this which has now come about, patriots ? We signed that certain acts should be done, and we see that others have been substituted. We said that both for political and military offices the most worthy should be chosen, and they were all unanimous to nominate such, and now they are doing the very opposite."

At noon the same day I went to the village Silimna, an hour from Tripolitsa, and Ypsilanti was there also. Many members came to join us. We there proposed and passed a resolution not to attend to any of their orders, but that as many among us as were soldiers should act against the Turks, whilst those who were politicians should provide us with supplies, and in that way we would save our country; and as for them, let them sit. I saw that their intrigues aimed at getting rid of and weakening me.

Then they began a system of cajolery, and made Anagnostês Deligianni the mediator. He was one who took the middle course till he saw who would be likely to conquer, and he sent the professor Theodoros and Gianni Rakos to ask me to return, in order that the Government might not be ruined : "Come, and be the vice-president thyself." As Anagnostês Deligianni urged me to do so in order to avert a civil war, I did return, just to see what would come out of such a Government. I went to the executive department. On the first day of my appearance there I greeted Mavromichaelês and the others, when Petro Bey said, "So, then, art thou going to dance, Kolokotronês?" "As thou art singing," I replied, "I am dancing; cease singing, and my dance ceases."

*   *   *   *   *   *

Civil war began ; * they laid siege to Nauplia by sea and land, they sent soldiers to Tripolitsa, they besieged us ; we were besieged for a whole month. Londos, Giatrakos, Notaras, and others conducted the siege. When they laid siege to us they proposed that we should give up the executives, Petro Bey, Soter Charalampês, and Metaxa.. We answered that it was not possible to do that, but if they liked we would take one or two of the executive and try them, and whichever was found culpable among them he should be punished. This they would not agree to, and

---

* Panos Kolokotronês was holding Nauplia at this time for his father, who had put himself in opposition to the Government, and was at Tripolitsa.

several skirmishes followed. Koliopoulos went to act as mediator, and Petro Bey promised to remain neutral and go to Mani, acquainting us that we could easily leave Tripolitsa, as there were no soldiers on the road either from one side or the other. So I went from Tripolitsa to Karytaina, and Soter Charalampês went to Kalavryta. Nauplia was still besieged, and Niketas was in Bougiati; he had some conference with Kountouriotês, when the latter proposed that he, on his own part, should return; but he replied, "You must communicate with my uncle, and if he unites with the Government again, then I shall unite." I wrote therefore that I would go, and that we would talk the matter over together, and Kountouriotês wrote to me to go to Tsiveri with only fifty men of my own, and then I was to proceed on my journey with his men; but I had my suspicions, and did not go.

Whilst at Karytaina I got many soldiers to join me, and I made some descents on different parts and took three hundred prisoners, but no blood was shed. I then marched over to Tripolitsa and laid siege to them. Gennaios, Koliopoulos, and Niketas went to the help of Panos at Nauplia, and returned to us afterwards. Then Andreas Zaimês came to confer with me, and we met outside Tripolitsa. He asked me to write to Panos and order him to deliver up the fort. "No," I answered, "I will not consent that he shall give up the fort into the hands of adventurers like thyself; if thou wert fit to hold it I would give it up to thee, but I have three hundred grosia owing to me for my disbursements in pay." "We are fit to hold it," he answered, "and we will discharge all the outlay which you have been subject to." I wrote to Panos upon this, and told him to deliver up the fortress to the Andreidês and not to the Government. I had told it previously to put their own people in the fort of Palamedi, and not those wrong-headed people; but they placed Photomara there, and afterwards Grivas; hence arose all the after evils.

Panos came to Karytaina. In regard to Panos there was an amnesty given, and therefore he received an order to go and besiege Patras, in consequence of which he joined Zaimês and Londos, and they, being very much displeased with Kountouriotês, united with us. Pappa Phlessas was sent to subjugate the districts of Arcadia, Phanari, and the rest. The loans that had been advanced by Kountouriotês strengthened the Government, and power made everything legitimate. I wrote for Panos and Gennaios to come to Karytaina and oppose Pappa Phlessas. The districts drove him out, and he retired to Nauplia. A force of eight hundred under Vasos was then sent, and the soldiers came up with Panos, and he was killed.

Zaimês had arrived, and we were going to Tripolitsa. The Tripolitsans were alarmed on account of Panos having been killed, and resisted. Kanelos Deligianni had frightened them. The Government being strengthened by Kountouriotês sent into Roumêli for Gkoura to come, and he, with the other captains of Roumêli, went to Corinth and routed Notaras; thence they went to Kerpeni, a village of Kalavryta, and surrounded Zaimês, whilst Karaiskakês and Tsavellas also going against Zaimês, he was defeated, and with Niketas and Londos fled into Western Greece. Karaiskakês and Tsavellas wrote to me to stay and have a conference with them, and they took it upon their own heads if I should suffer any harm. I was no longer in Karytaina, however, for Koliopoulos had come to me, being sent by the Government, and he had told me that we must go to Nauplia in order to arrange matters there.

We went to Tripolitsa; there was a committee there composed of Skourtês, Mavrommatês, and Zapheiropoulos, and they gave me to understand upon their oaths that I could go there safely, so that they might transact the necessary business. I trusted them implicitly, and went to Nauplia. There I saw that in two or three days they had driven away all my men, and had left me alone—under arrest, in fact, until they got hold of the others. They embarked us in the sloop *Gorgo*, Skourtês was also there, and took us to Hydra. We stopped there two days, and then they sent us to the monastery of the prophet, St. Elias.* We remained there four months. Twenty days after we were seized, Ibrahim came into the Peloponnesus. A society was formed directly by the people in Hydra demanding our release. Kountouriotês made himself ready to go to Patras, but when he heard that Ibrahim had got as far as Mothokorona, he gave orders that the armies should return to Neo-Kastro. Kountouriotês then went to Tripolitsa, and sent Skourtês forward as generalissimo of all the forces. He had with him half a million of grosia. The Roumeliote armies also marched forward, and went to Neo-Kastro. P. Giatrakos and G. Mavromichaelês were commandants at that fort. Ibrahim laid siege to Neo-Kastro; afterwards he disembarked at Navarino, where a thousand Peloponnesians were shut up, and being much distressed for want of provisions, they surrendered, and Ibrahim let them go free. Among them were Tsokrês and Tzametos. Ibrahim bore himself most amiably just at this time, in order to get the Greeks to submit. The people began to cry aloud, " We won't fight unless you give us back our chiefs." The Roumeliote and Souliote armies, and especially Karaiskakês and Tsavellas, appealed to the Government for our freedom, and all the soldiers framed a petition, asking for our release, and presented it to Anagnostaras, who was the minister of war; but he tore it up before

* See Note F.

them, saying, "Do not interfere in these matters, leave his business to the Government."

There was a battle at Kremydi, and our people were victorious. Karatassos fought a good battle. Then all the Roumeliote leaders gathered together, preparatory to going over to help Roumêli, and especially Missolonghi, the siege of which had now commenced. They then went to Kountouriotês and took their pay, and some departed for Eastern Greece, and others went to the Western districts. Ibrahim made a descent upon Sphakteria, and Anagnostaras as well as Tsamados were killed; many prisoners were taken at Sphakteria, and P. Zapheiropoulos was taken as a slave to Kremydi, and K. Zapheiropoulos, and Chrestos were also captured. Neo-Kastro was so sore distressed that it capitulated and was given up. The enemy permitted them to go out as soldiers, only without their arms; the officers were allowed to retain their arms, and two only were detained as prisoners, namely, Georgakês Mavromichaelês and Panagiotês Giatrakos.

Kountouriotês, hearing that Neo-Kastro had capitulated, embarked at Almyro for Hydra. The time was now come for our release. When they saw the dangerous position of the country, and the perseverance of the people who clamoured for our being set free, they set us free. We went to Nauplia, and upon our arrival there, the members, the executive, and ourselves all went to church, and took our oaths that we would let all the past go, and forget it, and uniting together, would have no other idea in the future but how we could best serve our country. Then they made me the national general. The deputies and the executive assembled, and I went also.

CHAPTER VIII.

A S soon as the deputies and executive were assembled,
they summoned me, when I thus addressed them :
" Revered Administration, will it please you to listen to
the advice which I proffer to you ? Let no Turk be found
anywhere in Patras, Korona, or Mothokorona—let the
whole be Greek ; but the fort of Tripolitsa we must
destroy, because it is not well in the middle of the Peloponnesus to have such a cradle where civil wars can be nursed,
especially now, when Ibrahim is in the Poloponnesus with
fifty thousand men, and holds the three forts of Messenia,
and is also keeping Patras, besides which he has won
many victories over the Greeks, and has killed Phlessas,
with his five hundred men; and had Phlessas had a thousand
men, he would have been killed ; he has also burnt Kalamata, and the armies have fled before him, he having conquered in so many engagements. He will surely now come
to Tripolitsa, and if he come to Tripolitsa, and seizes the
fort, then the whole of the Peloponnesus is lost, because
the fort is in its very centre."

" There are no funds," they answered.

" Give me permission," I replied, " and with the help of
the people I will pull it down in five days, and then Ibrahim will not find a place wherein he can make his nest, and
I can attack him from all sides. If he takes Tripolitsa he

will not need any other nest from which he can go forth and ravage the Peloponnesus, but if we destroy Tripolitsa, he will find no other nest, and I, with my armies, will drive him out of the Peloponnesus. The other armies will then join us, otherwise they will not join us, for they are afraid on every side." (And so it was.)

They suspected that I had some hatred to gratify by destroying the walls of Tripolitsa, and answered, "We will see." I went to Argos, and made an address similar to that which I had made at Tripolitsa, but I was not listened to. Then I massed eight thousand soldiers: the soldiers came at my bidding. The Argives came to Nauplia, and the Tripolitsans to Argos. I said to them, "Hasten, brothers, lest these Arabs make slaves of us; we shall have no help except from our own arms." Both men and women then joined in thanksgiving to the Most High. I then sent an order to all the districts, and thus, in three days, I assembled eight thousand men.

I was in Tripolitsa when the news came about Phlessas. The enemy had burnt Kalamata; he was powerful, and ruled all Messenia. I occupied Dervenia, and passed over to Leontari, and built furnaces in order to cook food at Dervenia; I also built a breastwork strong enough for them to fight Ibrahim from. He also had his spies, and he saw that he could not pass over Dervenia without much loss. There was a Leontarian Turk, a captive at Bolianen, who was a fugitive to Ibrahim, and he told him: "I know a way by which we can take the ranks through, and ascend to the plain above." I did not think that he would cross by that narrow pass, which I hoped could never be, yet it stirred me to find that the Messenians were moving to the hills, and I hastened on myself to secure that very place by which he had already passed.

Some captive Turks, who were natives of the place, had

fled to Ibrahim, and acted as guides. I had sent my nephews to take possession of it, and I moved on to Sampazika with eighty men, in order to raise the villages and secure the positions. Day dawned when I arrived at the village of Akova, and more men came from other villages so that we might occupy this post. They (the enemy) did not arrive until three o'clock that day, and by the help of his Turkish guides, he (Ibrahim) took possession of the hill before we came up there with our army. Every one who was in the village, when they saw that the hill was occupied, scattered and fled; and I, who was on a cliff, saw them flee before me.

The Turks went to Boliani, a village with two hundred and fifty inhabitants. The infantry set fire to the village, and the cavalry hunted up the children to make slaves of them; the army was coming up on the rear. I fired off a volley: the Turks feared something, and the people there were saved. This was at noon.

That hill whereon I remained was a strong post, so I sent word to Dervenia for the army to return and come to me, because the Turks had gone to Boliani, bidding them hasten so that the plain should not be taken. The army was six hours off, and night was coming on, so I stayed there like a watchman, to observe what the Turks would do. On receiving my message, G. Giatrakos brought up eight hundred men, and the others drew nearer, led by Gennaios, Koliopoulos, Deligianni, with the Arcadians and Tripolitsans. (Kolios had been killed.) I went back an hour's journey along the road by which my own people came up. It was about sunrise when Giatrakos reached me, and I made him occupy a village called Dyrrachi, for I suspected that the Turks would not pass through Mistra. He left, and went thither; I remained at the same post. Anton Kolokotronês, who well knew the locality, passed along a footpath and got before the Turks. Our armies came up in detachments. About a thousand arriving, I sent a body of five hundred of them to seize upon a height; among them were Kanelos, Gennaios, and Papatsonês. Koliopoulos came nearer with his Arcadians and the other forces. The Turks came down upon us early in the morning, but not by Dyrrachi; they met, but our own people did not resist them, and made their retreat to me.

Upon their coming to me, I made my resolutions accordingly, and despatched three thousand to the heights, that we might sustain the enemy there. The Turks came down straight upon Gennaios, and stood. He gave them no opportunity to advance, because they had left the main body in the rear. The battle began with Gennaios, Kanelos, and the others. Our own three thousand men built up breastworks, and the cannon was placed there ; but we could do nothing against them. I went half an hour's space forward in order to be opposite to the engagement, and I ordered Koliopoulos to take assistance to the base of that hill, the top of which was held by Gennaios ; and Koliopoulos went thither and fought with the Turks, but Gennaios descended and said, " Uncle, leave this place, and go to my father, so that you may strengthen his position." So Koliopoulos came to me, and the Arcadians also, and therefore we were a good force. Gennaios with his body was fighting throughout the whole day. Giatrakos, who was stationed in the village, when he heard the battle going on sent a reinforcement to one part ; but the Turks were many, and they fell upon him and routed him. There was no possibility of our giving him any aid, because rocks separated us. Giatrakos was wounded, and his force scattered. We expected help from the villages, but none came. Gennaios, with the others on the heights above fought all through the night ; but the Turks did not take the posts in front.

The next day I sent the Arcadians to occupy a footpath, because I saw that the Turks had seized all the heights. The Turks, seeing that I had sent to take possession of that narrow defile, moved thither. The Arcadians did not oppose them when fighting commenced, but came to me. The Turks took the plains. The Turkish cavalry then moved on to Leontari, burning the villages as they went along. About ten thousand were extended along the flanks of Gennaios, on the plain. When I saw that our forces were outflanked, I sent down Koliopoulos to a quarter a little distant from the Turks, to frighten them. The battle never ceased for two days and three nights. I saw that I was not able to give them assistance—there was a brook near, but I could not give any care about their going to get water, because they were in flight—I had neither ammunition, food, nor water—so I made a signal by lighting fires, that they should retreat. In that battle five of our own people were killed, and of Turks a good number. Our men fled to Tourkoleka, and thence marched to Dervenia. We went on to Karytaina, which was a strong position. The Turks marched towards Tripolitsa, and entered it. When we were in retreat, I sent Tsokrês in the evening to burn Tripolitsa, but he did not succeed in doing so. He had begun to burn the city when Ibrahim arrived. Tripolitsa and all therein were taken.

For ten days the armies of Ibrahim never ceased burning the country. During those ten days I got together Koliopoulos, Kanelos Deligianni, and Papatsonês. Kolios was killed on the night of the retreat, but not by the enemy; we made altogether four thousand five hundred men. We approached nearer in order to occupy certain positions, to prevent him (Ibrahim) from marching to Karytaina and laying waste the villages. Zaimês and Archontopoulos were at Torniki with two thousand men. The Mistriotes and

Agiopetritai were with Zapheiropoulos. Ibrahim did move forward, but he went to Argos. He left an army in Tripolitsa and went to Glykeia (a garden belonging to Miaoulês).

As soon as we learnt that Ibrahim had gone to Argos, I devised a stratagem, by which we, by going outside Tripolitsa, might fight with them, and spring over into it. I sent Koliopoulos with a thousand men to seize upon the water source secretly; but his army was not to appear. Gennaios with two thousand was to go to Perithori, and Kanelos Deligianni, Papatsonês, and the rest moved to the centre above the gate of St. Athanasius, where they were to be concealed, whilst I stationed myself in the centre. Kanelos, who was among them, was to have fifty men with him. My idea was that the Turks, seeing so few, would come out, and in that case Koliopoulos and Gennaios, who were concealed, could enter Tripolitsa by means of the Leontarian gate. But my device was of no avail, for the Turks within were few and never left the fort. There was some firing for about an hour, when the Greeks, seeing that the Turks would not come out, showed themselves. The Turks got possession of some redoubts.

At the same time I received a letter from the Government which was at Nauplia. The Government sent me word that Ibrahim had gone to Akro-Corinth, and that I was to take my armies thither. We had neither ammunition nor provisions. We had been feeding upon old rams and green corn, because the villages were deserted in consequence of their fears. The Turks of Tripolitsa wrote to Ibrahim to return. As soon as I received this letter from the Government, I directed Demetrius Koliopoulos to go to the Aphentikos Mills and obtain ammunition and provisions for us. I left Kanelos and Papatsonês with fifteen hundred men, just to terrify the Turks, and with another three hundred I went forward to obey the orders of the Government. On that day there happened to have been a great rising of the water springs, and there was quite a flood. The men got food from many villages, and drank wine, which got into their heads and intoxicated them, so that they delayed going on to Partheni. I sent Konstantinos Zapheiropoulos to number the forces of Ibrahim from a nearer point, and I also went myself. I marched forward, and about noon we arrived at Achladokabo. I went down to the Khan at Achladokabo to reckon up all our forces, and then moved on. I wrote to the Government to send me forthwith powder and bread to the Aphentikos Mills, so that I might go to Akro-Corinth.

Ibrahim went to Argos and slept at Vrysaria : the place had been dug out and ploughed. When we sent forward swift messengers, they came up with the advance guard of Ibrahim, and fled back to us, saying that the Turks were come.

I organized the army to form into four columns, and sent out Basil the trumpeter to make a reconnoissance. If the Turks were few in number, he was to blow his trumpet ; if all the force was present, he was to fire off a gun. He went, and he fired off his gun. Koliopoulos then went to Gyra, and G. Alonistiotês to the place of embarkation at Begi ; Gennaios was to occupy the pass of Partheni, and I was to be on the heights. We saw all the force of Ibrahim, numbering three thousand men, opposite to us, and he placed himself on the plain of Achladokabo. He formed his men into four columns, and directed the greater part of the cavalry to move towards Gyra.

The Greeks who were with me were broken because they had no breastworks. I quite expected that we should be routed. If we had received the news at night we could have made breastworks, and if Zaimês had come we should have had some good fighting. I was very anxious—the army was starving, and without powder ; so, to save the army,

I ordered a retreat. Koliopoulos marched to the monastery of St. Nicholas, which was a strong place. I blew my own trumpet so that Gennaios might move away; but he did not wish to retreat. Ibrahim, seeing that he remained, threw column upon column on the wild position which he held. I again ordered a retreat.

Going towards Partheni, accompanied by twenty cavalry, I went into a village at Pertsova to find some water to drink. Gennaios occupied the heights opposite this village, on the top of the hill, and had fifteen hundred men with him. I went there to drink water, but found none : there was a place excavated for a fountain, and I went thither to drink. The Turks were stationed in the vineyards of Pertsova until they all could assemble, and the Turkish cavalry who were scattered over the plain came down upon us at the fountain. We fired off our guns and fled. We continued to be fired upon for some distance, and then I went and waited opposite the place where Gennaios was posted. The other Turks did not take the field, but remained in the vineyards; they saw Gennaios, but did not attempt to ascend to him. In the twilight I summoned Gennaios with my trumpet to come down to us, and in the evening we met again. When they had rejoined us I said to them, "Kanelos and Papatsonês are encouraging themselves with the idea that the Turks are few in number; let us go forward and make them leave their positions so that they be not surrounded by the Turks." We reached them, and they arose, and we all went to Alonistaina together.

Ibrahim took up his quarters at Tripolitsa. I wrote to the different districts, and we assembled seven thousand men at Dervenia. Archontopoulos, Zaimês, and Londos had two thousand at Levidi, and I had five thousand with Koliopoulos, Papatsonês, and the Karytainan armies. We learnt from a Turk that his son-in-law had gone with a reinforcement of soldiers to Mothon, which was to move forward to give additional aid to Ibrahim. I then sent orders that Dervenia should be occupied, so that the reinforcement should not pass that way, and with this object, I seized on Vervena, and they were to come to our aid from Dervenia, whilst Zaimês was to go to Pano-Chrepa. I also sent Koliopoulos with two thousand men to seize on Valtetsi, and despatched Gennaios to occupy Trikorpha.

In the evening Zaimês came to Pano-Chrepa and lighted fires. The Turks saw the fires from Tripolitsa, and suspected that the Greeks were going to seize upon Trikorpha; so in the morning Ibrahim decided to send one or two thousand men to secure Trikorpha during the night. Gennaios had gone forward, but he did not succeed in taking the whole of the breastworks, but about half of them, and the other half was taken by Ibrahim. The battle began; I was at Pano-Chrepa, where the Kalavrytian and Corinthian armies were posted, and Koliopoulos endeavoured to take a reinforcement to Gennaios. Ibrahim thereupon sent out his cavalry, who were gathering in the harvests on the plain. They went to Sylimna, and turned Koliopoulos back; it was a plain, and Koliopoulos was not able to oppose himself to them there. There were seven thousand soldiers in Vervena; they heard the battle going on, and never went to render any assistance; if they had gone and given their aid, Ibrahim would not have sent his entire force against Gennaios. As soon, however, as Ibrahim sent to Tripolitsa for aid, I also had sent to get heip from the other side for our own people.

The battle lasted from early morn until two hours after noon—nine hours altogether. Cannon was brought opposite the breastworks of Gennaios. Twice did Gennaios sally forth from his breastworks to seize on the cannon, but he found too great a force arrayed against him, and was forced to return. The cannon of the enemy, however, did no damage. Papatsonês was killed in the breastworks, and two or three other chief men among us.

Ibrahim's whole force amounted to twenty thousand men. Gennaios had no fears as regarded the breastworks, where he placed himself, and when the Turks saw that they could do nothing in that part, they extended themselves to act upon the wings. ·Panagiotakôs Notaras, who kept the flank of Gennaios, went away, and Gianni Notaras then retreated amid great risk; the rear of Gennaios had been taken, and as soon as they saw that, they fled from the breastworks and came to us. The cavalry came up to them, and a hundred and eighty of them were lost, among whom were many distinguished officers—for instance, George Alonistiotês, Kostas Boura, Tambakopoulos, Christodoulos, and others, and the rest of the Greeks were all picked men. There were a hundred and ten men from Karytaina, and seventy from the other districts. I had sent Michalaki Zaimês' standard-bearer out with thirty men; he maintained his position well against the Turks, and our own men saved him. At night we went back to Alonistaina.

When Ibrahim saw that there were Greek soldiers there, he occupied both Piana and Chrysovitsi, about a mile the one from the other, with the mills of Davia between. He left Souleiman Bey there with five thousand men, and built twelve breastworks so as to guard the mills. Ibrahim spread his men all over the fields in order to harvest the corn, and to carry it when reaped into Tripolitsa, whither he now went. A hundred Arabs went to Alonistaina, but the Greeks fell upon them, and killed all except three or four who managed to escape, and carried the news to Tripolitsa. When Ibrahim found that we were at Alonistaina, he moved the whole of his army forward in five columns, both cavalry and infantry.

We had an intention of going to Demitsana, but we were not able to get there.

We left in the early morn, and Koliopoulos remained behind with a thousand men, but he was not strong enough to oppose himself to Ibrahim, who got to Vytina, and from Vytina went on to Magouliana. We were not able to stand up against him there, and the army was dispersed. As for the Karytainans, when Ibrahim reached that district, each one there thought about securing the safety of his family; the Corinthians dispersed; Londos himself got away.

At this juncture there remained myself, Zaimês, Kanelos Deligianni, Koliopoulos, Anagnostês Papastathopoulos, and Apostolês Kolokotronês. We went to Langadia.

Zachariadês came to us with letters, asking us to sign an address in which we asked for the intervention of England, because, on account of the position of affairs, we were not able to unite, and we were to sign this address. I and the six others put our signatures to it. We were all in despair in this conjunction of affairs, and therefore we signed it, and gave it to the person who was sent with it, who took it back to Zante.

Zaimês went away to Kalavryta. Gennaios departed to look after my son Konstantine at Psathari. Kanelos accompanied him, and they took their families, and carried them to Nauplia. Koliopoulos departed for Palouba, and secured the safety of his family, and took it to Monemvasia.

Thus this force was entirely disbanded, but I remained with thirty men, and crossed over to Phanari.

From Phanari I despatched my orders, and in three days I found myself again with two thousand men. This was what puzzled Ibrahim so much, that when he broke up one of my camps, in two days I set up another.

Ibrahim now went to the district of Karytaina; he also went to Kalavryta and Strezova, burning all before him, and making slaves everywhere. Having ravaged all those places he returned to Tripolitsa, and after stopping there one night he went to Mistra, and, having enslaved and despoiled that place also, returned again to Tripolitsa. Thence he went forth to Mòthokorona. I left two thousand men at Karya, and went myself to Vervena for the purpose of preventing the five thousand who were assembled there from dispersing. They scarcely set eyes on the Turks before they were broken ; at Vervena many were surrounded and shut up. Andreas, a son of Kontaki, fought well, and killed fifteen. When the Turks went back to Tripolitsa, we went to Agio-Petro, and the army was dispersed. Ibrahim had gone down to Mothokorona, and attacked the army which I had left at Karya. He attacked them, but had no great success, and thence he passed to Korona. Seventy Turks were killed.

Just see how the beginning of this address for the intervention of England came about. I once took a letter to Romas,* and he said that he would talk it over with Adam.† Adam asked him whether it would not be possible to detach Kolokotronês from the body of the chiefs. This body was supposed to be in opposition to England, and devoted to Russia, so the Mavrokordatoi gave out. Romas wrote to me, and said something to the same effect, and asked me to give him my opinion in writing under my own hand. "I am neither an opposer of the English, nor a worshipper of the Russian," I answered, "but I am the friend of whosoever is willing to do any good service for my country, and I will become a guarantee for this to his Excellency, Adam, and let Adam take my sentiments to his court."

Adam did send information about this to England, and

---

* Conte Roma. He belonged to a great Greek family in Zante.
† The English Lord High Commissioner of the Ionian Islands.

after some time he sent for Romas, and they were closeted
together for two days. The scheme of an address was then
framed: one was sent to me for my signature, and another
was sent to Miaoulês. We signed it. The nation understanding this, called for an assembly, and the members
and the executive signed as private persons, not as an
administrative body. By the rule as it now stood the presi-
dents both of the sea and land service were to execute it.
Thus I put my signature as president of the united districts
of Greece, and also as the generalissimo of Greece, and
Miaoulês as the president of the islands, and admiral of
the Greek forces on the sea. The nation ratified this
action as regarded the address to be forwarded, in an
assembly held at Epidaurus and Troizenos.

I again despatched my summonses to Mistra, Monemvasia, and Agio-Petro, for troops, and gathered together
ten thousand men, when I went and occupied Vervena.
The old lady—my mother (I had instructed Captain Chima-
riotes to take charge of her)—went at this time to Gior-
gitsi, and passed to the end of Mistra in order to go to
Nauplia. We had also with us the two sons of Senetzim
Bey, hostages from Tripolitsa, whom we put into a safe
place and guarded until we could exchange them for the
two Zapheiropouloi who were with Ibrahim. I then took
over the army to Vervena, and left it there, whilst I went
to visit my family. It is two miles from Vervena to Agio-
Petro. My troops saw a haze rising from the plain of Tripolitsa, and fancying that it was an army coming, thereupon
dispersed, and as I was returning I met them. I now saw
that it was impossible to make them serve, and so I sent to
the Government to enlist soldiers at Nauplia, and to give
them to Londos, Gennaios, and Kanelos, and they were
to be paid troops, when I, having the executive power,
would send for them, also myself collecting other soldiers.

They came, and altogether we assembled four thousand men. Londos and Kanelos arrived, and in this way we made up the four thousand which were at Agio-Petro.

I immediately ordered Anton Kolokotronês and those he had with him to go and seize the shepherds, and to attack the enemy in every direction. He did so, and got some flags, and also killed many, bringing us their heads, for which we paid the soldiers a dollar apiece. This brought Ibrahim with all his force to Tripolitsa. Leaving part of his army at Mylos, and part in Tripolitsa, he went on to Mistra with a force of thirty thousand. At that time I happened to be at Nauplia on military business, in order to give my opinion to the Government in respect to supplies of food and ammunition, in consequence of which a commission was formed of Konstantine Deligianni and another Roumeliote of the same name, and also Anastasês Londos, and sent to Astros to procure provisions, and to pay the chiefs and stipendiaries who had received orders payable there.

I then departed for Astros, where information was brought me that Ibrahim had gone to Mistra. I wrote, therefore, for my troops to move on to Mistra also, and I embarked myself in a boat to go to Levidi in search of soldiers. And this is what happened. Whilst I was at Levidi I succeeded in getting two hundred Levidiotes, and again going forward, I came up with some bodies of troops under Zaimês, Londos, Gennaios, and Panagiotakês Notaras.

Ibrahim again went forth, burning the country beyond Monemvasia, and afterwards returning to Apidia, he sent out his son-in-law into the country with a thousand men, and he entering into a village in that district, we harassed him there, and four of his men were killed, after which he ascended a hill and signalled from thence for aid, when some regular troops were sent to his assistance.

The Turkish armies moved thence towards Geraki, and our own force went to Kosma. I ordered them all to cross over to Agio-Basil and to prepare for battle. The whole of the paid troops accompanied the baggage : they were about three thousand in number, so we had only a thousand left with us. Ibrahim marched over to Marathonesi, thence to Polytzaravon : there he was met by the Maniotes, who fought a good battle, and the Turks were repulsed. Our men were surrounded in many strong positions, but they fought so well that the Turks gained no advantage. The enemy then marched back to Tripolitsa, and we returned to Vervena. Zaimês departed for Kalavryta, and Notaras went to Corinth to collect forces to oppose to the Turks if they entered those districts. Whilst the Corinthians were occupying Tsipiani, myself, with Gennaios and Londos, remained at Vervena.

At this time Theodore Grivas came from Nauplia to Doliana with three hundred men.

I made my resolves accordingly, and taking two hundred men with me, went to the Mills of Davia. When I left Gennaios, Londos, and Kanelos at Vervena, I said to them, "In so many days you will see fires lighted up all round ; have your sentinels in readiness, and as many fires as you see, so many thousands of soldiers shall I have with me. You must then kindle the same number of fires, so that we may understand that you have seen ours. At dawn I shall then attack the Turks at the mills, and you, during the night, must seize upon Trikorpha and prevent the possibility of any assistance reaching them from Tripolitsa."

I went to Doliana accordingly, and brought thence Theodore Grivas and his three hundred men, and we crossed over to Tsipiana, when I said to the forces assembled there :—

"If you see fires on the hills, let this force go and occupy Pano-Chrepa."

I departed to Alonistaina and sent a courier on foot to Zaimês, who was at Kalavryta, writing him that he was to come up with as many as he could get an hour earlier than was agreed upon. He brought six hundred men with him, and as I had fourteen hundred, we had thus acquired between us a force of two thousand. It was my intention to attack the Mills of Davia, so as by that means to cut off all food supplies from the enemy. I inquired of several Turks, whom the Greeks had captured, how many there were at the Turkish breastworks, and the answer was that they numbered only about eight hundred.

I made the signals as concerted, and as soon as the morning dawned the different bodies went out and seized upon the positions which I had indicated. Theodore Grivas wished to go to the post which Hassan Bey was occupying, so I gave him guides, and he went thither. Basil Alonistidês with his men went to his side. I ordered Anton Kolokotronês to take five hundred soldiers to Chrysovitsi, with instructions that if the Turks should make any attempt upon the entrenchments for the purpose of carrying aid to other bodies of Turks, that they should fall upon them from above; and this was the same spot where Konstantine Anastopoulos, my sister's son, intended to make an attack. Zaimês and myself, with two hundred men, stationed ourselves inside Piana, and we divided the Alonistainans among five positions. There is an old tower in Piana, and the Turks had made it into a fort, and a hundred and thirty Turks were in it. I had ordered the force to draw near to it during the night, approaching it either from the heights or from the village. The distance from one post to the other, whence we were to get there, was only about ten minutes' journey.

Konstantine and Lechouritês went down at sunrise to the village which had been destroyed by the Turks purposely that the Greeks should not take possession of it, but there were two companies of Turks at the foot of the village.

Firing was opened at Piana, and when we went forward to give them assistance those two companies came down upon us. When the Turks saw that we had ten of the cavalry with us they thought we were more numerous than we were, and retired. The Alonistainans came upon the lines of the Turks, but Grivas did not stop to fight when he caught sight of Souleiman Bey. Anton Kolokotronês with Petimeza rushed to seize Kephalovryso and the mills, but they were not able to pass the Turkish entrenchments.

My own standard-bearer, and also that of Zaimês', drew near to the wings of the Turkish army. Zaimês' standard-bearer was the first to break them, when he killed three with the spear of his banner staff. The Turks fell into disorder, and out of those two companies only four were saved. We took their flag and sixteen drums. The Turks who were shut up in the old tower were defeated, and the whole of the hundred and thirty were killed.

The body of the Verveni went to the post vacated by the men of Trikorpha; Londos, Giatrakos, Kanelos, and Gennaios were the leaders, and they had the cavalry. There were twenty horsemen, and it was the first time that we had begun to form regular cavalry. The Turks came out of Tripolitsa to go to the aid of those with whom we were fighting; they were attacked and driven back by our cavalry. Notaras then arrived at Pano-Chrepa, whilst forces from Tripolitsa and Sylimna came down upon Gennaios at Trikorpha, which is opposite Sylimna. A most obstinate battle ensued, and the Turks took to flight. About seventy of them were killed, and they got possession

of thirteen drums ; eleven breastworks were also taken, as
well as the little fort of Sylimna. On account of their
complete defeat they did not attempt to go on to
Tripolitsa.

The Turkish leader sent four of his cavalry to carry the
tidings to Ibrahim, who was then in Messenia making ready
to go and waste the Soulimo district. Upon hearing the
state of affairs Ibrahim pushed on to relieve the men who
were shut up in Davia.

Gennaios had no more ammunition or provisions. He
went to Valtetsi and I to the vale of Alonistaina. On the
third day I ordered Gennaios to take his force to the mills
below, near Sylimna. He went there and fought for four
hours, when he got possession of the fortifications and
burnt the mills. They killed about fifty and seized upon
the entrenchments.

On the other part, we, with Anton Kolokotronês,
Kolphinos, Grivas, Tsokrês, and others, destroyed all the rest
of the mills, and shut up those who were in the old fort
that was situated upon a rock which it was almost impossible for any one to ascend. We came to the opinion that
the best plan would be to cut off the water from them, and
that in two days they would then be forced to surrender.

At this juncture of affairs, however, Gennaios showed
a light, which gave us to understand that Ibrahim had
arrived. Gennaios marched to Vervena.

Ibrahim brought up two thousand cavalry ; they went
and released the Turks whom we had surrounded, and the
soldiers went through, fighting all the way from the rear.
We passed through Vervena, and Notaropoulos and Tsokrês
stayed at Tsipiana. We destroyed eight or nine mills on
the plain of Tavia ; and then the enemy went back to
Tripolitsa. The regular Turks in three days, and in
different places, lost five hundred men, twenty drums,

many muskets, four flags, and a great number of officers.

We fought there; but in all parts and in every district the Turks were continually being attacked, and not a single day passed on which Turks were not killed. I am writing here, however, only concerning the engagements at which I was present and in which I was the leader.

This was the only way in which the Turks could be successfully attacked, since I was not able to systematize a national campaign: first, because I had no food supplies; secondly, because there was no ammunition; and thirdly, because it was utterly impossible for us to conquer the Turks in a pitched battle on account of the overwhelming force of the enemy. I always, therefore, gave directions to attack the enemy from the front, from the rear, and from the sides, and to fall upon their camp at night, and I also ordered that our own soldiers should burn all our supplies when there was no means to carry them away, rather than leave them to be taken by the Turks; and by this system many Turks were destroyed without much loss to the Greeks.

There were not wanting some who called out upon this, and the Government had the same impression, writing to me to systematize a national camp and carry on a national campaign; but none of them knew our position. The Turks had seized upon the centre, and we were never enabled to centralize ten or fifteen thousand to oppose to the enemy's forces. Every district had to take measures for its own defence. Every part had become almost like a desert waste, for the war had prevented all husbandry and tilling of the ground, and so we had no bread. The Government was a Government only in name, and never sent us what we needed, because it had it not. For twenty and thirty days at a time we lived solely upon crabs, green corn, and flesh (*of rams*). If we had carried on a national warfare, and five or six thousand of us had been destroyed, it was not possible to amass another force; whereas if Ibrahim lost ten or fifteen thousand of his Arabs in a battle he could at once bring others into the field.

In such a conjuncture of affairs many shepherds greatly helped us, because the whole camp was sustained by the products of the people. In these skirmishing wars all assisted to the utmost of their power; all, but especially Antonakês Kolokotronês and Korelas from Akrodoremma, with Pappas Demetrius from Chrysovitsi. These killed sometimes twenty, sometimes thirty, sometimes forty, and sometimes even fifty of the enemy. Every district opposed itself to the common foe. The Arcadians and the Konto-vounesoi, and all the Messenians went to Mothokorona and attacked the Turks and slew them, often carrying off twenty, thirty, and forty mules; and in this way only could exist, because the Peloponnesians had no pay, and they could only live by the spoils taken from the Turks. The in-habitants of all the districts fled to a hill when the Turks came down upon their places; if the Turks followed them thither, they fled to another. All these things were done in 1826.

After I had destroyed his mills, Ibrahim had no longer any means for storing supplies; he therefore opened a road from Mothokorona to Tripolitsa, and sent beasts of burthen laden with supplies from Messenia. He took possession of Issari and made a camp there. In this manner he fed Tripolitsa for some time, and left there five thousand guards whom he had collected from different Messenian forts.

When I learnt from the captive Arabs whom the Greeks had taken that Ibrahim was making ready to pass over from Gastouni to Missolonghi, I wrote to the Govern-ment, and I gave them my opinion, with two alternatives—

namely, that they should either give me permission to go myself to Gastouni, or allow some one else to go, for the purpose of collecting all the provisions that could be found in Gastouni, in order to embark them for Missolonghi; and had they been but willing to listen to me, God knows how everything might have been changed, because Missolonghi would not have fallen if there had been any more food in it. The Government had time—there were twenty days—and I gave them information very early. Ibrahim supplied the three forts with soldiers and provisions, and himself moved into Gastouni. As to the Gastounians, some took to the hills, and others shut themselves up in Chlomoutzi. He burnt some provisions there, and the rest of the supplies he prepared to take with him on his journey to Missolonghi.

Thus the Gastounians who were shut up in Chlomoutzi had not the necessaries of life, for they had with them many women and children, and very few provisions. Three hundred of the Gastounians at Chlomoutzi, considering how they were thus surrounded, resolved to fall upon the camp of the enemy, to fall upon them very suddenly, and after harassing their enemies, to return to the fort. These attacked the Turks in this manner and destroyed many, but a spring of water had been occupied during the evening, and as they were returning they were enclosed in a village, and were all killed. They had slain as many Turks as they could, but they were lost themselves, and Chlomoutzi was given up. Michaelakês Sissinês was there.

Ibrahim now made ready to go to Missolonghi with his army. What took place at Missolonghi is well known, and has been told in another history. He united himself to Kioutahi. Another history also has taken note of the bravery of Missolonghi. A very few days after he arrived there, Missolonghi was lost.

When the enemy had gone to Missolonghi I went all round Tripolitsa, and was able to find out the narrow road leading from Agiorgitika and Pertsova, and burnt the houses belonging to the Turks. I measured out the ground for the purpose of making an entrenchment there, for it was winter time, and going down to the national mills, I sent to the Government to provide me with food and ammunition in order that I might be able to collect soldiers in the villages within a mile or so of Tripolitsa, from which we might find an opportunity for getting into Tripolitsa itself. And my Government told me to go to Nauplia ; but this was my answer :

" This is no time for me to go to Nauplia, but if you will let me have what I have asked for, I shall be able to do some hurt to the enemy, here in Tripolitsa."

Upon this the Government promised me that it would do so, and began to send me supplies, which I stored up in the village where I had made entrenchments.

I transmitted despatches to all the districts to bid them assemble. In one part they collected soldiers, and from another part they gave provisions. At the same time they sent to me Konstantês Mavromichaelês, who was a member of the executive, with a hundred men, and I went to the interior of Achladokabo, and gave provisions both for that place and for himself. The newspapers heard that food supplies had been sent to me to Tripolitsa, with the object of making an assault upon it. This got into the newspapers, wherein it was also stated that the national general had made agreements with the Government whereby it engaged to supply him with rations and ammunition, in order that he might make an assault upon Tripolitsa. This was what the newspapers made public before I had made ready my designs. Whatever secrets they had were always reported to the enemy.

In those days, whilst I was collecting troops, Petro Bey and his son Georgaki, who were in the Government, sent letters to Tripolitsa, by which an exchange of prisoners was effected. (We had given them up the two Pashas, and they delivered back Georgaki Mavromichaelês and Giatrakos to us.) They sent Philemon from the mills with letters, and he stayed a day and a night at Tripolitsa, until the Turkish commandant who was there should give him his answer to carry back. A closed answer was delivered to him after the same manner as the letter sent, and he went to embark at the mills for Nauplia.

"Where hast thou been?" I asked him.

"To Tripolitsa—with letters."

"Who sent thee?"

"The Government."

Then I said, "I am collecting soldiers and provisions, and I am the general, and yet the Government carries on a secret correspondence with the Turks." I seized upon his letters, and tore them up, and thrashed Philemon.

When the Government heard of my proceedings it was very displeased, and wrote me a reprimanding letter, which I answered by saying that it was my duty as a general to know what transactions the Government had with the enemy, lest I should be chastised," &c.

I began my campaign by collecting five thousand men, and I ascended to the camp by ladders, and passed one day there—it was near Christmas—and because excavations had been made by our own men from Tripolitsa, I divided the forces among the leaders. I sent Niketas to the gate of Mistra, Gennaios to that of Karytaina, Konstantês Mavromichaelês to the gate of Kalavryta, and Panagiotês Zapheiropoulos, with the Agiopetritai, to the gate of Sarai, and to the other gates I despatched other captains. I divided the scaling ladders among the commanders who

NIKETAS THE TURKOPHAGE.

were to mount the fort, and I had a body of men with me
who were to render any assistance that might be needed.
When we were all ready we marched forward, but when we
drew near to Tripolitsa some traitors (it was night-time) fired
off two guns—a signal to the enemy. Two Bulgarians had
joined us ; who sent them I know not. The traitors had
given this information : " To-night there will be an assault
upon you." The Turks, men, women, and children, came
to the walls and waited for the dawning. Niketas threw
down the ladders, and we, seeing that we were betrayed,
retired at daybreak.

When morning came the Turks saw that there were no
armies, and attacked the body of Tripolitsans under
Riziotês. Gennaios sent them a reinforcement, but ten
of them were killed. Gennaios had perceived the position
from Rizai. We were unsuccessful on account of those
traitors, and therefore, as we were unable to perform
any good service, we gathered our men together, and went
back to the villages, when they all began to disperse.

I then went down to Nauplia in order that we might
confer together upon the expediency of calling an assembly,
since the Government had ruled for a year in an unwilling
mood, and the term of its duration was approaching. "What
treachery is this that is going on ?" I said ; and then we
spoke of the imminent danger which threatened the country. The Government had issued a decree that no military
man should go to Nauplia, because, if he did, he would not
be received.

As soon as I knew of this decree I wrote to Zaimês and
to the districts that they had better gather themselves
together, and that we would hold an assembly in Argos.
The plenipotentiaries began their work, and came to Argos,
and we agreed forthwith to go to Piada, and went there.
The representatives from the islands of the Ægean Sea

came, and also the Peloponnesians, and we framed our assembly. This assembly then abolished the rule of Ypsilanti.

Having all met, we began our work: we placed the executive power in the hands of Andreas Londos, and constituted the elder, Panoutsos, our president, because, as one party wanted to throw out Petro Bey, and another desired to get rid of Zaimês, we thought the best way to put an end to this wrangling was to give the presidency to Panoutsos. And in these afore-mentioned labours there was a party among the Roumeliotes, and Ypsilanti, on his side, said, "We do not agree with that appeal which you have sent to London." They answered with one voice, "We have done that which the nation wished, and that cannot be made matter for his opinion." The Roumeliotes stood by Ypsilanti. Whereupon I rose up: "It is not just," I said, "to drive out Ypsilanti from among us, because it seems to me that at the beginning of the rising you had a writing sent to you from his late brother; and did we not make great use of that brother in the cause of Greece?" And with other words I endeavoured to pacify them in regard to him, saying, "He has opposed you, that is true; but let us look at the good work he has done." I succeeded in getting a remission, and the suppression of his official duties was limited to a year. We then went on with our business.

On Palm Sunday the heroic people of Missolonghi made a sally out of Missolonghi, through a host of many thousands, through all their cannon, their entrenchments, and their cavalry. Two thousand only were saved, and the women and children were sacrificed. The news came to us on the Great Wednesday, at evening time, when the meeting of the assembly was over, and the shades of night were closing round us. The news came to us that Missolonghi was lost. We were all plunged in great grief; for half an hour there was so complete a silence that no one would have thought that there was a living soul present; each of us was revolving in his mind how great was our misfortune. When I saw this great silence I rose to my feet, and spoke some words to encourage them ; I told them that Missolonghi had fallen gloriously, and that her bravery would be for ever remembered, but that if we gave ourselves up to mourning we should bring upon ourselves a curse, and that we should be guilty of sinning against all those who were weak. They answered, " What *can* we do now, Kolokotronês ? " " What *can* we do ! " I cried, " why, we will have a meeting at daybreak, and decide upon a Government with five, six, or eight persons who can govern us, and we must choose persons who will resolve to correspond with foreign Powers (the Minister, Canning, had then gone to Constantinople), the committee of the Assembly for Foreign Affairs must give their report to the Government, and to the people, and all of us meanwhile must disperse to the districts, and take up arms everywhere, as we did on the first day of the rising.

And so on the morning of the Great Thursday we assembled and chose eleven members for the Government committee, with Zaimês for President. We had Petro Mavromichaelês, Spiridon Trikoupês, and others ; and the duration of this committee (this was the 26th of April) was to be until September, 1826, and then, if we were saved, we were to meet and finish the sitting.

CHAPTER IX

WE had Gennaios with us at Nauplia lest there should be any opposition. The new Government, however, did not offer any opposition, and departed for Nauplia, where it began to attend to its business. I went down to Argos, and, collecting some troops, prepared to move them forward. The Government had arranged to make Gennaios chief of the garrison, and then afterwards it desired that Londos should be appointed. I said to Gennaios immediately, "Let be, we must save our country, and whatever the Government wishes, let it be done." Gennaios therefore exerted himself, and I got together some thousands of men, and occupied a village in Bongiati, six miles from Argos.

I sent out men to collect sheep for slaughtering. I wrote to the Corinthians to assemble, because Ibrahim Pasha was about to leave Missolonghi and go to Patras with the whole of his force, and I also told them what I had heard, namely, that he was about to unite with Kioutahi, who was also coming; but this report was false, for Kioutahi had gone to Eastern Greece.

When all his army had passed over to Patras—for he began to move immediately with the whole of his troops— the people of Patras, everyone of them, gathered together, and with their women, their children, and their effects, took to the hills. There were among them two Peloponnesian Turks who fled from the hill Chelmos, and betrayed it to Ibraham. Ibrahim went to Chelmos, and there was not a shot fired at him anywhere. He made slaves of about two thousand women and children, and took altogether four thousand captives. The rest were scattered like the winds, and there was a report that five thousand were killed. The Kalavrytians and the inhabitants of districts of Karytaina, Leontari, and Mani, fled ; horror filled the whole of the Peloponnesus, and Ibrahim passed· along and arrived at Tripolitsa, and I myself, when I received this information, had two thousand men with me, and we went over opposite Tripolitsa in order that we might see whither he would direct his arms, and then we marched to the district of Karytaina.

Ibrahim took his forces to the plain of Karytaina, when I sent Gennaios forward with five hundred men, and he occupied Stemnitsa, in which, being a strong position, he could shut himself up if Ibrahim should come down upon him. I meanwhile lay concealed with the rest of the army, so that if I saw that Gennaios was attacked by the Turks, I could fall upon them in the rear. Ibrahim did not come down upon Gennaios, for he had learnt that the female children had been taken to Mani, and therefore he followed them thither, leaving his camp on the plain. The people, hearing that Ibrahim had gone to villages on the rear, burning all before him, took refuge in Mani, until his army turned back. He marched through Messenia, and the Arcadians and Androusani, upon hearing of the ravages committed on the plain above them, also hastened to Mani. Wherever he went there was slaying, everywhere there was enslavement. He then fixed his camp at Nisi, in Kalamata.

When Ibrahim had left Missolonghi the Maniotes erected a strong breastwork at Armyro, where lie the homes of the Kapetaniani. It was built from the sea-shore to the rock, and was quite an hour's march in extent. Ibrahim went thither once, but the Maniotes attacked, and after killing a considerable number, repulsed him. About the same time I took three thousand soldiers to Derveni, and leaving them all there except eighty men, I went with this body into Messenia, and marched over the whole of the heights because Ibrahim and his camp were stationed at Nisi, in Kalamata. As I was on the road I blew my trumpet, so that everybody should know that I was there, and they knew me, and they were much cheered in consequence, and were encouraged to go back to their houses. And then going down to Armyro, I wrote to every part that the Peloponnesians had returned to their several districts, and thereupon they all came back, the women and children going to their homes, and the men going to the war.

I stayed eight days there, lest Ibrahim might again attempt to go to Verga. Ibrahim, however, marched away to the forts, so that his army might get a little breathing time, and also to leave the captured women and children there. I sent many inspiriting words to encourage the Maniotes, and many gathered round me at Armyro, when I went to the army which I left at Derveni, and led it to Manesi, between Leontari and Mistra, and when we were all united with the Mistriote forces we numbered four thousand. At Mistra I obtained some provisions.

Ibrahim sent his lieutenant to attack Verga in Armyro again, and at the same time despatched a force to fall upon the same place in the rear. Upon hearing of this movement of Ibrahim, and that he had gone to Verga for the second time, they sent word to me, "The enemy is upon us, come with a reinforcement." I moved forward directly to their assistance with two thousand men, but the distance was great, for it was ten hours' journey. The Turks marched towards the above place, but were re-attacked by the Maniotes, who again drove them back ; the Turks were at half-an-hour's distance both from Verga and Kalamata. We had ourselves reached Giannitsa, and the Turkish forces were an hour from us. As we were advancing I blew my trumpet, that our forces upon hearing it might act. I did not expect that the Turks would hear the trumpet because it was cracked. As soon as the Turks heard my trumpet, which they did, they marched off an hour's journey to the plain in the direction of the river of Kalamata. If we had succeeded in getting in time to the place where the Turks were encountered by the Maniotes, we should have been able to surround them, whereby numbers of them would have been killed.

After two days had passed the Turks went over to Nisi. I also marched to Manesi, where I had left the other part of the army, not being able to stay any longer where I was on account of a lack of provisions. In the space of ten or fifteen days Ibrahim took his cavalry with the intention of going from Armyro to Mani, and also to embark his infantry in boats to be disembarked again at Vero on the coast of Tsimova. The Maniotes, however, women as well as men, came out and arrayed themselves against them, driving the Turks into the sea, and causing a tremendous panic among them. They opposed themselves to the cavalry at Verga with the like fury, and Ibrahim, seeing that he could have no successes in that quarter, marched away to the Messenian forts.

I stopped ten days at Manesi, and whilst there I received a letter from the Roumeliote captains who were at Nauplia, namely, Karaiskakês, Tsavellas, Kostas Botsarês, and Lambros Veikos, with Georgios Drakos, and the other leaders who had been at the fort of Missolonghi, and they wrote to the effect that we should all of us meet and confer together upon the advisability of uniting, and of our all taking measures simultaneously in an endeavour to overthrow the enemy. I left Georgaki Giatrakos as my lieutenant with the army, and taking fifty men with me, I went to Argos forthwith. I sent word to Nauplia, and Karaiskakês, Tsavellas, and the rest came, except Kostas Botsarês and some others who held with Zaimês, who did not wish the forces to unite.

The grapes * were now getting ripe, so Gianni and Panagiotês Notaras began to harvest them; the reason of their doing so was that they were in the district of Corinth. The greater part of that district wished to have Panagiotês as its leader, but Gianni had got paid men, and tried to prevail upon the district to choose himself instead of Panagiotês, in consequence of which there was much discord between them.

The Government ordered me to go to Nauplia. I answered that I could not go thither, but that if they would go to Areia we would confer with them there, upon which Zaimês, Petros Mavromichaelês, Boudourês, and other members came to Areia. They asked my opinion whether it would be desirable for Zaimês to go to Corinth in order to put an end to the civil war still going on there. I told them that I thought Zaimês had better not go, but that they should transmit one order to Gianni, and another to Panagiotês couched in the following manner :—"The general of the nation has himself come hither, and you must obey what he enjoins ; and Zaimês as the president forbids you to do any damage, or to erect any camp." But they did not follow my advice, and departing into the interior the Roumeliotes made an encampment, whilst Zaimês prepared to go to Corinth. I meanwhile remained at Argos.

* The *currant* grape is here alluded to.

When Karaiskakês, myself, and the other captains mentioned above met together, we swore to be wholly united, that thus we might conquer the enemy. We transmitted a commission to Vostitsa and Corinth, and as many as they assembled there to go against the enemy were to be paid troops. Ibrahim was now moving his forces towards Tripolitsa, by the way of Agio-Petro, and arrived at Astros. Panagiotês Zapheiropoulos gave me information of this, so I sent Niketas forward with two hundred men, and he shut himself up in Kastrakî. The Turks swept over the whole of Tsakonia, whilst I with a hundred men went to the villages of Corinth, whither I had written for Gennaios and Koliopoulos to come. I sent Gennaios with a thousand men to the assistance of Astros, and when Koliopoulos came up with another thousand, I sent him thither also. Kanelos Deligianni arrived with five hundred, he having despatched three hundred to help Panagiotakês Notaras (the reason of the Deligiannis helping him being that he was their co-father-in-law). Zaimês and Londos at the same time aided Gianni.

We united, however, with Zaimês and the other leaders at Klêmentokaisara, as Karaiskakês had gone for a campaign into Roumêli. Panagiotês had some of his men at Sophikos, whither went Gianni, and in order to drive them thence he burnt the whole village, such was the way in which they conducted themselves.

We next had a talk about the currant harvest. The soldiers who had come from Missolonghi hoped to receive their pay out of the grapes, because we had no funds. I told them that we would appoint a commission to gather them in, and that we would reckon up their value. We were now six thousand in number, so we wished to go nearer to the enemy, and therefore I sent Gennaios, Koliopoulos, and Niketas forth, announcing that when we had attacked the

Turks every man who served should receive his pay. They did not oppose my counsel, they only said, "We will stay here until we get our pay, and afterwards we will unite and go against the Turks." "Now," I answered, "now is the time to act, whilst the Turks are burning the villages ; if we allow them to be burnt, of what use is it to act afterwards ?"

We strongly opposed Kyr [Mr.] Andreas Zaimês, and came to words.

" Why didst thou not send to thy nephew Gianni, Kyr Andreas," I said, "to bid him not to burn Sophikos, which was the chief village in the district? "

He answered me that he had not got a man to send.

" What sayest thou, Kyr Andreas? Thou hadst four thousand men with thee, and yet thou couldst not send one horseman to stop the burning of two hundred houses!"

Many were the other words which passed between us, when he called out before all the captains, "Kolokotronês, Kolokotronês, for six years thou hast been trying to unite the armies, and neither have I let thee unite them, nor will I let thee do so now." No one made any answer to him ; clapping my hands—

" Bravo, good patriot!" I cried, "thou who wilt not have the armies unite! If they were united Ibrahim could not burn the villages nor enslave the inhabitants!"

I saw that there was no use arguing with them. Zaimês then sent Kitsos Tsavellas and Notês Botsarês and others to me, who said that I was to take seventy thousand grosia for my expenses—that money being the produce of the currants.

"What! " I said, "not only will I not receive seventy thousand grosia, but I would not receive seventy millions, if there were so many. I have served my country so long without pay, that I will serve her still to the utmost of my strength."

I remained there five or six days longer, and then departed, having Hadji Michaelês and fifty cavalry with me. These remaining with me, they collected four hundred thousand grosia, and divided the sum amongst themselves.

CHAPTER X.

AS soon as Karaiskakês reached Roumêli he wrote asking
for assistance, when the Roumeliote captains moved
forward, and Gianni Notaras came to Phaleria.   This time
Ibrahim burnt all the villages of Agio-Petro and Prastos
(the people saving themselves by fleeing to Levidi), and
thence he went to Mistra, burning everything as he went
along on his way back to Tripolitsa. Gennaios, Niketas, and
Koliopoulos did not, however, allow any opportunity to pass
for engaging in frequent skirmishes with him. Gennaios
passed on to the villages of Corinth, and I sent Koliopoulos back to his old quarters again, so he went to Alonistaina. Thither also went Meletopoulos and Petimeza ; and
they had some very good skirmishing, when a good number
of Turks were killed. Koliopoulos then occupied Atsicholon,
which is situated near the country of Karytaina, in order to
prevent the Turks from going to Liodorai.   I called upon
Niketas to join me, and we went to Argos, and sent for
Almeïdas, who was the leader of about ninety of the regular
cavalry with about fifty irregulars besides. I went with
them to Agio-Petro and collected a force of about two
thousand of the Agiopetrians, Mistriotes, and Tripolitsans.

The Turks who were in Tripolitsa had a habit of going
every day to the plains, and there they reaped and gathered

in the corn. I sent out scouts to watch them. One night
I rose up and divided the irregular cavalry, putting Hadji
Michaelês at their head, and also Niketaras, who was put over
another thousand men, and they all passed along in secrecy,
whilst Panagiotês Giatrakos had a force of a thousand men
likewise, and Captain Almeïdas had his regular cavalry. I
took four men with me, and remained in the centre, with this
agreement, that when I saw the Turks I would immediately
make a signal for them to go out of their ambush and
surround them.

On that day the Turks did not go to the place where we
were expecting them. On the contrary, they sent out
three hundred of the regular troops with the view of
scouring through the villages to ascertain whether the
Greeks were lying in ambush anywhere, ready to
fall upon the large bodies of Turks who were reaping
in the fields, because the Greeks had for some days
past been lying in ambush, and had killed five or six
Turks every day; and I gave one dollar to every
Greek who brought me either a head, a gun, or a
captive.

The Turkish force went out to make their circuit and
came to a village called Meimetaga. There was a tower
there, so in order that they should not be able to shut themselves up in it I made no signal, but left them undisturbed
until they had spread themselves all over the village.
Then I gave the signal, when out flew the cavalry, which
was under the command of Niketas, and, with a sudden
rush, fell upon the Turks. The Turks endeavoured to
make a stand on the plain by forming a square, but when
they saw our cavalry, and beheld the infantry pouring in
on all sides, they returned to the village. They were not
able to reach the tower in order to occupy it, and so in
half an hour only four out of the three hundred were able

to save themselves. Never in my life before had I seen such slaughter.

The whole of the Turkish cavalry came to their assistance when they heard the battle raging, but none of them got away alive. I had told our troops on the previous evening that if I saw the Turkish forces coming down I would make a signal for them to hasten to the place which I held. I made a signal, but Niketas did not follow out the orders which I had given him. The Turks, towards evening, advanced somewhat nearer, when Niketas, with thirty of his men, made a stand, and a Turk of distinction was killed, and then the Turks drew back and retired, and we all rejoined each other safe and sound at Agio-Petro. The muskets and drums were sent to Nauplia.

I went to Nauplia myself afterwards in order to obtain ammunition, and then I intended to return immediately for the purpose of continuing these ambuscades. The Greeks were much inspirited, and whenever we had cavalry they went down to the plain. In that battle they all bore themselves with courage, but Theodoros Zacharopoulos was especially noteworthy, because he fell upon a house wherein there were twenty Turks and killed them all. Stamatês Mêtsas was wounded in the foot by a bayonet. The regular cavalry now went back to Areia. Almeïdas promised me that he would return, but he received an order to go to Damala, which he obeyed.

Ibrahim marched away to Messenia. He came in the month of September, and in October I went to Nauplia in order that we might have a conference respecting the Assembly. I told the commission of the Assembly to gather together because I wished to address them. They met accordingly, and I presented myself there, and spoke to them concerning the state of affairs in somewhat the following manner:—"Now is the time for you to announce (being the Committee of the Assembly) that the plenipotentiaries who are known to us should come together to complete the meeting of the previous April, when we only lost our time. Now is the fitting season—it is winter—and we cannot fight, neither can Ibrahim." "Where can the Assembly take place?" they asked. "Let the Assembly take place on the heights of the Peloponnesus. There we can keep Ibrahim in ignorance of all that is going on, and we can give military help upon any emergency, because we have the enemy at our own door." To this they replied, "Where can we find a secure place there to hold an Assembly in?" "At Lenidi, at Kranidi, at Kastri," I answered; "and then there is Piada, and among those four places you could take your choice." "We will ask the Administrative Committee," they said; and so those two bodies met together and consulted, and deceitfully resolved to do according to their own wills as regarded the Assembly, being bent upon holding it either at Poros or Ægina, when they would be able to embark any representative whom they desired, and whomsoever they did not desire to have they would also be able to decline to receive into the island. The committee therefore replied to me in respect to the conversation which I had had with the other body of the Government, that the Assembly would be held either in Poros or Ægina. I, however, would not receive this proposition, and made my resolution known to them in the following manner:—

"I will not embark on the sea, for I took an oath when they had me in Hydra that I would act no more on the seas. If I am not in the Assembly I should be the one person whom that would not injure. I have, nevertheless, many votes, and among the armies and the politicians I have also others who would not wish to go thither."

After this. I got up and went to speak with Kyr Andreas about the place of assembly, for he was the President of the Executive Committee, therefore I went to his house and had some conversation with him. "This plan of having an Assembly in the islands is not praiseworthy," I said to him, "and not well as regards the Peloponnesus, nor for the whole of the nation generally considered, because when we sail away from the Peloponnesus, then the Peloponnesus becomes cold and indifferent, but as soon as we are on dry land again we give them all new hearts."

Kyr Andreas sat down by the window looking out therefrom, and not looking at me; he kept shaking his foot.

"Kyr Andreas," I cried, "I am discoursing to thee, and thou art looking another way! Farewell, brother, I talk to thee no more on this subject."

So I immediately went to my own house, and afterwards galloped off and got Tsokrès to join me with two hundred men, and, accompanied by Nikolaki Poneros and Anagnostakos, went to Agio-Demetri. As soon as I reached Hermione I assembled four hundred men. When the two committees heard that I had gone to Hermione they removed at once and went to Ægina and announced that the Assembly was opened. I also, at the same time, announced that we should open an Assembly at Hermione. I sent Nikolaki Poneros to Hydra, to Kyr Georgios, and the other Hydriotes, and the Hydriotes came straightway to our Assembly, and we had ninety representatives, whilst that one at Ægina with its two committees only had fifty.

This division was continued for three months. At this time Hamilton came over and went to Ægina, and then he came to us to persuade us to unite, and to form one Assembly only. We said in answer, "Let the Ægina people come hither, for we are the most numerous, and we will receive them;" and they on their side said the same thing. They were quarrelling over the matter, and wrote as a committee to the Minister, and I wrote also, but as a private person. They received their answer, and I received mine. There was some rioting at Hydra about Hamilton, when some people were killed, and Hamilton was very much annoyed with the Hydriotes. Hamilton came one day to the camp which I kept at Hermione. He had Count Andreas Metaxa for his interpreter, as he did not know our language. Hamilton said to me one day—

"I hear that it is the intention of your Assembly to send for Kapodistria."

"Whoever has told you so has been joking," I answered, "because Kapodistria was once the Russian Minister of War, and as he did not lend us a finger to help us then, there is no reason why we should be induced to invite such a man over now ; time will show us what to do, because we are depending upon England, who has promised us her protection." Hamilton then went away.

In the month of March, when we had ninety representatives, we began our work, and made Sissinês our president.

Cockrane* then arrived, and we at once voted him high admiral in the three departments of Spetsai, Hydra, and Psara. Church† came about the same time. As the Assembly at Ægina had said that I, Kolokotronês, wanted to become generalissimo all over Greece, I resolved that they should not find this disposition in me, and I threw aside all personal ambition for the love of country, and the three islands also cast down whatever ambition they also might have had, and signed that Cockrane should be high admiral.

Cockrane then coming to Poros he took Metaxa to accompany him, and I met him on board, when we conversed upon everything which our Assembly had decreed.

* Lord Cockrane.　　　　　† Sir Richard Church.

He also asked for the union of the two Assemblies, and we made the same remark as formerly, "Let the Assembly at Ægina come here and we will receive it." I saw by the style of his conversation that Cockrane had some ideas of his own, and therefore I answered him as a Greek, who also had ideas of his own too. We parted and went back to Hermione, and we had General Church at Hermione with us, and then Cockrane joined fellowship with Church, and they gave it as their opinion that they would be able to bring about a reconciliation.

At that time letters came from Athens that they were terribly distressed there for want of soldiers, and the Assembly charged me to procure forces and send them thither; so I despatched Gennaios to all the districts, and in twenty days he went there with three thousand men, and the Assembly promised me that the Assembly itself, that is, the nation, would give them their pay, and so we remained content.

The two commanders by sea and land, who were desirous to unite the two Assemblies, did so by finding a third place wherein they could finish the remaining business of the Assembly, and this place was Troizen, also called Damala. We made answer to this proposition of the leaders that we would go thither, but everything which we had made law must remain the same, and the forts must be in the same hands, and if they ratified all this we would go. The Æginetans ratified everything. We therefore rose, and the two parties went to Troizen and became re-united there. We immediately began the required work ; all that we had done remained unannulled, and we prosecuted the business in hand. We made a resolution to vote in three persons to act as a Government Commission to overlook the army, and fifteen for the Senate. When we voted, the greatest number of votes fell to Georgaki Mavromichaelês, Marki, and Nako. There was to be a committee appointed at an early date for the purpose of choosing a president. The committee went to Poros, and the Assembly was left to complete its business.

We had some thought of sending for Kapodistria in the year 1827. They had all tried their hands at governing, and the whole nation was going from bad to worse on account of our dissensions. So I spoke out openly, saying, "We have cast away all our personal ambition in regard to the army, and we have put the Englishman Church over us, and our brave seamen have taken Cockrane; it behoves you politicians also to throw aside your ambition, so that we may choose a president who can govern us, for the English have promised that we shall have our independence."

One of those days I saw that they wanted to invite Kapodistria to the nation, and some of them came armed to see if they could frighten us, so that they could take the matter in hand; the secretary, Spêliadês, was one. I perfectly understood with what view they came to me. They had a meeting at the house of Mavromichaelês, and asked me to attend it; so I went by myself, when they began to talk to me about the Assembly, saying that they could not perceive that any good had come forth from it. I replied to them with some anger, that the nation had willed it, and whoever was not satisfied with it, let him try to ruin it if he were able, and went away without saying another word. Seeing that they had no power by themselves, and that, if they had endeavoured to do anything, they would certainly be put to shame, they dissolved.

Two days after we had finished the work of the Assembly, we resolved in the morning that after dinner we would sign a paper for Kapodistria, and so I went to my tent and ate some bread, and threw myself down to sleep. I looked up and saw Kyr Georgio Kountouriotês with Karakatsanês the Spetsiote, and Mark the Psarian, coming to speak with me about the Kapodistria proposition, which we were to sign in the afternoon. They said—

"We were to sign for Kapodistria this afternoon, were we not?

"Why do you ask me? I am neither the president, nor do I represent the nation. The President Sissinês and the nation resolved upon that measure this morning."

"It will be a good plan for us to send and ask for the opinion of Hamilton, who is at Poros, he having lately come from Smyrna."

"What! shall we send some adventurer to him to say things quite opposite to those which he will report to us, and thus ruin the position of the nation? Where will you find a suitable person to send? If you would trust me, I will go myself."

"We do trust thee, we do trust thee!" Three times they called out, "We do trust thee!"

Kountouriotês was of opinion, that as I had spoken to Hamilton, and as we had not at that time chosen Kapodistria, that I might meet with some opposition on the part of Hamilton, but I answered him, "Go in peace."

I then made myself ready, and called for Metaxa, and ten of his men to come at noon, and as I did not know any one else who could go with me, except Niketas, I sent for him, and told him that he must behave himself with discretion, and not cause any scandal whither I was going. The Assembly wondered, but had no idea where I intended to go. We went to the river of Poros, where the ships of Hamilton were taking in water; we there embarked on a boat and drew near the frigate. Hamilton received me and we sat down to converse. I opened the subject by saying, "How does it appear to you now, since the Assembly has united and the sitting is nearly over?"

"I rejoice at your union; you have done well."

"Captain Hamilton, we have come to ask your advice, for you have always counselled us best in our endeavour to acquire our freedom, and we know that, above all others, you are our greatest benefactor."

"Place your opinion before me, and if I am able, I will answer you in accordance with that opinion."

"Captain Hamilton, I have reflected that you have known the Greeks for many years. We throw over all those who govern us, for they never govern us as they ought, and seeing that we have no political man fit to rule us, we have come to ask for your advice, and because, whatever is decided by the Assembly, we dismiss: it has been decided to make Cockrane high admiral, and Church generalissimo, and now we want a politician. Will England give us a president, or a king?"

"No, that will never happen."

"May France give us one?"

"That's likely."

"Russia?"

"No."

"Prussia?"

"No."

"The East?"

"No."

"Spain."

"No, that can't be."

As I had mentioned all the kingdoms, I said, "Well, then, if all those Courts are not to give us a ruler, what are we to do?"

"Look about and find a Greek."

"We have no Greek who is sufficiently worthy; we can only choose Kapodistria."

When he heard the name of Kapodistria he turned and looked fixedly at me.

"Was it not you who told me that you would not have Kapodistria because he had been in the Russian ministry?"

"Yes, that was upon another occasion, but now it is different, because we have the protection of England. The sea is the right hand of Greece, and we have put an Englishman at the head of the navy; her left hand is her power on shore, and that we have also put under an Englishman. If England will now give us a politician we will take him, and then we shall no longer break our heads one against the other; but if this cannot be, as you say, we must then choose Kapodistria."

"Take Kapodistria or any other devil you like," he replied, warmly, "for you are quite lost."

I wanted to hear this from his own mouth, and I did hear it, and in this way our conversation terminated, and I left immediately. I had lost a great deal of time on board the frigate, and the drum of the Assembly began to beat. When the plenipotentiaries from the three islands heard the drum, they left and went away to the Panagia, in order to go to Hamilton. Hamilton saw them with his glass and embarked in his cutter for the Panagia. As the representatives went on purpose to question him, Hamilton first put the question to them, saying, "How is it that you have left the Assembly?"

"We were coming to ask your opinion."

"I gave my opinion to Kolokotronês," he replied; "do what he tells you," and then he returned to his frigate.

Panagia was half an hour distant from the Assembly. As soon as the Hydriotes returned they called for me, when I related to them all that had passed. We again met together at early morn, and signed an address to Kapodistria. The letters of invitation were begun and finished and sent away to three parts, and so that business was completed. We met the next day to resolve upon a president for the Senate, and the members voted for a presidency. On the day following, rushing to the Assembly, one was for Zaimês, another for Basla, and another for Piasa from Androusa, and there was a complete division. The next day succeeding that there was the same thing going on. Seeing how great was the division and caprice of every one around, I rose straightway to my feet. " Honourable Assembly," I cried, "we are sitting and quarrelling about a president of the Parliament, whilst our country is in danger of being ruined. We have had an Assembly sitting for seven months, whilst Kioutahi is president in Eastern Greece, and the president of the Peloponnesus is Ibrahim, and yet we are sitting and wrangling. May is now here, and Athens is in great danger, and the Peloponnesus is also imperilled: shall not one out of so many Greek representatives be spared that we may make a President? Are we still to go on sitting and wrangling?" I looked around and saw a nice old man who was sitting amongst the Cretans. I did not know his name, nor did I look to see what it was, but sprang up in the middle of the Assembly, took hold of him, and leading him in front of the seat of President Sissinês, I put him on a stool. " This man is worthy!" I cried; and with one voice the Assembly cried aloud, "He is worthy, he is worthy!" and there was great clapping of hands, and thus it was settled. They blessed the memory of my father, but Renierês seemed as if he were frightened. The Assembly was then dissolved.

On one occasion I went to Nauplia and said to the Government, "The Roumeliotes receive their pay, whilst the Peloponnesians are stripped of their all by Ibrahim, and have not where to lay their heads—why do you not pay those who have lost so much?" They then resolved to form twelve thousand disciplined soldiers; this number was to be reckoned as fifteen thousand, and with the overplus the proportion could be so reckoned as to afford thirty grosia a month to each. They told me that they would be required to serve three months beforehand, at the expiration of which they were to go and receive their monthly pay. Three months passed, and I sent to take the month's pay, when I received for answer that " a small donation of two and a half millions (of grosia) has arrived, but the Government had other necessary affairs to attend to, and they have used it. Your experience," it said, "will be able to prevail on the soldiers to have patience."

Our rising was totally different from any which had ever taken place in Europe before our day. The revolutions of Europe had always been against their rulers—they were civil wars. Our war was more just than any of them —it was a nation rising up against another nation—it was a war with a people whom it never desired to acknowledge as ruling them; to whom it had never taken oaths of fealty, except when made to do so by force ; neither had a Sultan at any time any inclination to regard the Greek people as his people, but only as his slaves. Once, when we had gone to Nauplia, Hamilton came to see me. " You Greeks must have a treaty," he said, "and England will act as mediator."

" This will never come to pass," I made answer; " with us it is *freedom or death.* Captain Hamilton, we have never yet made a treaty with the Turks ; they have killed some of us, others they have enslaved by the sword ; but the rest, like ourselves, have lived free from generation to generation. Our king was killed, he made no bond, and his

NOTÉS BOTZARES, A SOULIOTE CHIEF.

citadel has carried on a never-ending battle against the Turks—and there are two fortresses which have never surrendered."

"Where is this royal garrison—which are your fortresses ? "

"Our royal garrison is with the bands called Klephts; the fortresses are Mani, Souli, and the hills."

He said no more.

The world said we were fools, because if we had not been fools we should not have made the rising until we had first got together our ammunition, our cavalry, our explosives, our powder magazines, and our stores ; we would have reckoned up our own powers as against the Turkish power. Now when we have conquered, when we have successfully terminated our struggles, we are praised and we are applauded ; if we had not succeeded we should have been reviled and cursed. We are like a small heavily-laden boat which, lying in a harbour where fifty or sixty large ships are waiting with their cargoes, cuts herself adrift, spreads her sails, and goes on her voyage in the face of a strong gale blowing; she goes on her errand, and she sells her merchandise, makes a good profit, and comes back to port safe and sound. Then all the ship's captains who were left behind, cry out aloud, saying, " Here is a true man; here is a pallikar; and a wise one, unlike us, who are sitting here idling and are full of fear ! " And those captains are upbraided as being worthless ; but if the little boat had not been successful, then they would have said, " What an idiot to go out with such a burthen, in such a wind to be lost ! "

The commandership of a Greek army was of necessity a perfect martyrdom, because he was made to be both leader, judge, and adviser, and therefore they had to run to him to and fro each day ; he had to hold his camp together by cajolery and promising tales ; to him was left the procuring of supplies and ammunition, and no one listened until the leader called. In Europe, on the contrary, the commander-in-chief gave his orders to his generals, the generals to the colonels, and the colonels to the majors, and so throughout. The general formed his plan of campaign, and it was carried out. If Wellington had given me an army of forty thousand, I could have governed it ; but if five hundred Greeks had been given to him to lead, he could not have governed them for an hour. Every Greek had his caprices and his hobby, and to get any service out of them, one had to be menaced and another to be cajoled, according to the nature of the man.

CHAPTER XI.

IN November, 1826, when I went down to Hermione for the Assembly, I left Gennaios behind, in order that he should endeavour to impéde the devastation which Ibrahim was carrying on. The captains and chief men of the district of Karytaina at that time made a proposition to him: "If you will build up the fort of Karytaina, Gennaios, Karytaina could be guarded on all sides as well as Phanari and all the middle districts." Gennaios was himself persuaded of this, but he answered, "I must send and ask my father's opinion, and then we will see about it." So he despatched a foot-messenger to me with the proposal about a fort, and I gave him permission to build it. As soon as he received my permission he set about it earnestly, and paid for lime, and got four lime-kilns made, and he also sent about to find out masons, so that the fort might be immediately commenced. When they began to build they came across four or five hollow places, which they filled with powder and exploded, and on account of this it was said that cannon had been discovered, and so the report spread about. He never allowed any one to go over his fort, because there was in every place a traitor to be found, and therefore Ibrahim, having been told that cannon had been found, and that they were fired off daily, made no attempt to go thither lest, indeed, it might so happen that cannons were really there. Gennaios had the gates built first and then the cisterns, when he commenced carrying up the fort as far as it was possible at the time. He at once had the furnaces set to work and baked biscuits, which he sent to Demitsana in exchange for three or four loads of powder. When he happened to have no lead, he sent into Zante and bought five or six hundredweight. He also purchased two cannons, which were transported to the fort, and then got carpenters to make gun carriages also, which were placed on the fort.

The fort being thus strengthened, the districts of Phanari and Karytaina carried their property thither, and deposited it in the fort for safety. They worked at it throughout the whole winter until April came. They erected three caserns, and finished the interior, and at this time, at the battle of Lala, he had the two cannons brought from Cephalonia. They were fixed up in one place. They were brought over and put into the fort at considerable expense. He placed two hundred soldiers in it when it was completed. It was near two rivers, and whilst they were erecting it they found some helmets that belonged to the Crusaders.

Niketas had a sentinel on a hill near Tripolitsa, who, when the Turks went forth on their pillaging expeditions, as they did in every direction of Messenia—making slaves all round—gave a signal that the Turks were out, and as soon as this was known, the fort also made a signal, when the surrounding families came to the fort, bringing in their animals. When the signal on the hill was seen the two cannons were fired off, and thus all knew that the Turks were out again ravaging Messenia, and thus the people near the fort were protected. He had sentinels also at Derveni of Leontari. The people became more emboldened in consequence of this, and the husbandmen began to till their fields again, as they were protected in this manner from any sudden surprise by the enemy. Before this they were dying of hunger, for if agriculturists owned any oxen they did not dare to take them out to make use of them; but now they could do so, being under the protection of the fort. The sentinels were always at work night and day attending to the lights, so that throughout these districts there was no more ravaging going on, and the people were much inspirited, and worked to help the masons until April. Gennaios was still carrying on this work when, in April, he received the order to go to Athens.

On the part of the Assembly of Troizen, we sent Karaiskakês and Hadji Michaelês, with a hundred and twenty horses, and twenty-five thousand grosia and cavalry.

I was freed from the Assembly in the month of May, and went to Argos. The camp at Athens was broken up, and the Peloponnesian soldiers returned. As soon as I reached Argos I sent orders to all the districts in which there were no Turks. I did not send to Messenia because there were three forts there, and the Messenian armies were therefore always impeded by the enemy. I left the troops of the surrounding country at Tripolitsa, for fear of Ibrahim. I despatched, however, my commands to Mistra, where there was no apprehension concerning Ibrahim, as he was at Patras at this time; and I also transmitted my orders both to Agio-Petro and Monemvasia, and they replied to them by asking me to build a camp for them, and then I might command them, and they would come. I marched over to Corinth. Grivas and all the rest of the Roumeliotes were at the fort of Nauplia, and did not move at my summons, and Nikolas Tsavellas was at Corinth; they were holding the forts there, namely, at Corinth, and did not leave them; they seemed to look upon those forts as an inheritance. I therefore found myself on the hill of Corinth (Agio-Georgio) with two hundred and fifty soldiers only; but Zaimês had a force also, and he, with Panagiotês Notaras, looked forward to fight with those malcontents who were in Corinth.

"Leave them alone," I said; "we must gather soldiers together for the sole purpose of aiding the fatherland."

At this very time Ibrahim sallied out of Patras and summoned Nevekos to submit, and Nevekos made his submission, when Ibrahim despatched him to prevail upon others to submit also, when two parts of the Kalavrytians submitted, together with the whole of Patras and some parts of Vostitsa. He then came to Kalavryta, two hours beyond the capital Kalavryta, with the object of the whole of that part making its submission also.

Ibrahim now endeavoured to conciliate the people. A Turk was not permitted to cut or to burn the standing corn, and in consequence of this many were gained over, and he gave papers of submission to numbers of them. The whole of the captains submitted, and even the captains belonging to the chiefs also gave in their submission. The Petimezaioi and others formed themselves into a force, the submitted people went to Megaspêlaion, and others to the hills, among which they were shut up. Following upon this, and being incapable of doing anything, Basil Petimeza was one night, through some treachery, surprised, and barely escaped with his life. He immediately sent out his brother Nikolaki, who came to me where I then was in the villages of Kortho. "Hasten to Spêlaion," he cried, "for Spêlaion is betrayed, and the whole district will be lost." I resolved to despatch my adjutant, Photakos, directly, and also my standard-bearer, Karachalio, and gave them to Nikolaki Petimeza to go with him to Megaspêlaion. I got together the Corinthian forces, and they went to the monastery.

In the space of three days I amassed fifteen hundred men and despatched them under Panagiotês and Georgaki Cheliotês and their captains to the villages of Vostitsa, and I myself went to Agio-Georgio, in Phonia, and although we did not get very near them, they were able to fall upon the submitted soldiery and the Turks, and wholly ravaged Diakophto, taking many captives and also a good portion of spoils. On their return they attacked the monastery, and killed there about sixty Turks, after which they went back to the camp at Kalavryta. Ibrahim took fifty of his cavalry and came opposite the monastery to reconnoitre, but after making a good survey of the position through his glass, he saw that he could not possibly lay siege to it, as the place was a most difficult one, and therefore retired.

It was through our prisoners that we suffered in the Peloponnesus. They were Turkish prisoners, who betrayed the Petimezaioi, at Chelmos.

Whilst I was at Agio-Georgio I wrote letters to Gennaios and Koliopoulos, who were together, and ordered them into Livartzi, a submitted district of Kalavryta. My mandate was, "*Fire and sword to those who have submitted!*" And so they passed over to Livartzi.

Ibrahim now sent out spies to see where I was, and what was the amount of the force that I had with me, and he gave three hundred pieces of money to a Greek to learn where I was, so that he might fall down upon me suddenly. I seized the spy, however, and sent word to the public authorities, and hung him at Kalavryta, two miles outside the town; I had him hung up with a paper upon him which detailed his crime—"*a traitor to his nation.*" I sent two other men whom we had seized to the monastery of Megaspêlaion, because they were not clearly traitors, and then I went to Spêlaion myself.

Ibrahim heard that there was an army of five thousand men gone into Livartzi, and that I was in another part with two thousand. Spêlaion is about two hours distant from Kalavryta. Gennaios and Koliopoulos with the other body of men were also about four hours off. Upon Ibrahim learning that the Karytainan armies had arrived, he marched with his forces towards Tripolitsa and Karytaina, and sent for Deli Achmet Pasha, who was to march into Patras with the submitted soldiers, and they, going along the road, came across the man whom we had hung up, and he went up to him and read the paper fastened to his breast and on his shoulders, and he plucked his beard, and terrified the whole of Karytaina, and taking a force of eight thousand cavalry and infantry—a picked force— went forth for the purpose of chastising Akovo and Langadia, and with an intention of burning the villages of Demitsana, Zygovisti, and Stemnitsa, whence, it was said, the Greeks, who were with Gennaios, had gone. Gennaios and Koliopoulos, when they heard that Deli Achmet Pasha had gone forth and would pass over to Patras, and that Ibrahim was on his way to Tripolitsa, turned back, and coming across the advance guard of Ibrahim, had a skirmish and killed about fifteen.

Whilst Ibrahim was marching to Tripolitsa, his force, which had been sent to the villages, Akovo and Langadia, arrived at those places. Akovo and Langadia had already been burnt, but what was left of them they burnt over again, and the Turkish army stationed itself on the plain of Demitsana. Gennaios and Koliopoulos, not knowing whither it had marched, Koliopoulos returned and went to Heliodora, and Gennaios marched by night, and with only five hundred men took possession of Demitsana and built

up breastworks to fight from, whilst the rest of the Karytainan forces dispersed to the hills where their families were,
for the purpose of protecting those families.¯ The Turks
arrived as they were passing over to go to their families, and
passed the night on the plain of Demitsana, when the
soldiers below fell upon them for plunder, and began to
shoot them, and the soldiers on the hills sent for a reinforcement either from Gennaios or Koliopoulos. Gennaios
not knowing that the Greeks were all round the Turks, and
seeing the Turks on the plain, resolved to attack them at
night with his little body of five hundred soldiers, and
moving forward he arrived at the plain during the night,
and when he got near the Turkish army he fired a volley
into them. When the other Greeks heard this volley they
were at once convinced that Gennaios must be there, so
that every Greek fired off his gun whenever he found himself opposite the Turks. When the Turks saw that they
were thus encircled they collected on the plain and passed
the night in camp, sending out some cavalry as scouts.
The number of the Turks was eight thousand. Gennaios
marched forward and seized upon the road which led to
Demitsana, so that when the morning broke the Turks
would see that there was no way for them to depart, as if
they tried to go into the country they would come up to the
breastworks which he had built up to fight from.

When the Turks heard the volleys of the Greeks they
were convinced that they proceeded from the armies led by
Gennaios and Koliopoulos. They were therefore much
alarmed, and turned back towards Tripolitsa. Gennaios
and his band advanced nearer to them, and the Turks
marched to the vale of Alonistaina in order to pass at
that place. The Alonistainans came in front of the vale
and drove them back into another road, when the Turks
endeavoured to cross near to Akrodoremma, and then

the Greeks, who were approaching in that quarter, forced them to go in like manner to Trikorpha. In that pursuit many Turks were killed, and many horses were taken before the Turks got back to Tripolitsa.

As Ibrahim had his whole force in Tripolitsa, he marched out to go to the forts of Messenia, and Gennaios with four thousand Karytainans went straightway into Messenia in order that they should not be able, as they passed along, to make all the people slaves. Phourtzalokamara is about two miles distant from Kalamata, and it was there that Gennaios took up his station. When I learnt that Ibrahim had sallied out from Tripolitsa, I marched into the villages of Kalavryta, which had submitted, and sent Basil Petimeza with fifteen hundred men to Agio-Vlasi, one of the submitted villages, to take from the inhabitants all their papers of submission and send them back to those who had given them, and to tell them that I would give them in exchange the papers of submission of the nation. Five hundred Argives came at the same time, and I sent them also to Basil Petimeza. Tsokrês was at their head, and Nezon, his wife's brother. Agio-Vlasi was seized, and the papers of submission were sent to me.

There were with me at Spêlaion—Londos, all the Petimezaioi, Lechoritês, Soter Theocharopoulos, and Benizelos Rouphos. The vacated army of Gianni Notaras was with Londos. I said to them, "Let us go to the submitted villages, and march on to Patras?" They answered, "Go forward, to-morrow we will follow," and the four hundred remained at the monastery. I took my own men, and Kolphinos Petimeza his four hundred also, and we went together to a village called Petzakos. I sent word to the submitted villages that if they would deliver up the papers of submission which they had from the Turks I would give them papers from the nation. Before I moved forward to those submitted villages, and whilst still at Agio-Georgio I wrote a letter to the Government asking them " to send me both soldiers and ammunition, because the country is in great danger from submission ; and if you know any invention by which an army can be fed upon air, please forward it. If you should also know of any other invention for making gunpowder out of earth, and lead out of stones, send this machine also, and we will use it, for the men about here have not yet discovered such. I pray you send me all these."

I entrusted this letter to a monk, and exhorted him to speak to the Government about the danger which was thus threatening the country. The monk went to Nauplia and told them to assemble the Parliament, as he was charged to read aloud to them that of which he was the bearer, and also he had to tell them somewhat from my part. They therefore assembled the members, and he read them the letter, and also delivered to them by word of mouth all that he was commissioned to say. One of the members said, " What can he want with ammunition when he has only fifty men ? " The monk assured them that I had four thousand, but they did not believe it. The Parliament sent Anagnostês Zapheiropoulos from Zygovisti, and Anagnostês Papagiannakopoulos to see the condition of the armies and districts. They came to Agio-Georgio. I said, " Our country is endangered." They on their side told me all which they had been charged to say to me, which was— that I should go to Argos, in order that we might all unite our arms there, and then the whole force could move on together. If I had listened to them and gone to Argos the country would have been lost, because in that case the greater part of the districts would have submitted directly they heard that Kolokotronês had gone to Argos.

" Go back to them," I said, " and tell them by word of

mouth that I will do according to their plan, that they also must send forth as many as bear arms, believe in Christ, and love their country. Cretans, or whatever kind of soldiers they may be, let them come, and we will meet this great danger, and I—I will become of the smallest account amongst them all ; let them but send me ammunition, and as for provisions, we will do what we can ; with water and the bodies of sheep we may be able to manage."

They went back, but they sent me no reply ; neither ammunition, nor provisions, nor paper whereon to write despatches, and not even did they send one consolatory epistle to the districts, and thus they abandoned both me and the Peloponnesus together. When I saw how great was their indifference I moved on to Megaspêlaion and exerted myself as I have related before.

Deli Achmet Pasha, going out from Patras with the submitted Corinthian soldiers, and part of the submitted Vostitsanoi, pressed on to Agia-Paraskevy and killed about a hundred Greeks—most of them were from Corinth, under Cheliotês ; two good captains were also killed. The Pasha returned afterwards to Patras. When I arrived at Petzakos the men who had submitted went to the Pasha and told him that Kolokotronês and Basil Petimeza had only a few soldiers with them, and that they could go and easily destroy us. Deli Achmet fell in with this opinion and marched with six thousand submitted Greeks, Neketos accompanying him with two thousand of the submitted Greeks. He came to Lapatês, which was three hours from where Petimeza was stationed, and one hour distant from myself. I had written to Megaspêlaion for Londos, Theocharopoulos, Nickolas Petimeza, and Lechoritês to come, and they sent word to-day or to-morrow, but they had not yet arrived. A captain of the submitted armies from the village in which I was, that is to say, from Petzakos, went o the Turks and said, "Kolokotronês is at Petzakos with only four hundred men, and we can easily go and attack him." When the Pasha heard these words of the captains, he immediately, that same evening, summoned all the captains to receive his counsel about going against me. When all the captains were gathered there the Pasha said, "Information has been brought to me that Kolokotronês is down at Petzakos with only four hundred men, and we will go and attack him." There was one captain present, one of those who had submitted, whose name was Stamatês Botiotês, who, hearing this, called out, " We will not go to Petzakos, we have a king, and we will not go and destroy him." He addressed these words to the Pasha; and the Pasha laughed, saying, "Whom do you wish, then, that we should go against and destroy?" The same captain answered " Why, we will go against Petimeza, who is at Agio-Vlasi with two thousand men." So his resolution was taken, and it was agreed to go forth by night and attack Basil Petimeza.

Two brothers deserted from the submitted ranks and came to us, saying, "They are coming upon you." I did not repeat this to the Greeks, but I left my adjutant and Oikonomopoulos from Stemnitsa, and Karachalio, my standard-bearer. I left them in the village, saying to them previously, "I shall go out to sleep—for the village was a strong position to fight from, according to my judgment. If I am outside, I thought, I can go to them to help in case of need; but if I am within, and with them, they cannot bring any aid to me. I went therefore to the heights of the village, to a rock, and I stationed a watch with ten men, who were to remain there the whole of the night.

At daybreak the Turks advanced upon Basil Petimeza and the Argives at Agio-Vlasi, and there was some little skirmishing, when our people departed. There was no blood shed either upon one side or the other. The Argives went away to Argos. Basil Petimeza did not see them, neither did I. So Basil remained in his post at Agio-Vlasi, and the Turks with the whole of the submitted soldiers returned to Patras.

The next day Londos, Nikolaki * Petimeza, Theocharopoulos, Rouphos, and Lechoritês, with the four hundred men who were in the monastery, came to me, and then I arranged to leave Petzakos, because I did not know who had submitted, and who had not, therefore I determined to go to Kerpeni, which was a much stronger place for defence. Londos and the other leaders said, " Old chief, let us stop here all together." I answered, " You are untrustworthy, the whole of you, and I know not what to do ; I shall go away and make an army for myself, and you can stay instead. When I arrived at Kerpeni I sent my adjutant, Photakos, to seek out Gennaios and Koliopoulos, and to bid them join me. Gennaios at that time was at Phretzali, and Koliopoulos gathered the soldiers together, and within the space of five days came to me with five thousand men.

When Londos and his company heard that my own soldiers had arrived they went over to Argos, not because I had got my own army again, but because they learnt that Deli Achmet Pasha had gone to gather in the currants, and having lost all hope of being able to get the currants for themselves (for which purpose they had been waiting), they departed. I spread my soldiers all over the submitted villages, and made the following proclamation : " Every village that does not return shall have all its houses burnt, its vineyards shall also be burnt, and I will sweep it from the face of the earth ; but if any of them shall

---

* The termination *aki* is an addition frequently bestowed on names out of familiarity or affection.

turn back to us, the nation will forgive it everything," and many other threats, as, for instance, " If you imagine that Ibrahim will give you five hundred men to guard your villages, you are deceiving yourselves, because he has no such force, and if you flee from one part to another for safety, we shall come down upon you nevertheless, and shall burn and slay you all." When I distributed these proclamations they were shown to Ibrahim, and he said, "I will have a battle with this Kolokotronês." The submitted villages, however, did turn back, and we received from them their papers of submission, and gave them in exchange those of the nation. So they returned and went back to their villages in order to save their houses from being burnt.

I marched forward with eight thousand men, and we took our way to Vostitsa, and upon reaching Vostitsa, opposite the heights, we placed men there, so that we might ascertain if the enemy were coming, in order to fight. But the Turks had no intention of fighting at that time, but had gone there solely to harvest the grapes, and had stationed cavalry at the extremities of the plain so that we could not fall upon them. We stopped there two days, and I challenged them to combat, but they had no mind for a battle. Seeing that it was useless to remain, and having no provisions to allow of our staying there, I took Gennaios and half of the army with me and went to Agio-Vlasi, and left Koliopoulos, Meletopoulos, and the Petimezaioi to look after Patras and the villages of Vostitsa.

When I arrived at Agio-Vlasi I received a letter from the fort of Karytaina, which read thus: " Messenia is preparing to give in her submission " (I had left Niketas in Messenia with an army, but his soldiers, out of sheer hunger, had left him), "only come to us as quickly as possible, that we may not have to suffer this." I left

Gennaios thereupon, and announced to Koliopoulos that they must stop and watch the movements of Deli Achmet Pasha, and the submissions that were being carried on in Gastouni and Pyrgos, and that I should go forward with two hundred of my body-guard. The Pasha collected his troops at this time, and, joining to them the submitted bodies, left Patras to go against Koliopoulos in Kaukaria, a strong place. Koliopoulos was there alone, for he did not send any information to Gennaios, who was six miles farther off, because he had no idea that the Turks had any intention of going to attack him, and thus they fell upon him unexpectedly; but he fought a good fight. A hundred and fifty Turks were killed, but among our men no harm was done. Chrestos Photomaras, Meletopoulos, Nikolas Petimeza, and others were among them to the number of two thousand: the Turks were eight thousand. So Deli Achmet Pasha returned in the direction of Patras and Gastouni, and going down to Divrês, that and the neighbouring villages immediately submitted.

As soon as Gennaios, who was at Livartzi, heard about the Turks and the submissions, he encamped at Paralongous, about an hour distant from the Turkish camp; Chrysanthos Sisinopoulos and Thanasês Koumaniotês were with him. When the Turks saw Gennaios they broke up their camp and went to Lala. Gennaios sent different bodies against them, who attacked and harassed the Turkish rear, which was also attacked by a cohort at the bridge of Nemouda. In this skirmish forty-five Turks were killed and five captured, three Greeks also were slain. The Pasha had made a forced march from Gastouni and Patras thither, and Gennaios turned with his arms to Divrês for the purpose of chastising those who had submitted, as also to get them to go back to the Greek side, and in consequence of this they and all the villages round about came back to the nation. Pyrgos had submitted, and Gennaios wrote two letters to them, but they not only did not heed him, but persuaded the districts of Phanari to submit also. Wherefore Gennaios was forced to go and take severe measures with them. and he burnt some houses by way of giving them an example, and also that others might profit by it. I marched forward, as I said before, and crossing over the districts of Kalavryta, Karytaina, and Leontari, arrived in Messenia, and went to the village Zavazika, where Niketas was, two miles from Kalamata. I accumu-lated many soldiers on my road, and we mustered some thousands of Arcadians and one thousand Androusani in three days; I had no provisions for them, but sent to the villages for supplies, and in this way received two hundred dishes of corn and a thousand animals for the use of the army. The submitted people of Patras, Kalavryta, and a part of Phanari wrote to Ibrahim. Ibrahim took his measures, and sent his lieutenant with a force of some thousands with weapons and axes into Messenia, with orders to go with fire and with hatchets through all the district. What they did not destroy by fire they were to cut down with their hatchets. Olives, fig-trees, and mulberry-trees were all destroyed. Five thousand of the cavalry were stationed upon the heights, so that the Greeks should not go down to the plain, and do battle. " With thy life," Ibrahim had said to Kehayas, " thou shalt pay for it, with thy life if any one be slain, because I send you thither not to fight, but to burn and destroy." He himself went with the remaining part of his army to Zacharo, and ordered the submitted districts to assemble for the pur-pose of going out to destroy Karytaina. He gave his lieutenant injunctions first to send to the Messenians, calling upon them to submit, and if they did not submit, to begin his work directly. He gave this order in writing to two captured Gastounian slaves, who brought it to the place where I was stationed.

Upon reading this decree, which was in itself so terrible, I answered him, not on the part of myself, but on the part of the people of Messenia, " This action with which you would terrify us, threatening to cut down and burn up our fruit-bearing trees, is not warfare; the senseless trees cannot oppose themselves to any one; men alone who have soldiers and slaves can be arrayed in opposition to each other; and this is legitimate warfare—with men, not with trees; but we will not submit—no, not if you cut down every branch, not if you burn all our trees and houses, nor leave one stone upon another! What, and if you do cut down and burn up all our trees, you cannot dig up and carry off the earth which nourished them; that same earth will still remain ours, and will bear them again. If only one Greek shall be left, we will still go on fighting, and never hope that you will make our earth your own—dismiss that from your mind."

As soon as Kehayas received this answer he began his work in earnest with fire and axe. We endeavoured to force his army into a battle, but they were not to be incited to battle, but only to execute his work. Some Greeks during the night seized upon four Bulgarians, and I had them under examination, when they told me that their orders were, not to have a battle, but only to look that this work of destruction was carried out. I then went over to Armyro and summoned the captains and other Maniotes, bidding them find a boat so that we might send Ibrahim's letter to the admirals, and also the answer of the people to him, to be opened outside Messenia or wherever they were met with. Captain Panagiotês Gianneas had a schooner, and we gave fifteen dollars and the letters, and also another letter of my own, in which I said, "Behold what the enemy of the Greeks has done!" And she went, and was to return to us when she had found them.

I then marched out, and I and Mourtzinos joined together, when I said, "What are you doing, brothers? shall we not occupy Armyro with the thousand of Peloponnesian soldiers which I have?" Upon this they assembled again, both Anastasês Mavromichaelês and other captains of Mani, and all went to Armyro. On the very same day I received a note from Basil Alonistiotês, who was at Karytaina, saying, "Phanari is beginning to submit; only take some measures." I immediately summoned Mourtzinos and the captains, and Niketas also, and I took two hundred men myself, to go over to Karytaina and Leontari to collect an army to take to Phanari, for I had an idea that Ibrahim was at Zacharo collecting soldiers also. And so in twenty-four hours I found myself at Karytaina, and sent forward soldiers to Phanari.

The schooner succeeded in meeting with the French squadron, and upon making a signal was reconnoitred by the three admirals, who read the letters, but did not believe that it could possibly be true that Ibrahim had done the things alleged, because they had sent to him strict orders that he was to cease all warfare; but that dog did not heed them, and in this way he showed the enmity and ill-feeling which he bore towards the Greeks. They then called for the late ever-to-be-remembered Hamilton, and a French and a Russian frigate set sail for Armyro in order that they might be able to ascertain with their own eyes if that which had been asserted was really true. When they reached Armyro they disembarked, and found the captains who were still remaining there. From Armyro to Kalamata is only half an hour, and they saw truly that the districts had indeed been cut down and burnt, for the captains showed them all that Ibrahim had done.

The three commanders embarked in three cutters, and went as far as the river of Kalamata, which is about half an hour from Armyro, and summoned Kehayas to put an end to his work, " with fire and hatchet." And his answer was, " My orders from his highness are to cut down and burn."

" The three Powers have sent him a letter, telling him that he must make an armistice, and now he has done that which is contrary to all the laws of war, as well as contrary to humanity."

" I know nothing about that; I receive my orders from one who is above me. Let the admirals and Ibrahim do what they choose."

The commanders upon this departed, and made sail, and went to the admirals, and acquainted them with all they had seen, and also what they had heard from Ibrahim's lieutenant, Kehayas.

Following upon this, the most gallant Codrington and the gallant Russian and French admirals went to Neo-Kastro,* and burnt his (Ibrahim's) fleet, so that if, when they arrived at Navarino, there had been two thousand Greeks, they would have annihilated the fifteen thousand Turks, who were in this place, and were reduced to despair at the burning of the fleet. The burning of the country thereupon ceased, and he (the lieutenant) went to Neo-Kastro, and Ibrahim, who was encamped there, intending to go to Karytaina, departed for Navarino. The rage of war now ceased. This was in the month of October.

About that time Karytaina gave nine hundred thousand grosia to the armies for their pay during the five months' service of June, July, August, September, and October. Nothing was sent to me, however; neither to the districts

* Neo-Kastro = Navarino.

of Messenia, Leontari, Patras, Kalavryta, was there anything disbursed. I had had for six months a body-guard of
two hundred men, who had gone everywhere with me. I
myself was ill through the amount of intriguing and cabal
going on, my feet swelled, and if I had not had Agamemnon with me, I should have died. That summer I had
used twenty reams of paper in letters and despatches.
The Government had gone to Ægina, and took no care
about anything, and there it remained, resting all its hopes
upon the mediation of Stratford Canning at Constantinople.
I had six secretaries, and I wrote day and night, but it was
of no avail.

During the time when they were submitting all round I
feared for my country, but only then—at no other time,
not even at the commencement of the struggle, nor in the
time of Dramalês, who came with a chosen army of thirty
thousand men—not even then; but I did fear when all
around me were giving in their submission. The whole of
Roumêli had submitted, Athens had fallen, the Roumeliote
army had dispersed, and only the Peloponnesus and the
two islands were left to us. Kioutahi had got his submission tickets with him; he worked hard to spread them,
and Ibrahim was about to send them to Constantinople in
time, so that if the minister of England, or of any other
Power, should have gone to the Sultan to mediate for
Greece, he should have been able to answer, " What
Greece? Greece has entirely submitted; here are her
papers of submission; there may be still a few evil-dis-
posed men standing out; but see, all the others have given
in; " and in that case the Powers would have had nothing
to answer, and we should have been ruined; because, if I
had not exerted myself against the submission which was
being carried on, the Peloponnesus would also have submitted, and then what could Hydra and Spetsai have done?

They would have been lost. I held everything up until the naval engagement at Navarino, after which the governor came, and the French expedition took place. In 1826 I began to put them all in heart when I built up houses and a fort outside the camp, for then every one said that " if Kolokotronês did not feel sure that we shall get our freedom, he would not build up houses, nor plant vineyards on the national soil ; " and when the people saw this, and saw the houses that were being built, their hopes revived, and that was the way I gave them courage.

CHAPTER XII.

THE governor (Kapodistria) arrived at Nauplia on the
6th of January, and stayed there one day (Theodore
Grivas being commandant), and then went to Ægina. The
Parliament and Executive received him as Kapodistria
only.

I delayed going to Ægina, so he wrote for me to go. I
had just gone from Karytaina to Argos, where Gennaios
and the other soldiers were, when the messenger who bore
the letter came to Gennaios. "Give it to me, and I will
deliver it myself," said Gennaios, and brought it into my
tent to me. After reading the letter I took two hundred
men, and went with the other captains to Epidaurus, and
thence to Ægina. When I got there and presented myself, he received me at once, because we were known to
each other since 1807—at that time when he came over
from Russia, and I had met him again at Corfu, when he
came to pay a visit to his father. Afterwards, when he
went to Pisa, and took a station there, many of our friends
in those years of the rising sent some letters to him con-
taining matter against me, and there were false reports (as
lately when our king came), averring that possibly I might
have done some good to the country, but that I had also
done more evil. His ear, therefore, had been filled with
lying representations, such as, that I had played the tyrant,

and the like evil sayings, so that he did not look upon me
with any favourable eye. I understood it, however, for I
said when he came, " Such a man as he is, experienced
and far-seeing, will know in one or two months whether I
have done good or evil to my country."

*　　　*　　　*　　　*　　　*

As soon as he began to reorganize the affairs of the
nation, he made twenty regiments out of the Roumeliote
soldiers, but not one from the Moreotes. When he returned from doing this I said to him, "Your Excellency,
why have you made no regiment out of the Peloponnesus ?
what will become now of the armies of the Peloponnesus ?
what will result to them but of all their labours ?" He
answered, " Theodoraki" (he always spoke to me thus), " you
do not understand foreign affairs, nor why I do this. You
must know that the three Powers have only taken the part
of the Peloponnesus and the islands thus far, and have no
intention of widening these limits. I am acting in this
manner, so that the Roumeliotes may find themselves possessed of armies in their own districts, but if I form the
Peloponnesians into Peloponnesian armies, my coadjutors
will say, " Why does the governor wish to arm the Peloponnesians when the Peloponnesus is free ? He is looking
forward to the strengthening of his own army, and does
not regard us who were the defenders of Greece, and so I
should be doing harm rather than good. But tell the
soldiers and the captains of the Peloponnesus that we shall
see what time will teach us, and bid them be patient."

He then gave me a letter to all the submitted parts of
Patras, saying that the Government would forgive them
everything, and that they must separate themselves from
the Turks.

In the month of May the French army, a force of fourteen thousand, under Maizon, arrived with all the materials

for war, either by sea or land. The governor (Kapodistria) went by sea to Petalidi, and when I, who was then in Karytaina, heard of it, I took a hundred men with me, and went to Messenia. Niketaras was also there.

The governor and General Maizon had some conversation together, in consequence of which General Maizon sent letters to Ibrahim, saying that he had arranged with the three Powers that he should go with his army into the Peloponnesus, "and so, as I have now arrived there, I write to you to bid you gather up the remnant of your vessels and soldiers, and march away from the Peloponnesus forthwith; and if you do not march away, I am come prepared to fight you both by land and by sea." And he threw the whole of his army into Petalidi, and began to build works, with fascines, and every other preparation needed for batteries. He also asked the governor to leave him a general and two or three guides, so that his armies might have reliable people who knew the place. Niketaras was therefore left. He then despatched a part of his forces to Koron, and another body was sent to Neo-Kastro. For myself I went to Karytaina.

All this time, as many Turks as were at Koron, some two or three thousand, seeing the strength of the French army, and the corresponding weakness of Ibrahim, deserted from Ibrahim, and marched forward for the purpose of seeking a conference with me, so that they might be able to secure a safe passage for themselves through the narrows to Roumêli. They came up to me on the frontiers of Arcadia. When Ibrahim heard that they were gone, and had learnt what their intentions were, he sent in pursuit, and there was fighting between them, in which about a hundred regular soldiers were killed.

As they desired to have a meeting in order to procure an agreement from me, which would allow them to pass, I accepted their proposals, and sent Gennaios and Koliopoulos into Derveni of Leontari to confer with them. They consented in the first place to set at liberty all their captives and slaves. They then assembled on the plain of Karytaina, whither our own soldiers also came. The Beys also gathered together, and I met them there. Thence they marched towards Tripolitsa, and encamped outside it. They wanted to get possession of Gennaios and Koliopoulos, and to hold them as hostages, and I warned them both not to go to their camp, but Gennaios actually went there one day quite unattended (yet I would rather he should have been killed than have been made a captive), and I rose up and went down to Tripolitsa, and there was some fighting in consequence. A Greek spy had been to them, and had said, "You who are purposing to go to Derveni, beware, for there are pitfalls dug there in order to slay you."

The Turks then turned back to the plain to go to Argos, and I took my army to Achladokabo. I always followed in the rear of their flanks. They then went down to the mills, and pitched their camp there.

The French general who was with the governor at Messenia, said to him concerning this, " Do not let the Peloponnésians kill the Turks, but send your brother there." The governor, in consequence of these words, sent his brother to the mills, and he drew up a writing by which the Turks were to be allowed to pass over unharmed. Augoustinos met me there, and gave me the order which the governor had written to procure boats, when I also sent Augoustinos to give them a safe conduct ; but I likewise said to him, " We have made a treaty with them to allow them to go, but they must first set free all their slaves."

"What you have said, see that it be done," he said.

Whereupon I summoned the Beys, and told them about

the agreement concerning the slaves, when they answered, "Send out your men; and as many children as they can find, let them take them."

I immediately sent out two captains, and they brought back eighty children who had been carried off by the Turks, and also a hundred and twenty women. There were three or four women who were dressed in male garments; these we took by force, and set them all at liberty. Then I gave them guides, following them close in the rear, Augoustinos also accompanying me, and we consented that they should pass by Corinth. They pitched their tents at Agio-Basil, when Augoustinos said to me:

"Let us go to the same place too."

"This is not thy duty," I answered; "they might use some treachery. If they fell upon us, they could do whatever they willed, as our force is only four hundred."

I then went to Agio-Georgio, which was about an hour's journey in a straight line, and on the day following the Turks went down into the country. There was a Greek garrison at the fort, and the country was held by Greeks. We went along with Augoustinos, and had a tent below the fort, because we always had some fears regarding them. We also sent to Ypsilanti, who was at Eleusis, to come with his regiment to Lontraki, that we might speak together about the permission that the governor had given for them to go to Derveni, and pass by that route. He came at my request, and I and Augoustinos met him at Lontraki. Then the French sent a corvette to see if we were going to let the Albanians cross (from Patras), and also to observe our own movements. Ypsilanti wished that they should leave their arms and horses behind them, and then cross over, because we could press on them in the Peloponnesus; but if we had wanted to kill them, we could have killed them in the Peloponnesus; but the order of the governor was that they should pass over, and I had given them hostages for their safe passage. The Turks seeing this disorder in the state of affairs, moved off with their hostages one morning at daybreak, and crossed from Vostitsa to Patras. We followed with our soldiers, in order to attack them because they transgressed the conditions by taking the hostages with them. If we had seized upon the Black Rocks no one could have passed.

Captain Chrestos Alexandropoulos from Stemnitsa told me what follows: "The Turks had encamped outside Patras; Deli Achmet thereupon sent a man with whom their leaders had a conference. 'Why,' he asked, 'are you leaving Ibrahim?' 'Because he does not give us our pay.' 'I will give you your pay if you will remain with me.' The Albanian Bey then went to persuade the Pasha to remain; but the Pasha had no wish to stay with him, and struck him with his sword, upon which he called out, 'Strike me not,' and drew his pistol and killed him." The name of the Bey who was killed was Mousam Bey. After six days the Albanians fled from Patras and went to Juannina, and the hostages also fled. Upon this, Augoustinos and myself went to Trikala, and afterwards returned to Nauplia, when Augoustinos persuaded the governor to raise the seat of government, and move to Nauplia.

I forgot to say that Ibrahim, when he heard in April, 1827, that the French army had come over, went with his whole army to Tripolitsa, and utterly destroyed it, pulling down all the walls to their very foundations, and after that was done he sowed the place with salt. On his return he seized twenty-six of our own people, the Alonistainans, all of whom were our relations.

Ibrahim once charged me with avoiding coming to an engagement with him. I answered him that if he would meet me with five hundred or with as many thousands, and I had equal forces, we would then fight; or if he liked to come and engage with me in single combat, I should be most willing to do so; but he did not answer this. If he had been desirous to meet me, I would have done so with all my heart, because I said to myself, if I am killed— well, then I am gone; but if he should be killed, my nation is saved.

CHAPTER XIII.

THE governor arrived at Nauplia on the 6th of
January, and afterwards went to Ægina, where the
opposition committee and the Parliament were sitting.
He went to church, where a thanksgiving service was held,
but he would not take the oaths until he had made some
remarks. "If you wish me to govern," he said, "the
Parliament must be dissolved, because I cannot be under
it. Our country has enemies as well as friends; but if
you do not wish this I will remain and will serve you as
far possible as a private individual. He told them that
there were foreign causes that rendered this measure
necessary. He dissolved the Parliament himself, and
every member that was discontented was to receive
more than his pay. He organized the State and sent
out governors to the districts; he instituted commissions
of inquiry and began a regular system, so that each
might know his especial duties—a military man what
military duties were required from him, and a politician
what was demanded of him as a politician. He systematized the Panhellenic union, and placed all the chiefs;
Kountouriotês he made member of the administration, and
Zaimês of the interior. Upon all these things comments
began to be made, and a reaction set in, although in
secret. Even before the governor arrived there were many

who were prepared to act against him, because they feared that an orderly Government was about to be systematized, when every one would not be able to do what he pleased.

* * * * *

[The governor had gone to Messenia.] Whilst he was in Messenia, Maizon (the French general) came to Nauplia, and I being in Karytaina, the governor sent me with a hundred men into Derveni of Leontari to escort them to Nauplia. As it was Passion Week, and I did not know on what day he would come, I sent a scout to Derveni, who, as soon as he knew that Maizon had arrived, was to send me information by signal, and then I would go to Leontari. The baggage belonging to the army of Maizon came to Derveni, when my men made inquiries concerning him, and were told that he had gone to Ithomê in Messenia in order to see the ancient remains, and that he would come on the morrow. He went to these antiquities with the utmost speed, and whilst they signalized to me that he had arrived, he had passed over to Tripolitsa and had fixed his tents at the Nauplian gates, and did not go into the country. I immediately, therefore, hastened forward and got near to where he was stationed, when, taking five or six men with me, I went to offer him my apologies, saying that I had been ordered by the governor to receive him at Derveni in Leontari, and that my scouts had deceived me, and so he had passed without my knowledge, again begging him to forgive me. "Oh," he said, "I did not come as a general, but as a private person ; there is no harm done."

* * * * *

At this time as many of those who were discontented with the governor because they saw that he would not embroil himself with the state of affairs, met together to concert a new assembly with the object of driving away the governor and reducing us to the same anarchy as before. The governor heard that an assembly and a constitution were talked about, and he consequently arranged that an assembly should take place at Argos; wherefore they immediately began to assemble. He sent for me, and I went down to Argos, and the governor also arrived there, and he stayed awhile in Tsokrês' house. We were one day together, and the inhabitants showed us a garden, wherein it was proposed that the assembly should be held. It was in the beginning of July, and they had been making a good many fires there, and so I gave it as my opinion that the assembly ought not to take place in the garden, but that we should build a theatre near Panagia for the purpose. "That means expense," he answered. "Let the expense be made," I replied; "they who come here from Europe to look at those stones can defray the expense: it will be an honour for us to clean up those stones and show them, in order to have our assembly." Upon this he sent for wood and other materials and erected a magnificent place for the meeting, and the entire body being assembled the work began, and it ratified all the actions of the governor at Troizen, of whatever kind they were, the basis of the assembly being a complete ratification of the opinions held by the governor.

At one of their sittings there was a question raised about the Order of the Redeemer, which I opposed; "the Cross is a sign of the enfranchisement of every one of us; but if we succeed in getting a king he can do as he likes regarding it."

So with the full consent and entire agreement of the Government we decided upon giving the governor the full powers bestowed on him by the three Powers, and that he was to render an account to the assembly of what he received and what he expended. The assembly expressed their satisfaction with what he had done, and also passed the same resolution on the festival of the Saviour. What could it do? It gave him full powers, for he was the only fit man.

KLEPHTS AGAIN.

Klephts at Gastouni, Patras, Vostitsa, Kalavryta, and parts about Karytaina and Phanari—in all the districts together about a hundred and twenty. These went about the roads; among them was a son of Kostantês, and one of Anagnostês Petimeza; some from Soudena, Konto-vounesios, the Perameresioi, the sons of Karalês, about fifteen Gastounians, the Charilaioi from Patras, and three or four from Phanari. On account of these men scandals got abroad that there was a great number of Klephts. They arose on account of the collection for the revenues and the manner of taxing the herds, &c. Thirty men were sent to Katakolo, where there was one Phrangoundês, a revenue officer, and seized him and his family and all that he possessed. The father of Lycurgus was also an abettor of Klephts at Pyrgos.

When the governor heard of these disorders in the Peloponnesus, he gave a very severe order for me to carry out—namely, that I was either to kill them, take them prisoners, or to make them submit, for there had been a report given out that they numbered from three to five hundred. I sent to the captains whom the governor had in his service, and assembled them at Tripolitsa. There were Captain Georgaki Driva from Tsakonia, Prastos, Captain Georgaki and another captain from Kranidi, Nikola Lambros, Stamatês Metsa from Kastri, Tsokrês and Nezo from Argos, Captain Anagnostês from Nauplia, who was in the service, Georgaki from Korthos, Cheliotês, and others, so that we mustered about a hundred officers altogether. I gave an order to Koliopoulos to bring a regiment—Tsavellas' regiment—to Kalavryta, at the head of which was Gianoulês, and I commanded Gennaios to collect the captains of Karytaina and others. These crossed over Langadia and Akovo and drove the Klephts from those parts; and Gennaios arranged that Thanos Koumaniotês from Patras should go to the frontiers there, whilst I moved forward with twenty irregular cavalry, which I took from the cavalry at hand.

When I got to Phanari I seized two Klephts and imprisoned them in the same district. I afterwards marched on to Pyrgos, because there were two, three, or four Klephts in Pyrgos on account of the father of Lycurgus being there. When he heard that I had gone to Pyrgos he tried to escape to Nauplia, but I sent four of the cavalry, who seized him at Tripolitsa and brought him back to Pyrgos. I had learnt that he abetted the Klephts before he went to Katakolo. When the Klephts heard that myself, with Koliopoulos and Gennaios, had arrived, they dispersed. I marched into Gastouni, drove the men into a corner there, and imprisoned six of them. The people whose oxen and horses had been stolen made their complaints to me, and I, who knew the Klephts, became also their judge—for this the position of affairs necessitated. Then each man took back what belonged to him. We then went by night to Patras, and on the frontiers of Patras we met with some merchants of Pyrgos, who had been despoiled, and the Klephts who had robbed them were from Soubara.

An order then came from the Government to the general of the commune concerning the despoiled frontiers, demanding that he should call upon the surrounding villages to deliver up the Klephts. I at once searched all those villages where the Pyrgiot merchants had been robbed to find either the Klephts, or the ten thousand grosia which had been given out by the receiver who had bought the merchandise at Patras. The robbers came quite near to me at Patras, for in those days when I was sojourning there one Charmêlas, who was among the Klephts, came into Patras openly, and as there were many there who had been despoiled, and who recognized him, they gave me information, and I sent and had Charmêlas apprehended, when he bore witness against others who were also in the same place. When the Klephts heard that Koliopoulos and Gennaios were on the heights they came down to the frontiers of Patras, and I sent some soldiers and seized them also, and drove out others who went to Kalavryta. Koliopoulos with his regiment and with the half of the Petimezaioi pursued them and gave them an alternative when they surrendered. There were fifteen of the Petimezopoulai.

I despatched a messenger to Nauplia to obtain advice as to what I was to do with them—whether I should send them to Nauplia, or take sureties that they would not any more follow the same practices. I received an order that if the sureties were reliable they should be accepted, but as it would be an act of folly to forgive them all, as many as had no good sureties should be sent to Nauplia. There was one whom I had seized in Patras, when I went there by night with three hundred soldiers, and waited at the place till daybreak; for these Soubariotes had gone to the heights on account of the surrendering going on. I surrounded them during the night, and they were seized, and I took their spoil which had not been divided. The captain, who was not a native of the place, had gone to find a dealer to sell it. As soon as I went to Soumpara I resolved to hang one of them, and the captains were all incensed with me lest I should do so; therefore I took him

and another away with me. I then arranged in the
several districts about the sureties, and they gave me their
word and promise that they would be careful in the future.
The sureties were their neighbours.

Thus terminated this expedition. I made five hundred
decisions in the course of it, which, if they had been
carried to the lawyers, would have taken them three
hundred years to decide upon ; and so I put the districts in
order and quieted them. Of those two Soubariotes whom
I took, the one escaped from me with his irons on, and the
other, who was taken to Nauplia, was condemned to two
years' imprisonment ; he was the brother of the fugitive.
When I returned I presented myself to the Government ;
the manner in which I had pacified the people pleased the
governor, and then he disbanded the captains.

CHAPTER XIV.

THE votes of the Assembly at Argos formed the basis of a constitutional Government. When the Senate was chosen the governor organized a committee to prepare the constitution. Many members were displeased, especially the Hydriotes, because the governor had not immediately declared what he had spent upon the rising, and the Chiotes because he asked for their accounts. He was ill-spoken of by many literary men on account of the freedom of the press. They asked for a constitution, and yet the discontented united with the Hydriotes and others who were disaffected to overthrow the constitution before it was made.

The Klephts being overthrown, and the districts at peace, the Hydriotes endeavoured to make the islands revolt ; and they promised that they would return to Hydra, for the Hydriotes, who had become suspicious that the governor would send the Greek fleet against the Hydriotes, commissioned Miaoulês to go and destroy it. He accordingly burnt two ships and set fire to the harbour, but some servants of the Government succeeded in quenching it. Miaoulês by this deed darkened his reputation, for until then he had not mixed himself up with any of the divisions (of party), and his reputation was spotless. The vessels were the property of the nation, and not of Kapodistria. They succeeded in throwing down the masts and filling the sea with the pieces, and there they remained.

The governor was killed on the 27th of February, 1831, as he was going into church, by Konstantine and George Mavromichaelês. That family had poured out much of its blood in the cause of our independence, but it was a family which always had a propensity to commit assassinations. The late Elias killed his uncle, Theodore Koumoundouraki, whose wife was his father's own sister, and Georgaki and Katsako invited Nikolaki Pierakos one day to have some conversation with them, and whilst they were talking together they threw themselves on him and wounded him in the belly, and it was with difficulty that he was saved. He was, however, healed in six months.

Some other events, however, happened before the governor was killed. A committee was sent from Speliotopoulos, and others from Hydra to Mani when the constitution was announced, and the Hydriotes also sent three vessels to support the movements of the Maniotes. I was at Karytaina when I received a note from the Government bidding me send soldiers to Kalamata to guard the city from any spoliation of the Maniotes. I sent Gennaios with a regiment of Roumeliotes and many Peloponnesians. He went to Kalamata, and the Maniotes came and laid siege to Gennaios. The Roumeliote regiment of Alexakês (Kostas was not there) was perfidious and turned to the Maniotes. Rikordos came, and the committee itself burnt two national boats, and Rikordos also captured a Hydriote vessel.

I set out with four hundred cavalry, both regular and irregular, and got together about four thousand men from the districts. When the French learnt that I had been gathering soldiers in order to subject the Maniotes they sent a regiment without any orders from the Greek Government and occupied Kalamata, and proclaimed that they should not receive either one side or the other. I went to Nisi, and thither came a French regiment, and its commander told me that he had received a commission from his general to go to Nisi. I said, "If you have a commission from your general I also have a commission from my Government to occupy Nisi. If you like I will receive you there, and give you anything you may require."

"It is ordered that you are to leave, and that we are to enter into this place," he replied.

"I am also ordered by my Government to remain; if you wish, your general can write to the Government, and then if the governor orders me to do so I go away."

"We will go away," they answered. "If war is the consequence, the burthen of it will be thine."

"If I begin the war the burthen of it will be mine," I said, "but if you begin it the burthen is yours."

They thought to intimidate me, and that I should march away. We stopped three days outside Nisi, when it rained, and I told them to go in and occupy a warehouse and write to the Government, and if it sends me an order to leave I leave directly, even from my own house, if such be the order.

Seeing that we were not to be compelled they all marched into Kalamata.

When Gennaios had left Kalamata the Maniotes sacked it, and only spared the houses of some members of the Government. The Hydriotes saw that Rikordos had burnt two shops which belonged to the nation, and that the third, which was private property, he had left unhurt, and had taken possession of. The Maniotes robbed the committee sent from Hydra, and all the Hydriotes who had fled from the ships, whom the French took care of and transported back to Hydra. This commission when it came to Mani announced a constitution and freedom, and that Mani was not to pay more than one part in ten, and then it seized nine parts out of ten, and Kalamata was to be mulcted in five hundred thousand grosia—such was the constitution it announced, a constitution of rapine. I learnt that Rikordos had then gone to Armyro, and I moved thither with all my cavalry, both regular and irregular. Kalergês was at the head of the regular cavalry, and Hadji Chrestos commanded the irregulars. I met him and returned to Nisi, Rikordos went to Tsimova ; the mother of Mavromichaelês came to speak with him there, whence he moved to Nauplia.

When Miaoulês burnt the boats, all the nation murmured upon the injustice which he had committed in destroying the national vessels. Many men, seeing that they could effect nothing either by committees or revolts, resolved thereupon to kill the governor. At this epoch I received orders to go to Nauplia with my cavalry, both regular and irregular, and to take the infantry also, and leave it with Gennaios at Messenia, in order to keep watch over the movements of the Maniotes, lest they should go and ravage the place. Petros Mavromichaelês had fled secretly from Nauplia during the winter in order to cross over to Zante, so as to reach Mani. After a space he came down to Katakolo, and Anagnostopoulos, the primate there, had him seized, and sent him back to Nauplia, where he was put into a prison sufficiently commodious, in which he was supplied abundantly with necessaries. He seized Gianni Katzi and sent him to Palamedi, and Konstantine and George Mavromichaelês and Katsakos found themselves in a prison in the village of Nauplia. Katsakos escaped and got to Mani, and their constitutions were framed simultaneously with their designs for murdering the governor. Thousands of dollars and other things had turned his head, and if they had not been incited by very great promises it is certain that they would have been saved from this, and would never have attempted it.

As I said before, the governor was entering the door of the church on Sunday morning early, when these men greeted the governor. He had only two persons with him, a one-armed man and another. As he was going through the door Konstantine fired off a pistol at his head, whilst George plunged a knife into his belly, when the governor fell dead in the doorway. As soon as they had done this they attempted to fly, but Konstantine was wounded to the death by the one-armed man—a Cretan, and Georgaki fled to the house of Valianos. He saw that he could not remain there, and then took refuge in Rouan's house. The mayor of the city did not disturb himself much at this crisis, because he was himself mixed up in the affair. Zerar also, who regulated the regular Greek army, was in a position of cabal with his adjutant at Platonos, where the army then was, and he merely said, "It is nothing—nothing—keep quiet." Almetas, who was the governor of the fort, having with him a sworn and faithful army, shut the gates; he divided this force between the redoubts and the other posts of the city, and divers other citizens seized their arms; and thus it was that Nauplia, which was in danger of being lost, was saved.

The Senate and secretaries met immediately, and prepared to form a committee of three: namely, of myself, Augoustinos and Koletês. Augoustinos had sent a messenger directly to give me information of the death of the governor, and I went to Nauplia. I was at Tripolitsa at the time. The Senate communicated its proposition to Augoustinos, but he said that he could not accept the position until Kolokotronês had come and talked it over with them. I received the information from this messenger in the evening of the same Sunday, to the effect that the governor had been killed by the Mavromichaeli, and that one of them was also killed, and that the other had taken refuge in Rouan's house; I knew nothing more. I then remembered that the governor had ordered that if he should die suddenly, an assembly should immediately be held. I summoned Karorês, the prefect of Tripolitsa, and his secretaries directly, and wrote despatches to the armies everywhere, to march forward with Gennaios, stating that I should remain in Tripolitsa. For myself I did not at that time know whither to march, or what to do, for I was in ignorance of what had occurred at Nauplia, but I sent letters to the cavalry and infantry in all parts to oblige them to come at an earlier date. When morning dawned on the Monday, two foot regiments, one closely following the other, brought the news that the Senate had voted a committee of three, that the people were laying siege to Georgaki Mavromichaelês in the house of Rouan, asking Rouan to give him up, that he had delivered him up, and that he was taken to Palamedi, and asking mé to go as soon as it was possible.

I had kept it secret the evening before, and had not communicated the death of the governor to the city. At daybreak, when the citizens of Tripolitsa heard of it, they were all like dead men—paralyzed; they left their work, abandoned their employment, and wandered up and down the roads like madmen. I sent messengers bearing second letters to every one of the districts, bidding them all to remain quiet, and enjoining the prefects to keep at their posts and to continue their work. I gave them information that a committee had been chosen to govern the place, and that the necessary measures would be taken to ensure quiet and order in this critical moment. The prefects of the town of Tripolitsa came to me before I set off to go to Nauplia, and said to me, " What is to become of us ? We fear that we shall have to go through some trouble

here, because our city is open and accessible." I told them
to send out heralds to read out aloud what I had written
to the other districts. They besought me then to send
heralds, and as the citizens had assembled in the school,
would I go there and address a few words to them ? I
agreed to do so, and going to the school whither the
citizens were gathered, I spoke to them for one whole
hour, and told them as many things as it was proper to
tell them under the circumstances.

I put in Sisinopoulos with a hundred cavalry to ensure
the peace of the place, and left, and in six hours I arrived
at Nauplia. I had a hundred and fifty cavalry with me.
The people asked permission, and the gates were thrown
open for my reception, at the spot where our king afterwards disembarked, and the inhabitants conducted me
thence to my house. Some who met me were weeping,
others were in a great frenzy ; to all I said but one word—
"Peace." · When I got to my house I turned to them.
"Greeks," I cried, "go to your homes and fear not;
the power of God will take care of all things." Then I
went to comfort Augoustinos, who was sitting alone,
mourning, and when I went to him, we both consoled each
other, and at last he said, "It is to thee that I cling, both I
and the nation ; we will all do what thou judgest to be right."

I then returned home. I spoke with Almetas, the commandant of the fort, who was at the head of the regular
cavalry, and instructed him to send out heralds, and that
every one was to remain quite quiet in his own house, and
keep his arms (for all the citizens were armed), and "Go
on in the same way as thou hast borne thyself in the last
few days," I said, "for the conservation of peace. The
regulars stand to their oaths faithfully, and have prevented
fire and slaughter ; make your oaths now to the committee,
until we see how the affair will turn out."

The next day the Senate and secretaries met, and we took our oaths to abide by the powers over us. The people clamoured for the murderer Georgaki. "Either kill the murderer, and seize his accomplices, or we shall take our revenge ourselves, and we shall do what we can." We then resolved upon a court-martial, and condemned him to death, and the result was left to Providence. His two servants and Kaklamanos were thrown into prison, because they knew of the society which had pledged itself to kill the governor. We forced Zerar to make his declaration, although we did not wish to convict him as an accomplice. He gave his testimony, and he was thrown into prison also as well as the son of Kalamodartês, and others who would not give in their declaration. A number of fools came to me, calling out, "Kolokotronês, revenge us; kill all the murderers." I drove them out of my house, saying, "Go to your homes, this is no affair of yours."

At Hydra they had scarcely heard that the governor was slain, before Speliotopoulos, Papalexopoulos, and others rushed to Nauplia expecting to be able to do whatever they had a mind to, and so bring everything into disorder. We seized them at once, and put them in prison in the castle. All the districts and islands with the exception of Hydra sent addresses, lamenting the death of the governor, acknowledging the Executive Committee, and praising the action of the Senate. Those who were in Hydra sent a committee, but we did not receive it. If God had enlightened the Senate, and it had chosen another man in the place of Koletês, we should possibly have done better. We directed affairs for three months, and we announced by proclamation that there would be an assembly inviting the nation to attend at Argos, and it met there. Others came from Western Greece, and by the help of the devil

Grivas made it up with Tsokrês, with whom he was always quarrelling, and they all came together.

The whole nation having thus met together, I ran over in my mind that if we constituted ourselves another government the foreign courts would consider that we were all in agreement in regard to the murder of the governor; because by killing the governor, and changing the government in order to advance others, the world would plainly see that we must be all of one accord, or else that the governor was a tyrant. We had tried in past times the government of the many, so I said that Augoustinos had better be made the sole president, and that the Assembly should appoint a senate to consult with the president to govern until such time that the Powers would send us a king, and I made a proposition in the Assembly to that effect. Koletês, when he heard of this proposition of mine, was not well pleased that he was excepted, and began to agitate, so that both Eastern and Western Greece began deserting, and civil war was imminent. We had made an assembly, and the tents where the plenipotentiaries and captains met were thrown down by the body of the nation. They actually began to divide the tents among them, and Grivas, fool as he was, built breastworks at the tents, and thus was the whole society in parties. The Assembly took possession of the fort of Kitsos Tsavellas, because they had an idea that they would come upon the Assembly and destroy it, but they did not.

Day after day our troubles increased, but still we always carried on the Assembly. Augoustinos sent once or twice to Koletês. "It is not well," he said, "that the nation should be disunited; let there be harmony and peace, and let the Assembly finish its work."

*   *   *   *   *   *

At last we learnt that the King of Bavaria had consented

to send his son Otho to us—this was in June. I then made representations to the three Powers that Grivas should be prevented from interfering, for Grivas had gone to Tripolitsa, and was trying to stir up a civil war. They did not, however, attend to my request. I therefore sent a declaration to the Senate that we were bound to protect our honour, our lives, and our property, and that we must not recognize a tyrannical government.

This administration saw that it was powerless to control the present state of affairs, and asked the three resident ministers to allow the French army to occupy Nauplia and Patras. What a government to hand over national fortresses to foreigners to keep! General Genek, therefore, took a French force to Patras. Kitsos Tsavellas would not receive them, and said that he should deliver up the fort when the king came, adding, "If you want to take it by force, you will first have a battle," and hoisted a flag. When the French general saw the firmness and resolute bearing of Kitsos, he retired, and the French went to Nauplia and turned out the national regiment, and then shut them-·selves up there, and occupied it; if the French had not been invited Koletês must have fled to his own place, Juannina.

The soldiers who had gone against Kitsos Tsavellas formed themselves into an alliance with him, and said that they would prevent any civil war, and had sent messengers to the governor of Nauplia to reorganize matters. These messengers passed through Valtetsi where Gennaios was. As they were journeying along I met them at a certain village, and stopped to speak with them. I had made a proclamation, and Arcadians, Phanarites, Karytainans, and men from every district came to occupy different points to prevent those districts from being ravaged, and these also allied with them. They passed

over to Tripolitsa and conferred with Grivas and Hadji
Chrestos, thence they went to Nauplia, where they
gathered together in order to form a new Assembly, and
choose a committee to come to confer with us also. When
Grivas went to Tripolitsa very few of the inhabitants remained, the others were dispersed over the different districts
because they were frightened when they saw the evil which
he had wrought in Argos and Corinth. I sent a messenger
on foot to Tripolitsa to command them not to fight, and
Grivas seized him, and had him beheaded. I then went
from Karytaina to Valtetsi. I said to myself that they
had something in view.

Evangelês Kontogianni was at war at this time with the
inhabitants of Agio-Petro and a part of the district of Mistra,
and was in some danger. He had about three hundred men
with him, eighty of whom were Turks. Gennaios, when he
heard of his position, went and saved him, and took him
away with him to Tsiveri, where he left him, and then
proceeded to Roumèli. Niketas had defeated Katsakos
in Messenia, and was besieging him in Phourtzalokamara,
and if the French had not come up he would have taken
him prisoner, but he purged all this part and despatched
Apostolês Kolokotronês to Kantela in order to stop
Karataso from making any progress there. When I went
to Valtetsi I sent to Grivas to march on. The answer was,
"We will have a battle." I then directed Gennaios to go to
Mantzagra, when they came forth from Tripolitsa to besiege
him there, whilst at the same time our own people went from
different districts to go to Tripolitsa. Gennaios being at
Mantzagra, and Grivas being opposed to him, I gave the
signal for attack, and they went back fighting all the way
to Tripolitsa. I there received word that it was not his
intention to destroy that city, and I had a personal
interview with Hadji Chrestos, and as if I had allowed

the soldiers to enter with arms in their hands the houses would have been ravaged, however much order might have been imposed by sentries. Grivas at last fled, along with Hadji Chrestos and the calvary, and got to Argos. . I went into Tripolitsa, and in five days all the scattered inhabitants returned to their homes. A few days afterwards Tsavellas came. In all the skirmishes at Mantzagra there were only fifty killed. I brought all the army together, and after the Roumeliotes had left, I gave an address to them on discipline. During all this interval I had daily correspondence with Zaimês, Metaxa, Koliopoulos, and others.

An order came from Trikoupês that Gennaios should take part in the commission which he had arranged to go to Bavaria to invite the king over, and accompany him to Greece. I could not give my consent that Gennaios should go to a government where he was not known, and I resolved to go to Nauplia myself to see how this proposition was to be carried out. I went to Astros, and there I got some information from Rikordos, who sent me a cutter to bring me to his frigate. I had scarcely arrived there in the evening, when Koliopoulos came to ask my permission that he himself should go. He pressed me so earnestly, saying that the English vessel which was appointed to take out the commission was in haste to be gone. So what could I do more? I said, " Go in peace."

We reflected afterwards that we ought to have sent a commission from the whole nation to Bavaria, with an armed body accompanying it, but the circumstances did not permit this ; if they had told me exactly how it was, I should have ordered Gennaios to go, and he would have gone. I saluted the two captains, English and French, and they asked me why I had not sent my son to Bavaria ; when

I said, "I did not know enough of the Administrative Commission to accept its proposition." Zaimês and Metaxa came, and we all conversed together in the frigate. My view was that the senate should be left free to choose a government from the different parties after the protocol of London.

I returned to Astros and thence to Achladokabo, when Tsavellas and other Roumeliote officers came to us. We wrote with one accord to the different captains who were with the regiment to come and confer together at Tsiveri. They came accordingly, and we went thence to Argos. We resolved upon a commission of the army, in order to diminish the existing evils, and we wrote to Grivas to go out of the Morea. Grivas went to Koutsopodi upon this, and committed great abuses there. We thereupon decided upon forming a military commission, with a view of collecting the revenues, and dividing them in proportion and according to rule, so as to prevent the great abuses which had hitherto occurred. Zographos had written to them that discipline must be maintained, but who listened to him!

Whilst we were at Argos, the Senate wrote for me to go, and Zaimês and Metaxa with me, so that it might choose a third member, in order that the place might be arranged upon where the King was to disembark. I did not agree to this because there were so many officers there, and we were not in accord.

There were soldiers in every district, and they committed many excesses, and there was therefore a great necessity for a commission to collect as much revenue as the districts were entitled to give, and which were to be divided among the different officers for the purpose of getting supplies, and to establish a good state of discipline demanded by these anarchical circumstances. Each went to his post. Tsavellas and Notês Botsarês were stationed at Patras. Myself and Hadji Chrestos went to Tripolitsa, and the rest remained at Argos. A French regiment upon this resolved to occupy Argos, in order that the King should disembark at Mylos. They moved forward from Messenia, and came to Tripolitsa; I paid them every attention that could be offered, and then they went down to Argos. I don't know what they did there, but the men of Tsokrês and Griziôtês fell upon them; there was fighting, and more than two hundred innocent lives were sacrificed. The French seized upon my son as a hostage, lest the Greeks should go and kill them all. The Executive sent a commission to me to see if I had any information concerning how it came about. When they arrived they inquired into it themselves, and I wrote to the French general to say that I could have no view in harassing the French, for if I had been so inclined, I should not have let them pass through Tripolitsa, but should have awaited them at Derveni in Leontari, and that I had no cause to be the enemy of soldiers who were my comrades in arms, asking them why they had seized my son as a hostage. If I had thought that it was needful for my country's weal to attack them, I should have done so, and I would have let them have my son for a hostage, but they were quite convinced that I knew all about it, and the French thought that I was their enemy, although I had never given them any cause to think so. Koletês and the opposite party had filled their heads with the idea that I was against them, and that I was devoted to Russia.

Ten days later on, the fleet which carried our King came to the Gulf of Argos. Before this occurred, however, the French had seized upon the house of Tsamados, the President of the Senate, and treated him very badly. On account of this circumstance and other outrages which were committed on the senators, they resolved to go to Nauplia. I had gone down to Astros to speak about the position in which we were placed. Many of the senators had an idea of going to Astros also, in order to choose a fresh administration, consisting of three members, and to call upon Zaimês and Metaxa to make Rikordos a provisional president until the King's arrival. The Senate left Argos, and suddenly one morning at daybreak I saw them arrive at Astros. I did not accept their proposal, for I said matters had better stand as they were until the coming of the King, whereupon the Senate went to Spetsai, and remained there until the King's arrival.

When the Senate went to Astros they ordered Konstantinos to go to Nauplia and make a convention. By this convention they agreed to throw half their (military) strength into the several districts, a part of which would be composed of our men, and to regulate the accounts of their pay and other matters. Koletês was in accord with this, because he did not know anything outside the Senate, and there was the difficulty for him, that I did not wish to accept all the propositions that were useful to myself only, and abandon my senatorial comrades. These asked that there should be an administration formed, without waiting until the arrival of the King, because they said that the King might delay his coming for three or four months ; and again, that when the King did come, he would find these matters before them, and that he could then take only those representatives whom he found in their places, and by this way all the errors which had been already committed might be concealed, such as the burning of the fleet, the stirring up the districts to revolt, and the murder of the Governor; whilst, if there were a new administration formed by the Senate, which, until then, the resident ministers and the King of Bavaria had considered legitimate, this new administration would give full assurances regarding the deeds of those before them, and it would know what kind of men they were, and if Koletês and the secretaries should be left to consider themselves an administration, the King would find two governments, and might not listen to either, but follow his own way. No one in the so-called Government ever imagined that the King on his arrival might not take him to his heart, or that he would rather be indifferent to him, for each thought that the King would incline to him before those who had been faithful to the only regular government, which the nation had had since the commencement of the rising. Every one of the senators had such ideas, and in fact all those who were in any way connected with the Government.

Whilst I was in Tripolitsa I had been in correspondence with all the military both of West and Eastern Greece as well as with the Peloponnesus and the islands, especially with Spetsai and Hydra, urging them to prepare proper representatives to go and welcome our King on his arrival. My view was that all of them should assemble at Argos, and receive the King there, and that each of them should have an address prepared, in which should be stated all the evils which had arisen from having so many constitutional forms (so-called). Since the Greeks had attacked the French at Argos, I had changed my opinion, and I wished that he should land at Mylos. I did not know at what time the King would come, and upon this account I did not compel the representatives to assemble.

The King came to Nauplia.

CHAPTER XV.

IT is now time to speak of certain matters which have
reference to my unjust prosecution. Thersius and
other foreigners had made a tumult in Bavaria by saying
that I was the leader of a Russian party, and that I,
being the leader of a faction, did not wish for a king, and
other things of the like kind. They were foreigners who
said so, although Koliopoulos had fully shown to the King
and Queen all my sentiments in respect to a king, and
Koliopoulos had told them that he himself would remain
as a hostage in Bavaria until their son should arrive in
Greece. Notwithstanding this they had some suspicions.
On the English boat where the King and the Regency
embarked there might possibly have been something
brewing, on account of the impediment caused by Gennaios going away to Monaco. The King came first to
Corfu, when he heard that the Senate had left Nauplia,
and had left with bad intentions. He then reached Mani,
and there he heard that the French had been attacked by
the Greeks, and that those Greeks were the men belonging
to Kolokotronês, and that Kolokotronês, with a force of ten
or fifteen thousand, wanted to prevent the disembarkation
of the King: all these things excited in their minds a
feeling against me. I was written to from Nauplia, and
thus this was all made known to me. I was very sorry to

see that the intriguers had been so successful in perverting
the truth, and I left it to time alone to make clear to the
King all about men and affairs. I went to Rikordos on his
frigate, and said that I desired to present myself to the
King and the Regency, and I sent Koliopoulos to ask
permission for me to do so, when he brought me back for
answer that the King did not receive any one yet *specially*,
and that I should be informed concerning the place where
the King would disembark. Rikordos gave a dinner, and
we sat down with the General of the Bavarian armies,
with the uncle of the King, and with Smaltz, but I saw
that they were suspicious of me.

The day for the King's disembarkation arrived, and I,
with Koletês and Kountouriotês, went down down to
meet him. The King came: we all went to Nauplia. There
we were presented. Every day the committees met, but
things were changed, there were no addresses—nothing.
The King said that the Greeks had borne themselves with
bravery during the rising ; that he had left his parents and
his fatherland to go to a new country ; that he intended to
work for the welfare of Greece, and all the kind of things
which kings are accustomed to say, and he also made a
proclamation to that effect. After two or three days had
passed, I dismissed all my old officers, my soldiers, my
clerks, and my secretaries, and said to them, " Go in peace,
stay quietly in your own homes until the hour shall arrive
when the King may wish to know about certain men, and
some doings on our part, in order to reward each according to his deeds and his past services."

I then prepared an address, and offered the King the
fort of Karytaina, which I had built at my own expense.
I said in my address that I had built the fort to be useful
in any necessities of my country, but now, as I required it
no longer, I wished him to accept it. My view was that I

should thus give an example to all the others who had built towers and forts to give them also, on account of the position of affairs. I received a gracious answer that he would keep my building. As far as I could I had always done my duty to my country, and not only myself, but all my family. I now saw my country free. I saw that which I, my father, my grandfather, and my whole race, as well as all the Greeks had so long desired. I resolved therefore to go to a garden which I had outside Nauplia. I went there, and passed all my time in husbandry. I rejoiced greatly to watch the small trees which I had planted myself grow and flourish.

After a little while I sent a sword to the King's brother, Prince Paul Louis.

I left to pass two months at Tripolitsa, because I was afraid of being ill from the great heat in Nauplia. I was at Tripolitsa, and went thence to a festival at Agia-Monê, whither I went every year, because that was my own property. When I returned to Nauplia I found that intrigues had not been wanting in their influence upon the Government, and that many false statements, such as how Kolokotronês had himself made assemblies, got abroad. Zographos, who was the prefect of Arcadia (and he ought to have known if there had been anything of the kind), went to the Regent, and declared that all such reports were false. When I came back to Nauplia I went to pay my respects to the King and the Regent, and I saw that they looked very gloomy, but I did not understand anything about it.

I stayed in my garden. On the night of the 7th of September, Kleopas, the commandant, with forty soldiers, came there, and arrested me, carrying me off to Its Kalé, and delivered me to the governor there, who cast me into a secret prison, where I was six months without seeing one person except the gaoler. All those six months I knew nothing of what was going on, neither who was living, nor who was dead, nor why I was in prison ; for three days I did not know that I even existed, everything seemed to me to be a dream. I often asked myself if I were really the same man, or some other. I could not understand why they had shut me up.

In time a thought came into my mind that perhaps the Government, seeing the credit which I had with the people, had confined me in order to cut off that influence, but I never thought that it would go such lengths as even to procure false witnesses.

After six months the accusation was communicated to us * that we had frequently made addresses opposing the whole Regency, and again opposing the two members, and in favour of Armansberg, that we wished to make a rising, and with this view we had stirred up robbers.

When these accusations were communicated to me, I immediately suspected that the hand of the Government was in it, and that they would destroy us. They brought us before the tribunal ; many unworthy men of no account appeared there as false witnesses against us, who stated that they had seen the addresses, and other like falsehoods. Honourable men came from all parts—householders, who said that all these things were lies, and that those men were bad characters ; but they would not listen to them, they wished to see their aim—condemnation—carried out. I heard afterwards that Schinas, the Minister of Justice, had compelled the president, Polyzoïdes, and Tertsetés, with fixed bayonets, to sign it in the Court.

They took us down, and read the sentence to us. I had seen death near me so many times that I did not fear it— not then ; better that I should be killed unjustly than

---

* Koliopoulos was also arrested, as will presently be seen.

justly. I was sorry for Koliopoulos, because he had a large family. We ate in the evening; at daybreak I made my will, and prepared for the hour of death. After two hours we learnt that the King had granted us our lives.

They took us to Palamedi as a more secure place, and there we were kept eleven months. When the King came to the throne he gave orders that we should be released from prison, as it was an injustice. I went forth from Palamedi, and the reception which the people gave me made me forget all the troubles through which I had passed. I saw that some were weeping, others laughing for joy, and they all shouted together, "Long live justice! long live justice and the King!" I stopped two or three days at home, and then I went to Athens, and paid my respects, and expressed my gratitude to the King, and to Armansberg, after which I remained in peace and quiet until now when I relate all these events.

NOTES.

—♦—

A.

THE false representations of Russia that led to the disastrous rising of 1770, which, although it spread itself over all Greece, was particularly felt in Mani, occasioned the Porte, who greatly miscalculated the strength of the insurrection, to call in the aid of the Albanians. When, through the desertion of the Russians, the revolt was successfully quelled, the Albanians who remained in the Morea carried on the same cruelties towards the submitted people as they had exercised during the time when they were actively engaged in putting down the rebellion. For nine years the whole of the Peloponnesus was ravaged and desolated by those savage and faithless hordes, who became so emboldened that at last they threw off all nominal allegiance to the Porte, and aimed only at securing the whole Morea for themselves. To quell this outbreak, which threatened so greatly the safety of the Porte, the Kapitan Pasha, Gazi Hassan, was sent with a strong force to drive them entirely out of the Peloponnesus. This he effected with the help of the Klephts and Kostantês Kolokotronês, and pursued them so relentlessly that the whole Morea was cleared in a very short time, when the heads of the unhappy wretches who fell were devoted, some to adorn the court of the seraglio at Constantinople, and others to build a wall at Tripolitsa.

B.

Hassan Tzezairlês, the Kapitan Pasha or High Admiral of the Porte, was undoubtedly one of the bravest of the brave, and as capable as he was brave. This truly great man, who is supposed to have been of Algerine extraction, was captured by the Turks when quite an infant, and being afterwards sold, became the property of a man who employed him for a long time in the capacity of an oarsman. Fleeing from this service in the company of other fugitive slaves, he took service with a Greek, and thence went to Smyrna, where he enlisted among the recruits of the Prince of Algeria. In the different expeditions in which he was engaged he suffered untold hardships, and upon two occasions being badly wounded, was left for dead in the loneliness of a desert, exposed to all the horrors of a tropical sun, combined with hunger and thirst. He escaped, however, with his life from these dangers, and re-entered the service of the Prince, but the intrigues and envy which surrounded him impelled him in the end to abandon it, when he took himself to Spain, and after passing through many vicissitudes, travelled to Constantinople, where, falling under suspicion, he was cast into prison. The Sultan Mahmoud happened to pay a visit of inspection to the prison in which he was confined, when Hassan undauntedly appealed to him to the effect that he, being an innocent man and a foreigner, had been unjustly thrown into a dungeon as a malefactor. The Sultan was impressed with his boldness and his general appearance, and taking him straightway from confinement, appointed him to the post of commander of one of his vessels, when he quickly rose to the highest post in the fleet. The Kapitan Pasha does not appear to have been ill-disposed to the Greeks as a people. There was a great friendship between him and the celebrated Nikolas Mavrogenês, the Hospodar of Wallachia, who, although he was in the service of the Porte, did not always forget that he was himself a Greek, and possibly this friendship influenced Hassan. It is the opinion of the Greek historian Sathas that Greece owes much to him, for it was due to his interposition that a wholesale massacre, by which the entire annihilation of the Greek race was to be effected, was not decreed by the Divan. When all expóstulations on the score of humanity had failed to turn this purpose, Hassan simply remarked, " If all the Greeks are slain, where will your taxes come from?" And this proved conclusive in its logic, and so Greece was saved. His measures against the Albanians were too sweeping to be just, and he was almost disposed to be as inexorable towards the revolted Maniotes in the following year when Kostantês Kolokotronês lost his life. Besides the dignity of Kapitan Pasha, Hassan had the title of Gazi (conqueror), and, on account of his luxuriant growth of moustachios, received also the cognomen of Mustakos.

C.

The promontory of Mani is considered by many writers to be inhabited by descendants of the ancient Spartans, and until its submission to the Kapitan Pasha in 1779, never to have been entirely subdued by either Frank or Turk. Its rugged hills, its sterile soil, and its proximity to the sea conduced to make it in all ages the appropriate nesting-place for brigands and pirates. Its inhabitants were indisposed to industrial pursuits, and were by nature warlike and somewhat fierce, whilst their extreme poverty incited them to lives of rapine and plunder. It has even been stated that they were equally impartial in their incursions both to Christians and Mohammedans, and that their galleys by sea, and their bandits from the mountains, swooped down on both alike. The coast, indented with small creeks, was a safe hiding-place for the piratical row-boats, and the steep ridges of Mount Taygetus were a safe refuge upon the invasion of an enemy. The very women were ready to fight, in order to repel a foe, as is seen in regard to Ibrahim Pasha's troops, whom they attacked and prevented from landing. There were no Turks resident there, and they kept their own institutions, and were virtually self-governed. The districts were divided between the chiefs or Kapetani, and the taxes were sent to the Porte, being collected by themselves; but it need hardly be said that they were not always *regularly* paid, and from the inaccessible nature of the country, and the determined character of the people, attempts at compulsion had always been unsuccessful. Mani only produced acorns and oil, and these were almost a monopoly of the Bey. This wild, barren district has been called the nursery of the Revolution, and its untamable sons its chief promoters. After 1779 Mani was governed by the Kapitan Pasha.

D.

Among those who were shut up in the Acropolis of Argos was one Karagianni, a Maniote who, in the midst of the universal panic occasioned by the approach of Dramalês, had displayed spirit and courage; for he, hearing that the Turks left in Argos were enjoying themselves in supine ease as if they were having a holiday, fell upon them with ten companions of the like mind as himself, and after slaying some, drove the rest forth and planted the Greek flag on the Acropolis. When Kolokotronês, upon their subsequently being besieged by the Turkish force, achieved their rescue, as he narrates in his Autobiography, poor Karagianni, worn out with fatigue and hardships, was asleep on the floor, and knew nothing of what had transpired until he was awakened by the voices and entrance of the Turks, who were seeking for spoils in the deserted fort. The brave, quick-witted fellow started up, and seizing a large copper vessel which happened, fortunately, to be lying within reach, he put it over his head, and went out dancing as though he, a Turk, had chosen that for his share of the booty.

E.

Ali Pasha, whose name is inseparably connected with the Klephts and Armatoli of the close of the eighteenth century, was born about 1745 at Tepeleni, the son of one Veli, the most notorious of the bandits of Albania at that time, who, being devoted for a long period of years to the prosecution of his nefarious profession, amassed considerable wealth, and eventually became the Aga of his village. After a life of frightful crime and profligacy, he died when Ali was quite a youth. Educated as a bandit, Ali was noted at an early age for his skill in shooting, for his swift running, and for his bold riding—for all those acquirements, in fact, which were invaluable in a brigand. He was also inured to every toil and hardship. From the possession of these qualities he was at length attached to the service of the Beys, and he made a good marriage. He was able and he was ambitious, and rose by successive steps to the Pashalik of Trikala in Thessaly, and to the post of Derven Aga, or inspector of roads. This position was the chief origin of his future power. He was as crafty and subtle as he was able and daring, and he managed to attract into his service many Klephts and Armatoli. The Porte, becoming alarmed at the large body of men which he attached to him by good pay and better promises, was pacified from time to time by his representations that this force was required in order to suppress the robbers. By his enormous wealth, acquired in his former expeditions of rapine, he was enabled to purchase (all posts being saleable at the Porte) the government of Juannina. Once established there, his next object was to get rid of the most dangerous of his enemies, the Klephts, and by cajolery, and gold, and protestations of his devotion to the cause of Greece, and his desire for her emancipation, he succeeded from time to time in inveigling many brave but unthinking chiefs to second his designs. The manner in which he obtained possession of the persons of several of the most renowned of those brave men is told in the introductory history of the Klephts. His dealings with the unhappy Souliotes, and his subsequent treason against the Porte, with his fall and decapitation when in extreme old age, are matters of history.

F.

There is frequent mention in the Autobiography of monasteries used for garrisons or strongholds. The old monasteries of Greece were all built so strong as to enable them to take the place of citadels in war time. Megaspêlaion, in the north of the Peloponnesus, about two hours distant from Kalavryta, is the largest monastery in Greece, and the next in size is Taxiarchi, about an hour and a half from Vostitsa. Besides the fortress style in which these edifices are constructed, they are provided with natural defences from their situation, especially the former, which on one side has a precipice of four or five hundred feet. There are many lesser monasteries of the same character scattered over the Morea, which were used by the Klephts as places of retreat. It is seen also how Kolokotronês availed himself of their libraries in order to make his cartridges. The monastery of St. Elias, where Kolokotronês and some of his colleagues were confined, was one of the same character as the above.